RED ZONE DISCOVERED

BOOK 1

JANET ELIZABETH HENDERSON

ALSO BY
JANET ELIZABETH HENDERSON

Romantic Suspense Books

Reckless

Relentless

Rage

Ransom

Rich

Run

Invertary Romantic Comedy Books

Lingerie Wars

Goody Two Shoes

Magenta Mine

Calamity Jena

Bad Boy

Here Comes The Rainne Again

Caught

Invertary Too

Come Fly With Me

Sinclair Sisters Romantic Comedy Books

Can't Tie Me Down

Can't Stop The Feeling

Can't Buy Me Love

And more on my website

Janet Elizabeth Henderson

PRAISE FOR RED ZONE DISCOVERED

"I really, REALLY loved this book. From plot, to characters, to setting, to banter - **it was all so much fun** to read! I stayed up way later than I should have to finish it and have no regrets." - Kylie, Goodreads review

"...**filled with action, suspense, excellent [banter]**, and great humour with well developed and likeable characters." - Kantami B., Goodreads review

"Let me tell you that **I was hooked from the start** of Red Zone! I am not a big Sci-fi reader but the premise had me very interested and I am so glad I gave it a chance. I really enjoyed this book." - Sue, Goodreads review

"I am giving this all the stars! I recommend this book for when you want to be **completely swept up in a different world**." - Quinn F., Goodreads review

"**I was absolutely blown away!** Her story is engaging and fast paced. The world she builds is unique." - Katrina, Goodreads review

"Her words paint **vivid action scenes with unconventional characters**. The sultry and witty dialogue gives you sizzling sex scenes and laugh-out-loud moments." -Sandra B., Goodreads review

"I LOVED, LOVED, LOVED this book! **I read it in one sitting and devoured every word!** I think this may be her best book to date." - Beverly B., Goodreads review

"Red Zone delivers a page turning experience with characters that are engaging, funny and passionate about their journey. **A most definite MUST READ!**" - Laura T.,Goodreads review

"The story **had me hooked from page one** and I just couldn't put it down. The future world was as clear in my mind's eye as any contemporary romance setting. I believe that takes true talent as a writer." - Deb., Goodreads review

A NOTE FOR MY READERS

Welcome to the first book in my Red Zone series, Discovered, a romantic thriller set in an alternative future. This book was previously published under the title of Red Zone. So, if you have that, you already own this book. If you don't have a copy, I really hope you'll enjoy this one.

Janet Elizabeth Henderson

THE RED ZONE WARRIORS

In 2022 the world went to war.

One side of the fight wanted their citizens to have neural implants, enabling them to connect to the computer-driven world with just a thought. The other side wanted to outlaw the implants, fearing the damage they would cause to the human race. The United States, driven by the ambition of its tech companies, was firmly on the side of implanted tech.

To assure their victory, America and its allies deployed an experimental weapon to end the conflict.

They couldn't have predicted the outcome.

The weapon ended the war. It also produced a toxic fog, a thick, red mist that blanketed the U.S.-Mexico border, killing everything it touched. After a few days, the fog retreated from the water, and scientists predicted it would disperse from the land within a year…or two.

They were wrong.

It's been one hundred years since the war ended. One hundred years with the border shrouded in toxic mist. It's called the Red Zone. And nothing can enter it and come out alive.

Nothing except the men and women who were created within it.

A team of Army Rangers was left behind when the bomb dropped. They should have died, betrayed and killed by their own government, who didn't care enough to pull them out of the blast zone. But they didn't.

Instead of dying, they…changed.

And when they woke up a century later, they discovered the world had changed, too.

The Red Zone warriors, as they now call themselves, have been displaced from their lives and time. In a world where scientific advancement means everything, the secrets locked inside of their mutated genetics are priceless.

They cannot afford to let themselves fall into the wrong hands.

RED ZONE DISCOVERED

CHAPTER 1

Fourteen hours, thirty-six minutes, and ten seconds after
Friday Jones injected herself with a lethal dose of a slow-
acting poison, she stood in front of the most notorious
smuggler in the Northern Territory and asked him to
save her.

"Now why would I want to do that, chère?"

Friday knew her face showed none of the surprise she felt
at discovering Striker's accent was twenty-first century
Cajun, an accent she'd only ever heard in historical
documentaries because it was thought to be extinct.

"I'll pay." Don't ask how much, don't ask how much…

"How much?" It was a sexy purr.

She peered into the shadows of the dimly-lit bar where he
slumped out of view. All she saw was bulk. Raw. Male. Bulk.
It wasn't reassuring.

Mentally crossing her fingers, she gave him the bad news.
"Three thousand credits."

"Chère, that's an insult. I get ten times more doing a
standard job, and what you're asking sure ain't standard."
There was a smile in his voice. "You need to do better if you
want my…services."

She blinked at him steadily for a moment. "Is that innuendo?"

"What it is, is boredom. If you've got nothing else to offer, I'm outta here."

Flicking her tongue over her dry lips, she said the words she'd hoped she wouldn't have to say. "I have information. You can have it. Auction it. It's worth more than my credit stash."

"Information?" There was interest in his tone. "What kind?"

"CommTECH." She named the largest governing tech company in the world while silently chanting, don't ask for more details, don't ask for more...

She heard his sharp inhale over the noise of a bar crowded with miners who'd come off nightshift eager to unwind. Unlike most bars in the big cities of Texas, this one in the border town of Munroe wasn't entertaining its clientele with round-the-clock news. Instead, entertainment came in the form of one dais in the center of the room. It held one pole and one weary naked dancer. Friday knew her type. She'd grown up with women like her—underfed, glassy-eyed, and numb—working one of the only options available to the unenhanced. An option Friday would have had to consider if she hadn't signed with CommTECH.

The air shifted in front of her as the shadows solidified. Large hands hit the tacky surface of the small round table. There were scars on the knuckles. Bare biceps bulged as he leaned forward onto his elbows. A black, sleeveless tank barely covered his wide, muscle-filled chest. His jaw came into the light first, stubble-covered, with a scar curving his chin. His cheekbones were sharp as honed flint. Skin the color of aged mahogany invited a person to touch as the dull light gleamed off his shaven head. His left eye was covered by a black flexi-patch. His right was the color of a smoky quartz pendant she'd once seen in a jewelry store window. From the warm wood tones of his skin to the sparkling gemstone eye, everything about the man called to her senses—which was purely a scientific observation.

Maybe.

She caught the amusement in that one good eye. "Like what you see, chère?"

Very much, but she focused on the logical explanation for her reaction to him. "Your features are astonishingly symmetrical. Well, apart from your eyepatch, obviously. Your shoulder muscles are strangely disconcerting. I can't be the only person who's distracted by them. You should probably cover them up to allow your clients to better focus on business. Also, you're younger than I imagined. What are you? Thirty?"

His smile was lopsided. His shrug was Gallic, drawing attention back to those powerful shoulders. The movement made the head of the life-size Western Diamondback rattlesnake tattoo that curled up around the side of his neck nod in agreement. It was the same tattoo that gave the man his name—Striker. Nothing else. Just Striker. For a moment, Friday lost herself in her thoughts about the tattoo. The colors were incredibly vibrant. The only way that could have been achieved with his skin tone would be to bleach the epidermis before applying ink—a painful process.

"Don't you worry none about age, chère. I'm older than I look. And I'm still the best." His uncovered eye turned laser hard. "Now where's this information you have on CommTECH? I need proof that you have it, and that it's worth something, before we make any kind of deal."

He just had to ask about the information. Friday knew her next words would either save her life or hasten her death. "You would need to mine for it. I'm a Passive Recorder."

In an instant, the easy charm was gone. With a move too fast to follow, a gun appeared in his hand. It pointed at her chest. "You might have mentioned you were recording everything before I came into the light. See, now I have a dilemma. My pretty face is in your databank, waiting to be mined along with all the other information you're holding in that head of yours. What do you think I should do about that?"

She wet her lips, grateful she wasn't dead. Yet. "I went off-grid. Almost fifteen hours ago. No one knows where I am. No one can track me. No one can download the information stored in the data chips in my brain. I have roughly four days until that changes."

"Are you blackmailing me, chère? Sayin' if I don't help you, the authorities are gonna find out who I am?"

"No." She held his cold, hard gaze. "I'm saying that in four days I'll be dead, and no one will get access to the information in my head."

He arched a brow. "What makes you so sure you'll be dead in four days?"

"I took Interferan-X."

"You poisoned yourself?" Did he look impressed? It was hard to tell.

"It was the logical thing to do. There are people after me. Interferan-X blocks all access to my implants, remote and internal, and ensures I can't be tracked. Right now, the information I hold is locked inside my head."

"You plan on taking the antidote?"

"Not here. The clinics with the antidote are too closely monitored in the Territories. If I tried to get into one, the Enforcement agency would detain me in a heartbeat. My only option is to go to a clinic outside the Territories." She stared at him. "That's why I need you to take me to La Paz, Bolivia."

He didn't move. He just sat there considering her while pointing a gun at her heart.

"So you die if you don't get to the middle of South America within the next four days." It wasn't a question, therefore didn't require an answer. The noise of the bar was a quiet hum behind her as people waited to see if Striker would take his shot. "You want to tell me how you expect me to get you over the Northern Territory wall, through forty miles of poisonous Red Zone, and past an EMP barrier that will fry every circuit in your pretty body?" He shrugged again. "It can't be done. You're a dead woman walking. If the poison doesn't get you, an escape from the Northern Territory sure as hell will."

"I heard that you have a way over the wall and through the Red Zone. That you've done this before, many times. I heard you can get people past the barrier without it blowing their implanted tech and killing them."

"You sure have heard a lot about me, chère. How is that exactly?"

She didn't blink, and she didn't answer. Her secrets were staying inside her head, whether he liked it or not. What was he going to do about her defiance? As he kindly pointed out, she was a dead woman walking no matter what she did.

He considered her for a moment, making her fight the urge to squirm. "What's your job at CommTECH?"

This she could answer. "Research. Biotech."

His jaw twitched, and his eye narrowed. "Science? Huh. Genetics?"

She nodded. Bioengineering was one of the most common areas of research. She was nothing special. Although Striker seemed to think so. If she thought she had his full attention before, she'd been mistaken. Now she felt as though she were being stripped naked by his gaze. Her cheeks heated.

"What information have you got stored in your pretty head that would make this worth my while?"

She worked to hide the quiver when she exhaled. "Honestly? I don't know. I can tell you what I've been working on, but other than that, the information I have stored needs to be assessed to see if there's anything of value. All I know for sure is that, as a Passive Recorder, everything I do, say, and see while inside CommTECH is stored in my data chips. I know I've recorded something someone didn't want recorded. Whatever it is, it must be worth something."

"That's a lot of unknowns you got in there. A man can't sell an unknown. What makes you think you saw something you shouldn't have? Something worth my while?"

She resisted the urge to brush imaginary lint from her regulation black jumpsuit. "Someone wants access to whatever I saw, heard, or know. They want it badly enough to send Enforcement after me." Although she tried hard, she couldn't look him in the eye any longer. Couldn't take the chance that her fears had slipped past her controlled facade.

His muscles went taut. "You were followed?"

"I lost them."

His expression made it clear he didn't think much of her covert skills. "Are you sure?"

"Yes."

Yep, he definitely didn't believe her. "Are they still looking for you?"

She nodded. "There have been teams out searching, asking questions of friends and colleagues. A General Message has gone out on the public communication network, requesting information on my whereabouts."

His lips twitched slightly, as though he were amused. "The cyber equivalent of a wanted poster." He cocked an eyebrow at her. "Looks like you're an outlaw, chère." He sat quietly for a few moments, watching, the gun still pointed at her chest. "Let me get this straight. You've got Enforcement after you. CommTECH is pushing to find you. You think you slipped your tail. You somehow, mysteriously, knew how to track me down. And on top of all that—which I have to say, doesn't reassure me, chère—you want me to smuggle you through the border, take you overland to Bolivia and make sure the Red Zone doesn't kill you while we do it. In return for the risk, effort, and time involved in rescuing your ass, you're offering barely enough credits to hire a shuttle. Or, I can get the unknown information stuck in your head that might be worth selling. I gotta tell you, bébé, you ain't much of a negotiator, and that ain't much of an offer."

Friday fought the urge to let her shoulders droop. She wasn't defeated yet. She'd known seeking him out was a long shot. Unfortunately, it was also her only shot. "I need to get out of here. I need to get to La Paz. Please help me. You're my only hope."

"Yeah, yeah. Don't go all Princess Leia on me."

"Who?"

He gave her a look that implied she was the crazy one. "Star Wars? Help me, Obi-Wan Kenobi. You're my only hope. Ring a bell?"

She stared at him blankly.

"It's an old movie."

Movies? She didn't think anyone still watched those.

"Never mind." He waved the conversation away with the muzzle of the gun. "Unless you can up your payment offer, this discussion is over."

"I don't have anything else to offer you."

He stared at her for a few long minutes, considering. She refused to fidget. She was used to scrutiny. She wouldn't crumble. At last he nodded slightly, as though coming to a decision. He leaned toward her.

"I wouldn't say that." His eye skimmed her body as he smiled, slow and knowing. "You do have one thing I want."

She felt the color drain from her face as the room swayed. "You don't mean…"

His expression was unreadable. "I want you, chère."

CHAPTER 2

Striker waited for the inevitable blush to cover her face. Three, two, one…and there it was. He smirked. When he'd first come back to the former United States, he'd discovered it held only three types of women. There were the unenhanced, who were impossible to shock as they'd seen it all, done it all. The wealthy enhanced, who tended to indulge their every whim and were looking for something to shock the hell out of them. And then there were the ones like Friday Jones, who'd sold their souls to the companies and didn't have time for anything but work. Those women, he scared the hell out of.

He tended to avoid the glassy-eyed unenhanced, but he'd had his fair share of fun with the rich women. Friday was the first little worker bee who'd intrigued him. He wasn't sure if that was because of her hour-glass figure, her milky skin and wide blue eyes, or the way she stood in front of him, terrified, yet asking for help. Not to mention she intrigued him, purely on the merit that she'd managed to find him. He wasn't an easy man to track down.

"You can't mean…" she blustered at last. For a minute, he'd thought she'd turned mute.

"Mean what, chère?"

"Mean me." Her fair skin was a dark pink now, the flush running down into that ugly, formless jumpsuit she wore. "You can't want me."

"Oh, but I do." Not for the reasons she had in mind, but it sure was entertaining to watch her think it. No, he might be a bastard, and he sure as hell had done some questionable things in his life, but he'd never forced a woman to have sex with him. And no matter what was going through Friday's head, he wasn't about to start now.

She gaped at him like a pretty fish stuck in an aquarium. She knew she was caught. He laid the gun on the table, within easy reach. This woman wasn't a danger, but if she was being honest, she had a large chunk of Enforcement on her tail. If they crashed the bar, he wanted to be able to shoot his way out of trouble. Something he'd become adept at during his lifetime.

"Sit down." It was an order. He didn't need her fainting in front of him.

She sat slowly and cautiously, as though dazed. Long dark lashes fluttered as she stared at him.

He leaned over the table. "I want a year of your time. That's my price. Take it or leave it."

Her throat bobbed as she swallowed hard. She licked plump, ruby-colored lips that made his cock stand to attention, and he willed it right back down. This negotiation wasn't about sex. It was about survival.

"A year? Of me?" She no longer sounded like a programmed auto-voice. There was actual emotion in there now. Okay, so it was shock, but it was still better than listening to the lifeless tone she'd had going a minute ago. "You want to use me for a year? Can't you get other women? Is it because you only have one eye?"

He laughed loud and hard, attracting the attention of wary customers. "No, chère. I have no problems getting women. Believe it or not, some women find the eyepatch sexy.

You wouldn't believe the number of times I've been asked to play pirate. There are a whole lot of women out there who want to pretend they're being raided and pillaged." He cocked an eyebrow at her as he smiled, but she obviously didn't think he was amusing.

She gaped at him again, her eyes wide. Cute. Seriously cute. "Then why?" she whispered.

"You don't need to know my reasons. You just need to know the price if you want my services. And my price is one full year, starting right now. A year in which you do what I want, when and where I want, no questions asked."

"I-I-I…" She swallowed again. "How can you ask that of me when I don't even know what you might want? What if you plan to harm me?"

She needed parameters. He could do that. He just couldn't give her the details of why he wanted her and what he expected her to do. "Okay, here are the ground rules. I won't do anything to harm you in any way. I won't cause pain. I won't inflict emotional or mental torture. I only want a year of your time and your compliance. It's up to you. Just how desperate are you to live? Desperate enough to sign yourself over to a real outlaw?" He folded his arms and waited, confident she would make the right decision, considering she was seriously out of options.

As she thought it over, he signaled to the waitress for a water. A moment later the glass was placed in front of Friday and she snatched it up as though she were dying of thirst. As she drank, her eyes stayed on him. When the glass was empty, she clutched it to her chest. The cool, controlled facade she'd had in place since walking into the dive was gone.

"You can't be serious, I can't offer myself up as payment. It's"—she cast around for the word, color leeching from her face as she did so—"wrong. No, barbaric. It's barbaric." Her blue eyes were wide with shock—or horror at the thought of spending a year in his tender care.

"You got some other way of getting me the credits you'd owe?"

He watched her eyes flicker as her agile mind raced through options. "I can pay you off over a set amount of time."

"A payment plan?" He laughed again. She was too much. "For how long? Considering what you'll owe me, bébé, you'll be paying it off for the rest of your life. What's one year compared to a whole lifetime of debt?"

"But it's one year of…" The poor, sheltered little bee couldn't even say the words.

"Of whatever I want," he supplied helpfully.

"I can't." She shook her head. "I can't."

He shrugged. It was a pity, but not unexpected. "Then you die."

Her eyes snapped to his. "There are no other options that you'll accept?"

He knew his smile was feral and wasn't surprised when it caused her to shiver. "Chère, you ain't got nothing else to offer."

He watched realization sink in and her shoulders slump. Striker didn't like to see a woman defeated, but reality was sometimes a hard pill to swallow—he knew that better than most.

She licked her lips. "What happens at the end of the year?"

"I'll take you wherever you want to go and leave you there."

"Unharmed?"

"Unharmed." But not unchanged.

Her hand shook as she put the glass back on the table. Out of the corner of his eye, Striker saw the owner of the bar head toward them. Glen studied Friday thoughtfully, but wisely kept his conclusions to himself.

"Got incoming. Enforcement." Glen cocked his head

toward Friday. "They're after her. They got a tip-off she was here." He scowled as he scanned the room full of cash-strapped miners. "Not unexpected. They're offering a reward."

Friday sucked in a breath but didn't freak out. Striker appreciated that.

"What do you want me to do?" The bar owner rubbed his jaw. It wasn't a nervous action; it meant he was already thinking of scenarios and countermeasures.

"What's it gonna be, chère? You need to decide. Time has just run out."

"This isn't much of a choice," she snapped, showing some spine.

He liked it. "It's the only one you have."

She swallowed, bit her bottom lip, then straightened her shoulders. He'd expected to find dull acceptance in her eyes. Instead, he saw determination.

"Okay. I agree." He could see her heartbeat throb rapidly in the curve of her throat. "One year, starting right now."

He wanted to pump the air. He'd secured a geneticist for the team. Instead he inclined his head. "Good decision." He turned to the bar owner. "The bike's out back. We'll need twenty minutes."

"I've got you covered." The big man strode away.

"Let's go, chère." Striker stood, holstered his gun in the rig strapped to his thigh, and held out a hand to her.

With shaky fingers, she curled her hand in his. He couldn't suppress his grin of triumph as he strode toward the back of the bar, dragging his new acquisition along with him. Once they were somewhere safe, somewhere they could talk, he'd explain exactly why he needed her and put her mind at ease. Until then, he'd just have to let her imagination run riot, because they had more important things to deal with—like staying alive.

———

What have I done? What have I done?

Friday focused on Striker's back as they hurried through the room. Her stomach clenched in waves, and she knew if she'd eaten any food at all that day it would have been decorating the floor.

A year with the smuggler, or death? What the hell kind of choice was that?

She'd signed with CommTECH to ensure that she wouldn't have to sell her body to live, like so many of the women she'd grown up around, and here she was, doing it anyway. Forced into it by a pirate with a black heart. A year! What would he do? What would she have to endure? It was too much to contemplate. Part of her wondered if she wasn't better off letting the poison run its course instead.

She'd gone from one form of slavery to another in the space of a breath. At least with CommTECH, she'd had an idea what she was getting into. With this man, she didn't have a clue. Did he expect her to be his sex slave for a year? What if he meant to sell her and earn his money that way? Was she to spend her year servicing strangers to pay him back for saving her life? Fear hit her hard, making her trip over her own feet.

"Come on." He tugged her hand, his huge fist swallowing hers and reminding her of exactly how strong he was and just how helpless she was in comparison.

They pushed out into the humid air of the desert. Night had fallen, but the temperature hadn't. He tugged her into a lockup, hidden in the alley behind the bar.

"Wait." She dug her feet in and fought to stop.

With clear irritation, he turned on her. "You want to die here? In an alley? Because that's what's gonna happen as soon as Enforcement arrive."

Blood rushed loudly in her ears, making it hard to concentrate. Sweat pooled in the small of her back.

"I have to know." She stared him in the eye, looking for reassurance. "I have to know if you plan to sell me to make your money."

He hung his head and let out a long sigh. When he looked back up at her, his jaw was clenched. Anger? Frustration? She wasn't sure which.

"I don't pimp women. Your time will belong to me for the year. No one else will touch you. We'll talk more about the details of our deal once we're safe. But I won't do anything to harm you. Got it?"

Relief made her tremble. "Got it."

"Great. Now can we leave before someone burns a hole through my chest?"

"Wait. You said no one will touch me. But will you let other people watch us when we're sexually active?"

He stared at her, dumbstruck for a second. "Woman, you have a sick mind. I'm not sure if I'm impressed, insulted, or worried. No, there won't be any audience to any sex we might have. Happy?"

Might? What did that mean? Did he have something else in mind for her? If so, what?

He pressed his thumb to the entry-scan and opened the door to the lockup. It was dark, but Friday could make out the covered shape of a bike.

"Catch." A helmet thudded into her stomach. She tugged it on.

He pulled the cover off the machine as she fumbled with the strap of her helmet. That wasn't a hoverbike. The questions about his intentions fled, now that she was faced with something else she didn't understand.

"What is it?" She watched as he straddled the machine.

"This, bébé, is a relic. It's a fully restored, slightly adapted, Ducati."

She must have looked blank, because she felt blank.

"It's a motorbike. Vintage. Get on."

"Where?" She looked for the passenger capsule, but there wasn't one.

He looked down and shook his head. "Sit behind me. Wrap your arms around me and hold on tight." When he looked back up at her, it was fierce. "Now."

The word acted like a whip. It hit her hard, making her rush into action. She fastened the helmet and climbed onto the back of the bike. Sitting with her legs spread wide wasn't comfortable. Having a strange man between them made it worse.

"Wrap your arms around me. When I lean, you lean, too."

She did as she was told, although her face burned at the thought of being so close to him. But then, it was something she'd best get used to. The man owned her now.

"Tighter." It was an order.

His muscled back was a furnace against her chest. She pressed her breasts flat against him, scooted forward until her hips were flush with his, and wrapped her arms tight around his middle. She clung to fistfuls of his shirt. He smelled of citrus and sandalwood, a heady combination that made her already roiling stomach quake.

The bike roared into life. She gasped at the noise. It sounded nothing like the low hum of the hover vehicles.

"Don't let go." With that last order, the bike shot forward, taking them into the balmy streets of Munroe.

They headed out of town, toward the glowing lights of the thirty-foot-high wall that marked the southern edge of the Northern Territory and the start of the Red Zone.

The world's deadliest no-man's-land.

And Friday's only hope of escape.

CHAPTER 3

After three tries to remote communicate with her helmet using her now-defunct implants, Friday realized she'd have to turn on the audio manually. Getting used to life without her enhancements was going to be hard. Hopefully she'd have more than four days to work on it. A green light blinked in her visor to let her know she could now talk with Striker.

"Why are we using this machine? It's noisy and attracts attention. You may as well send Enforcement a message giving them our location."

There was a pause, and then deep rumbling laughter sounded in her ears. It surrounded her, making her shiver.

"This baby is faster on the ground than Enforcement hoverbikes, that's why we're using it."

"But if they can hear us, they'll just send someone up ahead to cut us off. I thought you were good at this outlaw thing. Was my information wrong?"

There was more laughter. She was beginning to wonder if she'd put her life in the hands of an idiot.

"Trust me. I know what I'm doing."

Yep, she'd get right on that. She looked over her shoulder. The beams from the Enforcement bikes blinked in the sky as they skimmed the rooftops. Her fingers clenched tight on his stomach.

"They can see us." She leaned to the side, peering around the smuggler. Up ahead more red lights cut through the night. "They've cut us off."

A strange stillness overtook her. So much for her great rebellion. It was all for nothing. She'd failed. There was no way they could get out of this. There were too many Enforcement personnel to count, and they were hopelessly outnumbered. She had no doubt that if either Striker or she was connected to the public communications network, they would have been flooded by messages telling them to surrender. But they weren't connected to the network. And there would be no warning. Instead, she'd get blasted by laser fire and die, without even knowing it was coming. It was over. Her life was over before it had even started.

"Promise me…" Her voice cracked a little. "Promise me you'll kill me before you let them take me."

"Why so dramatic, chère? Nobody is gonna get you."

"Promise me. I can't let them tamper with my memories or my personality. I'd rather die than live like that. Promise me you'll kill me."

He sighed. The sound wrapped around her, easing her anxiety. "We're gonna have to work on what you think of me. I don't know what you heard, but I don't kill innocent women."

"Even to save them?" Her throat became thick. "Please."

His muscles tensed under her hold. "Okay, chère. I won't let them take you alive. But you gotta work on your faith in me. They aren't taking us at all."

With those words, the bike skidded, taking a sharp right into a tight alley. She gasped as her knee lightly skimmed the old brick while they drove straight toward the wall at the end.

"Striker!" She clenched her eyes shut tight. They were going to die.

She waited for the inevitable crash. It didn't come. She opened one eye and looked over her shoulder. There was nothing behind her but the telltale shimmer of a holo-shield where the wall should have been. Fake. The wall had been fake. Just an electronic projection meant to fool the eye.

"No faith." Striker shook his head as the bike stopped suddenly. "Get off."

The alley was narrow, with barely enough space to stand beside the bike.

"You know what to do," he said to the space behind her.

She spun to find a man and a woman. They were tall, dressed in black, and clearly amused. The woman smirked at Friday.

"You sure she's worth it?" she asked Striker.

He ran a hand over his bald head. His white teeth shone in the dim light. "I hope so. Come on, chère." He nodded at the huge man as he took her hand. "See you back at camp."

The giant grunted, climbed on the bike, and revved the loud engine. The woman climbed on behind him. A second later, the bike roared forward through another shimmering holo-shield, which projected the image of a solid wall. Friday looked up. The wooden beams overhead seemed real. They also stopped anyone flying over from spotting them.

"Let's go." Striker pulled her toward a door cut into the wall of one of the buildings. It led to a narrow staircase that went steeply down into the earth.

"Your friends are decoys."

He raced down the stairs, dragging her after him. "Yep."

"The end walls, they were camouflage—holo-shields. Was the roof real or another holo-shield?"

"It was real."

They reached the bottom of the stairs, where he opened a reinforced door—twenty inches of steel. A tunnel lay behind it. It was narrow, barely wide enough to fit Striker's shoulders, and the ceiling skimmed his head. She silently said a prayer of gratitude that she wasn't claustrophobic.

Her mind distracted her from the small space by working on other problems. "They'll detect the energy signature from the holo-shields. They'll know where to look."

"Not until they've chased the bike for a while." He still held her hand tight in his. For some strange reason, Friday didn't want him to let go. "And if they do find the shields, as soon as they open the door in the alley, the staircase will blow. They won't find the tunnel."

"You sound awfully confident." And she wasn't sure it was merited.

"We set up this escape route when we started using Glen's dive bar as a meeting point a couple of years ago." He glanced at her, clearly amused. "This isn't the first time we've had to use it, and if the assholes don't blow it up, it won't be the last. This isn't my first rodeo, chère."

"I don't know what that means."

He just laughed, which was seriously irritating. Her life was on the line and the guy was continually amused.

"You know that's rude, right? Every time I say something, you laugh."

"Really? You're taking issue with my manners? We're about a hundred feet below ground, running from men with guns, and you're annoyed with my attitude. Is it any wonder I laugh?"

She scowled at his back but vowed to keep her mouth shut. "Does this tunnel run under the border?" Drat, that vow didn't last long.

"They monitor the earth under the wall. You can't tunnel there."

So where did the tunnel go? Why were they using it? How were they going to get past the wall?

There was more chuckling. "I can hear you thinking. That brain of yours never stops, does it?"

Now he was just trying to irritate her. "Do intelligent women threaten you, Striker?"

The sultry look he cast her way made her stumble. "All the damn time, bébé, but my luck's held out, and so far, they've never carried through with it."

"That's not what I meant, and you know it."

As she opened her mouth to continue berating him, the dim lights blinked out. She gasped and, without thinking, closed the distance between her and the smuggler. He stood still, blocking the space in front of her—a solid wall of taut muscle. Behind them, the unmistakable sound of laser fire echoed through the tunnel. Enforcement was breaking through the door.

"Run." He yanked her forward as he matched his order with action.

"I can't see." Her nails dug into his hand as she struggled to keep up with him.

"I can. Hold on tight."

"How?" How could he see? It was pitch black. It was impossible. Unless her information was wrong, and he was enhanced somehow.

"No time for questions. Store them up for later. Right now, run."

The ground was rough beneath her feet; the darkness, all-encompassing. Their panting breaths warred with the thudding of their footsteps, filling the small space with noise that echoed and surrounded them. The intermittent thump of laser fire hitting metal was a timer on a bomb behind them, the creaking of metal a signal that the door was about to blow. They were about to be trapped. Underground. In the dark. With armed Enforcement agents.

Friday's lungs burned from gasping for air. Her heartbeat pounded loud in her ears. Her thigh muscles cramped. Too much time sitting in front of a computer. No time exercising, not even the recommended thirty minutes a day. She'd been too busy to fill her quota.

There was a loud blast. Metal crashed. Voices shouted. Footsteps pounded the dirt behind them.

Striker suddenly stopped, making her slam into his back. "They're in. We won't make it to the end of the tunnel." Large hands clasped her shoulders. "We need to fight. Do you know how to use a gun?"

"Of course." She tried to ignore her roiling stomach. She could do this. She didn't have a choice.

"Take this." He pressed a gun into her hands. It wasn't one of the laser guns Enforcement used, but one that fired bullets. They weren't uncommon, but she'd never used one before. She was grateful for the darkness, as it meant Striker couldn't see her tremble as she took it.

"All I do is pull the trigger, right?"

He swore. "You said you knew how to use a gun."

"A laser gun."

He cursed again. "Point and shoot. The trigger is in the same place as a laser gun, but it isn't coded to a print, and there's no projection to help you aim for your target. The only real difference is there is more recoil with this gun. Be ready for that. Only shoot if they get past me. I don't want you hitting me in the back."

She nodded, even though it was too dark for him to see her. She could do this. Point and shoot. Easy. Just don't think about the target being people.

"I can't see where I'm shooting." But she could hear. The running feet were getting closer.

"Just face the way I point you and fire when I shout. Or, if someone who isn't me comes at you, feel free to pull the trigger then too. You'll know it isn't me because Enforcement wear lights on their vests. But remember, if you hit me, the deal is off."

How could he joke? "You're huge and take up all the

space. I can't fire around you." *Oh God, if he dies, what will I do?*

"If this goes as planned, you won't need to fire at all."

"You have a plan?" It was impossible to hide her disbelief.

He chuckled as she felt fingers trail over her cheek, startling her with the gentle offer of reassurance. "Yeah, I have a plan. Don't worry, bébé, I've lived through worse than this."

The pounding steps got closer. Friday's eyes shot in the direction of the noise even though all she could see was endless black.

"We're gonna wait until they get closer," he whispered against her ear, the feeling oddly intimate. "Then we'll fire at their supply packs and hopefully blow them and the tunnel around them."

"Do they carry explosives?" she whispered back.

"Enough to do some damage. Hopefully enough to bring this baby down on top of them. Remember, they can only come at us one at a time. The tunnel isn't wide enough for more." He stilled. Listening. "It's time. Crouch down. Point the gun. Fire when I tell you."

She took a deep, shaky breath and did as she was told. "What are you going to do?"

"Scare the crap out of them." She could have sworn he was smiling as he spoke. "Off you go," he added, which didn't make any sense.

"Go where?"

"Not you. You stay."

Who then? She didn't get a chance to ask because that's when the screaming started.

CHAPTER 4

FRIDAY CURLED HERSELF INTO THE SMALLEST BALL SHE COULD manage, while still aiming her gun in the direction Striker had pointed her. Flashes of light illuminated shadows around her as laser fire rang out. Dirt fell. Dust billowed. Through the thick cloud, in the hazy flashes of light, she could make out Striker's back as he crouched a few feet in front of her.

"Snake! Snake!" someone shouted. "It bit me. Fuck. It bit me!" A gut-churning wail went up, echoing off the walls as it traveled down the tunnel.

Friday stilled as the cry sank in. There were *snakes* in the tunnel. Slithering, venomous, snakes. In the darkness. With her. Her breathing turned into shallow panting as she fought the very real urge to run screaming. *Still*—she had to stay still. She had to protect the man who stood between her and Enforcement as hysteria reigned.

"I'm down, I'm down. It bit my neck!"

"Where is the fucker?"

Another bone-chilling scream.

"What the hell kind of snake is that?"

"Where did it go? Where is it? Can anyone see it? I can't see it."

A panicked roar. "It got me!"

"Shoot it!"

"I can't see it."

"Where the hell is it?"

Fire blasted out, random and unfocused, as Enforcement agents succumbed to panic. It was agony-filled chaos. Friday concentrated on breathing evenly in an attempt to steady her hands. Focus. She had to focus. Don't think about the snakes. Don't think about the snakes…

"Stop shooting!" The order came from farther down the tunnel. It was a bark of absolute authority that made Friday shudder. "Get the injured out of here. Pass them back. The rest of you move forward."

"There it is! It's huge. Run! Run! It's above us." Another shriek filled with agony, followed by more flashes of blue light from laser blasts.

Friday bit back a cough as dust filled the tunnel and clogged her throat. In the dim glow from the lights attached to the Enforcement uniforms, she watched Striker's silhouette as he stood. There was a whistle. It might have come from him. The shadow of a man stumbled into sight, his bulk hazy through the dust-filled air. He stumbled and fell, sobbing, wailing, clutching his neck. Another scream echoed along the tunnel. Someone shouted orders. Shots went off, fired aimlessly.

And through it all, her protector stood like a statue.

The fallen man writhed on the ground before them. Why didn't Striker fire his weapon? Why was he just standing there? He whistled again. The light in the tunnel grew brighter as more men closed in on them. Striker's silhouette shuddered before he stilled. His arms lowered, and his hand reached for his gun. He rose slightly on the balls of his feet, took aim, and fired. He hit the utility belt on the waist of a dead Enforcement agent. The blast blinded Friday and sent her rocking onto her backside.

The ceiling above the rest of the Enforcement agents began to crumble. They fired blindly, scrambling over each other to get out from under the falling earth. Friday closed her eyes against the biting dust. She wished she could close her ears against the panic and screams of pain as erratic laser blasts echoed through the tunnel.

Striker fired again, hitting a second officer. Another blast. This time it triggered the belt of the man behind as well. Two blasts in quick succession. Friday's ears were ringing. She shook her head. Dizziness, disorientation—she wanted to double over and retch. A hand grabbed her arm. The air was thick. Unbreathable. A voice at her ear. Distant. Faint, as though she listened through water.

"Cover your mouth," Striker hissed. "Run!"

He pried the gun from her grip and grabbed her hand. She pulled the neck of her jumpsuit over her mouth. They rushed forward into blackness as the tunnel fell behind them, crushing Enforcement agents and snakes alike. Dirt and stones rained down. The earth creaked and moved, groaning in protest, pressing in on them.

She stumbled. Striker pulled her up. She ran blindly, her lungs burning, her legs rubber, her heart racing. All the while, the tunnel crumbled behind her. The roar of falling earth was an agonized wail of protest. The earth was angry at having been invaded. It wanted to swallow them whole as punishment for their trespass.

Striker suddenly yanked her to the left. She stumbled, fell against something wooden, and tripped over a step. A door. They'd gone through a door.

"Up. Hurry. Don't quit now."

He dragged her behind him, moving fast and pulling her along. She fell too many times to count, too high on adrenaline and fear to feel pain.

"Nearly there." Striker's voice was an echo in her damaged ears. "There!"

He pushed forward, and suddenly artificial light enveloped them. Friday fell to her knees, panting, desperately sucking in air that was stale and thick but blessedly free from dirt and dust.

Striker threaded his hands under her arms and yanked her up. "Not yet. We need to get out of this building. The tunnel could collapse beneath us."

They raced up more stairs and out into an abandoned store. Striker scanned the street beyond the windows while Friday bent double and gasped for air.

"Okay, we're good. Come on." He motioned for her to follow. Unlike her, he wasn't out of breath.

They sneaked out into the street, hugging the walls of the buildings, keeping to the shadows. Striker took her hand again to ensure she kept pace with him. His eye restlessly scanned the area as he led her across the road. They were in a suburb full of cheap prefab houses with tiny rooms and even smaller windows. Boxes for storing the poor, out of sight of the rich, where they couldn't offend.

"In here." He elbowed the door to a darkened house.

There was a crack and the panel gave way.

He shoved her inside and quietly shut the broken door behind them. As he spied out of the window to see if anyone was following, Friday surveyed their surroundings. They were in the main room. The kitchen area was in the corner. The furnishings were sparse, cheap but neat. Someone had tried to care for their home, and it had been invaded. Guilt assailed her.

Striker turned away from the window. "We're good here for now."

He strode to the kitchen area, opened the refrigerator, and pulled out two bottles of water. He thrust one at her. "Drink. But spit out the first few mouthfuls. We ate a lot of dirt."

She followed him to the sink and did as he ordered. Her first swallow of ice-cold water was a balm to her abused throat. Without another word, Striker fetched two more bottles and passed one to her. She sank down the wall to sit on the cool stone floor. Her mind was blank, and every inch of her body began to ache. Leaning her head back, Friday closed her eyes. It felt like her eyeballs had been rolled in sand. The grit had worked its way under her comlens and rubbed relentlessly against her eyeball. She made a mental note to take the damn thing out, first chance she got. The lens was useless to her anyway, now that she was disconnected from the grid.

"You did good."

She snorted. It wasn't ladylike and she didn't care. "I did nothing."

"Which is exactly what I told you to do. Hence the good."

She opened her eyes to find Striker crouched in front of her. "You could have told me there were snakes in the tunnel."

He shrugged, but that wicked smile was back. "The only predator you need to worry about is me."

"How did Enforcement get past the staircase? You said it was rigged to blow."

"I don't know. But I'll make a call and ask a few questions."

That made her weary body move. Her hand shot out and her fingers curled around his wrist.

"You can't call anyone. The public communications network and all the messaging systems are being monitored. They'll be on us within seconds."

"You have a lot to learn. I keep telling you, I know what I'm doing."

He reached into his back pocket and came out with a small metal box. He pressed a button on it then put it to his ear. It took her a few seconds to realize what it was—an old phone. A museum piece.

"Those don't work anymore," she said when the shock passed. "They haven't worked for over eighty years."

The infuriating man winked at her. "Keep drinking, then we'll clean you up and get out of here."

She opened her mouth to say something else, but he suddenly started talking into the phone. Guess they did still work after all.

"We were made. What the hell happened?"

He turned away from her, his focus on the call, leaving her to wonder who her rescuer was, exactly, and if they were going to make it to La Paz in time to save her life.

CHAPTER 5

Striker worked to control his rage. The urge to hit out at something, anything, burned through him. All he needed was a target. Instead, he had a bunch of questions and a woman he'd promised to protect. He watched Friday gulp her water. Just watching her calmed him. She'd done good. No hysterics. No acting out. She followed orders like a pro. Although her fitness needed work. Something he intended to help her with after they made it to La Paz.

If they made it to La Paz.

"I don't know what happened," Mace said in his ear, bringing his attention back to the phone conversation.

"Enforcement should have followed you two, not us."

He peered out of the window as he spoke. The street was quiet. "Did anyone chase you?"

"A couple of units. It took about ten minutes before we realized we didn't have everyone's full attention. By the time we'd doubled back, the tunnel was gone. Glad you made it out, man. You had us worried for a minute there."

"I wasn't worried," Sandi shouted in the background, making him smile.

His second-in-command huffed. "The more-human member of this duo was worried."

With a shake of his head, Striker interrupted, otherwise the siblings would fight all night. "When things settle, we need to look into why the stairs didn't blow."

There was silence for a beat. "Seriously? You're telling me that plume of smoke wasn't from the charges we laid?"

"Nope." He pinched the bridge of his nose. "I blew up a couple of Enforcement vests."

"Fuck, Sergeant."

"Thanks for the offer, but you don't float my boat."

"Where are you now?"

"Holed up in an empty house in South Munroe. We can't stay here." He watched Friday as she pulled herself to her feet, rolled up her pants, and started dabbing at the scrapes on her legs with a wet cloth.

"We'll get a transport to you asap. I'll text when we're close and need more specific directions." There was a pause. "You don't think she lied about taking Interferan-X, do you? They could be tracking her. That would explain why they found you so fast."

The siblings had been his backup in the bar during his meeting with Friday and had monitored everything that was said. But Mace hadn't been able to see her face. The woman couldn't lie worth a damn. There was no way she was an Enforcement mole.

"I'll talk to her. But I don't think she's lying."

There was a heavy sigh. "I'll get the rest of the team onto this, and see what we can dig up. We'll bring your transport."

"Make it fast. The clock's ticking here."

"Yeah, I heard. It's gonna be tight getting to La Paz on time. I hope you know what you're doing, man."

"So do I, but we need answers, and the little scientist may be able to provide them. It's a chance we have to take."

"If we can get her out of this alive."

"Yeah, there is that." He hung up and stared out into the night as he tucked the old phone back into his pocket. It was a relic. Just like him.

Rubbing a hand over his bald head, he turned back to his latest job. Friday had found some new-skin spray and was dousing her scrapes. He strode over to her and took the spray from her hand.

"Let me." He crouched in front of her, spraying the cuts she'd missed, watching in fascination as skin-colored patches appeared where the abrasions used to be. "This stuff still blows my mind. It's like magic."

He grinned up at her, and her brow puckered—a clear sign she was thinking. Again. The woman spent a whole lot of time thinking.

"It isn't magic." She held out her hand for him to spray the palm. "The new-skin adheres to my skin and is gently absorbed into my epidermis over the time it takes for the wound to heal. While that's happening, it transmits sensation as though it were actually part of my skin."

"So, if I were to do this?" He traced a finger over the palm of her hand in the spot he'd just sprayed.

She shivered and cleared her throat. "Then I'd feel it the same way I'd feel it if you touched me somewhere else."

Her cheeks flushed, and he wondered if she was imagining all the other places he could touch. He sure as hell was. The little scientist was far too much temptation for her own good. He'd be wise to put some distance between them, before he forgot their deal was only for her brain and not for the rest of her.

Friday shifted in front of him, and his mind went blank again. She had a way of doing that, of stealing his thoughts and focusing his attention solely on her.

She cleared her throat. "Meanwhile, under the layer of new-skin, the product is working to speed up healing in the damaged areas." She blinked down at him as he crouched in front of her, her hand resting in his. "It increases the healing rate by roughly seventy percent."

"And in the meantime, it feels exactly like normal skin."

"Exactly." She swallowed hard enough for him to see.

"Are you sure about that, bébé? Have you tested the hypothesis?"

"I don't need to test it. I'm familiar with the research."

"Mm, I always find that doing your own research is the best way to be certain." He looked up at her. "Close your eyes."

Her eyes actually got wider, making him chuckle. "Close your eyes. See if you can tell the difference." He cocked an eyebrow at her. "Remember our deal, chère. What I want, when I want it."

She sucked in a breath. Fear and irritation flashed in her eyes before she did as she was told and her lashes fluttered shut. Her breathing sped up, her cheeks were flushed and it almost killed him when she licked her dry lips. He traced a circle in the middle of her palm with his index finger and her whole body became taut, waiting for his next touch. He took her other hand, the one that wasn't damaged, and drew another circle in the exact same spot. She shivered.

"Well?" he murmured, his voice suddenly hoarse.

She trembled as he moved closer to her, but her eyes stayed closed, as though she'd forgotten she could open them.

"The same." The words were a croak. "The same. It felt the same."

"What about here?" He trailed his fingers over the inside of her wrist, first on her left arm, then her right.

With a gasp, her eyes flew open, and dark pupils looked down at him. "There isn't any new-skin there."

"You sure? Maybe I should do it again. Just to make certain."

She snatched her hands away, slid to the side and out of the kitchen, away from him. But not before he's spotted more than a hint of curiosity, and heat, in her gaze. Seemed he wasn't the only one feeling the burn when they touched.

Striker got to his feet and headed for the pantry, where he rooted around until he found some meal replacement bars. Strawberry sundae flavored. He shuddered. He'd rather have a real sundae. No matter how many vitamins and minerals these things had added to them, they still tasted like flavored cardboard. What happened to normal food? The kind that didn't come pre-wrapped. He handed a bar to his pretty little client, who perched against the arm of a chair in the dark living room.

"Thanks." She took the bar, unwrapped it, and bit into it without once looking him in the eye.

Everything about her was fascinating, even the way she ate. "We need to talk about what happened. The Enforcement agency knew where we were. I have to ask, are you sure you're cut off from your implants?"

"Yes. I'm sure. I took Interferan-X."

"Would that affect a tracker that's been placed under your skin? One that wasn't an official implant?"

Her head snapped up as she frowned—thinking again. "You're suggesting I've been tagged without my knowledge?"

"It happens." It was a lot more common than most people thought.

"Even if I had been tagged, it wouldn't work. Interferan-X works a little like a gel. It finds the implants, or in this case any tech parts under my skin, and surrounds them, essentially cutting them off from the outside world and from my neural network. The tech still works, but it's been isolated. It no longer records, it can't be accessed remotely, and it doesn't communicate with me."

"There's no way any tracking device in your body would work."

"No."

"What about your clothes? Could they be bugged?"

She glanced down at her regulation jumpsuit, one he'd seen on thousands of busy little worker bees going to and from the companies.

"I changed clothes as soon as I knew I was coming after you. I don't have anything on me, or with me, that I owned while working at CommTECH. I bought this in a small store on the outskirts of Houston and left all my old clothes there."

"Okay, it isn't you. Did you tell anyone where you were going? Who you planned to meet?"

"No one."

"No family? Friends? Someone looking after a cat for you?"

"There's no one. I was a foundling. My mother left me on the doorstep of CommTECH." Unreadable, luminous blue eyes stared up at him. "I was found by a security agent called Jones. On a Friday. Hence the name. I then spent my youth in various institutions."

"I get it. No family. What about friends? Boyfriends?" The thought that she might be involved with someone grated on him. It seemed he was fast developing possessive urges when it came to Friday Jones, and in his line of work, there was no room for them.

"No time for either friends or romance. My colleagues are just that—people I work with. We don't socialize."

"You're telling me no one outside of CommTECH knows that you've gone missing?" He ran a hand over his head as he tried to get his brain around someone being so completely alone. Without his team, his brothers, he'd be lost.

Her eyes flicked away for a second before returning to his and he tensed, instantly alert.

"Not exactly no one," she hedged.

His mind raced through the facts as he knew them. "There's the person who told you about me."

Her shoulders slumped. "Yes."

"Who is it?"

"I can't tell you. But they would never betray me. They want what I want."

He crossed his arms and glared at her. That answer was unacceptable. "And what exactly is it you want?"

Wide, sad eyes looked up at him. "Freedom."

He sucked in a breath and then cursed on the exhale.

"You're part of Freedom." Her cheeks flushed, but she nodded once. He clasped his hands on top of his head. No wonder Enforcement was so hot to catch up with her. She was a rebel. A member of Freedom. Part of an underground revolution.

Or, in the eyes of the Territory governments—a terrorist.

CHAPTER 6

CommTECH Headquarters, New York City,
Northern Territory

"WHAT DO YOU MEAN YOU LOST HER?" MIRIAM SHEPHERD, CEO of CommTECH, asked the holo-image of the Enforcement agent.

The man stood to attention, large as life, in the middle of her office. This was the way Miriam liked to deal with the dirt that came with her job. At least a holo-image didn't leave marks on her priceless silk rug.

"She may have been buried under the rubble, ma'am. We're checking for bio-signatures right now." The man's voice had all the emotion of a drone.

"When will you know for certain if she's dead?"

"Within the hour."

Too long. She could be out of the Northern Territory by then. Especially if she'd obtained the services of a smuggler. No. Not just *any* smuggler. *Striker.* The man had been a thorn in the side of CommTECH ever since he'd mysteriously appeared three years earlier.

"Keep searching. This is a priority order. Stand by for

further communication." She waved her hand and the image disappeared.

"We need to make sure the girl is no longer a threat." Ju-Long Lee, master of the obvious, and CEO of Lee-Chan Medical, smoothed a hand down his pristine oriental-style suit.

"What do you think I'm doing here?" Miriam let none of her frustration show in her tone. If the man hadn't insisted on a meeting in person, none of this would have happened. He didn't believe there was such a thing as an un-hackable conference call, and they were all suffering because of it.

"I think you are trying to correct your mistake." His black eyes were icy cold. "You should have ensured the building was empty for the meeting."

"I did." The scientist had sneaked in to work. Something she did all the time, apparently. Something her supervisors had failed to mention.

"We need to contact our source." Serge Abramovich nursed his ever-present whiskey as he lazed on the cream leather sectional in the corner of her office. His sarcastic smile was as much a fixture as the scotch. "The source will tell us if the woman is still alive."

"Yes," Miriam snapped the words. "Why didn't I think of that?"

The owner of Abramovich Metals and Alloys laughed into his drink.

Miriam waved her hand over her glass-topped desk, used her implant to communicate remotely with the virtual screen that appeared in front of her, and sent a message to their source. A second later, a shadowy figure manifested as a ghostly silhouette hovering above her desk. She didn't know the identity of her contact, only that he called himself "the Broker" and made a living trading information to the highest bidder.

"We have a problem," Miriam told the person who was

costing them a small fortune. "Enforcement lost them. Are they still alive?"

"I'm adding this to your bill," the modified voice said.

"Of course." She folded her arms over her cream silken dress and resisted the urge to tap her toe. The image in front of her froze while their source contacted someone else. A few seconds passed before it moved again.

"They're alive. They're holed up in South Munroe."

Before she could say anything else, the image disappeared. She mentally contacted the head of the Enforcement team. The holographic man appeared in the middle of the room. This time Miriam noticed he was injured. Blood trailed from his temple.

Not her concern.

"They're in South Munroe."

His jaw clenched. "We'll deal with it."

"See that you do." She cut the connection, and the man disappeared.

"Is this really necessary?" Sandrine Cherbourg asked. The lithe woman headed up the Southern Territory's largest conglomerate. "Perhaps we should invite the woman in for a download. You *do* download your Passive Recorders periodically, non? Such a request wouldn't arouse suspicion."

"It's too late for that, my dear," Ju-Long told her. "Now the world is watching a manhunt unfold live on their newsfeeds." He gestured to the soundless images running on the wall behind him. They showed live footage of Enforcement officers speeding through Munroe. Someone had gotten hold of the details concerning the chase, and they were running it as a hot news story. To make things even more difficult for them, a photo of Friday Jones appeared in the corner of the screen. "The girl isn't going to come in willingly now."

Sandrine shrugged. "Then cut the satellite feeds."

"Yeah, like that won't attract further attention," Serge drawled.

"You should have called her in for a routine download," Sandrine chastised.

Miriam didn't appreciate the reprimand, especially coming from someone she considered to be an interloper within the leadership ranks. "A routine download was the first thing we tried. As soon as it was reported she'd been in the same building at the same time we were, I sent a message requesting her presence for an upgrade." She eyed each of the most powerful people in the world in turn. "She ran."

Sandrine stared at the image of Friday Jones, which was frozen on the screen. "Why did she run? Did you order something out of the ordinary?"

"No." Miriam had personally supervised the request. "I even added the incentive of a promotion."

Ju-Long stood, clasped his hands behind his back, and paced the room. He was the oldest of the four. Miriam didn't know his exact age but estimated it to be somewhere in his eighties. The only signs of his advanced age were his white head of hair and a slight stoop to his shoulders. Other than that, his long, stick-insect proportions had changed little over the years. Neither had his merciless nature. "Are we sure she even saw anything? This could all be for nothing if the woman didn't see anything incriminating."

Miriam waved a hand, and a recording played on the screen taking up one wall of her office. It showed a bumbling woman hurrying along a corridor. Her attention was firmly on the data pad in her hand, her lips moved as she read the information on it. As she turned the corner, she stumbled, and instead of looking left, she looked right—straight through the open door at the end of the corridor. Straight at the six people who were meeting covertly.

She didn't pause when she saw them, didn't stop at all. She had barely more than a glimpse, but it was enough time for the image to be stored in her databank and for her to have recorded any conversation she'd overheard. The woman carried on, still reading her handheld. The meeting hadn't consciously registered with her. She was completely unaware of the time bomb that was now residing in her head.

"She saw all of us," Ju-Long said.

"Yes. I didn't get this visual record until our meeting had concluded. As soon as I saw it, I ordered a download session at the clinic. She should have come in as usual. We would have downloaded the images, wiped her memory, and the incident would have been dealt with."

"Instead, she ran," Sandrine said again. "Do you think she's a spy?"

The four of them froze before turning in unison to stare at the image of Friday. Miriam felt a chill climb up her spine. She waved her hand in front of her desk and mentally brought up the chief of Northern Territory Enforcement.

"Yes, ma'am," the woman barked. She'd been born into the military and breathed Enforcement in all its forms.

"Friday Jones. Full investigation. Leave nothing uncovered."

"When do you want it?"

"Now."

"Yes, ma'am." The image disappeared.

Miriam stared at the blank glass of her desktop.

"You think she's with Freedom," Ju-Long said the words everyone else was thinking.

"I hope to hell she isn't." Serge thrust his fingers through his overgrown hair. "If she is, then this just got a million times worse for all of us. Because this comedy show"—he pointed at the newsfeed—"has let her know how important the information inside her head is to us."

Miriam had to clench her teeth to stop herself from thanking the man for pointing out the obvious.

Their four companies might control the civilized world,

but if the scientist was working with Freedom, she had the information inside of her that could ignite a war. Freedom needed something to unite the people behind it. And Friday Jones could do exactly that.

"We'll get her." It was a promise. Miriam held the eyes of her peers.

"Yes." Ju-Long stared back at her. "Yes. We will."

There were no other options.

CHAPTER 7

"You're a terrorist." Striker folded his arms and glared down at the woman he'd claimed. The woman who was now his responsibility, and whose expertise he badly needed to help his team come to terms with the anomalies in their genetics. Anomalies that would get them all killed if they were ever discovered.

She shot to her feet. "I am not."

"Yet you admit you're involved with Freedom?"

"I pass on information. That's it. And the information I've been able to give them hasn't even been that useful. It's mainly about the work I'm doing. Nothing earth-shattering or innovative, only run-of-the-mill biotech."

He pointed at her head. "They download your data?"

"No. CommTECH would know if someone else accessed it. I had a secure communications link, and I contacted them once a week to share what little I knew."

"They're looking for a way to take down CommTECH."

It wasn't a question. Freedom was very vocal about their aims. They wanted a world run by elected officials—the way it used to be—instead of a world run by big business.

"They intend to take down the big four. To wipe the slate

clean. Start again. Build a system that favors the poor. One that gives people like me choices. Right now, there aren't any. You either sign away your life to a company for an education, or you scrape a living doing whatever you can. That isn't a choice. It's slavery."

"Yeah, yeah, Freedom is noble. They're fighting the good fight. Let's arm the proletariat and rise up against our oppressors." It was the main theme of every history book he'd been forced to read in high school.

"You're being facetious."

"It's one of my many skills. I'm surprised you didn't hear about it when you were making inquiries with your Freedom buddies. Did they tell you where to find me?"

"Yes, they gave me your location when I messaged my contact after I got the order to come in for an upgrade. They said you had the skills to help me. For a price."

Striker didn't like that one bit. He thought he was flying under the radar—from official and non-official organizations alike. "They told you to get to La Paz?"

"I worked that part out on my own. Where else would I find the antidote?"

The look on her face said she thought he was a complete idiot for asking. That attitude would help her cause. Not.

Striker's eye shot to the window as he heard the low hum of an approaching hover-vehicle. "Don't move."

He strode over and glanced out to find Mace riding up. He headed to the broken door to let his teammate in, checking the street behind the big man. It was empty. "Where's your other half?"

"She'll be here soon. She's busy spreading misinformation." He held up a thin scanner. "I brought this. Better safe than sorry."

"Yeah." Striker motioned into the room. "Friday, this is Mace, he's is gonna scan you for trackers."

"I told you it's impossible for any electronic device to work in me right now."

"Humor him." He was seriously beginning to regret his decision to take the woman, and her many problems, on.

"Arms out, honey." His second-in-command grinned down at Friday. At six-and-a-half-feet tall, Mace towered over her, and yet, she clearly wasn't intimidated. In fact, she seemed more interested in the tech than the man.

"That's a DC-120." She pointed at the scanner. "There's a more up-to-date model. You need to get one."

"I'll get right on that." Mace ran the scanner over the curve of her waist.

"You're doing it wrong." She frowned. It was cute.

With an irritated growl, the big guy glared at her. "There's a right way?"

She huffed out a breath. "Yes, there's a right way. That scanner works best when you work your way down in a circular motion rather than a straight line. It has a limited field of operation, which means it can sometimes miss items. A circular motion ensures there isn't any chance of skipping even an inch of skin. Do you want me to show you what to do?"

"No, I think I got it." Mace shook his head, then resumed the scan. Making sure to do it properly this time. "Clear," he told Striker when he'd finished.

To her credit, Friday didn't point out that she'd told him so. Although the look she gave him was the same one his kindergarten teacher had given him every time he'd tried to eat the paste.

"Could just be luck," Mace said, referring to Enforcement knowing their whereabouts. But his face made it clear he believed in luck about as much as Striker did.

"They're getting information on her whereabouts from somewhere. There's no such thing as a coincidence."

"She tell anyone what she was doing?"

"*She*," Friday said pointedly, "is standing right here, wondering why you're talking about her instead of to her. And no, I didn't tell anyone." Friday folded her arms over her ugly jumpsuit and glared up at Mace, who seemed bewildered by her.

"She told Freedom." Striker felt the need to point out.

It was his turn to be on the receiving end of her glare. "They don't count. They would never sell me out to CommTECH or Enforcement."

"Freedom?" All amusement drained from the big guy's face. "You have got to be kidding me?" He railed at Striker. "She's a terrorist. They're never going to stop hunting her. Or anyone who helps her. You need to cut her loose." He looked back at Friday. "You're on your own."

"No." Striker strode forward, unconsciously positioning himself between Friday and the man who had the dubious honor of being his best friend. "We have a deal. I promised my help. And we need her."

"We can get someone else. Genetic scientists are a dime a dozen. We can get one who doesn't have the entire Enforcement organization on her ass."

"It's not that easy. You know how hard it would be to get one we could trust."

Mace barked out a mirthless laugh. "Trust? Are you listening to anything I'm telling you? She's in league with a terrorist organization. She sells secrets. She spies. She's the last person on the planet we can trust."

Friday pushed out from behind him, trying to get to Mace. Striker put an arm around her waist and pulled her to his side, uncertain why he felt the need to protect their client from his teammate, but unable to stop himself from doing it anyway. Mace watched the move with narrowed eyes.

"I'm standing right here," she snapped. "*She* is perfectly capable of talking for herself. And *she* has a name. My name is Friday." She struggled, clearly wanting to face-off against

Mace—a man who was more than a foot taller than her and had at least four times her bulk.

"Okay, *Friday*," Mace growled. "You want to tell us how we can trust you? How you're not going to put our whole team at risk? How you wouldn't sell our secrets to the highest bidder? Or spy for Freedom, if you thought anything you found out about us would help the cause? Tell me, Friday, tell me exactly why we should trust you. Why we should help you." He didn't wait for an answer before looking back up at Striker, his dark eyes flashing with anger. "Cut her loose. This is a mistake. We can't take the risk."

"I don't sell secrets." Friday's outrage made her voice rise.

"You spied for Freedom," Mace said. "You're one huge walking, talking trust-issue, waiting to bite us on the ass."

She opened her mouth to object, and Striker squeezed her waist to silence her.

"This is my call." He kept his voice even, free of any emotion, wanting them both to know he was deadly serious. "You heard the deal I made with her. We have her for a year. No questions asked. We have complete control of her for a year."

He felt a shudder rush through Friday and could only imagine the twisted things going through her overactive mind. She paled as she looked up at Mace, making him want to reassure her again that she wouldn't be touched against her will. Not by anyone. Not ever. Not if he had his way.

"What happens at the end of the year, genius?" Mace wasn't cowed by either of them. "What's to keep her from spilling everything she finds out once the year is up?"

"I won't." Friday's confident answer might have meant a little more if she'd known exactly what her promise meant.

Striker ignored her assurance. It was easier than trying to ignore the heat of her body as it pressed against his. Even as he focused on Mace, he was still aware of her curves beneath her ugly jumpsuit. Her softness pressing against his hardness.

He shook his head to clear it, aware that his increasingly intense reaction to her wasn't in character for him. Sure, he found her attractive, but the need to keep her close and protect her was growing by the minute.

"Yeah," Mace mocked her. "You'll keep our secrets. There's no way you'll run to Freedom with them the first chance you get."

"I won't do that. I wouldn't." She looked up at Striker. "You have to believe me. I will never speak about what happens during our year together. You have my word."

Mace snorted.

"We don't have time to deal with this right now," Striker said to his second-in-command.

"Will you listen to yourself?" The big guy threw up his hands in disgust. "You're risking all of us on an unknown future. On a woman who is a proven security risk."

Striker held his friend's eyes as everything within him stilled. They needed Friday. He was beginning to think *he* needed her. His reaction to her was visceral. All of his instincts, his *changed* instincts, were telling him to keep her close. He broke the stare-off to look down at the woman in his grasp. She was pale, but stoic. A woman used to making the best of some crummy life situations.

"After you take the antidote," he said. "Will your implants automatically reconnect to the grid?"

"No." She glanced at Mace. "They can be removed and analyzed, but they won't reconnect. The only way to get any information off them would be manually."

He could see her big brain working overtime, trying to find a solution to their trust dilemma that would reassure them.

"Are you willing to sever your ties to Freedom in order to come with us?" Striker asked.

Mace scoffed at the question. "Like she couldn't contact them again in the future."

Friday's face paled further. Her huge eyes became more vivid as she watched them. He knew she was struggling with a decision. He also knew when she'd reached it. Her shoulders slumped slightly, but her chin remained high. There was resolve in her eyes.

"I will sever my ties." She licked dry lips. "I'll also agree to be implanted with a monitoring chip once the Interferan-X is out of my system."

Striker's hold tightened around her waist. His gaze flicked to his friend, noting the shock and reluctant admiration in Mace's eyes, before turning his attention back to the brave woman in his hold.

"You know what that means, chère?" He deliberately pitched his voice soft, soothing.

She swallowed hard and nodded once. "It means you will know everything I do and everyone I contact. It means you can control my communications—for the rest of my life." She looked away from him.

He heard the words she didn't say. It meant she would never truly be free. The hold CommTECH had over her would be replaced with his hold. Part of him wanted to shout his objection, to throw her over his shoulder and take her somewhere private where he could reassure her using his hands and mouth. The urge, the need, to keep her safe and give her the freedom she desperately wanted, rose in him like a wave. One that almost drowned him. Instead of doing any of those things, he looked at the man he trusted most in the world. "That good enough for you?"

"Yeah." Mace sounded a little stunned and a lot impressed. He considered Friday the same way he did those puzzles he obsessed over.

Striker understood. There was a whole lot about their client that got under a man's skin and made him think.

An alarm blared from Mace's wrist unit. His mouth

thinned as he checked it. "Enforcement breached the perimeter beacons I set up. We need to get out of here. Now."

They were out of time. Striker cursed, grabbed Friday's arm, and started to run for the broken front door.

"Wait." She shook free and rushed back across the room. Hurriedly, she dug into her pocket and came out with a credit chip, which she left on the counter.

When she turned back and saw them staring at her, she blushed. "We broke their door, ate their food, and drank their water. I don't have enough to cover what we took, but it'll help." She kept her eyes low and snapped the words as though she was ashamed of what she'd done.

Something cracked around his heart.

"Can you cover us while we run for it?" he said to his second.

Mace nodded as he frowned at Friday, who'd just added something else for him to puzzle over. "You take the bike. Sandi will be here any minute. I'll hold down the fort until then."

With a nod of thanks, Striker climbed onto the hoverbike. "Get on," he ordered Friday, who stood staring at the machine.

"Do you have something against passenger pods?" she grumbled as she climbed onto the seat behind him.

Hoverbikes weren't designed to take two on the seat, and it was a tight squeeze. He could feel her plastered flat against his back, her breasts pressed into his muscles.

"Be safe," he said to his friend.

The big man gave him a chin lift as Striker started the bike and headed southwest to the border wall, aware they had mere minutes of a head start. There was no time to waste; he had to get Friday past the wall and into the Red Zone before they were both killed.

Or worse, captured.

CHAPTER 8

THEY HEADED INTO THE DESERT AND FRIDAY WATCHED THE lights of the city fade into darkness. Munroe city lay behind them, and the border wall was a tall, gently glowing barrier on their left. Even at a distance, the wall seemed to loom over everything around it. A reminder that they were all caged in. Prisoners in the Northern Territory.

Sure, the wall had been built to protect the territory citizens from wandering into the Red Zone. At least, that was the theory when it had been put up a hundred years earlier after an experimental weapon had killed everything within the zone and rendered the area a no-man's-land. History class had taught Friday that the red mist the weapon dispensed should have dispersed over a year or two. The scientists had been wrong. Instead of dispersing, it had grown thicker, heavier, and more condensed. It was unmoved by wind, unaffected by rain, and deadly to any human who touched it. She'd seen satellite images of the Red Zone. It looked like a long, red gash on the planet's surface, a festering wound that wouldn't heal.

And she would have to go through it to get to the antidote she needed.

That was, if they could get past the wall.

"Shouldn't you enable the reflector shield on this thing?" Once again, she was communicating through the helmets they were wearing.

"Don't have one." Striker's voice sounded far more intimate in the confines of her helmet.

"You don't have one?" A reflector shield would obscure the vehicle and keep it from being visually identified. It worked by blurring the air around it and making it hard to see the machine. She would have thought it an essential item for a man who liked to stay under the radar.

"Don't have anything unnecessary, chère," he drawled. "Extra weight will slow us down, and we need speed to outrun Enforcement."

"But wouldn't a reflector shield mean we could hide from them?" Didn't he realize that if they hid, they wouldn't need to outrun them? Had she made a mistake in trusting Striker and his team? It was quite possible he wasn't as smart as her contact had told her.

His chuckle unnerved her, making her body tingle in places she didn't want to be aware of at that moment. Possibly ever. Her powers of denial were already stretched to the limit with pretending she didn't notice there was a man wedged between her legs, pressing hard against her. She felt overstimulated—mentally and physically—and really didn't need anything more to cope with.

"I know what I'm doing. If we needed a reflector shield, we'd have one. We don't need it."

"Why aren't we heading for the wall? We need to get over it."

"You say that like I wasn't able to think of it by myself."

She thought it wise not to answer that. "Everybody says the best places to get over the wall are in the crowded areas of the cities." Although, not that many people had tried to get over the wall, and those who did tended to get swallowed by the mist, never to be seen again. It seemed the general wisdom on the best places to get over the wall stemmed more from speculation than reality.

"Everybody don't know shit," Striker said.

A horrible thought occurred to her. What if she was totally wrong? What if this man couldn't get her where she needed to be? "You do know how to get over the wall, don't you?"

"No faith," he drawled.

Having no choice but to hold on and hope for the best, Friday tried to focus on the landscape rather than her fears. The desert wasn't what she'd expected it to be.

"I thought it would be barren," she whispered, more to herself than anyone else.

She felt his abdomen flex beneath her hands and regretted that she'd spoken aloud.

"You never seen the desert, chère?"

She shook her head before remembering he couldn't see her. "I'd never been out of Houston until I came to Munroe to find you."

That made his muscles clench and relax again.

"Someday I'll take you to the Painted Desert and let you see how unbarren the landscape can be."

She felt something melt within her at his declaration. And then she remembered that her chances of seeing anything in the future were slim to none. "Unbarren? I don't think that's a word."

His chuckle warmed her, and she fought the urge to rest her cheek against his back. The bike swerved, turning down a rough dirt road toward the wall, and her stomach clenched at the sight. It was much higher than she'd imagined it would be.

"How are we going to get past it?"

"Probably better if I don't tell you."

She opened her mouth to demand an answer but froze

when she caught sight of a sign at the side of the road. He was taking her into Scorpion Canyon.

Was he out of his mind?

"No!" She dug her fingers into his hard stomach. "You can't be serious."

"It's the only part of the whole damn territory that isn't walled."

"There's a reason for that. People die in the canyon. Everyone who goes into it dies. Everyone. They couldn't build a wall there because the work crew kept getting killed."

A hundred years had passed since the first attempt to block the canyon, and still the gap in the wall hadn't been closed. All the Territory authorities had done to deter people from trying to get through it was to make sure that no vehicle could enter the canyon. You only got so far before spikes and lasers immobilized your ride. If you were going to risk your life with the scorpions, you had to do it on foot.

Striker angled the bike down the trail into the canyon, completely untroubled by her protests. Unlike the Grand Canyon, this one wasn't large. But what it lacked in size, it made up for in mystery. The place was an anomaly for researchers to study because, when the weapon containing the red mist had detonated, scorpions had flooded the canyon. No one knew why. All they knew was that the creatures had been affected by the mist somehow and had multiplied, becoming even deadlier with each successive generation. The canyon was now home to millions of aggressive scorpions. It was their territory, and to enter meant death.

"Let me off this bike!" Friday thumped at Striker's shoulders. "I won't let you kill us both. Let me off. I'll find another way."

The bike skidded to a halt, kicking up dust behind them. The blue glow from the wall couldn't penetrate the depths of the canyon. There was only the flickering light of the stars above and the narrow beam from the bike's headlight to break up the black void that engulfed them.

As soon as the engine cut, she jumped off the bike, spun on her heel, and started up the trail they'd come in on. She didn't get far before a strong arm wrapped around her waist and tugged her back into a solid body.

"I know what I'm doing. This is the way in and out of the Red Zone. You think I haven't done this before?" Clearly, he was running out of patience. Which was fine with her, because she'd about reached her limit, too.

She pushed at his arm and gained enough space to turn in his hold. She glared up at him. "Have you done this before? Because you don't tell me anything. You just expect me to follow blindly."

"That's what you're paying me for. You're paying me to lead you out of the Territory."

"I'm paying you to keep me alive. That's why I need to get to Bolivia. Yet here you are, taking me into what is basically a death pit."

He had the audacity to smile at her. "You're forgetting one thing, bébé. I'm way more dangerous than any itty-bitty scorpion."

Of all the ludicrous things to say… "Are you way more dangerous than millions of itty-bitty scorpions?"

"Hell, yeah." He chuckled at the thought.

He was obviously insane. She'd trusted her life—what she had left of it—to a madman.

"Let me go!"

"No. Behave. We're on a deadline and I don't have time to deal with your freak-outs."

Freak-outs? "Let me—" His large hand covered her mouth.

"Quiet! Enforcement." The words were hissed against her ear.

She froze instantly, her eyes going to the canyon rim.

There were lights. Lots of red Enforcement lights. Striker reached out and, with a flick of a switch, disabled the light on his bike. They were suddenly shrouded in darkness, halfway down the canyon.

"We need to go," he said against her ear. "Trust me. If you can't believe that I wouldn't let you die, at least believe that I wouldn't let me die."

He had a point. She nodded, and he released her mouth.

"No noise," he hissed.

She nodded again, and he gently cupped her cheek.

"I promise you, I will keep you safe."

Her face tingled under his touch, and for one endless second, the world faded to the man in front of her. He wasn't like anyone she'd ever known, and much to her own shock, she wanted to trust him.

"Desperation," she whispered her reasoning aloud.

His lips twitched. "Probably." He stepped away from her, grabbed her hand, and turned toward the canyon depths. "Come on." He tugged her forward, down the narrow, rocky path that led to the bottom of the ravine.

And to the scorpions.

Voices echoed through the night. Floodlights came on above them, casting sharp shadows on the canyon walls. They hurried downward as the sheer rock face rose up either side of them. Water trickled, and she thought there might be a stream at the bottom. Were they going to walk through the water to safety? Could scorpions swim?

She clutched Striker's hand when he dragged her past an official warning sign. Even if there hadn't been a huge skull-and-crossbones on it, or the word Danger hadn't been written in large red letters, the photos would have sent her running. Two boards detailed what a scorpion sting would do to a person, showing photos of corpses that had been stung multiple times. It was horrific.

But instead of running at the sight, she felt a strange calm sweep through her and recognized it instantly. She'd experienced the same sensation in the past, when things were out of her control. It was acceptance. Either she would die in the canyon, or she wouldn't. There wasn't a whole lot she could do about it. One thing was for sure—she wasn't going to climb out of the canyon and take her chances with Enforcement. If she was going to die, she'd do it on her own terms. And she'd do it attempting to be free.

The path narrowed and twisted down to the bottom. Friday could barely make out shapes around her as the lights from the wall above them dimmed. Soon, the light wouldn't be able to reach them, and she would be left in the dark— with the scorpions. Her breathing became shallower with every step she took, and she clung to Striker's hand as though it were a lifeline. Their descent defied logic. There was no evidence, in over a hundred years, that anyone had survived this trip. And yet, here she was, desperate and terrified, going further into the canyon with each passing step.

It didn't take long to reach the bottom. The crevice wasn't as deep as she'd thought. But what it lacked in grandeur, it made up for in atmosphere. There was an eerie stillness that made her skin crawl with the awareness that something was waiting, watching and thinking, in the dark nooks and crannies.

Scorpions.

Her hands started to tremble as the darkness engulfed them and her other senses became acute. She heard the first scurry of tiny feet as they made their way along the water's edge toward the gap in the border wall.

"Shouldn't we walk in the stream?" she whispered. Although, common sense told her that the arachnids already knew her exact location and she would give nothing further away by talking.

"The scorpions in this canyon don't mind the water." Striker didn't whisper. Nor did his voice tremble with fear.

In *this* canyon. Like they weren't normal scorpions at all.

"Do you have protective suits stashed down here?"

"There isn't a suit on the planet that would keep out thousands of determined scorpions."

More scurrying to her left made her head snap around. She pressed closer to Striker. Without breaking his stride, he wrapped an arm around her waist and tugged her to him. The darkness became thicker. Friday stumbled on the uneven ground.

"I can't see," she whispered, aware her voice was shaking.

"I can."

"You keep saying that. It doesn't help."

The scurrying sounds came from every direction now. Her breathing grew shallow, making her a little lightheaded. She felt Striker squeeze her waist and she curled a fist into his belt, to hold on tight.

Her mind whirled, throwing facts at her, reminding her of everything she knew about scorpion stings. Their venom was a neurotoxin, which attacked the nervous system. She'd feel pain when they first struck, but it wouldn't be agonizing. The agony would come later. First there would be vomiting, followed by muscle cramps, paralysis, and convulsions until her lungs and heart stopped working. It was an excruciatingly painful death, and that was assuming she only received one sting. Each additional injection of the toxin would speed up the process. Maybe it would be better to be attacked by several scorpions, rather than just one—less time suffering. Images of herself lying on the ground, covered in scorpions, flashed in her mind, and she decided one would be enough. She couldn't even think about her body becoming food after she died…

"You're gonna be fine. Just focus on breathing normally." Striker's words cut through her impending hysteria. "Once we're around this bend, I'll turn on the flashlight, and you'll be able to see where you're going. That will help."

There was no sign of the bend he was talking about, or even a path in front of them—it was that dark. She shook hard now, each step on the uneven path becoming perilous. It was difficult to concentrate on anything other than the sound of scurrying—a hurricane of tiny feet, building in volume and speed, all coming straight for them.

They swerved to the right, and the flashlight came on. Instantly, she scrunched her eyes closed, terrified of what she would see.

"It's okay," Striker said calmly. "You can look."

No.

She couldn't.

Instead, she turned into him, pressing her face into his chest, wishing she could crawl inside him and hide forever.

But the noise wouldn't let her.

All she could hear was the scurrying. They were surrounded, and the sound was deafening.

"Open your eyes," he said gently. "You're safe, I promise you. You gotta open your eyes, bébé."

Clasping her fists into his shirt, she managed to look up at him, terrified of glancing anywhere else.

"Not at me." He smiled at her. "Look around you."

Her lips were trembling, making it impossible to speak, to tell him that she didn't want to look. That she might die if she saw millions of tiny, hungry eyes staring back at her.

"Bébé, trust me. If you look, you'll feel better."

It was his tone, more than his words, that convinced her. The gentle conviction. The power in his voice that said he'd stand between her and her fear.

Swallowing hard, she forced herself to glance down at the area illuminated by the beam of light. At first, she didn't see anything, only rocks and dried-out grass, but then, at the edge of the light pool, she saw them. Scorpions. She stopped breathing at the sight, shaking so hard she thought she might pass out. Her eyes shot back to Striker.

"No, no bébé. It's okay." He nuzzled the top of her head. "They won't come any closer. I promise. Look but you'd best breathe while you do it, or I'll have to carry you outta here." His smile was reassuring.

For a minute, she stared into his dark eye while she fought to get air into her lungs.

"That's it," he soothed. "Deep, even breaths. It's gonna be fine now." He rubbed her back, slow and firm, in time with her breathing. "See? That's much better."

Friday's fists were still clamped in his shirt, her fingers over his steady heartbeat. She felt the calm rise and fall of his chest and tried to follow his lead, breathing when he did.

"That's good. You're doing good. Now, look at the scorpions. See how they stay a few feet away? They won't come closer."

She followed his gaze and shuddered at the sight—thousands and thousands of moving bodies, black and red, a carpet of arachnids as far as she could see.

But none within touching distance of them.

She gasped, and her eyes flew to his. "Is it the light? Are they afraid of the light?"

"No. Scorpions are nocturnal and don't like the light, but it isn't the light that scares them." He paused. "It's me."

Her mind reeled at his quiet assertion. A million questions flooded it, the first and foremost being, why were they afraid of Striker?

He unpicked her fingers from his shirt and took her hand. "We've got a long walk out of here and no time to waste. Stick close to me, and you'll be fine."

At his words, her attention flew back to the ring of scorpions and she held him tightly as they trekked alongside the stream bed. Slowly, they moved deeper into the canyon, all the while surrounded by a crawling carpet of arachnids. The noise was something she would never forget—the sound of a million scurrying feet as they clambered over rocks and dirt, the faint clacking of pincers as they rubbed together. It was unnerving. The sound of nightmares.

"I'm glad I can't see their eyes." The thought of millions of eyes reflecting through the darkness was too much to contemplate.

"Especially seeing as they have about twelve each."

She poked him in the ribs. "That doesn't help."

They walked on in silence, making steady progress. When they reached the narrowest part of the canyon, the spot that should have run under the border wall, the scorpions raced up the sheer faces on either side of them, forming a moving gate for them to pass through. Friday and Striker inched forward, passing the scorpions while crossing under the cool glow from the wall lights that came from the edges of the ravine. Heart stuttering, she crossed the few short feet that took them past the border wall. She was officially out of the Northern Territory.

And heading into the Red Zone.

"Just a little farther and we'll be done with our eight legged stalkers," Striker said.

"Why do they stay away from you?"

He shot her a look she couldn't quite read. "Maybe, if we get that poison out of you and you survive, I'll let you in on that little secret. Right now, we gotta focus on getting out of here. Soon, we're gonna start the climb out of the canyon and the scorpions will stay behind."

"They never leave the canyon?"

Now that her terror had eased, she wondered if someone had studied the creatures. Their behavior was off. But then, she didn't know a whole lot about arachnids in general. She glanced at Striker out of the corner of her eye. It seemed he was something else that might need some investigation. In the logical part of her brain, the part that never stopped working, she was already trying to figure out a reason for the scorpions' aversion to the man, and she didn't like any of the theories she came up with. Because each one meant she was in far more trouble with the man than she would have been on her own.

"No, they never leave," he said, turning her attention back to the scorpions. "Why would you leave a cushy home like this when your prey keeps walking in and presenting itself to you?"

It was hard to believe anyone would be that stupid. "You can't mean that people still try to get through the canyon?"

"People, animals, insects. They all wander into Scorpion Canyon, but very few wander back out."

As they climbed the steep path out of the canyon, the sound of the scorpions following them began to fade. By the time they had reached the rim, she was fairly certain they were alone. She grasped the hand Striker held out to help her climb up onto the ridge, and with one hard yank, she was out of the canyon.

And into something far worse.

In front of her, not more than twenty feet away, was the cloud of poisonous mist that made up the Red Zone. It sat before them like a thick fog, heavy and impenetrable and dense. She looked up but couldn't see where it ended. To the right and the left, it seemed to go on forever. There was no getting past it. No going under it, or around it. And Territory restrictions meant flying over it was out of the question. That left Friday with only two choices—allow Striker to lead her through the red mist or head back into Scorpion Canyon to take her chances with the arachnids and Enforcement.

With a shaky breath, she looked up at him. "I've changed my mind. I want to go back. This isn't going to work."

"Have a little faith," the reckless outlaw said.

CHAPTER 9

CommTECH Headquarters, New York City,
Northern Territory

"WE BELIEVE THE SUSPECT IS HEADING FOR GALVESTON." THE life-size image of the Enforcement agent tasked with retrieving Friday Jones stood at attention while he gave his report.

Miriam Shepherd was unmoved by his disheveled appearance and obvious injuries. The man deserved pain for having failed, yet again. Actions had consequences. It was a rule the CEO of CommTECH lived by. And she especially enjoyed the consequences when she was the one dispensing them.

"You believe?" Miriam arched one perfectly groomed eyebrow.

The perspiration on the man's brow pleased her. He was right to sweat. He should be the one to feel stress from this grossly mishandled operation. Not her. It grated that this mess had landed in her lap for her to solve. If it hadn't been for Ju-Long's fears, the incompetence of her staff, and Enforcement's mishandling of the situation, Miriam wouldn't have had to get involved. Once again, she was cleaning up after other people. And she did not like it. Not at all. There would be consequences for everyone who'd dragged her into this mess.

The Enforcement agent cleared his throat. "We lost the suspects in South Munroe. There was a firefight. Our agents were attacked."

"By the smuggler?" Sandrine asked from her perch on the sofa.

"No, ma'am. We think it was drug dealers. They mistook our hunt as an attempt to shut down their operation, which was not our aim at that time. In the confusion that followed, the suspects slipped out of Munroe. Agents were dispatched, and we thought we caught sight of them heading west into the desert. I sent a team to check the lead, but it went straight to Scorpion Canyon."

Serge waved his whiskey in her direction. "If they're in the canyon, they're dead."

Miriam clenched her jaw to stop from thanking him for stating the obvious. Unfortunately, because of the vast number of scorpions in the canyon, attempts to scan for bioreadings were always pointless. There was no way to know for sure if anyone went into the canyon. But they did know for certain that no one ever came out.

"Did you find evidence they'd taken that route?" Miriam asked the officer.

"No, ma'am, and while we were scoping the area, word came in from another team. The duo had been spotted on their way to the coast. With this new information, we've concentrated our efforts in the region around Galveston."

"Do they think they can get to the Southern Coalition countries by boat?" Miriam shook her head at the stupidity. "Shut the coast down. Turn all satellites to that area and identify every person they reveal. Arm the drones and send them out to cover the gulf. Stop all shipping traffic. Find them. Do not fail."

The man paled at the clearly implied threat. With a disgusted shake of her head, she cut the link, and he blinked out of existence. If only it were as easy to get rid of someone in reality.

Before anyone in the room could give her more useless advice, Miriam contacted their mole within the smuggling organization. The shadowy figure of the Broker appeared almost instantly.

Miriam didn't waste any time with pleasantries. This conversation was costing her money. "Our information says they're heading for Galveston and the gulf. Is that correct?"

"That's what I heard."

She almost breathed a sigh of relief at having her facts confirmed. If they were headed to the gulf, she'd get them.

"If you hear anything different, please contact me immediately."

"At double the usual cost." There was a smirk in the voice. Their informant had them over a barrel, and they knew it.

"Of course." She inclined her head in polite acceptance of their new deal before cutting off the communication.

She looked over at her three co-conspirators. "As soon as this is over, I want to find out the identity of the Broker and have them removed."

There were nods of agreement, as well as smiles filled with relief.

CHAPTER 10

From a sealed box that had been left beside the canyon rim, Striker retrieved a lantern and switched it on. He also pulled out two bottles of water and yet more unappetizing meal bars. He offered both to Friday. She took the water but shook her head at the bar. Striker couldn't blame her. He tossed both bars back into the box.

Friday sat on the ground, her back to a rock, staring at the thick red cloud in front of them. Her face, which had been filled with emotion minutes earlier, was now carefully blank. The mask she wore when she was terrified. Obviously, she was resolved to follow him into the Red Zone but didn't think she'd make it out the other side alive.

The lack of faith in his abilities was depressing.

"It's so thick," she said, her eyes glued to the sea of red. "When they talk about it, they always call it a mist. It's nothing like a mist."

"Yeah, it's more like deadly red cotton candy."

She glanced up at him, then back to the red cloud. "I don't know what that is."

"It's bright pink spun sugar. You eat it. It looks like fluff, but it's sticky and thick. Like the cloud."

"Is this something you've seen in the Coalition Countries outside of the Territories?"

"Something like that."

Silence fell again as she stared at the red void. Striker was familiar with the sight, but for someone who'd only heard about it, he could imagine it would take some getting used to.

"Six million people." The whispered words broke the unearthly stillness that permeated the Red Zone. She looked up at him, her eyes glassy with unshed tears. "That's how many people were killed."

He felt a strange tightening around his heart at the sight of her grief. In the three years he'd been taking people through the zone, it was the first time anyone had commented on the destruction the cloud had caused. And it was definitely the first time he'd seen someone moved by the overwhelming loss of lives.

She wiped away a tear that had fallen onto her cheek. "The people couldn't get out of the blast zone in time."

"They weren't given any warning."

"There was warning. But there were too many people to evacuate."

He knew better but kept his silence. This wasn't the time, or the place, to argue about the past.

"They're still in there," she whispered.

For a second, he could see the Red Zone through her eyes. It must seem like one vast graveyard.

"The people who were responsible for releasing an unknown and untested weapon were put to death shortly afterward," she said, as though he didn't know. "Theirs were the last executions carried out in the old United States." Her eyes held heartbreaking sadness. "The government shouldn't have done that. We needed to keep the scientists alive to find out what they'd done in order to undo it. Such a waste.

"They destroyed their research when everything went wrong, and their deaths took their knowledge with them. It was only years later, when the cloud didn't disperse as the scientists had promised, that the authorities regretted their hasty actions. Now we'll never know what's in the mist, and we'll never be able to combat it. It's impossible to get close enough to study it. It's like a huge time bomb from our past, just sitting there waiting to go off. What if it expands? What then? We're no better equipped to deal with it now than we were a century ago."

"It's dispersed some," he pointed out. "It retreated from the water pretty damn quickly after it was released."

"Another mystery. Why disperse from the water, but not the land?"

"At least the rivers run clean."

They fell silent again, contemplating the evidence of mankind's arrogance, his belief that he was in control of his world and could do what he liked with it.

"Do you know what this is? The red mist?" Friday finally asked. "It's a monument to how greedy and evil mankind can be. A permanent reminder of what we're capable of. A red scar on the face of the planet. That's us. We're a plague. A blight. We don't deserve to be here."

"Okay, Susie Sunshine." Striker crouched in front of her. "Should I bother trying to save your life, or would you rather end it all here and now?"

Her cheeks flushed. "Too much?"

"Just a bit."

She chewed at her lip before talking. "I'm worried what will happen when we go in there."

That was priceless. He threw back his head and laughed, long and hard. When he wiped his eye and looked at her, she was glaring at him. He held out his hand and tugged her to her feet.

"Bébé, you're either gonna die in there, or the poison's gonna get you out here. You got nothing to lose. Now how about trusting me for a change? Didn't those Freedom contacts of yours tell you that I'm the best? Have a little faith, huh?"

She batted those thick eyelashes at him. "How about I keep my more maudlin thoughts to myself instead?"

———

Friday blinked at him, unsure she'd heard correctly. "What?"

His smile was pure wickedness. "I said, get naked, chère."

He folded his arms, making those unnaturally large biceps of his bulge. The snake tattoo on his neck glinted in the blue light from the lantern and for one fanciful moment, she thought it watched her, too.

"Remember our deal," the devil said. "You do anything I want, anytime I want."

She gaped at him. Opening and closing her mouth like a fish stuck on dry land. "You want to have sex? Here?" She pointedly looked around them, first at the rocky ground beneath her, then at the rim of the canyon behind her and, finally at the cloud of heavy red fog on her other side. She could see this was going to be just as romantic as her last sexual encounter. "The ground is too rough. It will rip up my skin. I could get an infection."

When she looked back up at him, his grin was all teeth, and his shoulders were shaking.

"Are you laughing at me?" She was outraged. There was no way she was having sex with him under these conditions. She didn't care what their deal was. She'd rather walk into the red than surrender.

"Bébé." He closed the distance between them and clasped the top of her arms. "I don't want to have sex here. I never even mentioned sex when I negotiated our deal. But I find it highly entertaining that no matter what I tell you to do, you assume it will lead in that direction." She felt her cheeks burn as he leaned in to talk against her ear. "Now strip."

"If you don't want sex, why do I have to strip?"

He turned his back on her to dig around in the storage box, coming out with a tub of body cream. "I need to cover your skin with this, to help protect you from the mist."

She eyed him and his magic cream suspiciously. As far as she was aware, there was nothing that would keep the red mist from being absorbed into the skin. This sounded like a childish ploy to get his hands on her body.

"Whatever you're thinking right now," he said when she looked up at him, "don't tell me. Save it for later. I know from the look on your face that it's going to be good, and we don't have the time for me to fully appreciate it." He cocked his head. "Now strip, or I'll do it for you."

"This is embarrassing."

"Not for me." He grinned, obviously having fun.

"What is that cream? And do you honestly think it will save me from the mist?"

He rubbed a hand over his head in a gesture she had come to realize meant he was losing patience. "It's kind of like a barrier cream. One of my team developed it. It won't protect you from the mist for more than a few seconds, at best. But that's more time than you'd have without it. Think of it as another layer of defense under your protective suit."

"You must be insane if you think I'll be able to walk through that"—she pointed at the mist—"protected by a suit and some sun cream."

He looked up at the starry sky for a second. "Woman, can't you do one thing without knowing the ins and outs of it?"

She thought about that for a second. "No."

He mumbled something under his breath that she couldn't quite catch, and then he took a step toward her. "You're going to find out anyway." He lazily reached for the hidden fasteners down the front of her suit, before hooking his fingers under the seam and peeling it apart. All the while, his eye stayed on hers. "There are paths through the red cloud."

Friday gasped. She wasn't entirely sure if it was from the shocking information or from the heady experience of him undressing her. Even though she knew she shouldn't be attracted to the man who held her life in his hands, she couldn't help the pull she felt toward him. He fascinated her with his confident grace and his easy sexuality. He wasn't like any man she'd ever known, and the urge to get closer to him was almost overwhelming.

"Paths?" Her voice seemed more husky than usual.

His eye darkened. "Like a maze. You need to know the right paths, and you need to stick to them. You can't touch the cloud. If you do, bad things happen." The last fastener on her suit popped open and the front gaped apart, catching on her breasts but baring her from throat to navel. "Think of it as something similar to the tunnel we went through, only deadly."

"The tunnel we went through was deadly, too." She could still hear the roar of the earth closing in behind them as they ran, a strange contrast to the feeling of the cool night air on her skin.

"Yeah, but not like the mist can be." He trailed his index finger from the hollow of her throat all the way down her body to the indentation of her navel. "Never felt anything softer."

Her skin burned in his wake.

"How will the suit and barrier cream protect me if I touch the mist?" She stepped back, away from his touch, grasping the edges of her suit to hold it together and feeling a modicum of regret that she'd removed herself from his touch.

"It will buy you time." His gaze was intense when he looked at her. "There's a way to counteract the mist while it's still on the skin, before it's absorbed. The cream buys us the time we need."

Everything within her stilled. "You know how to counteract the mist?" she whispered.

That kind of knowledge was priceless. It was worth far more than anything she had in her head. He didn't need her or the money she could make him. He had the potential for riches at his fingertips.

"I know how to stop the mist from being absorbed. I don't know how to counteract it once it's inside the body."

"You make it sound like you know something mundane. What you're describing is the biggest breakthrough concerning the mist in a hundred years. It could blow the scientific community wide open and change what we know about the Red Zone. Not to mention, it could make you rich. You could sell that knowledge." Her voice began to rise at the thought. "There isn't a ruling body on the planet that wouldn't pay for it. Not to mention pharmaceutical companies. They would be falling over themselves to own your research. You would be famous."

"I don't want to be famous. I don't want to sell what I know. I just want to live peaceably."

"But—"

"—no buts. This is set in stone. I ain't gonna change my mind. There's too much at risk. This knowledge stays with me. You got that?" The deadly tone from the bar was back, and it made her shiver.

"I understand." She thought about it for a second. "No, I don't understand, but I respect that's what you want."

He studied her, as though trying to assess if she meant what she said. "Good enough. Now strip. I'll rub this on your back, and you can do your front." He gave her a smile that would charm the pants of a saint. "Unless you want me to do both."

"No!" The word came out like a shot, but she wasn't entirely sure she meant it.

"Don't worry. You're safe with me." He stepped closer. "For now. You need help getting that suit off?"

With her cheeks burning, Friday let the black suit drop to her ankles. She kicked off her boots and stood there dressed in nothing but her plain white panties. The chilled night air nipped at her skin, leaving goose bumps in its wake.

"Underwear, too." His voice was hoarse; she felt the words as breath on the back of her neck.

Quickly, as though ripping off a taped dressing, she pushed her underwear down and kicked it to the side.

He groaned behind her, and Friday felt her body flush. She was standing naked. In front of a fully dressed man. Outside. It was almost too much to comprehend. Definitely too much to deal with.

"Get on with it." The words were harsher than she'd intended.

"My pleasure."

She felt the warmth from his body at her back and then cold cream touched her shoulder. She jerked.

"Shh, bébé, it's gonna be fine." He cooed the words to her, intending to soothe, but instead causing tingles of sensation to ripple over her skin.

Slowly, methodically, his hand skimmed over her shoulders and down her back. He didn't linger. Didn't turn his touch into something lecherous. He was gentle, but thorough, making sure to cover every inch of her skin. She found herself swaying into his touch. Her eyes drifted closed. The silence and darkness became like a cocoon. A safe place where she could just be. Where she could live without expectation and feel without reserve. For once. She felt Striker's breath on her skin as he moved down her body. She trembled when he traced the curves of her rear, fighting the urge to arch into his touch as he caressed the cream onto her skin.

Large hands worked their way down her thighs and over

her calf muscles. By the time he'd finished, she was trembling —a boneless, dazed, and disorientated mess. She felt his presence in front of her, and she had to fight to lift her suddenly heavy eyelids.

"Beautiful." He reached for her, but stopped midair, snatching his hand back. "Damn it!" He snapped the words before turning on his heels and striding away from her.

She couldn't take her eyes from him as an unfamiliar longing swept through her. She recognized the need on his face and suspected it was on hers, too. He let out a low stream of French that sounded like curse words, then strode toward her. He thrust the pot of cream into her hands before turning away.

"Do the rest," he ordered.

Friday studied his back as he bent to rummage through the box. She didn't have much experience with men, and she wasn't sure what his change in mood meant. Did it mean she'd done something wrong? Or did it mean she'd done something very, very right?

"You need to finish the job and get dressed." His harsh tone snapped her back straight. He threw a containment suit at her. "Put that on once you're done. Don't forget to cover your face and your eyelids with cream, too."

With a nod, she reached into the jar for a handful of cream. She slathered it onto her breasts, trying hard not to notice how sensitive her nipples were or how needy she felt deep inside her body.

"Just so you know," his low, rumbling voice said behind her. "We were about ten seconds away from having sex on the desert floor. I'd advise you speed things up unless you want me to pick up where I left off."

Slowly, facing the darkness, Friday smiled.

CHAPTER 11

SHE'D GONE FROM BEING NAKED TO BEING WRAPPED IN SO MANY layers she could barely move. Her skin felt oily from the cream, and her jumpsuit stuck to her body in a way that definitely wasn't comfortable. On top of her jumpsuit, she wore a body protection suit—full head mask, elbow-length gloves, and knee-high reinforced boots. She knew from her student days that the suit was made up of three layers. The one closest to the skin was a heavy cotton, chemically treated to neutralize as many dangerous biogens as possible. Then came a fine metallic mesh, to protect against rips in the suit. Lastly, the whole thing was fused together by a synthetic polymer that repelled most liquids and filtered gases.

The viewscreen on her mask was made of reinforced glass. It could stop a bullet if it had to, which made the helmet heavy and cumbersome. Her boots were reinforced with alloys, as were her gloves. The gloves were the sort used in refineries to pick up molten metals, which meant they were insanely thick and difficult to maneuver.

"I feel like I'm going into space," she said through the communication outlet in her helmet.

"Yeah, I think spacesuits might be easier to move in."

Striker adjusted his boots. They weren't the same as the ones she wore. In fact, now that she really looked, there seemed to be quite a few differences in his suit. For one, it seemed to have more flexibility than hers, and the gloves appeared thinner, enabling greater dexterity. It worried her that familiarity with the Red Zone might have made him blasé about the dangers.

"Why is your suit lighter than mine? Surely you haven't cut back on protective measures in your arrogance?"

He stilled and curled up from checking his boots. He studied her for a moment, his expression difficult to read through their respective helmets. "Nobody ever noticed that before."

That didn't answer the question, so she asked it again. "Are you taking unnecessary risks?" The thought of him playing recklessly with his life bothered her on a fundamental level. She wasn't entirely sure why. Maybe because if he was hurt, there would be no one to save her.

"No."

"Then why is your suit thinner?" She frowned at him, working through her memory of the moments earlier. She'd been focused on the strange vulnerability of being naked in front of someone and hadn't paid any attention to what he'd been doing. "Did you put cream on, too? I don't recall you doing it."

He made a move to rub a hand over his head, as he usually did when he was cornered, only to remember it was covered.

"Time is ticking. We need to get going. Stay right on my heels. As close as you can, without getting hurt. Do not move to the left or the right. Stay on the path. There will be times when we have to crawl. Don't put your head up unless I tell you it's okay."

"But, your suit—"

He cursed in French before storming toward her and

grabbing her upper arms. The fury that poured from him made Friday shrink back. He seemed taller, bigger, more intimidating than he'd been a moment earlier.

He gave her body a sharp shake. "This isn't the time for questions. You need to focus. You need to follow orders. If you can't do that, then I'll take you back to Munroe."

She felt her blood rush through her veins. He oozed danger and violence. A man capable of anything. She'd become too comfortable with him. Too reliant on him. She'd forgotten that she didn't know him, and she'd definitely forgotten how deadly he could be.

"Got it?" he snapped at her.

"Yes. Yes. I've got it." She jerked back, trying to break his overpowering hold. Even through all of her layers it felt like her arms were in vices.

"Do as you're told. Keep that big brain of yours focused on following orders. If we make it through this alive, you can ask all the questions you want. Until then, all you have to do is exactly what I tell you to do. Your life depends on it."

"I understand." His one good eye seemed to glow as it reflected the light from the lantern. For a second, the yellow flecks in the brown seemed to take over, making him look eerie. Making him seem other than human.

She shook her arms free—aware that she'd only managed to shake off his hold because he'd allowed it.

"Stay at my back. When we aren't crawling, hold my belt. Follow close, right behind me, in my footsteps."

"I will."

His bulk seemed to shrink back to normal, which was still huge. He studied her for a moment, as though trying to ascertain whether he could trust her word or not. He nodded when he came to his conclusion. "Let's go."

Friday's limbs shook, completely thrown by their interaction. She still had questions. Her brain wouldn't stop just because he'd ordered it. There were too many anomalies. If she had the time, if this were a different situation, she would have fought for answers. But there wasn't time. And this wasn't the right situation. Which meant she had to bury her concerns and focus on doing exactly what he'd told her to do, because her life was, literally, in his hands.

Striker switched the lantern off and placed it in the box.

"Turn on your suit lights." His voice was cold, distant. The musical sensuality from earlier was gone.

With a tug at the chord on the front of her suit, the small directional lights sealed into it came on.

"Okay." He nodded his approval once he'd checked her lights. "We're heading that direction." He pointed along the endless red barrier. "Stay on my left. I want to be between you and the cloud. I'll let you know once we hit the path we need to take."

Friday nodded, then realized that with the bulk of the suit he probably wouldn't be able to see the gesture. "Stay on your left," she repeated instead.

"Good." He turned in the direction he'd indicated and strode forward, checking to make sure she was at his side, where he'd told her to be. The black night swallowed them as they made their way along the narrow strip of barren land between the high border wall and the red mist. She looked up at the wall, noting the dim glow of the lights along the top of it.

"They don't monitor this side of the wall?" she asked before she could stop herself. "I know you said to stop questioning everything but I can't help it. It's how my brain works. I promise you, I am completely focused on what we're about to do and will follow your instructions to the letter. I just can't help that there are other things in my head at the same time."

His long-suffering sigh came through the commlink. "Let's keep the questions to a minimum. You need to concentrate on what we're doing. There's no space to screw up."

"I will. I promise."

"You drive me crazy, chère. I worry that you'll distract yourself to the point of getting killed."

"I know." There wasn't much else she could say.

He let out another little sigh, resigned, she supposed, to having to deal with her inquisitive nature. "There's no need for them to monitor this side of the wall. Nothing lives over here."

She couldn't help the pleased smile that escaped when he answered her question, although she wasn't sure he was right. She looked at the thick red cloud and shuddered. It was only a feeling, but she could swear that the cloud was aware of their presence. Which meant something definitely lived on this side of the wall.

"Here." Striker stopped suddenly. He pointed to the ground where there was a small tunnel-like opening in the red mist. "We're going through one of the narrower parts of the mist, around ten miles wide. It's gonna feel like fifty by the time we're on the other side. We crawl for about half an hour and then we get more room to move around. Okay?"

"Okay." She fought to keep her questions to herself, but it actually physically hurt to do so, and she was pretty sure keeping them bottled up inside of her would make it harder to concentrate on doing what she was told. "I have a couple more questions."

"Are they relevant to what we're doing? Because, remember, no wandering off in your head. It's too dangerous."

She nodded, forgetting he couldn't see. "Yes, they're relevant. The tunnels and paths, the parts of the Red Zone where the mist has receded, do they shift? Are we likely to climb into a tunnel that suddenly disappears in front of us, or swallows us whole?"

"It happens. We monitor the paths and know instantly if anything changes. The mist is slow-moving, it wouldn't shift fast enough to trap us inside."

"Good, that's good." The air in her suit had become oppressive. The building heat made sweat run down her back and gather under her breasts. "Is the air where the red mist has receded contaminated or is it okay to breathe?"

"The air is good. You could take off your helmet and breathe normally. The only reason you're wearing it is to offer some protection in case you brush up against the mist."

"To buy time for you to counteract it before it's absorbed?"

"That's right."

She desperately wanted to ask how he was going to do that exactly, but she figured that was one of those discussions he would deem as not immediately relevant.

"Let's go." He took a step toward the red.

"Wait." She put a hand on his arm to stop him. "You said you've taken other people through here before me. If that's the case, why doesn't anyone know about the paths through the mist?"

"Chère." His voice was back to that irresistible southern drawl that made her shiver. "I know you're stalling, but you ain't ever gonna be ready to go in there, no matter how long you give yourself."

"No." She blinked several times. "I want to know. It's important." Had the other people he'd taken through died? Is that why no one knew about the paths, because no one had lived to talk about it?

"Well, seeing as it's important. Usually we knock our customers out before we take them through the mist."

"What?" She could have been unconscious? That was an option? Now he told her. "Don't they have to stay awake to ensure they don't touch the mist?"

He shrugged. "I get paid up front. Doesn't matter to me what condition they're in at the other side."

She felt bile rise to her mouth at his nonchalant answer.

"You about ready to go now? I mean, it's your life we're literally wasting while you stand here analyzing everything, but I'm happy to hang around until your curiosity is satisfied before we get on with this."

Now he was just irritating her. "I prefer your anger to your sarcasm."

"Good to know. How about you get to your knees and follow me into the Red Zone. If you're finished with your questions, that is."

"Yes. I'm finished."

"Fantastic. I'm thrilled." He gave her one last pointed look. "Don't screw up." Then he dropped to all fours in front of the gateway into the mist.

With a shaky breath, Friday did the same. Her own shallow breaths were loud within the confines of the helmet. Sweat trickled down her brow and into her eyes, and she wished it was possible to brush it away. Her movements were awkward and stiff, restricted by the suit. Her heart pounded hard and fast, making her fear she would have a heart attack. Somewhere in the back of her mind that never stopped, she wondered if an increased rate of blood flow would speed up the activation of the poison in her system and cause her limited lifespan to end even earlier than she'd predicted.

"I can hear you thinking." The voice in her ear was reassuring, and she realized that since she'd met the man, she'd spoken to him more over helmet comms than in person.

"I can't help it," she said through gritted teeth.

"I know, bébé. I know. Now let's play follow the leader." With that, the crazy man crawled straight into the deadliest area on earth.

CHAPTER 12

FRIDAY DIDN'T LOOK UP FROM THE SOLES OF THE FEET IN FRONT of her. Not once. Her terror at the thought of moving even an inch off the path he'd designated kept her mind firmly on the man in front of her.

"You doing okay back there?" Striker didn't sound stressed or bothered by their dangerous journey.

"Fine," was all she could manage to say.

Sweat poured off her body, pooling in the low points of her suit. She was sticky, hot, and the air was oppressive. She had to keep reminding herself that she could breathe and that her circumstances wouldn't last forever. It was a fight to keep her mind from wandering. The red glow, caused by the light from their suits bouncing off the mist, made her want to turn and look into the cloud. Questions. She had so many questions. There were few people on the planet who had managed to get this close to the red cloud. Her scientist's brain wanted to study it and find answers to the mysteries it held.

"Don't get distracted." The words made her already-warm face blush.

"Trust me, the last thing I want to do in here is get

distracted." Although it was increasingly difficult not to let her mind wander.

"You might not want to, but that big brain of yours must be buzzing by now. I'm surprised you aren't asking about a million questions."

It amazed her to hear amusement in his tone. "I'm trying not to die."

"Yeah, that will focus a person."

They carried on. Her head bent, her eyes firmly fixed on the ground beneath her and the man in front of her.

"Okay," he said. "You can stand now."

She was still afraid to move. "Can I put my head up?"

"Chère, you have to, if you want to stand." There was a grin in his voice.

Fantastic. They were in a death trap, and he was teasing her.

Slowly, cautiously, Friday lifted her head and looked up the body of the man standing in front of her. He held out a hand.

"You'll be stiff from crawling so long. Let me help you up."

She took his hand, grateful for his aid, and he tugged her to her feet, wrapping his arms around her while she steadied. "You good now?"

"Yes." Safe in his arms, she looked around her for the first time since entering the Red Zone and her knees gave way.

His hold tightened. "Like when Moses parted the Red Sea. Only it's literally red, and instead of walls of water on either side of us, we've got deadly mist."

"You think you're Moses?"

Her attention remained focused on the red mist. It was a deep red, like dried blood. The consistency varied. In the thinner places, she could make out hazy shapes, but they weren't clear enough for Friday to tell what they were. In other parts, the red mist was so thick, it was a solid wall of impenetrable fog. There was a stillness to it, an oppressive heaviness weighted with foreboding. She peered closer at the section nearest her. It seemed to glimmer when it caught the light.

"Mesmerizing, ain't it?"

"I swear," she mumbled, "you can almost see patterns in it."

"Bébé, you stare at it long enough and you can see anything you like in it."

She reluctantly pulled her gaze from the mist to look up at her protector. "Someone could lose themself completely staring into it."

For a moment, they stood there in the red glow, looking at each other. It was as though they were the only two people on the planet.

Striker cleared his throat and stepped back from her, although he kept his hands on her arms. "We need to move out. You dehydrate fast in that suit and I'd rather we didn't have to remove the mask to get some water into you."

"Of course."

She let her hands drop to her sides and waited for further instructions.

He wasn't slow in providing them. "I'm gonna turn. Hold on to my belt. Stay close. We'll move at a faster pace now we can walk."

She nodded as weariness began to overtake her. She'd barely slept since she'd run from CommTECH. Only adrenaline kept her going, and now she could feel her body shake as it worked its way out of her system.

"I understand," she said, to make it clear she was listening. "But once we're out of here, I need to find somewhere to nap for a couple of hours."

"I know a place." Of course he did. The smuggler-for-hire was a master at preparation.

They walked in silence for a long time. Friday lost track of exactly how long. Time didn't seem to exist in the Red Zone. There was only the mist, closing in on them, swallowing them whole. The red walls on either side of them went up far into the sky. If she looked up, she could see a strip of black night above her. Other than that, it was one long, endless sea of red. The unchanging surroundings were almost hypnotic, and she found it hard to keep her eyes open. She stumbled, falling against Striker's back.

"You okay?"

"Sorry. I'm tired." And it felt like the inside of her suit had turned into a sauna.

"Hold it together. Not long until we get to camp."

"Camp?" The red mist seemed to swirl in closer, disorientating her with its shifting patterns.

"Sleep. Water. Cold shower. Sound good?" He moved around until he stood behind her, supporting her with his hands on her waist. Not that she could feel them properly through the thick layers of her protective suit. "Just hold on. We're nearly there. I'll keep you on the path."

"I'm okay," she protested.

The air inside the suit was thick and hot. Her mouth was dry, and the world seemed to tilt with each heavy step she took.

"Five more minutes." Striker's voice seemed to come from very far away. "You can do it. We're nearly there, bébé. Just put one foot in front of the other. I'll do the rest; don't you worry none."

"I'm fine." Did her words sound sluggish? Had she even said them aloud. She couldn't remember, so she said them again. "I'm fine."

"Base," he snapped the word. "Come in base. I'm coming in hot. Package is dehydrated and disorientated. Medical assistance needed."

"Base here," a voice she didn't recognize echoed through her helmet. "What's your ETA?"

"Eight minutes. We're in the northern channel."

His words weren't making any sense, and she tuned them out. Instead, she concentrated on putting one foot in front of the other as the red mist sparkled and shifted in the light.

"Sending assistance," the strange voice said. "Doc is on his way. ETA two minutes."

"It's so pretty," she said. "Like a cloud at sunset."

There was a pause. "That her?" the strange voice said.

Friday no longer cared what the voices in her head were talking about. She only cared about the beautiful swirling mist.

"Yeah, that's her. She's losing it." Striker moved to stand beside her, wrapping an arm around her waist to hold her up.

Surely the path wasn't wide enough for them to stand side by side. She looked sideways at Striker, and everything within her exploded in a rush of pure, ferocious terror.

His arm was in the mist.

"No!" Her scream was ear-shattering in the confines of her helmet.

She lunged forward, pulling his arm back. Her foot slipped. She lost her balance. Striker's hold tightened on her, but not before her gloved hand and part of her forearm plunged into the red swirling haze.

"Fuck!" His voice was a roar. "She touched the mist!"

CHAPTER 13

"Doc?" Striker heard the quaver in his voice but couldn't stop it.

He lowered Friday to the ground and ripped off their masks.

"You got this," Doc said through the comm unit in his ear. "I'm two minutes away. I have an IV. How big an area was contaminated?"

He pulled the glove off the hand that had gone into the mist. Her fingers had a dusting of red on them. The mist had already made its way through the thick material. He tossed the glove aside and frantically yanked at the fasteners on her suit.

"I think it's only her hand and arm."

"Get everything off."

"On it."

She groaned as he shifted her body in order to strip the suit from her. Curses he hadn't used since he was a kid playing on the bayou poured from his lips. The layers of protective clothing were necessary but there were too many of them. It took endless seconds to get past the protective suit, and the jumpsuit beneath it. His eye ran over her body, relieved to see that the damage had been contained to only one arm.

"We've got red mist sitting on her hand and arm. The hand's taken the worst of it."

"You know what to do." Doc's voice was steady. "Get started. I'm nearly on you and I'll help once I get the IV hooked up."

"You need…get…help." Her weak voice made his eyes shoot to her face.

"It's gonna be okay, bébé. I promise you."

"No!" Her contamination-free hand reached out and grabbed his wrist, her grip weak. "Get help for you. You need to get the red off you. You need to survive."

He trailed a finger down her cheek. "Don't worry 'bout me. I'm fine, me. We're gonna get you sorted."

He lifted her contaminated hand to his mouth.

"No! Don't. It isn't safe." She struggled against him.

"Stop! You need to lie still." He couldn't get through to her. All she could hear was her own panic. "Doc, she's losing it. She's going to hit the mist again at this rate."

"I'm here." The team medic slid to his knees beside them. "I'll hold her. You get rid of the red." His face paled when he saw how much of it coated Friday's arm. "Hurry!" He leaned forward and used his body to pin her chest and flailing arm to the dirt.

"No! No!" There were tears streaming down her cheeks as she pleaded with Doc. "Help Striker. He was in the mist. You need to help him. He said there was time. Please"—she sobbed—"please."

"Damn it, man, get on with it." Doc looked traumatized by her distress.

The barrier cream Doc had developed would buy them a couple of minutes at most. Holding Friday's hand tight, he lifted it to his face and licked the red mist off her skin.

The horror and distress, in her eyes was almost too much

to bear. "You can't! I'm not worth dying for. Make him stop!" she pleaded with Doc.

"I can knock her out." Doc's voice was strained.

"Can't," Striker said around licking the red mist off her skin, making sure he didn't miss any, knowing his saliva would counteract any trace amounts that were left behind. "Interferan-X remember?"

Their medic cursed as he pressed down on Friday, keeping her immobile. Suddenly, her eyes rolled back, and she went limp. Striker felt the bottom fall out of his stomach.

"She's not—" He couldn't even finish the question.

Doc checked for a pulse. "She passed out. I'll hook up an IV line while you finish up."

There was no time to lose. He focused on cleaning her skin, one tiny inch at a time, grateful the mist had only touched a small area of her body. He was also irrationally grateful that he didn't need any help to remove the red from her skin. He only wanted his mouth on Friday, no matter what the circumstances. And that made him feel like a complete bastard.

His eye stayed on her face as he worked. She was pale, far too pale. She looked almost peaceful, lying there. The kind of peace reserved for death.

A flash of panic raced through him. "You sure she's okay?"

"Yeah." Doc held the bag of fluids high above her, the line from it feeding into her arm. "I don't think this is a reaction to the mist. I think it's a combination of exhaustion, dehydration, and whatever the hell that poison she took is doing to her insides."

Striker licked off the last of the residue and began checking every inch of visible skin, to make sure he hadn't missed anything. "I thought the Interferan-X lay dormant, sealing off her implants until it activated days later?"

"I thought so, too, but it isn't my area of expertise." The

medic rubbed the back of his neck. "Nothing in this new world is my area of expertise. I'm making things up as I go."

"We all are." He checked Friday's arm one last time. There was no telltale discoloration of the skin that would let him know the red mist had been absorbed. They got to it in time.

"She's okay, we got it. She's okay." His hands trembled as he gathered her to him.

He'd promised he'd keep her safe, and he'd failed. He wouldn't fail a second time. One way or another, he'd make sure Friday had the long life she dreamed of.

A firm hand clasped his shoulder. "It's not your fault. She must have been disorientated. It's no wonder she stumbled into the mist."

He shook his head. "She didn't stumble. I was walking beside her, to keep her upright, and she must have seen my arm touching the mist. She lunged into it to save me. She pulled my arm out of the damned mist."

Doc's eyes grew wide. "She was trying to save your life?"

"Yeah, she almost killed herself trying to save my life. I was never in any danger. I should have told her before we even entered the Red Zone that I wouldn't be at risk. I should have come clean with her."

"No, you couldn't have. She wouldn't have believed you anyway, and you can't give out that kind of information unless you're in a safe environment. You made the right decision, waiting until you got to base."

"A decision that could have cost her life." He brushed a strand of pale hair off Friday's face.

"You didn't know she'd try to save you."

"No, I didn't. But now that I do, it changes everything." He ran his knuckles across her satin cheek, reveling in the warmth under his fingers that meant she lived. "We can't let this woman die. No matter what it takes, she has to live."

Because she was his responsibility, and he owed her.

CHAPTER 14

Friday's eyes snapped open, but she was blind to her environment. All she could see was the image in her mind. The one of Striker touching the red mist. She bolted upright, ready to run. To save him.

"Striker!"

"Shh, bébé, I'm here. Everything's gonna be okay." Firm hands held her shoulders as she looked up into one unpatched eye of the deepest, most luscious brown.

"I thought you were dead. I never intended for anyone to get hurt because of me. I'm sorry." Her eyes scanned furiously over his body, checking for damage. None. There was none. "You're okay. They got to you in time. You're okay." She sagged into his hold.

"I'm good, me. It's you who's had us worried. Ain't that right, Doc?"

For the first time since opening her eyes, Friday looked around her. She was in a cave. A cave that had been fitted out to look like a barracks. There were metal framed cots along one wall, a makeshift kitchen near the cave entrance, and a medical area—complete with examining table and supplies. She looked down at the bed she sat on.

Make that two examining tables. She occupied the other one.

"Where am I?" She eyed the sheet covering her. "And why am I naked?"

"You're in the Bat Cave, chère." Striker's grin was pure, seductive mischief. "And you're naked so I can have my wicked way with you."

"Seriously?" She looked around, noticing the two men who stood at the entrance to the cave and a third man walking toward them. "You want to have sex? Here? When I feel disorientated and we have an audience?"

The men started laughing, and she frowned at them. This wasn't funny. She'd joined CommTECH to ensure she wouldn't have to perform naked in front of strange men—like the woman back in Munroe's bar.

"You promised people wouldn't watch us," she hissed.

"Bébé." The word rode a long-suffering sigh. "You're in the medical area. You just woke up after being out for hours. You're in no state to have sex, public or otherwise. But I'm beginning to wonder why that's always the first thing on your mind. I'm thinking somebody wants me bad."

"You're insufferable."

He gave her that Gallic shrug as his eye twinkled. "I call it how I see it. You're obsessed with getting your hands on this fine body." He motioned to his body, as though there were any doubt he was talking about himself.

"Why am I here? You were the one who touched the mist."

"Actually," said a tall, rangy man who stopped at the end of her bed, "you were the one who touched the mist. Fortunately, we got to you in time. You're going to be fine."

"But..." She stared at the men. Was she losing her mind? She could have sworn she'd pulled Striker out of the mist.

"This here is Doc," Striker said before she could question them further. "And before you ask, you ain't having sex with him, either."

The two men over at the door thought that was hilarious. She ignored them and looked at the doctor. He was long lean muscle and overgrown sandy hair that he kept brushing out of his eyes. He looked like he would have been more at home on the back of a horse, patrolling the plains of Montana, than cooped up in a cave tending to her medical problems.

"You're a doctor?"

"Army medic, ma'am. But as far as medical help goes around here, I'm as good as it gets." He reached into the utilitarian metal shelves beside her and pulled out some clothes. "We had to dump your things. They got contaminated. These will have to do. The boss here will show you to the shower, and then you can get some food into you. You were pretty dehydrated when you came in, but we're on top of that now. If you've got a headache, we can talk about pain meds. I didn't want to give you anything while you were out, in case it interfered with the poison you took."

She brushed her fingers over the soft cotton T-shirt in her hands. It was old, worn smooth with wear, and must have cost a fortune to buy. Real cotton was more expensive than silk—rarer, too. It made her wonder how much the team made from smuggling. And why, if they made that much, were they holed up in a cave?

"Nothing will affect the Interferan-X. Except the antidote." She looked at Striker. "How many hours did I lose?"

"A few. It's late afternoon now."

"A few?"

He smiled but his jaw was tight. "Twelve."

She trembled at the word. Too much lost time. "I have about three days left to get to Bolivia."

He put his hand over hers and brushed her knuckles with his thumb. "The hardest part is over, chère. You made it past Enforcement and through the Red Zone. All you've got to deal with now is the EMP barrier and a trek to La Paz. Three days is more than enough time."

She swallowed hard as she looked back down at the faded sheet covering her. "You're right." It had to be enough time. It wasn't like she could ask for an extension. She either made it or she didn't.

"Come on." He tugged at her hand. "Let's get you cleaned up. Everybody turn around," he ordered, and the men complied.

With help, Friday wrapped the sheet around herself.

"You okay to walk?" He lifted her and placed her on her feet, ready to catch her if she began to fall.

"I'm fine. I don't feel weak. I can definitely walk."

He didn't seem convinced, but he turned toward the back of the cave and she followed. "We've got a few smaller rooms back here. The cave system is a labyrinth. We've only mapped a fraction of it." He pointed to a large, well-lit space on the left. "That's the training room." There were mats on the floor and various weights and weapons dotted around the cavern. "This is the lab." The large area had metal benches set up with various lab equipment.

"Who works the lab?" And would they let her in to see what they were doing? For no other reason than professional curiosity. She glanced up at her host. Probably not. She couldn't exactly be trusted around their secrets. Not until her data chips were removed and the monitoring chip was implanted. She forced thoughts of being monitored from her mind. She'd volunteered to have the implant, and she'd take responsibility for that decision. Even if it meant she'd have to give up hope of ever experiencing freedom.

If she lived.

"Doc works the lab." He put his hand on the small of her back to lead her into another tunnel. "He trained as a pharmacist before signing up for the military. He isn't just good-looking." He cocked the eyebrow over his unpatched eye. "Don't bother denying it, I saw you notice."

She cocked an eyebrow back at him. "I don't remember

our agreement including a clause telling me I couldn't look at other men."

His hand skimmed down her back to rest on the curve of her hip. "I think I'm gonna add that clause now." His eye seemed to glow.

She stared at him, wondering if she was seeing things and the poison in her system had started to kick in earlier than expected. No, his eye was definitely glowing, and it also looked more yellow than usual.

"I was teasing," she said softly. That strange, intense eye of his was mesmerizing.

"I like teasing." His voice lowered, the drawl a lazy purr. "I like playing. You can play with me anytime." He nuzzled against the side of her head before moving closer to her ear. She stopped breathing when his lips touched the sensitive shell. "But just me, bébé, okay?"

She was afraid to move, to breathe, to think. She clutched the sheet tight to her body and waited to see what he would do next.

"You bewitch me." He whispered the words against her ear, making her shiver. "I close my eyes and dream of how you might taste. Will you taste like sunshine, all warm and light, like your hair? Or will you taste like an aged bourbon, all passion in a concentrated bottle, ready to blow my mind with one little sip?"

A tiny whimper escaped at his words. He had it wrong. He wasn't the one who was bewitched. It was her. He'd somehow entranced her, and she was under his spell. His hand threaded into her hair, gently caressing, running the silken stands through his fingers.

She leaned into him as her eyes fluttered closed at his touch. She desperately wanted to ask him to kiss her, to dare him to discover what she tasted like, but the words stuck in her throat, trapped by her own lack of courage.

"Boss man," an amused voice penetrated the daze in Friday's head. "You sure you want to fool around with the client in the corridor?"

Striker growled his annoyance and stepped back from Friday, leaving her cold.

He turned toward the intruder. "What do you want, Sandi?"

"Well, mainly I want to make sure you keep it in your pants until the mission is over. Or, at least until you get to your room. I'm fairly certain none of us could cope with the trauma of seeing you go at it in the tunnel."

"Smart-ass," he grumbled with a smile.

Friday looked past him to find the woman from the alley. The one who'd acted as her decoy with Enforcement. She was tall, muscled, and dressed in black, with a weapon strapped to her thigh. She studied Friday in a way that made her wonder if she should feel intimidated. She almost snorted at the thought. After a lifetime dealing with CommTECH, it would take more than a female mercenary to intimidate her.

"I'm taking Friday to the showers," Striker said.

"So I see," Sandi drawled. "I'll do it. You're wanted in comms."

He hesitated, running his knuckles down her cheek. "I'll see you once you're sorted. Sandi'll take care of you."

He gave his fellow soldier a deadly look before he strode back toward the main cave. Friday pulled the sheet up tight around her and clutched the clothes she'd been given to her chest. She felt like a bug under a microscope as Sandi continued to stare, and it annoyed the life out of her. Who cared if she'd made a deal with the team's boss, one that gave him rights to her? It didn't mean she was less of a person. She lifted her chin and stared Sandi in the eye.

"Do you have something you want to say to me?"

Amusement flickered in the woman's gaze. "Yeah." Sandi

closed the distance between them. With the heels on her leather boots she was almost a head taller than Friday. She came to a halt just inside Friday's personal space and folded her arms. "I want to know if it's true."

"Want to know if what's true?" She would not cringe if the woman asked if she'd sold her body to Striker for a chance at survival. She'd done the right thing. The only thing she could have done. She was proud that she'd had the courage to make the decision, and she wouldn't let someone take that from her.

Sandi cocked her head. "Did you dive into the mist to save the boss?"

It was the last question she'd expected.

"Yes." She didn't see the point of lying. It wasn't a secret.

Sandi nodded. "You got courage." She turned toward the interior of the caves. "Come on," she called over her shoulder. "I've got some pants you can wear that are closer to your size. But you'd better wear Striker's tee. I don't think he wants to see you in anyone else's clothes right now. The boss is a little possessive."

Friday trotted after the Amazon. "Is he like that with everything he owns, or is it just me?"

"Oh, you're different, sugar. There's no denying it. You're something none of us were expecting."

Sandi led her into a smaller area that had been set up with shower heads. A heating system had been rigged up, and pipes led to the back of the cave, where she could hear running water.

"What am I?" she asked, unable to help herself. "What weren't you expecting?"

"Hope." Sandi turned on the water and stepped back. "We weren't expecting hope. That's what you are to Striker. You're hope."

For a minute it felt as though Sandi could see right through her, and she fought the urge to swallow hard or run.

"I don't understand."

"I'll get you those pants." Sandi turned away, disinclined to clear the matter up. "Use any of the soaps you find. There are towels on the shelf. I'll be back."

With that, the woman disappeared into the caves.

CHAPTER 15

After she showered, a barefoot Friday followed Sandi back into the main cave area. The smell of food hit her hard and her stomach growled in response. There were more people in the room now. Several men sat around a dining table, laughing and talking while they ate. Without exception, they were huge, muscled, and armed to the teeth.

The conversation died as she entered the cavern, and she found it hard not to shuffle in place. She wished she were dressed in her regulation jumpsuit. The jumpsuit was like armor—it deflected interest. Instead, she wore combat pants, rolled up to stop her tripping over them, and the soft cotton T-shirt that hung to her knees. She felt like a child in a room full of adults.

"Chère!" Striker's voice had her head whipping around to see him come out of the training room. "Let's get you something to eat."

He gave her attire a look of approval before wrapping an arm around her waist and tugging her toward the kitchen area. She recognized the man on kitchen duty—Mace, the guy who didn't know how to work a scanner.

"I only make one thing," he told her. "Chili. If you don't like it, you go without."

He picked up a bowl, ladled a steaming serving of chili into it, and handed it to her. He nodded his head toward the table against the wall. "Bread and utensils are over there."

She looked down at the bowl then back up to the overgrown man. "Is this safe? Are you better at working a food unit than you are a scanner?"

Striker barked out a laugh as Mace narrowed his eyes at her. "Just because you threw yourself into the red to save the boss doesn't mean I trust you. Or think you're worth the hassle."

"Now I really want to eat your food."

"Come on." Striker wrapped an arm around her shoulder. "You need to eat. Don't worry about Mace none; he don't know a thing about poisons. The food is safe."

"I'm completely reassured."

That earned another chuckle. They grabbed forks and freshly baked bread from the table before Striker led her over to the dining area. He pulled out a seat in the middle of the table and gestured for her to sit. She kept her eyes on the food as she did so, and not on the half dozen men who were staring at her like she'd arrived from Mars. Striker sat beside her, poured a glass of ice water from the jug on the table, and placed it in front of her.

"Keep up your fluids," he ordered.

She rolled her eyes at his bossiness as she hesitantly tasted the chili. She'd grown up with the food. Versions of it were a street staple in the areas around CommTECH. It was considered too lower class for most of the residents in the Territories, but to her the food meant home. And this one was good. She groaned her delight, closing her eyes at the bite of rich pepper and cumin, savoring the heavy amount of garlic.

When she opened her eyes, everyone was staring at her, and she felt her cheeks heat.

"Good chili, huh?" Striker sounded hoarse.

"Better than meal replacement bars."

He snorted his agreement. "Eating dirt is better than meal replacement bars."

He reached for his fork, and his arm brushed against hers, making her whole body tingle. He was far too close. Their shoulders rubbed, their thighs pressed together— it was intensely distracting, and she couldn't afford to be distracted in a room full of strangers.

She shuffled her chair away from him and relaxed. For a second. Because, without hesitating in his conversation with the man facing them, he grabbed the seat of her chair and yanked her back—even closer than before. She scowled up at him and wondered how he'd like a bowl of steaming hot chili in his lap. As though reading her mind, he grinned at her. Infuriating man. He was amusing himself. Again. She'd never met someone with his sense of humor, and she wondered if she'd ever get the jokes.

"You need to watch that one," a man across the table said. "She's plotting your demise."

Friday turned her frown on the blond stranger.

His eyes crinkled with amusement. "I take it back. She's plotting against all of us."

There was nothing to say to that—he was completely right.

When they were finished, the men cleared the table, and she expected them to disappear, going back to whatever they did in their cave. Instead, they helped themselves to mugs of coffee and sat back down. All eyes on her.

She elbowed Striker and whispered, "What have I done now?"

"Nothin' Chère, unless you count those wicked thoughts you've been having about the two of us." Of course he made it sound like her wicked thoughts were sexual instead of her trying to come up with ways to maim him.

"I don't like being the center of attention." It made her want to run, but seeing as she didn't know where she was, or where she'd run to, there wasn't much point.

"Don't panic. We just got some things we need to tell you."

That was not reassuring. And it didn't ease her mind any that the people gathered were serious and intense. There weren't any smiles. No teasing looks. Shoulders were tense. Eyes were dark. Whatever they were going to tell her, she wasn't going to like.

"It's about our deal, bébé." He toyed with her hair. "It's about what I expect you to do to pay off your debt."

And just like that, she felt the color drain from her face. She swayed, her mind going places she really didn't want it to go. Her fingers clenched tightly together in her lap and her mouth was suddenly dry. Striker's eye sparkled as he leaned into her. He whispered against her ear, "You're thinking about sex again. Bébé, you got to get your mind out of the gutter. This has nothing to do with that. If that happens, it will just be between me and you."

"Okay." She didn't believe a word of it. Not when there was obviously something going on that she didn't understand. She swallowed hard as he sat back in his chair, giving her an indulgent smile that said he found her amusing.

Striker shared a look with Mace, then took a deep breath. "We need a scientist." He ran a hand over his face. "We want you to work in the lab with Doc during your year here."

Okay, she wasn't expecting that. "But...I thought you wanted my body."

He threw back his head, his laughter echoing through the cave, and her cheeks burned. Well, this was humiliating. Apparently, wanting her was a laughing matter. She couldn't believe she had an audience for this.

When he'd calmed down, Striker ran his knuckles down one of her burning cheeks. "I do want your body. But I also want your mind. Your body was never part of our bargain. I just couldn't tell you what the bargain was, exactly, out there in the world."

She glanced at the men, who were amused by her exchange with their leader. They weren't anything like the men she was used to, and she didn't quite know how to deal with them without feeling foolish.

"What do you want my mind to do?" She tried to sound as detached and professional as possible.

"Before I answer that, I gotta tell you a story." He leaned forward and placed his elbows on the table. "Do you know where you are?"

The question threw her. "Mexico? The Southern Coalition? Your base of operations?"

He shook his head slowly, his eye on her. "I told you earlier, we still need to get through the EMP barrier into the Southern Coalition."

As his words penetrated, it became hard to breathe. "You can't mean…"

He pointed up. "Look, chère."

Anxiously, cautiously, she did. There was a hole in the cave ceiling. Someone had made a wooden trap for it, presumably to keep out the weather. The trap was open. It was daylight.

And the sky was red.

Her hands shot out to grip the edge of the table. "We're in the Red Zone?" It was a whisper. It wasn't possible. It couldn't be. But, above her, there was a thick cloud of red covering the large opening where the sky should have been. She shot to her feet as panic hit her like a blow to the stomach, making her nauseous. "We need to run. It isn't safe."

A strong hand grasped her arm, holding her firmly in place. "Sit down. You're safe here. You think I'd let something bad happen to you?"

She forced herself to look at Striker instead of the exit. "I think you'd be willing to let me die if it suited your purpose."

"Ouch!" someone said.

He glowered at her. "Well, it don't suit my purpose none. Now sit your cute ass down and listen."

She looked at the rest of the team. No one else seemed in a hurry to run screaming from the Red Zone. In fact, they all sat calmly watching her. Slowly, she lowered herself to her seat, grasping Striker's hand and holding on tight. Suddenly his penchant for invading her personal space was a comfort rather than an irritant.

He muttered something in a reassuring tone in a language she didn't understand, before switching to English. "Good girl. I know this is a lot to take in. Are you okay?"

She swallowed. "Don't say 'good girl.' It's patronizing."

There were chuckles, and he smiled wryly at his team. "Guess that's a yes." He turned his attention back to her. "Remember I told you that the red mist lifted from the water first?"

She nodded, although that conversation seemed like a lifetime ago.

"It lifted from other places, too. It just took a little longer. This cave system is one of them. The mist sits a few feet above it."

His words acted like a switch in her mind. It flicked from scared to curious. In an instant, the adrenaline flooding her system and telling her to escape rushed to her mind and prodded her to demand answers. She relaxed. This was her comfort zone—analysis, research, study.

"Did it leave residue? Is it safe? What if it moves again and comes back down? Are you monitoring it? Are you sure the cave system is empty?"

"And she's back." Striker's smile made her insides warm in a way she didn't fully understand. "Nothing stops that big brain of yours for long."

"The mist won't come back into the caves." Doc pulled up a chair on the opposite side of the table. "It's been steadily dispersing from this area for years. We monitor it closely. Its distance from the cave increases each day. It's slow, but it's definitely moving away. If it changed direction and suddenly started to fall again, we'd know instantly. There is no residue in the caves. The red mist only lingers on biological matter. All of this"—he gestured to the furniture—"was salvaged from the mist. It's safe. If it wasn't, you'd be dead already."

It didn't slip her notice that he'd said she'd be dead, not they'd be dead. She added that little slip to the list she was compiling of things she needed more information on.

"How long have you been here? How long have you been monitoring the mist over the caves? How did you find this place? How did you find out about the paths through the mist, anyway?" Now that she thought about it, that should have been a question to ask a whole lot earlier.

"One question at a time." Striker held up a hand to slow her down. "Okay, first, we've been monitoring the mist over the caves for about three years. That's the same amount of time we've been mapping the paths through the mist."

"Are you out of your minds? How could you do something so dangerous?" She gaped at them. "Do you all have a death wish? How did you know when you followed a path that it wouldn't close in on you? How did you know you'd be able to get out without getting hurt? Are you stupid?"

"The stupid part is something we can debate another time," Striker said wryly. "As to how long we've been here." The room suddenly grew serious, heavy even. The words he was about to say were there already, hanging in the air between them. The hairs on Friday's arms stood to attention. She knew whatever he said would change her life forever— what she had left of it.

"We've been here, in these caves, for about a hundred and

three years. Give or take a month or two. But we've only been awake for about three years. The rest of the time we were unconscious."

There was an expectant silence as everyone waited for her reaction. She couldn't speak. She could barely comprehend what he was telling her. It didn't make sense. It wasn't real. She was hallucinating. A side effect of the poison she'd taken.

"It's not possible," she whispered. "You were unconscious for a century?"

She looked at each of them in turn. There was no humor in the room. The atmosphere was deadly serious. As shocked as she was, her eyes still scanned for data. They appeared healthy. They seemed to range in age from mid-twenties to mid-thirties. It wasn't possible that they'd been unconscious for a century. He was talking about stasis. And the scientific community had given up on that idea decades earlier. People placed in stasis didn't come out right once they awakened. It was too unstable a practice. Too dangerous. She shook her head. "It isn't possible."

"Yeah, we thought that, too." Striker gave her hair a little tug to get her attention. "All we know is that one minute we were fighting for the United States in the Technology Wars, and the next minute we woke up in these caves." He paused, clenching her hand tight. "And, we woke up changed."

Slowly, he reached up with his free hand and tugged off the flexi-patch that covered his eye. The eyelid on his hidden eye lifted, and she found herself staring into the vertical pupil of a bright yellow iris. It wasn't the eye of a human being. It was the eye of a reptile.

It was the eye of a snake.

CHAPTER 16

Striker had expected hysteria. Fainting maybe. He'd had Doc prepare a pressure injector with a sedative in case they needed it—now that Friday had assured them it wouldn't affect the poison. What he hadn't been prepared for was, well, nothing. Friday appeared frozen as she stared at him, her face expressionless. There was nothing there at all. She'd completely checked out.

He shot a worried glance at their medic. "Doc?"

The man ran a hand through his sandy hair. "I don't know. This is a new one. Never seen anybody react like this before."

"Is she a cyborg?" Mace reached for his coffee. "The Territories fill their people with all sorts of cyber shit. Maybe she's rebooting."

"Not helping," Striker snapped.

What if he'd broken her? What if she couldn't cope with the secrets he'd shared? No. She was stronger than that. He'd seen her in action. She was sheltered, sure, but braver than most people he knew. He shook her gently. Still no reaction.

Mace stood taking his coffee mug with him. "I'm getting a refill. She's been like that for fifteen minutes, and it doesn't look like it's going to end anytime soon. Might as well get comfy."

Striker turned to their medic. "Is there anything you can give her to, you know, get her started again?"

"Like what?"

"I don't know. An upper?"

"You think I have speed in my med kit?"

"I don't even think they make speed anymore," Sandi said. "You guys are about a hundred years out of date when it comes to drugs."

Striker took Friday's hand in his and patted it. There was no reaction. She was blinking, but that was about it. "We've got to do something. Look at her."

"Try slapping her," Sandi said.

He gave her a death glare.

"Bucket of ice water over the head." Mace sat back down at the table.

Maybe…

"That could shock her into cardiac arrest," Doc said, killing that idea.

"Kiss her." It was a grumbled order from Gray Hanson. Their lethal teammate rarely spoke but never missed a thing, which made everyone listen to anything he had to say.

"Kiss her?" A shock went through him at the thought. Find out how she tasted? Know for sure, instead of imagining, and bring her back to him at the same time? "I can do that."

He cupped her cheeks in his hands. She was so damn small compared to him. Fragile. Easily broken. He needed to remember that. Slowly, softly, he lowered his lips to hers. It was like touching lightning.

Her lips were satin soft and gave easily under his touch. But she didn't react. Cold fear slid through him, and he fought it back, redoubling his efforts to rouse her. Angling his head, he gently teased her lips with his, staring into her vacant blue eyes, willing her to come back to him. His tongue nipped out to stroke along her lower lip, tasting, teasing. He thought he felt a faint sigh brush against his mouth. His heart raced as he pressed his lips more firmly against hers.

And then her eyelids fluttered closed.

A surge of hope welled up inside him, and he teased the seam of her lips with his tongue. A gasp of breath was his reply. A heartbeat later, her lips moved against his. Striker wrapped his arm around her, pulling her tight against him as he threaded his fingers through her hair. When her tongue snuck out to touch his, he poured his relief into their kiss.

She tasted just as he imagined she would. Of sultry nights spent on the bayou. Of teasing words whispered into the ear of a lover. She tasted of everything he'd thought he'd lost.

She tasted of home.

Slowly, as if coming out of a daze, she pressed her hands to his chest and pushed. Reluctantly, he ended their kiss.

"Why are you kissing me?" She blinked several times before glancing away from him. "And why are you doing it while people watch? We talked about this. No audience. Remember?" Her cheeks turned a lovely shade of pink.

He couldn't help but grin at her indignation, while fighting the urge to pull her close and hold her tight, until his heart stopped racing. "Bébé, that agreement was for sex."

"Same thing."

"If you think kissing is the same as sex, then I need to spend some time educating you. It will be my pleasure." He cupped her cheek. "You scared me."

She nuzzled his palm for a second before lifting her head. "Why?"

"You've been comatose for the past fifteen minutes."

"Oh." She frowned and then shook her head. "I didn't realize. I have no idea what to tell you. I don't think that's ever happened before."

"Is it the Interferan-X?"

That damn poison was a time bomb ticking away inside her. Who knew what kind of problems it could cause.

"No. I think it was shock." She trailed a fingertip under his mutated eye. "You're part snake. It's a lot to take in."

"I get that. It scared the hell out of me when I woke up. Come here, bébé, let me hold you until my heart stops racing."

He gave her his best puppy dog look.

She huffed out a sigh but climbed into his lap. "You use that charm of yours to get your own way far too often."

"You sayin' I'm irresistible?" He grinned at her.

"You're something all right." She snuggled in closer to him, relaxing in his arms.

He nuzzled at the spot behind her ear that fascinated him, while his team laughed. They thought he was joking, teasing her, seducing her. But he wasn't. He needed to hold her, to reassure himself she was okay. "Don't blank out on me again." It was a foolish order to give, but he couldn't stop himself.

"How am I supposed to do that? It's not like it's something I can control. Maybe I should get out of your lap? You seem calm now."

He tightened his hold. "You changed your mind about touching me, now you know about the snake?" He was joking around, but still found himself holding his breath for her answer.

She rolled her eyes dramatically. It was cute. "Don't be stupid. And I never decided to touch you in the first place. You blackmailed me into it."

"Bébé, I didn't blackmail you for your body. I did it for that big brain of yours. But, having your sweet body would be a nice side benefit."

"Striker!" She smacked his chest. "Let me go. I have questions."

"Chère, that ain't no surprise. You always have questions.

Ask away. But how about you ask them from right where you are? That way if you check out again, I can kiss you until you check back in."

She relaxed back into him. Obviously, she was just as eager to break their contact as he was. "That is not an appropriate way to deal with a person who's in shock."

"As entertaining as this dynamic is," Mace cut in, "we have some things we need to deal with."

"He's right." He kissed Friday gently. "You okay?"

She softened and nodded, her focus on his yellow eye. "Does the changed iris affect your vision? Is it the reason you can see in the dark? How did it happen? Is that why you're hiding out? Have you been seen by a doctor?"

"And she's back again." He relaxed into his chair but kept an arm around her waist to keep her close. "Doc? You want to take it from here?"

"Sure. We can't see anyone in the medical profession because we don't want word to get out about us."

Jeremiah, the ex-army chaplain, interrupted, "They'd lock us up and turn us into experiments. Not a great reward for a bunch of soldiers who died for their country. None of us are keen on being dissected in the name of science."

The fact Friday didn't even try to argue against Jeremiah's logic was telling. She knew, just as much as the rest of them, that their secrets would get them killed.

"Far as we can figure," Doc continued, "the mineral composition of these caves is unique, and we think it interacted with the red mist to form something new. Something that had never been seen before or tested. The mist inside the caves reacted differently than the mist outside of them. Instead of killing all biological life within the caves, it adapted it, merging species that sheltered in the cave during the blast."

"Merged?" Friday interrupted as she gently smoothed a fingertip under his eye again, staring at it in fascination.

"Yeah," their medic said. "Snakes, bears, mountain lions, pretty much everything you'd find in this region. Everything that'd taken to the caves during the conflict. When we got warning the bomb was being dropped, we were near the caves and ran into them, too. Next thing we know, it's a hundred years later and we wake up alone. No animals. At least, none we could find."

"What we think"—Striker rubbed his hand up and down her arm, reassuring her, or maybe himself—"is that our DNA merged with the animal closest to us. We kind of absorbed the DNA of the other creature."

She inclined her head, considering. "The stronger DNA won out."

"Yeah."

"You merged with a snake." She traced the tattoo on his neck with her fingertips. "A diamondback. Do you have a poisonous bite? Can you detect heat signatures? Do you have to eat live rats now?"

He couldn't help but grin, and the mood in the room eased. "No rats, bébé. But I can see in the dark. My instincts are acute, and I can pick up heat signatures. There's no poisonous bite, though."

"Did you get the tattoo in honor of the animal you merged with?" She skimmed her fingers over the head of the snake as it curved around his neck.

He hesitated with his answer. Once the rest of the story was out, there was no taking it back. She would never look at him as a normal man again. Would she see him as a freak? As repugnant? Would she still want him to touch her? He looked into her intense, intelligent gaze and took a deep breath. All or nothing. She had to know everything. They needed her. He needed her.

"I woke up with the tattoo, bébé."

Her touch trembled against his skin. "It isn't a tattoo, is it?"

"No."

"Is it an impression of the animal you merged with? The remnants of the snake melted into you, like a brand?"

"No. It's something else."

A little pucker appeared between her brows as her quick mind raced over the information he gave her. She was getting ready to ask for an explanation, but there was no explaining this. This, he had to show her. Lifting her, he sat her on the chair beside him, and then stood. He reached for the bottom of his vest top.

"Be certain," Mace warned.

Striker eyed the woman in front of him, considering what he was about to do. Her pale cheeks were flushed pink. Her eyes darted around as though following every thought zipping through her mind. Her hands shook, her breathing was rapid, but she didn't run. There was no hysterics. No revulsion. No fear. Only shock, wonder, and curiosity. She was brave and vulnerable at the same time. She was beautiful.

"I'm sure." He yanked off his shirt.

With his eyes still on Friday, he held his arms away from his body and called to the snake. He felt a tingling in his spine. Dull throbbing pain raced through his muscles, making them clench tight. Friday's eyes widened, and she tugged her bottom lip between her teeth. She clenched her hands together tightly in her lap. Striker felt a wrenching sensation deep inside him, then the sharp pain of separation made him break out in a sweat. There was a snap, and his other half landed on the table beside him.

Friday gasped. She shot to her feet and backed away from the table. Striker lowered his arms. His eyes were on the woman instead of on the live diamondback curled in the middle of the dining room table.

She stared at him, then at the diamondback, then him again.

"Turn around." Her demand was little more than a shaky whisper.

He did as she commanded and heard her sharp inhale when she saw his unblemished skin. There was no sign that there had ever been an image of a snake on his body.

"How?"

He felt her touch, ice cold and trembling as she traced over his shoulder where the snake had been. The diamondback on the table hissed at them. His other half wanted Friday's attention, too. He felt her jerk away from him, which made the diamondback hiss louder. He turned to find Friday staring at the reptile.

"Is it real?" She reached a hand out toward the snake.

"Don't!" Sandi took a step forward. "It will bite."

Striker shook his head. His connection with the reptile was buzzing. The diamondback wouldn't attack Friday. He had never been more certain of anything in his life.

"It won't harm you. It wants to be petted." A dull throb of agreement jangled through his mind.

"What are you doing?" Sandi snapped at him. "Are you trying to get her killed? I thought the whole point of this was to keep her alive."

Confusion and indecision flitted across Friday's face.

"The snake likes her," he told his teammate. "It won't attack. I'd bet my life on it."

"But you aren't," Sandi snapped. "You're betting hers."

"Bébé." He took a step toward Friday. He didn't know why, but he felt it was of the utmost importance that she believed him. That she trusted him. That she accepted the diamondback the way she'd accepted the man. "I promise you. The snake won't harm you."

"Damn it!" Sandi threw up her hands. "What the hell, she's already dying, right? What's the difference if it happens now, or in a couple of days' time?"

Friday looked up at him, those brilliant blue eyes of hers

seeing past everything that was irrelevant. Seeing to the core of the man.

"I promise," he whispered.

She swallowed hard and turned back to the snake, which had inched across the table toward her. Slowly, she reached out to touch the diamondback. The team held their breath. Her fingers trembled. As usual, she didn't let her fear stop her, closing the distance between herself and the deadly predator. Striker felt the moment she made contact. The touch vibrated down his back, in the spot where the reptile normally lay.

Deep in his mind, he felt a smug preening. The snake was proud and showing off for Friday. It wanted her to like him. If the damn thing had been a cat it would have rolled to its back and offered its belly for a rub. Instead, it brushed against her hand, making her caress the length of it. Striker shivered at each touch as though she were caressing him.

The diamondback wriggled forward and wrapped itself around Friday's arm. Slowly it worked its way up to her shoulder. She froze in place, her eyes wide with fear and wonder. Striker felt a giddy delight deep inside and knew it was the snake. It curled around her shoulders, snuggled its head into the crook of her neck and closed its eyes. Striker could have sworn he heard the damn thing sigh with contentment.

"What the hell?" Mace muttered.

Friday let out a nervous giggle. She was adorable, still frozen in place and trembling, yet delighted with that damn reptile.

"It likes you." As did Striker, and those feelings were growing by the minute. Seemed that neither the man nor the beast could resist this woman.

Deep inside him he heard a whisper of a word. *Mine.* His eyes shot to Friday and watched as she stroked the long length of the snake. Another word whispered through his mind. *Keep*. His jaw dropped as he realized what he was watching. His reptile half had claimed her.

"What just happened?" Sandi said.

"Snake whisperer." Gray was leaning against the cabinet, eating an apple and studying them. "An affinity for the creatures."

"Maybe." Doc stepped closer to Friday, earning a warning hiss from the diamondback. "Maybe the snake is picking up on signals from the man and doesn't see her as a threat."

"Or food," Mace added helpfully.

"It's warm," Friday said in wonder, petting the reptile. "Look at its beautiful colors. It's actually more vibrant when it's off your body. Your dark skin tone dulls the colors somewhat. It's so pretty."

Inside his mind the damn reptile gloated. He could have sworn it was telling him that Friday liked the snake more than she liked the man. His life was getting weirder than usual. He was used to an instinctive connection with the reptile. One that meant they could communicate without words, but this was stronger, clearer. It was almost as though his connection with the snake was growing.

Which brought him right back to the reason he'd made his deal with the little scientist. Somebody needed to get to the bottom of their mutated DNA. Somebody had to give them some answers. Otherwise, they were walking into their new futures blind.

"How long can you two stay separate?" Friday asked, her hand still on the diamondback.

"Twelve, fourteen hours, at most, then the urge to merge is painful. I don't know what would happen if we couldn't get back together." But he feared it would be the end of him and the reptile.

"Do you talk to each other? Telepathically?"

An inexplicable surge of pride went through him at her question. She was so damn smart. "We communicate instinctually, but recently"—very recently—"I've started to pick up words and emotion."

There were gasps from his team. He looked over at them, wondering if anyone else had experienced something similar. There was silence, and he knew they didn't trust Friday enough to share their secrets in front of her. He was the only one willing to take the risk, and he did it because his team needed the scientist. And, if he were honest, partly because something about the woman pulled at him. He wanted her to know about all of him. To accept all of him.

"Who's in charge in your partnership? You or the snake?" She nuzzled her cheek against the snake's head, and he could practically feel the damn thing purr.

"Me. Definitely me."

"Is it aware when it's on your skin?"

"It's sleeping, but aware."

Her eyes went wide, her back snapped straight, and her lips parted. "We can never have sex!"

The room erupted with laughter, and she turned a deep shade of red. There was really no stopping the woman's thoughts from coming right out of her mouth.

"Why can't we have sex, bébé?" This he had to hear.

She peered at the team from the corner of her eye. "We'll talk about it later."

"I think you need to say it now. Everybody's waiting to hear your reasoning." Something nasty gripped at his emotions, making the diamondback raise its head and narrow its eyes at him. "Is it because I'm a freak?"

"What?" She stepped toward him, her hand up as though to touch, but she remembered they had an audience and stopped. "Don't be an idiot. It's because the snake would watch."

Relief surged through him, followed closely by annoyance when his friends made no attempt to smother their amusement. Striker growled at Jeremiah, who was laughing hard enough to have tears rolling down his face.

"I meant to whisper that," Friday mumbled.

He mentally nudged his other half and told it to get on home. There was a second of protest before it slithered off Friday's shoulder, rubbing against her as though the snake was petting the woman, which made her squeak, then giggle. It climbed up Striker's body, curled around him, and he clenched his teeth in pain as they merged once again.

Friday was on him in an instant. Her hands running over his back to trace the body of the snake.

"Unbelievable." She was clearly awestruck. "Do it again!"

He put his hands on his hips and hung his head. This was not how he'd thought this would go.

"Can you make it wink at me while it's on your body?" She prodded the head of the snake on his neck. "Can it hear me? When I touch it, do you feel it or does the snake?"

"I take it back," Mace said. "She's worth the hassle just for the entertainment."

Friday ignored the comment. Striker wasn't even sure she was still aware there were people in the room. Her focus was on his weird DNA, and the little scientist was beyond excited. "Is this why you wanted my brain? You want me to study your genetic mutation?" Her voice bubbled with enthusiasm. "I didn't need to be blackmailed into this. I'd have done this for free. This is amazing. Scientists spend lifetimes waiting for an opportunity like this. This is a dream come true." She scanned the rest of the team. "What animals do you have? Wait! Does this mean you're immune to the red mist? What about aging? Do you age at a normal rate? I know you were essentially frozen for a hundred years but has your aging changed since you woke up?" She beamed at their medic. "Can we go to the lab now? Do you have some samples I can look at? Can I read your data? I've already been sworn to secrecy. I'm totally trustworthy." She looked up at Striker. "Tell him."

It was clear from the hysteria in the room that he'd had lost control of the meeting. He wrapped his arms around Friday and lifted her up against him, high enough to make her feet dangle above the floor. Without saying a word to the assholes he called family, he strode toward the back of the cave.

"Wait!" She struggled to get free. "I want to see what everybody else has. Who's got the bear? It's Mace, isn't it? He's huge, and he couldn't work the scanner. I hear bears are big and not that smart, so it would fit."

He tuned out the new wave of laughter behind him as he stomped his way to his room. Friday thumped his shoulder— the one without the snake tattoo, no doubt because she was worried about hurting the reptile. Obviously, she wasn't that worried about hurting the man.

"Take me back. I have questions that need answering. I want to get started on my research."

"We're going to bed."

"I told you, I won't have sex with the diamondback watching our every move. You promised we wouldn't have an audience. I don't care how attractive you are. Sex is off the table. I can't do it with a snake watching me."

He shook his head in wonder at the stuff that went on in her head. The team's laughter followed them down the corridor, telling him they could still hear every word coming out of her mouth. He took her into what was essentially a private room. His private room.

The cavern wasn't brightly lit like the communal area had been. Instead, it was filled with the dim yellow glow emitted by a low-beam industrial lamp. Furnishings were sparse and looked completely out of place against the rough stone of the walls. A set of metal shelves held his clothing, all neatly arranged, a habit left over from his army days. Against the wall nearest the entrance was a small table he used as a desk. On top of it sat a top-of-the-line computer console, the kind they used in the Coalition Countries because you didn't need implants to work it. Hunter, their tech guy, had rigged an old-fashioned keyboard to the state-of-the-art machine, making it a fusion of old and new— much like him.

He walked over to his bed and sat Friday on the edge. Her mouth was open, and her eyes were wide. "You were serious? You really expect us to go to bed now?"

"Yeah." He was so damned tired he could sleep standing, which meant they were definitely going to bed. But first he had to make sure Mace had taken care of their transport to La Paz and the paperwork they needed to get into the closed city. "Get ready. I'll be back in a minute. If you need the facilities, turn right out of this cavern and you'll see them farther down the tunnel on the left."

"I know where the facilities are." Her nose wrinkled in disgust. "What I don't know is why you're using something called a chemical toilet."

Man, she was cute, but these conversations tended to go on forever and he needed some shut-eye. "Bébé, this is a cave. The best we can do for plumbing is to heat the water that runs through it. The toilets are chemical because that's what works in here. Do you really want to discuss the toilets?"

"No." She sat up straight. "I want to talk about the animals. Have they changed your personalities?"

"Tomorrow." He pinched the bridge of his nose. "We both need sleep. Get yourself sorted and get into bed."

The color drained from her face. "I thought there would be more kissing and stuff first."

An alarm sounded in his mind. He was missing something here and needed to backtrack fast to find out what it was. "First, before what? Before sleep?"

She blinked up at him. "Before sex. Isn't that why you want me to get ready?"

"Bébé." He let out a sigh. "I already told you. Sex isn't part of our deal. You don't need to worry about it. Right now, we're exhausted and need to catch some sleep."

About a million different emotions seemed to race across her face—relief, confusion, disappointment, acceptance. And with that last disheartened look, he knew she'd come to the wrong conclusion.

Wide blue eyes looked up at him. "Don't you want to have sex with me?" Her words were like a punch to his gut. If the woman knew the effect she had with her vulnerably honest questions, she'd be dangerous.

"Chère, if you believe anything, believe this: I definitely want you."

She didn't look convinced, making him close the distance between them to crouch in front of her. "You've turned me into a desperate man, Friday Jones. It's been a long time since I wanted a woman as much as I want you. I want to strip you naked and lay you down on cool cotton sheets, then take my time exploring every inch of that smooth, creamy skin of yours." Her full pink lips parted with a little hiss of air that made him want to taste, and touch, and indulge. When they had time. "I want to tease you with my lips and teeth and listen to those little gasps and groans you'll make when I drive you crazy with need. And then, when you're begging me to take you, because you can't stand the pleasure no more, I'm gonna cover you with my body and slide into your warm, wet heat. Then, mon amour, I'm gonna take us both to paradise. Over. And. Over. Again. Until you can't think from wanting me. Because I can't think from wanting you." He stroked his thumb over her bottom lip. "Does that sound like a man who doesn't want you?"

She leaned into his touch, her eyes dark, her cheeks flushed. A perfect picture of pure temptation. "It can really be like that?"

"Yeah, it can really be like that. But, with you, I think it's gonna be something more. I'm not sure we're gonna survive that much passion." He gave her a slow, promising smile. "But I sure am willing to try."

She let out a shaky little breath. "I didn't know…"

No, from her reaction, he didn't think any man had taken proper care of her in bed. He'd change that. When they had time.

With deep regret, he forced himself to stand and move away from her. "Trust me, there's gonna be way more kissing in your future, but not right now. We're exhausted, and we need to get in some sleep before we head out again."

"Okay," she whispered, but she didn't sound convinced. "Maybe we could have sex then sleep?"

She was too damn tempting. And he couldn't resist. He leaned over, clasped her face, and kissed those soft lips of hers. He took his time, making it last, letting her feel the need he wanted to unleash, but couldn't. When he pulled away from her, she was dazed and swaying, her cheeks pink, her lips red. Beautiful.

"When we make love, I'm not going to rush to fit it in before something else. I want to take my time. I want to have hours, days, to spend making you desperate for more. Tonight, we sleep."

He forced himself to turn away from her and head out of the room. It was one of the hardest things he'd ever had to do. But he had to talk to his team and make sure they were ready for the rest of this mission.

They had three days to get to La Paz. More than enough time if they didn't have the entire Northern Territory Enforcement agency on their ass. They had to be prepared for anything if they were going to make it to the antidote in time.

And they would make it on time.

Or die trying.

CHAPTER 17

The Penthouse, CommTECH building,
New York City

Miriam Shepherd opened her eyes and read the personal message that flashed across her comlens. A message from the Broker. A message that had woken her up. And she didn't like what she read one little bit. For a moment, she stared up into the star-filled sky through the glass ceiling above her bed and wondered what her next move should be. Should she tell her fellow leaders that Friday Jones was still a threat? Or should she deal with the problem and inform them after the fact?

She pressed her fingertips to her temple and rubbed circles. Enforcement had let her down again. How Ms. Jones had evaded them in Galveston, she didn't know. But she was going to get to the bottom of the incompetency as soon as she'd dealt with her latest problem—whether to tell the other leaders or not. It was tiresome to have to consult others in such matters. Not that they would be of any use. Ju-Long would offer up outdated ideas for Friday's capture. Serge would most likely be drunk and fucking his way through one of the downtown clubs by now. And Sandrine would find a way to use the information to further her own agenda. Because Sandrine was power-hungry. Miriam saw the look every time she met the other woman's eyes. She recognized it because it was the same visceral need that drove each of her own decisions. No, she wouldn't inform the others. Not yet.

With a sigh, she rolled to the edge of her bed and reached for the silky robe draped over the arm of the antique chair. The white fabric was smooth and cool against her skin. Another reminder of the power and money at her disposal. A moan brought her attention back to the young man currently tied on his back to her bed. She'd been very careful to ensure that the wrist and ankle cuffs didn't break his skin. Not because she cared about damage, but because she couldn't tolerate the thought of her pristine white room becoming contaminated with his blood.

Her eyes slid down his muscular body, to the painfully stiff erection straining up from his groin. She had planned to use him again before morning. Now, with yet another mess to clean up, she found her mood had changed. With the slightest thought, she sent a command for her head of security. A moment later the door opened, and Kane strode through. The man was an uncanny combination of brains, brawn, and ruthless obedience. For years, he'd functioned as her personal bodyguard and head of her security. And he had never failed to please her.

He inclined his head in acknowledgment before eyeing the man on the bed. The muscle in his jaw ticked at the sight of the brutal erection.

"Please get rid of that for me."

Miriam turned her back on the young employee. He was nothing more than a perk of the job. Her position afforded her access to a never-ending parade of young men, each of them eager to meet with CommTECH's director in the hopes of advancing their careers. Of course, after a trip to the clinic the following morning, none of the men remembered ever having set foot in Miriam's apartment. Their time together was nothing more than a gap in their memories and a few unexplained bruises and scars on their bodies. She smirked at the thought. There was nothing more delightful than meeting up with one of her men during work and seeing their lack of recognition. In fact, on a number of occasions, she'd used the same man twice, enjoying that she could do what she wanted and the evidence would be wiped away.

"How much stimulant did you give him?" Kane asked. "He's sweating, and it looks like his balls will burst."

"I don't know. Enough." She looked over her shoulder as she walked across the polished wood toward her bathroom. "I had planned to use him again before he was removed." She smiled at her loyal employee. Kane deserved some perks, too. "You can do as you wish with him until he's taken to the clinic. No point in letting him go to waste."

The smile that curved around the man's lips would have made most people shudder. Miriam wasn't most people. She closed the bathroom door behind her and stepped into the cleansing chamber. A mental command to the unit made sure that her body was expertly cleansed, perfumed, and moisturized in a matter of minutes. Knowing she had an image to present, even if it was the middle of the night, Miriam pressed her face to the makeup mask and felt the tingle as it made up her face. A quick walk through her closet allowed her to select a white silk trouser suit and matching leather boots. Once dressed, she headed for her office.

"Director." The Enforcement agent bowed his head as soon as she had him on screen.

Miriam didn't waste any time. "Friday Jones is alive."

The man's jaw clenched tight.

"My source tells me that she's meeting a jet in Monterrey on Saturday morning. Early. The pickup is scheduled for before dawn."

"Do you know which direction she's coming from?"

"In other words, do I know where she is now?" Miriam's fingers flicked on the console, and she pulled up the Enforcement captain's file, aware he could see her actions. "No. But I think I've done enough of your job for you. Don't you?"

The man paled as Miriam sent his details to Kane. She was well aware that the rumors around Kane were particularly vicious. Often times, those rumors alone were enough of a threat to ensure compliance.

"Forgive me, Director. I'll make sure that there is a team waiting for her in Monterrey."

Miriam pinned him with a look. "A team of mercenaries. We can't afford to have Enforcement linked to operations in Coalition Countries."

"Of course."

"Make sure the orders you give to the mercenaries are clear. This is an elimination. It is not a capture."

"Yes, Director." He hesitated. "And if there is anyone accompanying her?"

Miriam almost wished the man were physically in front of her so she could slap him for his stupidity. "Let me be as clear for you as I can. I don't care who is with her. I want the scientist and her companions killed. I don't want any witnesses. I don't want any loose ends. Do you think you can manage that, Captain?"

"Yes, Dir—"

With a dismissive wave of her hand, she got rid of his image and turned to look out at the city's skyline. When would she reach a position where she wouldn't have to deal with petty issues? She'd thought being director of CommTECH would be enough. She ruled over the most prosperous and powerful Territory on the globe. But increasingly, these past few years, she'd found that other people's mistakes were disturbing her peace. It only reinforced what she had long believed. There were too many leaders on the planet. A peaceful existence, for her and her Territory, was dependent on there being one clear leader. Someone every nation rallied around. Someone so powerful that petty issues were beneath them.

That someone was her.

CHAPTER 18

AFTER A FEW HOURS OF THE BEST SLEEP SHE'D EVER HAD, CURLED safe in Striker's arms, Friday sat impatiently while everyone argued about her. Doc wanted to sedate her before they made their way through the red mist to the EMP barrier. Apparently, the consensus was that she was likely to throw herself into the mist again. She scoffed at the thought, now that she knew it didn't affect Striker, she was hardly going to save him from it. A fact she'd told his team. Unfortunately, they weren't listening to logic, and she'd resigned herself to waiting for them to talk themselves out.

She was bored. She wanted to get going. She didn't want to die. She mentally rolled her eyes at herself. Of course she didn't want to die. Did anyone?

"You don't know what effect a sedative would have on the poison she took," Striker shouted, even though she'd told them twice now that it would have no effect at all. Seemed no one was interested in listening to the expert in the room, so she let them carry on wasting their time—for now. "We can't take any chance of reducing the time we've got left to get to La Paz."

"You're being unreasonable," Doc shouted back. "If she

touches the mist again, you're gonna lose another damn day dealing with the repercussions."

"I won't touch the mist," Friday said again, and was ignored—again.

It was clear she didn't actually have to be present for the argument. She wondered if they would mind if she went to the lab and read through Doc's research. There was a lot of it, and she was eager to get started. The team fascinated her. Especially Striker. She shivered at the thought of his late-night kisses and the promises he'd made to drive her crazy with his touch. She couldn't wait.

"We can't take any chances with her," Striker's angry words snapped her back to the useless argument they were all set on having.

His shoulders rippled, and she could have sworn the diamondback looked straight at her. She leaned closer to stare at the thing. Did it move? Maybe it was just the tensing of Striker's muscles while he waved his arms around. The man gestured when he was angry. Great big over-the.top gestures. Strangely, she found it more amusing than threatening.

"We'll get through the red a lot quicker if she's out cold," Mace said. "She isn't exactly up to the team's standard of fitness. It will go faster if we knock her out and carry her."

She frowned at the huge man. That was insulting. She might not be able to run as fast as Mace, but she was a normal-size human being, not a freakishly large man with a tiny brain.

She tuned them out. She got the impression that they were more interested in venting tension than actually winning the argument. But she was so bored. She even wished she had the diamondback to keep her company. She'd love to get a closer look at the patterns on the snake. They were so pretty. She even liked how it felt to hold him. Was it a he or she? She should really ask Striker. When he wasn't shouting.

"Hey," she whispered to his living tattoo, entertaining herself, "come play with me."

Her jaw dropped when the head of the snake moved, and the body wriggled.

"What the hell?" Striker shouted.

The next thing she knew, the diamondback popped off his skin and was slithering across the floor of the main cavern toward her seat. The sudden silence was oppressive. Everybody in the room gawked as the snake made its way up her leg to curl in her lap. It butted her hand to make her pet it, which she did, turning red under the shocked stares of the team at the same time.

"Sorry," she said. "I was bored and thought I'd hang out with the snake. Carry on shouting. Don't mind us."

"Did she just…?" Mace pointed at her.

"What?" She petted the animal in her lap as it snuggled into her. She probably should have felt like prey, but mainly she felt comforted.

"Bébé, you called my snake off my body." Striker's voice was soft as he took a step toward her. His arms were folded over his sleeveless shirt, making those distracting shoulders bulge.

"I'm sorry?" It was clear from the reactions that she'd done something wrong. "I didn't mean to. I just asked him if he wanted to come play, and he did."

The men shared uneasy looks. Striker crouched down in front of her and put his hands on her knees.

"You don't understand. You shouldn't have been able to communicate with the snake, let alone call it to you and have it obey."

"Oh." She looked down at the reptile. "This has never happened before?"

"No." His hands flexed on her knees. "We've tried calling each other's animals, and we've tried communicating with them, too, but we can't."

"Then why did it come to me?" And why did that make her feel warm inside, like she was special? Her cheeks flushed at the childish thought. She needed to put her brain to good use. This was about analyzing the unusual behavior of the snake, not feeling smug because she managed to do something the men hadn't.

"Guess the man and the snake are both fascinated by you, chère."

That made her cheeks burn hotter.

"Maybe she's a snake whisperer, like Gray said." Mace came to stand beside them. "Some people have an affinity for animals. We should get her to try calling someone else's. See if it works with them."

"And while you're at it"—Friday frowned up at him—"maybe you can also stop talking about her as though she wasn't sitting right here."

"You're a pain in the ass," Mace said. "You know that, right?"

She considered the reptile snuggling in her lap. "I wonder if he'd bite you if I asked him nicely."

That caused laughter. Even Mace managed a smile. Wonder of wonders, the man didn't die from the effort.

"She can call to my animal." Gray, who was drinking coffee at the table on the other side of the room, stood. He put his mug down and sauntered toward them.

"You sure, Gray? It means she knows about you." Mace looked down at her. She couldn't read his expression. "She could still be captured by Enforcement. You have to assume that anything she knows is something they could know, too." He gave Striker a pointed look. "Which is why I suggested keeping the show-and-tell until after La Paz."

"I don't care about Enforcement." Gray stood beside them and tugged his T-shirt off. He was just as muscled as the rest of the men, but he was nowhere near as gorgeous as Striker.

She caught Striker glaring at her for studying Gray's chest.

"Don't worry," she told him. "You're prettier."

He choked at her words, and the team snickered.

"Seriously," Mace said to Gray. "Think about this."

"I told you. Let Enforcement come. I'll be ready." The cold look Gray's face made Friday think there wasn't a whole lot he cared about, least of all his own life.

She felt a surge of excitement as he turned to show her his back. She wanted to see all of their animals. She wanted to study the team, and their partner creatures, until she had all the answers they needed. She gasped as his tattoo came into view. It was a glorious wolf curled across his back as though sleeping.

"Call to it," Gray ordered.

She frowned at him. She didn't like taking orders. She also didn't like the pressure of performing while everyone watched her.

"Just try, bébé." Striker caressed her cheek, making her melt.

She took a deep breath and looked at the wolf. "Hey, you," she whispered at it, making the diamondback raise its head to see what she was doing. "Want to come play with me?"

The reptile in her lap head-butted her hand as though jealous, but the wolf didn't move.

"Again," Striker encouraged.

"Can I touch it? It might help. We've never met, so it might not listen to me."

His mouth tightened. He didn't like that suggestion at all, but he nodded tersely.

"It's okay with me." Gray's voice was devoid of emotion.

Gingerly, she reached out to trace the curve of the wolf. The detail was amazing. She almost expected to touch fur. Instead, all she felt was the warm skin of a strange man.

"Hey, wolfie, want to come play with me?" she whispered again, making the diamondback hiss its annoyance. But the wolf didn't react.

"Nothing." Striker sounded almost relieved.

Gray shrugged back into his shirt. "Maybe she can only call to reptiles."

Striker studied her. "Or maybe, she can only call to my animal. That's what the damn snake is telling me, anyway."

Eyes widened. Mace let out a whistle. "It's actually talking now?"

"Short sentences." Striker smiled ruefully. "It just told me I was an idiot, and that Friday is special."

That made everyone stare at her again. She held up her hands as though surrendering. "Trust me, the diamondback is wrong. There's nothing special about me at all. I am one hundred percent ordinary. Ask Striker."

His eyes warmed as he smiled at her. "I wouldn't call you ordinary, chère."

"Guess this is something we'll have to look into once you two get back from Bolivia," Doc said.

Friday glanced up at the hole in the ceiling. The red mist had lightened. "Can we go now?"

Striker let out a sigh. "Yeah."

"Great." She stood with the diamondback curled round her shoulders. "I'm going to assume that I'll be awake for the trip to the Coalition border and start putting the barrier cream on." She strode toward the tunnel that led to Striker's room. He'd brought a tub of cream and a new suit for her that morning.

"Friday?" he called out after her. "You forgetting something?"

She looked back at him. "Don't worry, I'll wait for you to do my back before I put the suit on."

His smile was devastating. "Can I have my snake back, bébé?"

Her cheeks burned. "Sorry. Go home now," she told the diamondback.

It hissed as though grumbling at her, but slid off her body and headed to his other half.

"I'll be damned," Mace said, and Friday realized she'd ordered the reptile around again.

"Don't blame me," she told them. "Blame the snake!"

With everyone staring at her, she hurried toward the bedroom. It was time to get out of the Red Zone and see if she had a future ahead of her.

———

Friday lasted almost an hour in the red mist before the questions started. Striker was impressed. He figured she must have been bursting to talk for at least fifty minutes of that hour.

"Does the mist have any effect on you at all?"

"Nope." He walked behind her, closely behind her, to keep an eye on every move she made.

Mace was in front of Friday, the hope being that if they kept the woman between them, she would be less likely to touch the mist. Their first priority was to guard Friday, which was why they hadn't bothered with the pretense of wearing protective suits. Without the suits, they could maneuver more easily and react faster if she needed saving again. Which he didn't want to even think about.

"Do you stick to the paths through the mist when you don't have other people with you?" Her voice had a strange echo, coming at his earpiece through the comm unit in her helmet.

"We stick to the paths. We're not sure what long-term effect going into the mist might have on us, if any. We've already had enough exposure to it. That's why we need a scientist. We have lots of unanswered questions."

"How did you find out your saliva combatted the mist?"

He smiled. He'd bet her brain was bursting with questions.

"Less talk," Mace snapped, "more concentration. I don't know if you've noticed, but we're walking through Death Valley here, and you're the only one that can be killed."

"What's your animal?" She sounded irritated. It didn't look like Friday and Mace were gonna braid each other's hair anytime soon.

"None of your business. You survive and get a security implant, then we'll talk."

"It's a bear, right? A grumpy, antisocial bear. Tell me I'm right."

Mace growled, kind of proving her point, making Striker smother a laugh.

"Were you this huge before you woke up?" Friday was undeterred by Mace's attitude. Striker wasn't sure if that made her brave or reckless. There weren't many people who'd confront the big man when he was annoyed.

"Woman, stop talking," Mace ordered.

"Of course. I'll get right on that." She sounded amused. "But first, did you wake up this size or were you this size beforehand? I'm wondering if you've taken on the bulk of a bear."

Her only answer was a deep, irritated growl.

"Striker," she changed tactic, pulling him into the mix. "Is his animal a bear? It is, isn't it?"

"I'm not sayin', chère."

"A coyote, then. A real bad tempered one. Oh, an alligator! Is it an alligator? They're antisocial, too."

"Are you sure she's worth it?" Mace said. "Maybe we should just toss her in the mist and cut our losses."

"Is Sandi really your sister?" Friday changed the topic fast enough to make a man's head spin. "You don't look alike. And I didn't think women were allowed in the special forces a hundred years ago."

"She was among the first wave of female Army Rangers," Striker said.

"She had to be tougher than the men to get through." Mace sounded proud of his foster sister, in a gruff kind of way.

"You were Army Rangers?" She glanced back, and he grasped her hips.

"Eyes front. Concentrate. If you can't do that while talking, you need to be silent. This is no game, chère. I will knock you out if you look back at me one more time. Hear me?"

"Yes, Striker."

Her soft words sent shivers down his spine. If they'd been alone, he would have been on her faster than a cat in heat.

"Keep it in your pants, dude," his best friend muttered. "Case you didn't notice, this ain't the place to get horny."

"Horny?" Friday said. "I missed something. Did I black out again?"

"No, bébé, he's is just being an ass."

"A perceptive ass," Mace muttered.

"You act like brothers." She sounded awed.

"We are brothers. We're family." And Striker would die for each and every one of them.

"We're the only family we got left." Mace reminded her.

The silence was suddenly heavy. Striker fought the memories that were brutally fresh. His parents, grandparents, sisters, cousins—all gone. They'd been gone for decades, but for him, it had only been three short years.

"I'm sorry." Friday's soft voice filled the silence. "I didn't think. It must have been terrible to wake up and find your families had been gone for such a long time."

They didn't reply. There was nothing to say. Striker wondered what was worse, that his family had mourned him as dead while he slept, or that he woke up to find them all gone. He hadn't even dared to research who was left, what descendants might still be around in the bayou. None of the team had gone looking for relatives. It was something they'd all agreed on when they woke. It was too dangerous for them to call attention to themselves and their families by digging into their pasts.

"Oh my," she whispered. "I never thought. Some of you must have been married, had children. Striker?" Her voice trembled as she asked.

His first instinct was to comfort. "Not me, bébé. I was single. I lost family, but not that, no kids." He paused. "You might want to keep your curiosity about our pasts to yourself where family's concerned. Some of the guys did lose partners and kids. It's hard on them."

"Of course; I'm so sorry."

They all were. Sorry didn't change a damn thing. They walked on in silence for a while longer, trying not to become distracted by the oppressive presence of the never-changing red mist.

"How do you map the Red Zone? You can't use satellite imagery, and there are no landmarks to keep you from getting disorientated." Friday's curiosity couldn't be subdued for long.

"We use drones to check the passages and to bring back changes in data," he said.

"Of course."

He watched her head bob, moving that huge protective helmet. "That means you must have people on the team who are good with the current technology, unlike Mace. It must have been a huge learning curve for you when you woke up."

Mace growled again, and Striker grinned.

"Is your animal a wild dog? You definitely growl a lot."

"Only around you," the big guy grumbled.

Friday looked back at him. "Is it an armadillo?"

His hands shot out to clutch her hips and stop her from backing into the mist.

"Wait up," he called to his partner.

When he looked through the glass shield in Friday's helmet, she was biting her bottom lip. "I won't do it again. I promise I'll be more careful and keep my eyes front. Honest, it won't happen again." She batted those big blue eyes at him.

It wasn't going to work. Not this time. Not when her life was on the line. He already had the pressure injector in his hand, ready for this moment, because he knew it would come.

"I know it won't." Moving too fast for her to stop him, he flipped the lock on her helmet, lifted it, and pressed the injector to her neck. "Mace. Catch."

The big man was behind her in an instant.

"No!" she shouted before her eyes rolled back and her body went limp.

It took seconds to secure her over Striker's shoulders, her arms tied to his waist to stop them from waving around.

"She's going to be pissed when she wakes." Mace walked behind them to ensure no part of her body entered the mist. "She just doesn't stop, does she?"

"Nope." He shifted her weight, holding her tight with one arm clamped around the back of her thighs and the other hand on her rear. She wasn't heavy, and he'd be able to carry her all the way out of the mist. For some reason that calmed him. The thought of letting anyone else hold her made him want to roar his displeasure.

"Never seen someone behave like that in the mist before. Normally people are terrified to touch the damn stuff and struck dumb because they're concentrating on staying alive. Not Friday. She's too busy asking dumbass questions."

Her questions weren't dumb, they were just…plentiful. "I'm telling the team she thinks your animal is an armadillo."

"Asshole."

Content to have a quiet Friday in his arms, Striker kept his focus on getting her out of the red zone in one piece.

CHAPTER 19

"I can't believe you sedated me. Are you aware of how ethically wrong that is? You can't sedate a person against their will." Friday tugged off the protective suit while she railed at the men. Her head was foggy, and her mouth felt like it was full of dry foam. "It's assault. That's what it is. Assault. I don't think I like you anymore."

"You like me just fine." Striker's smile was as smugly arrogant as his drawl.

"No, I don't. I like your diamondback, but you I could do without."

His smile grew wider, and her heart stuttered a little. She wished that eyepatch was gone so she could see both eyes. Somehow it was reassuring to see the snake staring out at her along with the man.

"You might change your mind if I tell you the snake agreed with me that we had to knock you out."

"No!" She kicked off the heavy boots and reached for the lightweight shoes Striker had dug out of their supply trunk. The soles were thick, but the upper part of the shoe adjusted to fit the wearer. They were ugly but functional— exactly what she was used to. There had been no need for fashion or vanity in her life; practical was definitely better for the labs. "Did the snake tell you that? Are you lying?"

He placed a hand over his heart. "Would I lie to you, bébé?"

"You'd do whatever you thought was best for you."

"And you." His smile turned to a frown. "And yeah, the snake cheered me on when I knocked you out. He said you don't listen too good to instructions."

"He did not." Now the infuriating man was making things up to justify his heinous behavior.

He shrugged then turned his back on her, rummaging around in the chest.

"Sit," Mace ordered. "Eat." He pointed at the nutrition bars beside her.

"I don't like you, either," she told him. "You were complicit in his behavior."

"Ask me if I care." The man-mountain sat down on a rock and started to demolish a large box of bars.

"Don't forget to drink." Striker sat down on a rock near to her. "Remember what happened last time. We can't afford you getting dehydrated again."

With her teeth clenched in frustration, she snatched the bottle of water he offered. "You want me to stay in the caves and study your genes when I get back from La Paz. That means getting in and out of the Red Zone at least twice more. Probably even more than that, as I'll need to go get samples and equipment. Do you plan to knock me out every time I have to go through the mist?"

They exchanged a look that made it clear they thought her question was stupid.

"Well, yeah," Striker said.

When she took a deep breath, ready to shout some more, he held up a hand to stop her. "You can't be trusted in the mist. Your mind wanders too much. You show me you can stop thinking, then you can walk through the mist."

"That's insane."

"That's the condition. You comply, or hello Mr. Sandman."

"What does that even mean?" She threw up her hands in frustration.

"That's what I miss most," Mace said around a mouthful of nutrition bar. "Nobody ever gets our cultural references. I feel like my sparkling wit is lost on the people of this new world."

"You have wit?" She glared at him.

"Can we knock her out again?" Mace asked his team leader.

"Come." Striker patted the boulder beside him. "Sit with me. We've still got a long ways to go."

"I'm very annoyed with you."

"I know." His eye danced. "And if Mace wasn't here, I'd make it up to you. But I know how much you hate an audience."

She blinked at him for a minute. "Was that a sexual reference?"

His chuckle made her want to kick him, but the heat had gone out of her anger. Mainly, she just felt weary. With a humph of annoyance, she sat down beside Striker but resisted when he tried to hold her close—even though it felt like she was cutting her nose off in spite of her face.

"Whatever I want, whenever I want it," he whispered against her ear, making her shiver. "And right now, I want to hold you, bébé."

"Unbelievably irritating, arrogant man," she grumbled as she moved closer to him, feeling his arm slide around her waist and liking it far too much. "I'm doing this under duress."

He pressed a kiss to her temple.

"You know," Mace said as he watched her, "the more I get to know you, the more I wonder why we're bothering to rescue you. Do you even know how to study our genetics? I mean, how experienced in this field are you? What did you do at CommTECH, anyway?"

She narrowed her eyes at the man. He was really beginning to irritate her. "I was nothing more than a cog in the wheel. There are a million or more biotech engineers who can do what I do. There's nothing special about me."

"Then what makes you think you can study our DNA and come up with answers?"

Part of her wanted to rattle off her experience and study credentials, in some misguided show of ego in the face of his blatant disbelief in her skills. The rest of her wanted to tell him to go to hell and find another scientist. Striker saved her from making a choice.

"Friday here graduated top of her class in genetics. She won a year's research scholarship to study with a Doctor Swanson in Germany, but she couldn't afford the rest of the costs to take it up. She had to go work off her study debt at CommTECH, instead. If her field of study had interested them, they might have paid for her to go to Germany, but it didn't. Tell him what your specialist area is, bébé."

"How do you know that stuff?" She stared up at him and, as usual, felt the world fade away. Having Striker's full attention made everything else feel as though it was a hologram and he was the reality.

"I had you researched. I read the report last night." He brushed her hair off her forehead. "I had to know who I was dealing with."

Of course he did. And it was stupid to be disappointed that he hadn't wanted to know just because he was interested in her. Pressing her feelings down deep, where they usually lived, she turned her attention to the giant, annoying idiot.

"I studied genetic anomalies. The scholarship would have let me take part in Doctor Swanson's study on how the slightest genetic manipulation could prolong the use of implants and make them less invasive for the host." She glanced away before looking back at them, wondering if she should tell them the area she was most interested in. Wondering if they would think it was a setup, her approaching them. She took a deep breath and gave them honesty.

"What I most wanted to study was the genetic impact caused by the low levels of chemical seepage and radiation that are emitted by the implants and absorbed into the host's system. In the implants I studied, especially the ones in the brain, I found significant genetic adaptation in relation to the host. Most of it was localized, but my hypothesis was that, given enough sustained exposure to the implant emissions, the overall genetic makeup of the host could, and would, change. I wanted to study these changes, to see what the implications were for the future. To, in essence, predict the genetic development of the human race in relation to the impact caused by the implants."

It was the men's turn to look stunned.

"In other words..." Mace recovered first. "Your field of expertise is genetic deformities caused by manmade chemicals."

"Yes." She whispered the word, and there was silence.

It was Mace who broke it, and his voice was ice cold. "That's a helluva coincidence. The one scientist who falls into our laps happens to be the one who is a specialist in chemically-mutated DNA." He glared at his team leader. "You still sure she isn't a spy sent by the Territory governments?"

To Friday's dismay, Striker didn't say anything at all.

CHAPTER 20

The Penthouse, New Amsterdam Hotel,
New York City, Northern Territory

"WHY AM I HERE?" SERGE ABRAMOVICH SOUNDED BORED AS HE lazed back on the decadent red sofa. "I'm a busy man."

Sandrine Cherbourg was certain he was a busy man—busy getting drunk and screwing his way through New York's elite. Instead of snapping at him to be serious for once, she poured him a glass of the hotel's finest Scotch and handed it to him.

"We're here to discuss the methods Miriam is using to deal with her missing scientist."

"I thought she'd sent an Enforcement army to head her off at the coast."

"Seems Ms. Jones slipped through their net."

Serge grimaced. "Not a good look for Miriam."

No. It wasn't. A fact that pleased Sandrine no end. She tossed her long black hair over her shoulder and sat back into the armchair facing Serge. She'd chosen the form-fitting red dress she wore because it flowed over her curves, showing her body to her best advantage. After all, her body, like everything else at her disposal, was simply a tool she could use to achieve her aims.

"I'm assuming you've jammed all comm devices in this room." Serge pointed with the hand that held the glass.

The man was even too lazy to use his free hand to gesture. If she didn't need his alliance, she wouldn't give the buffoon the time of day. But she did need him.

"Of course." She crossed her long legs, letting the spiked heel of her red leather shoe dangle like a lure in front of her. "We are in Miriam's territory, non? It would be foolish to assume privacy."

She watched Serge lick his lips as he followed her movements. "You won't mind if I check for myself."

She inclined her head. "But of course." She watched as Serge used his implant to attempt to communicate with an outside team.

His smile was wide, but his eyes were dead, when he discovered it was impossible. "Tell me what you want, Sandrine." He took another mouthful of liquor.

That was one thing she did like about Serge—the man didn't like to waste time on small talk. Not when he could be using that time to indulge his desires. If she hadn't seen him in action in the boardroom, where he was ruthless and cutting in his intelligence, she would never have imagined how such a man could retain power over his region.

"I want to align forces. I want"—she licked her red, red lips before continuing—"to find this missing girl before Miriam kills her."

His eyes turned sharp. "You want to download the information in the scientist's head and use it against Miriam."

"Oui." She purred the word and watched his face flush.

Men. Too, too easy.

"But, Sandrine darling, have you forgotten that you, too, were at the meeting? If you compromise Miriam, you also compromise yourself. You compromise all of us." There was a bite of warning in his tone that she dismissed.

"True. But if one were to leak other information at the same time, that person could make it seem as though their only role in the meeting was to undermine the nefarious plans of the group."

"You want to tell the world you were there acting as a spy? That your involvement was for the greater good?"

Her laughter was tinkling. "Well, at least we can say it was for my good."

"For the public to believe you were there with honest intentions, you'd need corroboration of your story." His smile was knowing. "You'd need me."

"We can spin the meeting any way we like. The way I would tell it is that we were invited to take part, but once we learned what they intended, we instantly made our views known. After that, our consciences wouldn't allow us to do anything else but go public with the information and undermine their plans." She ran her palm down her thigh, watching him follow the move. "It will weaken their companies' stock."

"It will leave a power gap that you can step into." Serge threw back the rest of his drink and placed the crystal glass on the table beside him.

"That you can step into, too," she told him. "The gap would be too large for one person to fill."

His movements were languorous as he climbed up off the sofa and closed the distance between them, coming to a halt in front of her.

"How do you propose we find this missing scientist? And how can you be certain she isn't already dead?"

"Miriam is not the only one with sources."

His eyes were sharper than usual. "You have a mole in the smuggler's organization. Or"—he laughed—"her mole is your mole, too. Don't tell me you're using this famous Broker, too."

Sandrine smiled at him, giving nothing away. Serge considered her for several long minutes before nodding to himself. Sandrine felt her heart jump and her mouth water at being one step closer to her goal. One step closer to ridding the world of Miriam Shepherd.

"I always did fancy expanding into the Eastern Territory." Serge rubbed his jaw as his eyes followed the line of her leg from ankle to thigh. "I've often felt that Ju-Long has grown tired of the region. He doesn't manage it with the same enthusiasm he showed in his youth."

"That would leave me with the Northern Territory," Sandrine wanted to clarify their agreement. There could be no haggling later.

"I thought that was what you wanted, darling."

She smiled at him. It was no secret the Northern Territory was the most powerful.

"Well, it seems we have an agreement," Serge said. "How do you propose we seal this deal?"

Sandrine uncrossed her legs and widened her knees. Her eyes on Serge, she grasped the fabric of her dress and inched it upward until she was exposed for his pleasure.

His cheeks flushed and his eyes darkened. "Ms. Cherbourg, I like how you do business." He fell to his knees in front of her. "You have yourself a partner."

CHAPTER 21

"She isn't a spy."

Friday barely stopped herself from sagging with relief at Striker's confident declaration. In the short time she'd known him, his opinion of her had come to matter more than almost anything else.

"Then explain her research specialty." Mace glared at her. "And the fact she didn't faint when you told her about our genetics. Or when you revealed your diamondback. Most people would have passed out at the sight. Not Friday—she took the whole thing in her stride. Almost as though she already knew about it. About us."

"She didn't know about us." Striker's certainty made her eyes well up with tears. The reaction shocked her. She never cried. There wasn't any point. Tears achieved nothing. "You didn't see her in Scorpion Canyon. You didn't see how freaked out and confused she was when the scorpions kept their distance."

"That doesn't mean she didn't know we were genetically different. All that means is she didn't know about our effect on the scorpions in the canyon."

"What about her saving me from the mist? Explain that?"

He shook his head as he pulled her closer. "She thought she was going to die. There's no way she could have known we'd save her in time. We almost didn't."

Mace stood suddenly, looming over them.

Friday couldn't help but shrink back, but she cleared her throat and faced her accuser. "I didn't want to tell you about my area of expertise because I knew how it would come across."

He snorted his disbelief. And just like that, something snapped inside of her, filling her with anger instead of anxiety. She jumped to her feet and glared up at the overgrown ape.

"You might think you understand the world you woke up in, but you don't." And she was going to give him an education he'd never forget. "You've done a great job adapting these past few years, but you still think like people from the last century. When you went to sleep, genetics and biotech were rare research areas. That isn't the case now. It's one of the most common scientific disciplines. And a big part of that specialization is research into genetic mutation caused by chemical bleed.

"There are literally thousands of studies being done on the subject at any given time. Thousands. You think we wouldn't study it? Half of the world's population is walking around with implanted technology. The companies who make the implants have to know how they will affect the users. They use the research to develop solutions for genetic fallout. With each new generation of implant technology, they get closer to combating the bleed effect. This is common practice. Ask anyone. Call up your Doc person and get him to research the subject. Let him tell you how common my research area is."

"If it isn't a big deal, why not come clean straightaway?" He took a threatening step toward her, and suddenly Striker was at her side. Protecting her. The thought was dizzying. People didn't protect her, they sacrificed her.

"Because, you big oaf, it took me about ten seconds to figure out you would jump to the wrong conclusion once you knew. I didn't lie. I've never lied. I worked as a drone in a low-level lab. I worked on the basic biotech function of communication implants. That's it. I was so far down the chain it's laughable. But my academic study was in a different area. And if I could work in that area, I would. That's why I was excited to study you lot. Excited about everyone but you. You need a different sort of study. Maybe you should contact a researcher who specializes in personality disorders and mental instability."

Striker barked out a laugh, pulling their attention to him. He stood beside them, arms folded, perfectly relaxed and obviously entertained. "You two about done bickering?" he said.

It took a second for Friday to realize she'd been facing off with an angry warrior who was double her size. Probably not the wisest thing she'd ever done, but she wasn't going to let that stop her now.

"Not yet," she told Striker before glaring back up at Mace. "As for my reaction to the news of your abilities. That's just how I react. If you were looking for hysterics, you picked the wrong woman. I've been shocked and stunned more times in my life than I care to remember. If I'd fallen apart every single time, I'd have achieved nothing. I'd still be stuck in a group home in Houston, praying I'd die of neglect before I had to prostitute myself to survive.

"So, no, I wasn't shocked at Striker's diamondback. I was thrilled. Thrilled that something exciting, something interesting, had fallen into my path for a change. Thrilled that I might have a chance to do what I love to do, rather than what I have to do. Thrilled that there was a group of people out there who wanted and needed me, instead of people who barely tolerated my presence. But"—she poked him in the chest—"when I find out what your animal is, I'll be sure to scream and faint, so you'll feel properly appreciated." She turned back to Striker, breathing heavily. "We need to get going."

"Yeah, we do." He reached out and clasped her nape. His eye was soft, and the smile was one she'd never seen before— she thought it might have been pride. In her? That couldn't be. No one ever felt something like that over her.

He pressed a soft, sweet kiss to her lips before releasing her. Friday turned away, picked up her water bottle, hoping the men couldn't see her eyes well up. Damn tears. She'd never been on the verge of crying so much as she had been since she'd met Striker. Or maybe it was just a side effect of the poison. She could only hope that's what it was because she didn't plan to turn into an emotional wreck anytime soon.

"Friday?" Mace called, making her tense. His tone had softened, but you still couldn't call it warm. "Jury's still out."

She didn't answer. He was kidding himself. The jury was definitely in, and it had already convicted her.

"Let's get going." Striker picked up his daypack. "You ready?"

She nodded and put some distance between her and Ape-man. They moved out in silence, walking across the rugged landscape toward the EMP barrier that indicated the border to the Coalition Countries.

The silence didn't bother Friday. It wasn't like she'd spent a lot of time around people anyway. The men might think she was a talker, but she was normally alone. The only reason she'd been talking since meeting them was because she had too many questions that needed answering.

They stopped now and then to replenish their fluids and energy with tepid water and dry nutrition bars. Friday actually craved the taste sensation of the spicy chili Mace had made, but she certainly wasn't going to tell the man. As night fell, the glow of power from the pulsing EMP barrier lit up the distant sky. The barrier was made up of a set of tall poles that emitted pulses of electromagnetic energy contained in laser beams between them, effectively forming a wall that would overload any circuit passing through it. All Coalition Countries used EMP barriers on their borders. No implant ready chips were legally allowed into Coalition Countries, and anyone who already had implants had to apply for a special visa to cross the border. Even then they were closely monitored.

As they walked up to the barrier, she noticed a concrete cube of a building on the other side of the glowing wall of light. Striker checked his wristwatch, another relic from his past.

"Any time now," he said.

"Time for what?" It didn't matter how much she wanted to keep the questions inside, they always found a way out.

He gave her a knowing smile. "I was wondering how long you'd last before your curiosity overrode your stubborn streak. It's been hours, I'm impressed."

"Not impressed enough to answer the question. What's it time for, and how are we going to get past the barrier?"

He jerked his head toward a man coming out of the concrete cube. "That's how."

The man walked over to the barrier. Although he wore the uniform of a border official, he didn't seem surprised to see them. The pulsing blue lights affected his skin tone, making him seem otherworldly.

"Smurf effect," Striker said, as though reading her mind.

"What effect?"

"We need to sit her down and let her watch some old movies," Mace grumbled. "This is embarrassing."

"I'm touched," she mocked. "It sounds like you've decided to let me stay, after all."

"Children," Striker reprimanded. "Behave or you'll get a time-out."

"Striker," the guard shouted. "You got my payment?"

He tapped his backpack. "Got it right here, Manny. Have I ever let you down?"

The guard snorted. "There's a first time for everything." He held up his hand, pressed a remote, and the beams between the two nearest poles stopped, creating a door in the barrier.

"Come on." Striker nudged her through the gap, and it closed behind them. He handed a credit chip to the border guard. "There you go. The vehicle was delivered?"

"It's waiting in your usual spot." The guy tucked the chip into his shirt pocket. "See you next time."

"Hasta luego, Manny." He saluted the man, took Friday's hand, and headed around the side of the building.

"Well, that was disappointing." She noted that there was only one vehicle in the cracked and desolate parking area—their ride.

"Bébé, you're through the EMP barrier. You should be ecstatic."

"Of course I'm pleased we made it past the border. I just thought we'd get through it in some magical way—like the way the scorpions keep away from you. Instead you bribed someone to open the barrier. Anybody could do that."

"Yeah, but it isn't just anybody who could have come through the Red Zone first before they made it past the barrier. There's a reason we can get through in this spot—nobody expects anyone to come in from the Red Zone. It wouldn't be so easy to bribe a border agent at one of the main crossings, away from the mist. I'm beginning to think you take my abilities for granted. You're becoming hard to impress, chère." His sparkling eye told her he was teasing. Yet another type of interaction she'd never experienced before meeting this strange and delightful man.

"Fix the seats, Mace," Striker said. The hover vehicle was large, the type where you could rearrange the seating to suit yourself. "Give us a bench seat up front."

"Fine by me. I don't want her behind me anyway." He stuck his head through the door of the vehicle.

Friday glared at this back. "Do we have to take him with us to Monterrey? Can't he walk back to the caves? I'm sure he'd be happier there."

Striker shook his head and tugged her against him. She went willingly, reveling in the sensation. He was tactile, needing to touch, and she was desperate to be touched. It was as though her skin were a desert and he was some much-needed rain. She hadn't been joking when she'd mentioned their team seemed like family. Just watching how they'd reacted with one another made her ache for everything she'd never had. She would have loved a family, any family, taking any form. What Striker and his team had was special, made even more so by the fact they'd been through a great deal to get there.

"Are you two going to snuggle all the way to Monterrey?" Ape-man complained.

"Yes." She challenged him to do something about it.

"You know, this must have been how my poor Maman felt when she had to referee between me an' my sister. This sibling rivalry is getting old. How about the two of you give it a rest until we hit Monterrey." Striker let her loose and threw his backpack into the car.

Friday froze, struck dumb by the sibling comment. There was a desperate ache inside her, a longing for exactly that, a sibling to argue with.

"Come on." He tugged at her arm. "You need to get some sleep. Might as well do it in my arms while Mace drives. Unless you want to snuggle up with him instead."

"No!" Mace and Friday said at the same time, making Striker laugh again.

CHAPTER 22

FRIDAY SLEPT DEEP, CURLED AGAINST STRIKER'S SIDE ON THE SEAT between him and Mace. She became increasingly tired the closer they got to the deadline for taking the antidote. Already the poison was having an impact on her system. But she never complained. He stroked his hand down her side. She was like a little kitten, sheltering against him, trusting him in her sleep. Trusting him with her life.

"I hope you know what you're doing." Mace's voice was barely a whisper, but Striker still checked that Friday wasn't disturbed by it before he answered.

"You were rough on her." There was more accusation in his tone than he would have normally used with his teammate. They were best friends for a reason. Striker trusted the man with his life. His arms tightened around the woman curled against him. It seemed he didn't trust him with Friday's, though.

"I don't like coincidences."

They traveled on in silence, covering the miles slowly in the inky black night. The vehicle they'd ordered wasn't the fastest on the planet, but it was quiet. Sometimes stealth was more important than speed.

"For what it's worth," Mace said at last. "I think she's telling the truth. I'll just be a whole lot more comfortable having her around once she's been implanted with a monitoring chip."

Striker smothered his wince at the thought of shackling Friday again. All she wanted was to be free.

"You don't like that plan." Of course his best friend hadn't missed his reaction.

"I trust her."

He felt the enormous weight of the words as he said them. But they were true. A core of honor shone out from her. It was clear she was a victim of circumstance. And who better to understand that than a bunch of soldiers whose lives had changed because they'd had the misfortune to be in the wrong place at the wrong time.

"My snake trusts her, too."

There was a snort of amusement. "Your snake has adopted her. I think your damn reptile sees her as his pet."

With a soft chuckle, he traced the dark circles under her eyes. Had they been there that morning? Was it another sign her body was slowly succumbing to the poison? He held her tighter, burying the surge of fear that followed the thought. He'd just found her. He didn't want to lose her. Not when he'd lost so much already. No, he wanted to keep her with him and give her the life she desperately wanted. But he was dreaming. He was a criminal, stuck in a world he didn't understand. If she stayed with him, she would never know freedom.

If she lived.

Helpless, that was what he felt. All he could do was get her to La Paz and hope the damned antidote worked. He couldn't even think about the alternative. Friday had become important to him. There was something strong between them. Something that needed a chance to grow. And somehow, instinctively, he knew he'd never get a chance like this with anyone else. Yeah, she had to live. For both of them.

"Your snake still talking to you?" Mace kept his eyes on the terrain.

If this had been a city, he could have programmed the vehicle with their destination and let it take them there. But it wasn't the city, and there were areas they had to cross that didn't even have roads. The only way to cover the ground was manually.

"Yeah. Does your animal talk to you?" Striker asked.

"No. Impressions. Emotions. Vague images. That's about it. This started with her, right?"

"You think there's a connection?"

Mace shrugged. "Maybe she woke something in the snake. Maybe her presence hurried that evolution along. Like I said, I don't like coincidence and the way she can call to your snake, the way it's taken with her, that worries me. I think she's having an effect—on you and the snake."

"I don't see how. All this stuff with my animal is probably just a natural development of our freaky genetics. That's the problem. We've got no way to predict what's going to happen to us next. Hell, for all I know, I'll wake up one morning and find scales covering my body instead of skin." He rubbed a lock of Friday's hair between his finger and thumb. Silk. Pure silk. "That's why we need her. None of us know what's coming our way."

"I'm not sure one baby scientist can give us the answers we need."

"You got a better idea?"

Silence was the answer.

Another few miles passed in silence, the hover car making barely more than a humming sound as it skimmed over the ground.

"I sure as hell hope we don't turn into our animals," Mace said. "That would piss me off big time."

Knowing what his friend had for an animal partner made that statement all the more entertaining. Striker tried to laugh quietly, but he couldn't prevent his chest from shaking. The movement disturbed Friday's sleep. She stirred, and he soothed her with gentle caresses and murmured words.

Once she was deeply asleep, Mace glanced over at him. "What kind of things does your snake say?"

"Mainly it tells me I'm an idiot and that Friday belongs to him." He let his head fall back onto the padded headrest. "When you were arguing with her, he told me he was going to bite you for upsetting her."

"Seriously?"

"Oh yeah. He damn near freed himself to do it. I was itching so much I had to fight to stay still."

"I thought they couldn't get free without us calling to them. Well, everyone else's animals, anyway." He sounded seriously pissed off about that, too.

"Still having problems?" Striker couldn't stop from sounding amused.

"Go to hell," was the terse reply.

"Never mind breaking free without us calling to them. I thought they couldn't talk." In all honestly, he'd been thrilled his snake couldn't talk. One voice in his head was more than enough. "And I thought it was only me who could call the snake. Friday proved that wrong."

Mace ran a hand through his hair, making it stand on end. "The crap we're dealing with is enough to make you lose your mind."

"Yeah."

"Sometimes, I wonder why us. Why were we the ones in that cave? Did God just up and decide we needed more to deal with?"

"Mainly, I wonder how we're gonna get through the day. Or how we're gonna stay safe. Or how we're gonna cope with what the future brings. I don't got no time for the why of things."

Mace inclined his head. "Well, if I figure it out, I'll let you know."

"Appreciated." With that, Striker closed his eyes and concentrated on the woman in his arms.

———

Friday woke to Striker's gentle prodding. "Are we there yet?"

"Kids," he scoffed, confusing her. "We're about five minutes out from the airfield. You need to have something to drink and eat."

She felt foggy as she sat up. Her limbs were heavy, and she could have slept for another twelve hours straight. She took the water bottle he offered and drank as she looked out the windows. They were on the edge of the city. The sun hadn't yet risen, but there was a glow announcing its arrival around a massive, strangely shaped mountain to the east of the urban sprawl.

"Saddle Mountain," he said.

Of course he would know what it was called. Next to Striker and his team, she felt incredibly ignorant. He'd traveled the world, lived in two lifetimes, and had experiences she could only imagine. All she'd done was survive.

"The city is bigger than I thought it would be." Lights seemed to extend as far as the eye could see.

"About eight million now. That's almost double what it was when the bomb hit."

He seemed so casual about everything. She could only imagine what it must have been like to wake up to a completely different planet. "You had to relearn the world, didn't you?"

"Some things never change." He pointed at the mountain.

"The sun still rises." He gestured to the city lights. "People still live. Still work. Still play."

The rumbled emphasis on "play" made her shiver. Without even realizing she was doing it, she leaned into him. His eyes softened. He placed his hand on the nape of her neck and urged her closer. His unpatched eye warmed, making her melt inside.

"Mornin', bébé," he said softly, before his lips settled against hers.

His kiss was slow and delicious, each taste stealing what little awareness she'd managed to gain since waking.

"I'm sitting right here." A disgruntled voice cut straight through her haze. "And I think I'm going to be sick."

With great effort, she broke the kiss and turned to the man who was fast becoming the bane of her life. "You're still here." And yes, she didn't try to hide how disappointed she was.

He arched an eyebrow as though silently challenging her to do something about his presence. "Airport coming up."

A horrible thought occurred to her. "Are you coming with us to Bolivia?"

"You can rest easy, little spy, I'm staying right here."

She pursed her lips and thought of all the nasty things she could do to him under the pretext of testing his DNA.

"She's plotting your demise, brother." Striker sounded proud.

Ape-man snorted. "Bring it on. I'll squa—"

There was a brutal bang, and the hover car shunted to the side. Friday was thrown across Mace as he fought with the controls. The vehicle swung wide as he struggled to keep it on the road.

"You okay?" Striker snapped.

He had his weapon out and ready, his eyes on the window. The car swerved right, and she felt something hit the back of it. They were under attack.

"Are you hurt?" Striker demanded.

"No." Shaken, not hurt. "Is it Enforcement?"

"No. Enforcement sticks to the Territories. These guys are private."

"Damn it!" Mace shouted as their car turned sharply, throwing her into Striker. "We're cut off."

There were vehicles behind them and what looked like a long-distance truck in front of them. It was the huge, driverless kind that tended to stick to the longer routes. This one had been used to block off the road. It was angled across their path, and there was no way around it.

"There." Striker pointed at the windscreen.

An alley. Mace aimed for it, hitting the building and scraping against the walls as they hurtled into the narrow space. They barely fit. Sparks flew from the car's body as they skimmed the brick. More shots hit the back of the vehicle, and suddenly they thudded to the ground.

"I've lost hover." Mace's fingers flew over the console. There was a grinding noise as the wheels engaged.

The car squealed as they shot out of the alley and careened into a highway. Horns blasted at them. Signs flashed above the motorway: *Slow Down!*

Friday held on tight to the console in front of her as they wove their way through the traffic, speeding past everyone else.

Striker's focus was on their rear. "Four behind us."

She snapped her head around to see he meant four vehicles were chasing them down, all still hover-enabled and fitted with weapons. As she watched, three more cars appeared from the road on the left. Seven. Too many.

And then the new cars blasted the ones who were already following them.

"What the hell?" Striker said. "Mace did you call in backup? Arrange cover?"

"No. I don't know who the new guys are."

The car screeched as he ran it up onto the sidewalk and through a pedestrian-only area, which was empty because of the early hour. Another vehicle blocked their path. A gun fired at them, hitting their rear as their car swerved left. There was a blast. Their car was propelled into the air. They hit a screen advertising nutrition bars and crashed to the ground beneath it.

With brutal efficiency, Striker produced a knife and stabbed the airbags that had popped out around them to protect them.

"Car's done." Mace snatched up his gun, pushed the debris of the airbag aside, and threw open the driver's door.

"Everybody out." Striker grabbed her arm and dragged her through his door.

Even though it was predawn, there were still some people about. They ran, screaming, desperate to get out of the way as two sets of vehicles descended on the square—firing at each other.

He thrust her into the doorway of an old stone building. "What's going on?" he called to Mace.

"Damned if I know," was the answer. "Feels like we're stuck in the middle of a turf war—and we're the turf." Mace aimed and fired at a vehicle that got too close. It exploded, smoke billowing.

Friday's stomach spasmed. They weren't fighting over turf. They were fighting over her. She was trapped in the doorway behind the two men, their bodies a wall protecting her from the attackers. Her fingers curled into the back of Striker's T-shirt as she made herself as small of a target as possible.

"Oh crap," Mace said. "That isn't good."

"What?" She tried to see past them. It was impossible. Their shoulders alone blocked out sunlight.

"Run!" Striker reached back, grabbed her hand, and

yanked her out of the doorway—just before the massive driverless truck hit the spot where they'd been standing.

The crash made the air vibrate and the ground shudder. Gunfire skimmed past them as the world seemed to explode, and Striker dragged her behind an old, ornate fountain.

"Stay down," he ordered as he knelt up and fired over the carved stone.

The world was in chaos. People were running and screaming. Floating communication screens flashed messages telling them to cease and desist. Police sirens wailed in the distance. There was shouting. Pounding feet. The ever-present blasts of gunfire. Smoke stung her eyes. Screams of bystanders made her nauseous.

"Don't touch the woman!" someone shouted. "We need her alive."

Friday felt faint at the words.

"That explains the two groups," Striker said. "Team one wants you alive, team two wants you dead. You sure are popular, bébé."

"Don't fire!" Mace shouted before landing in a heap beside them. He had his back to the fountain, his gun aimed toward the building behind them. "They're coming around behind us."

"Who?" Striker shot a few more blasts.

Someone screamed in pain, telling her that his shot had hit its target. He ducked down to avoid the return fire.

"The guys who're out to snatch her. That's who."

"Looks like they've taken out most of the team who're here to kill her." Striker fired again.

"Yeah, I saw that. We need to get out of here. We're about two miles from the airfield. We can cover it on foot if we have to."

"Contact the pilot, tell him to get ready for a fast takeoff. We'll be coming in hot."

"Copy that."

Striker shifted to study the corner of the building the truck had crashed into. "We make for the other side of the truck. I saw apartments. Private garages."

"We can hotwire a car." Mace finished typing out a message to the jet pilot on his wrist unit. "I'll lay down cover. You take Friday."

"If we get separated, you know what to do."

"Yep." Mace crouched low, looking over the fountain. "You ready?"

"Yeah." Striker took Friday's hand. "Stay down. Run fast. Keep to my side no matter what happens. Got it?"

"Got it." Her voice was shaky. She'd never felt more useless in her life.

He looked over her shoulder at his teammate, his friend. "Now!"

Mace pointed his gun over the fountain and started firing. Striker was on his feet in a second, running fast, dragging her along behind him. They jumped over debris and dodged fallen masonry. The air was thick with smoke, making it hard to see. Striker fired into the smoke with one hand while propelling her forward with the other. He was fast, nimble. She was slowing him down.

They ran behind the truck. Two dead men lay among the rubble. One had lost part of his face from a laser blast.

"Don't look," he ordered.

But she couldn't help looking. He'd been somebody's brother, father, son, and now he was gone.

"They deserved it. It was them or us." Striker blasted the lock on the secure parking area under the apartments.

With one mighty kick, the door swung open. He rushed her inside. It wasn't the biggest of buildings, and there weren't a lot of vehicles to choose from. Plus, most of the cars were controlled by biolocks to ensure no one could steal them. Without having the same DNA as the owner, it would be impossible to take one.

"There." He pointed to the far corner, where a family vehicle was stationed. The car was big, bulky, and obviously designed to seat a lot of people. It also had a biolock.

"It's got a biolock. They all have." This was hopeless.

"This model has a bypass mechanism." He thrust the gun at her. "Aim for the door. Shoot anything that comes in."

"What if it's Mace?"

"He'll forgive you."

He lay on his back and shimmied under the vehicle. Friday kept her eyes on the door as fighting from the street echoed around the cavernous area.

"Don't fire!" The shout came before the door slammed open. "It's me."

She fired. It was an automatic reaction that she couldn't stop in time. The laser blast hit the wall about three feet to the left of Mace's head. He paused mid-run to look back at the black hole in the concrete.

"It's a good job your aim is garbage," he said as he jogged over to them. "I shouted don't fire."

"Yes, but if I was the enemy, I'd shout 'don't fire' before I came in too."

He glared at her. "I shouted that it was me."

"Maybe you should have shouted your actual name, and I wouldn't have fired."

He narrowed his eyes. "You sure you didn't know it was me and decide to fire, anyway?"

"Yes, you oversized idiot, I wanted to shoot one of the two men protecting me from a team of assassins."

"Done." Striker came out from under the vehicle. "Get in. Argue later."

She climbed into the back seat, while Mace took the front passenger seat. Striker started the car and aimed for the garage entrance, knowing the door would open automatically.

They shot through the open doorway. And as soon as they

were outside, another car slammed into their side and they screeched to a halt. The door beside Friday was yanked open. Large arms grabbed her and pulled her from the car.

"Striker!" she screamed.

"No!" came the answering roar.

The driver's door on their car was wedged shut by the vehicle that hit them. Laser blasts shot through the air around them, pinning both Striker and Mace in place. There was frantic cursing as she was thrown into the back of a vehicle.

"I'm coming for you!" Striker's voice, filled with fury, rang out.

The door slammed with Friday trapped inside and the car sped off, leaving her with three huge me—one of whom had a gun aimed at her head.

CHAPTER 23

They had Friday.

They'd taken her from him. Taken her when he'd promised to keep her safe. He was going to paint Mexico red with the blood of the men who stole her from him. Rage was a cold blade inside him. Honed and ready to strike. Even as the door of the vehicle slammed shut, leaving him with the memory of her terror-stricken face, Striker knew nothing short of death would keep him from getting her back.

From his position, crouched in the driver's seat, he heard the gunfire ease. They had what they wanted. Killing Striker and Mace wasn't part of the plan. All they cared about was capturing the woman.

That didn't mean they wouldn't die.

"On three." He barked the order, knowing his teammate would already know what he intended. They'd been in this situation too many times to count and knew how to cover each other's backs.

"One. Two. Three." They sat up at the same time, firing over each other's shoulders, taking out as many of the enemy as they could.

When they were finished, there was silence.

"This side is clear." Mace threw open his door and they scrambled out. Keeping their backs to the car, using it for cover. "You go after Friday, I'll deal with this."

"This first—nobody walks out of here. Am I clear?" He couldn't take the chance that a survivor would come after his woman. And she *was* his. In a way he couldn't explain but felt deep in his soul. They were linked together, as though made for each other, and he wouldn't let anyone threaten her, or the thing building between them.

He ripped off his eyepatch and stared at the car parked at an angle behind theirs. Three men were hunkered down behind it, using it as cover, their heat signatures clearly visible to him through the vehicle. He took aim. Three shots later, they were no longer a threat.

"I should have put a tracker on her," Mace said. "I never even thought about it. Now we don't know which way they went. Shit, we need to get the team to hack into the camera grid. See if they can spot her."

"There's no need." Striker checked his gun. Empty. He strode over to one of the dead men and relieved him of his laser gun. "I know where she's heading. They're going south on the highway out of the city."

"Did you put a tracker on her?"

"No." He looked up at his second-in-command, his gaze icy. "My diamondback is with her."

It took a second for his words to sink in before his partner's eyes dropped to Striker's neck where the diamondback's head normally rested. "No way."

"It threw itself at her when she screamed my name. Damn near ripped me apart separating that fast. It's in the van with her now."

He started jogging in the direction the kidnappers had taken Friday. Behind him, sirens blared, and he knew the cops were looking for them. With the number of cameras covering the area, it wouldn't take long for them to be found. They needed to get Friday and get to the jet—Monterrey had become far too dangerous.

They ducked around a building into a quiet street filled with businesses that hadn't yet opened.

"We need another vehicle." He jogged to the end of the street, keeping his eyes peeled for anything they could take.

"You can communicate with your animal? Even over distance? We've never tried that. We don't know what happens if we get too far from each other."

"I don't think my snake cares what might happen if we get too far apart. Right now, he's pissed and planning to take out everybody who's a threat to Friday."

"Hell, how fast-acting is its poison?"

"Not fast enough. There's a good chance they'll kill the snake before it kills them."

The color drained from his best friend's face. "If the snake dies…"

There was no need to say anything more. His relationship with his animal half was symbiotic. If one went, the other went, too. They wouldn't be able to live without each other.

"I'm more worried about him striking the driver. They're speeding. If they crash, we can say goodbye to my snake and to Friday." He came to a halt and pointed to an old model delivery van. "There. It doesn't have hover, but we should be able to hotwire it."

With his teammate watching his back, he slipped under the van and rewired the controls. A few seconds later they were heading out of town in the direction Friday's captors had taken her.

"They're heading south, out of the city." Striker sped through the early morning traffic.

"Your animal can tell directions?"

"No, dumbass, it can tell me what side of the vehicle the sun is on."

"Oh yeah." Mace ran a hand through his hair, his go-to reaction when he was tense.

"It's also telling me that there are three men in the car. One is in the back with Friday and he has a gun pointed at her head." He gripped the steering wheel tight enough to turn his knuckles white.

"Have you told the snake to hold back?"

"That's another stupid question. I keep telling it to back off. To wait for me."

"What's it say?"

"It says it knows what it's doing and I'm a screw-up for letting them take her in the first place."

Mace barked out a short, sharp laugh. "Looks like your animal has just as much attitude as you do. Does Friday know the diamondback is with her?"

Striker glanced at his friend. "Not yet."

———

Friday's grand bid for freedom, such as it was, had ended.

Her captors were taking her back to the Northern Territory, where she'd be killed, or else they'd remove the offending information from her head, wipe her memory of the past week, and put her to work in a lab. She wouldn't remember Striker or his team. She wouldn't remember her attempt to change her life. She'd just carry on, as she'd always done, working as a drone for CommTECH. If she lived.

"Where are you taking me?" Not that it mattered, but as usual, her mind needed to question everything.

The man facing her answered with a sneer. His wide shoulders were steady as he held the gun that pointed at her head. He sat with his back to the rear of the car, while Friday sat on the seat opposite, her back to the driver. Through the tinted rear window, she could see the lights of Monterrey disappearing into the distance. They were heading south, in the wrong direction for the airport.

"Aren't you taking me to back to CommTECH? I thought you were Northern Territory Enforcement."

"Do I look like a fucking cop?"

No. He looked like someone who'd seen the inside of a cell and liked what he'd found there.

"If you aren't with Enforcement, who sent you?"

"What do you care? You're alive, ain't ya."

"For how long?"

"Don't care. I get paid to deliver you. What happens after ain't my concern."

"Quit talking to her." The guy in the passenger seat turned around to glare at them. His eyes were dead, and the corner of his mouth was twisted by an ugly scar. "We don't engage with the merchandise."

The guy with the gun grunted.

"And you—" the scarred man stroked a finger down her cheek, making her cringe away from his touch. "One more word and I knock you out." He laughed as he turned back around in his seat.

They were amused by her helplessness. She let her eyes drop to the floor. Striker would have knocked his teeth out for that laugh. But then, by now he would probably have killed everyone in the car and freed himself. Unfortunately, she wasn't the smuggler. There was no extensive combat training in her background. No special powers in her mutated DNA. She closed her eyes tight as she remembered his shout when she was taken. His promise that he would come for her. She trusted him. She believed in him. Which meant she had to stay alive long enough for him to get to her. Maybe, just maybe, her life wouldn't end after all.

Not yet, anyway.

A movement under the seat across from her caught her attention and she studied the shadows. Slowly, a shape materialized from the darkness, and her heart almost stopped dead.

Striker's rattler had followed her.

Her gaze flew to the man who held a gun on her. He was oblivious to the danger beneath him, too busy smirking at his captive to notice anything else. She glanced back down at the snake, her palms sweating as she struggled to keep from hyperventilating. If her captor saw the snake, he'd shoot it. Her stomach lurched. What happened to the man if the snake died? She didn't know, but feared the worst. How could they possibly live independently of each other now that they were fused together?

The snake peeked out at her from behind her captor's feet, and she could have sworn it grinned. She shook her head at it, in what she hoped was a subtle, but clear, message that he was to lay low and do nothing. She blinked in shock when it narrowed its eyes in reply. Just like its human half, the snake would do exactly what it wanted to do.

Its thin, forked tongue snuck out, tasting the air, scenting its prey. It was clear what it planned. But there were so many ways it could go badly wrong. If the snake bit the man with the gun, he wouldn't die straight away. He'd have enough time to shoot her or the snake. And even if the snake did manage to take one man out, there were still two more to contend with. There was no way the diamondback could deal with all three of them before they struck back. Not unless the first man he bit stayed silent. An impossibility when diamondback venom caused agony.

The snake opened its mouth, and those long fangs of his slipped down, ready to bite. Its eyes focused on her captor's ankle.

"Don't," she said, risking being drugged to warn the rattler.

"Don't what?" the guy in front of her asked.

"I told you about talking," the scarred man said. "This is your last warning."

She clenched her fists tight, helpless to stop the snake from striking without putting herself and the rattler in even more danger. The diamondback reared its head back. There was no stopping it now. She saw the split second it'd made its decision, and fast as lightning, it shot forward to strike at its target. She threw herself to the floor. The gunman screamed. The gun went off. The car's tires screeched as it veered off the road.

"Snake! It bit me!"

"What the fuck? You shot our driver!"

The car careened through the grassy wasteland beyond the road. Each bump tossing Friday around, banging her against the hard surfaces around her. She grasped for something, anything, to hold on to as the scarred man fought for control of the car. The driver slumped forward over the wheel, blood pouring from the back of his head. They bounced up in the air and came back down with a crash.

The gunman screamed. The gun in his hand waved wildly. He pulled the trigger. A bullet hit the floor beside her head. Another gunshot. Two. He didn't know he was firing and didn't care who he hit. Friday tried to wedge her body under the seat to get out of the line of fire, but the car was moving around too much. The gunman's screams reverberated around the interior. The horror of his agony happening right in front of her—it felt like he would never stop screaming. And then, suddenly, there was silence. He slumped to the side, his gun falling to his feet.

The car flew up in the air again. She grabbed hold of the seat beside her as the snake headed straight toward the last of her captors. It didn't hesitate, striking over and over, hitting the scarred man's neck with icy precision. The screams were chilling and endless, until they stopped, and all she could hear was the car's engine and the banging of bushes and rocks hitting the undercarriage as it sped across the rough terrain.

She felt the snake curl around her. Protecting her the best it could. The car hit something hard, jerked to the side, and rolled. Friday flew up to the roof and fell back down again with a thud that knocked the air out of her lungs. The world was tumbling, taking her along with it. She was thrown toward the narrow gap under the back seat. Desperately, she grasped for purchase, angling her body under the seat. Squeezing herself into that gap. Hoping she made it. There was an almighty crash. Followed by scraping. Bodies thudded around inside the car like rag dolls tossed about by a child. She made one last push toward that tiny space under the seat. Toward safety. Her head hit something hard. The pain was dizzying. She caught one last glimpse of the snake looking up at her. And then, she felt nothing at all.

CHAPTER 24

"THERE!" STRIKER POINTED AT THE SMOKE RISING FROM THE middle of a field beside the highway. He could just make out the wheels of a car pointing up to the sky.

They'd rolled.

"We can't drive out to them. Not in this," Mace said.

Striker pulled the van over onto the hard shoulder and was out the door and running before the engine fully stopped.

"Are they alive?" Mace shouted, bringing up the rear. "What's your snake saying?"

"Nothing. It's saying nothing." He jumped over a bush and sprang over some rocks, racing to get to them. To get to Friday.

"No flames." His partner had his gun ready in case they ran into trouble.

No flames was good. It meant an explosion wasn't likely. It meant anyone trapped in the vehicle had a chance of surviving.

"If that damn snake is alive, I'm gonna kill it." He knew he wasn't making any sense, but he'd spent the better part of his time since Friday had been snatched arguing with the reptile telling it not to bite anyone and being ignored. Yeah, they were gonna have a long talk about who was in charge of their weird little duo. Right after he turned the reptile into a pair of boots.

They slowed as they approached the crash site, aiming their guns, senses tuned to the environment, ready in case of attack. The body of a man was sprawled halfway out of the shattered window on the driver's side of the car. Striker toed him with his boot. Dead. A gunshot to the back of the head. Carefully, he rounded the car. There was no movement. No sign of life.

You there, you rat-eating bastard? he called out mentally to his other half.

No answer.

"Got one over here," Mace said from the other side of the car. "Dead. Looks like a collision between the windscreen and his head took him out, but there are bite marks on his neck."

Striker cursed a streak in English and French. He was seriously going to kill that rattler. He bent to look through the back window. It was tinted. He could make out shapes, nothing else. "You see anything in back?"

"No. Don't hear anything, either."

"Cover me, I'm gonna pop the door."

Mace came around to point his gun at the vehicle. Striker yanked at the door, but it was wedged in tight against the foliage. And there was no movement inside.

"I don't think anybody's gonna shoot at us." He tried to keep his mind away from thinking what that meant. Friday couldn't be dead. To hell with his snake—he was wishing the asshole gone. But Friday... "Push on the wheels. See if we can get it up off the ground so I can open the door."

Mace slipped his gun into the holster strapped to this thigh and pushed against the wheels. The car rocked under his strength, and Striker managed to yank the door free. He crouched to look inside. The massive body of the man who'd snatched Friday from him was sprawled over the roof of the car.

But there was no sign of the little scientist.

"What the hell? Where is she?"

"You think she was thrown from the car?"

"Better look around." He put his hand on the door to pull himself up. That's when he heard it. A slight rattling noise.

Dumbass? he snapped at his other half. *You there?*

Every muscle within him clenched tight as he waited for an answer.

Sore.

That one word almost brought him to his knees. *Where the hell are you? Is Friday with you?*

Small space. Dark. She's mine.

Striker breathed a shaky sigh of relief. Damn possessive reptile. He crouched down and examined the interior of the large car. It was the modern equivalent of a twenty-first century SUV, only it was fitted with adjustable seating and plenty of tech. He examined the seats. Of course. There was a gap under the back seat. He stuck his head into the car to get a better look and almost collapsed with relief at the sight before him. Friday was wedged into the narrow space, his snake curled around her.

"They're here!"

He heard a moan. Friday's moan. "I'm coming, bébé. Hold tight. We'll get you out of there."

Mace had been scanning their surroundings. He came jogging over. "How the hell did they get in there?"

He was damned if he knew. But their hiding spot had probably saved their lives.

Stuck. Sore. His other half complained.

Is Friday okay?

She's waking up. She's mine.

"The talking handbag says Friday was unconscious, but she rousing now, and he's in pain."

"We need to get them out of there if you plan to make accessories from your animal."

Another slight moan emanated from the car, and he had to fight panic. He had to stay clear-headed. He had to make sure he got her out without causing her any further damage. He swallowed hard at the thought. How badly hurt was she?

Is she bleeding? he asked the rattler.

Sore. We both sore.

Yeah, that didn't help at all. He eyed the dead man taking up all the space inside the car. "Help me haul him out."

They took an arm each and dragged him out onto the grass. There was no need to be gentle. He couldn't feel anything. And from the number of bites on the man, it was a fast death—although not painless. A fact that warmed his heart.

They dropped him like trash beside the car, before Striker crawled into the interior to get to Friday. He wanted his hands on her. He wanted to reassure himself that she was breathing. That she was alive. He reached into the space under the seat and gently stroked her cheek. Warm. Alive. *His.* She moaned again and turned her face toward him. Her eyes still closed.

"It's okay, bébé. You're gonna be fine."

A hand clasped on his shoulder, and he looked up to see understanding in his best friend's eyes. "Her feet are facing the open door. If I get her legs out, you can support the rest of her while we ease her out of the car. You want to hand your snake to me first, before we move Friday?"

"To hell with him. He can damn well crawl out of there on his own steam."

There was furious rattling in reply. He ignored the reptile and reached for the woman. She groaned as he took her weight in his arms and they maneuvered her out of the car. Pain, she was in pain. His stomach roiled at the sound.

"I've got you," he soothed, hoping like hell he wasn't causing more damage by moving her.

"Striker?" The whispered word sent relief flooding through his system.

"Who else, bébé? Don't you worry none, we got you."

He cradled her head. Bruises marred her pale skin. He hated the sight of them and wanted them gone before she felt the effect of them. His diamondback slithered around until it was curled on Friday's stomach, hitching a ride out of the car. He fought the urge to knock the damn snake from his perch.

Slowly, carefully, the two men lifted her out of the upturned car. Mace cradled her in his arms while Striker got to his feet. As soon as he did, he took the fragile bundle from his friend. If she was going to be in anyone's arms, it would be his. The urge to lock her away and ensure she never hurt again was almost overwhelming.

"Striker?" She sounded less disorientated this time. "The car crashed."

He kissed her hair. "I know. But we've got you now."

"My head hurts." It was barely a whisper.

"We're taking you to the jet. We'll get it sorted as soon as we're on board." He looked at his partner. "Is there a medic nearby we can use if we need one?"

"I'll make some calls, see who we can trust." Mace fished his satellite phone out of his pocket and did just that.

"Your snake saved me," Friday said softly.

Yeah, he wasn't so sure about that. In fact, he suspected the rattler had done more harm than good. He glared at the reptile, who was completely unfazed by his anger. *I'm gonna deal with you later*, he promised it. The snake closed his eyes and went to sleep.

"I'm tired." Friday slurred the words, already falling asleep.

Her system was overloaded and shutting down. Even

without the poison, the physical traumas of the Red Zone and the kidnapping were enough to send her into shock.

"Close your eyes, chère. I'll watch over you."

She gave a little sigh as she relaxed into him. A second later, she was asleep. As they walked over the field to their van, the diamondback decided it should merge with him again. It slithered over his shoulder, under his shirt, and fused with his skin. And it didn't do it gently.

"Hell!" Striker stumbled, clutching at Friday to make sure she didn't fall.

"What is it?" Mace had his gun out, scanning the area for threats.

"The scaly bastard just shared his pain with me."

Told you. Sore.

"I'm really beginning to hate that forked-tongued asshole." He heard the diamondback scoff at him before it fell back asleep. "Now I feel like I've been in a crash. This is another side effect of our new genetics that I didn't need to know. Your animal gets hurt, he merges with you, you get the pain, and he gets to sleep." He grimaced at his friend. "When are we gonna get to the upside of this new existence? 'Cause, so far, it sucks to be us."

"Amen, brother." Mace slapped him on the back, making Striker wince.

"Sore, damn it!"

"Sorry." The asshole laughed, making it clear he really wasn't.

Once the door to the van was open, he placed Friday gently on the bench seat. "Turn around. I'm gonna check her."

Mace gave him his back as he kept an eye on approaching traffic. Friday's captors might be dead, but that didn't mean the threat had been eliminated. They now knew there were two separate factions after her. And one of them wanted her dead.

He ran his hands over her head. There was a lump the size

of an egg above her temple. He assumed that was the reason she was still out cold, but he didn't know for sure. It could have been that her system just shut down under the assault. Who knew what the chemical in her body was doing to her? He wished like hell that Doc was with him. She needed someone with more medical knowledge than he had to check her out.

"We got anything in the jet's med kit that will wake Friday up? In case we need it." In case she slipped into unconsciousness.

"You worried she won't rouse on her own?"

"Yeah."

"I'll ask the pilot. Make sure he has the kit ready for us when we arrive. Do we need a medic? I can have someone meet us at the jet."

"Give me a second. I'll check the rest of her. Right now, I'm most worried about the lump on her head."

He pulled the T-shirt he'd given her over her head. There were bruises and red marks dotted over her torso. A scrape on her shoulder. He ran his fingertips over the abrasion. He should have been there. He should have prevented this. He should have protected her. Slowly, he moved his hands down her ribs, feeling for breaks. Releasing a tense breath when he didn't find any.

Gently, he removed the oversize combat pants Sandi had given her. There was a massive bruise covering her hip, but no broken bones, no cuts. No lasting damage. His fingers trembled as he dressed her again. She was pale. Too pale. Her body kept taking hits—the poison, the red mist, this. How many more could she suffer until she didn't bounce back? Didn't wake up again?

"We don't need a medic." He climbed in beside his woman and took her into his arms. "Not unless she doesn't wake up. But her injuries aren't life-threatening." They were just wrong. Her beautiful skin should never be marred by violence. Never.

Mace climbed into the driver's seat. "The jet is ready to go. We'll deal with her on board."

"Any sign of trouble at the airfield?"

"No. There's too much security there. That's probably why they hit us en route. They took us out in the quietest part of town."

"They shouldn't have known where we were to begin with. We screwed up." Striker's voice was tight as he looked down at the woman in his arms. "Somebody shared information. We have a mole. Or a traitor." The word left a foul taste in his mouth. They'd all been betrayed more than enough already.

"Once you guys are in the air, I'll hunt him down myself."

"And deal with him."

"Permanently." Mace's voice was steel.

CHAPTER 25

CommTECH Headquarters, New York City,
Northern Territory

"WHAT DO YOU MEAN YOU'VE LOST TOUCH WITH YOUR TEAM?"

Miriam Shepherd sat with her hands clasped on the top of her glass desk, her attention very much focused on the holographic image of the Enforcement captain standing in the middle of her office. The man had managed to fail her yet again. It would be the last time she allowed it to happen.

"The last communication we had from the mercenaries stated they were under attack." The man paled. His eyes kept shifting to the figure standing behind Miriam. She'd made no secret that Kane, her head of security and company enforcer, listened in on the report. The captain should feel nervous. After his update finished, he would have the pleasure of meeting Kane in person.

"The smuggler and his team attacked our men?" If they had, she'd seriously underestimated the group.

"No." The Enforcement agent shuffled anxiously. "It was an unknown team. They seemed to be after the scientist, too."

"Interesting. Did your team manage to find out who these opponents were?"

"Negative. All we know is that the other team was trying to take Friday Jones alive."

Miriam felt cold rage work its way through her, turning her blood to ice. Obviously one of her esteemed fellow leaders had decided to pick up the scientist and download the information in her head. Yes, she could see the potential for scandal. Played the right way, information of the meeting could help someone usurp Miriam's position of power.

The Enforcement captain cleared his throat. "Do you have further instructions, Director?"

"Not at this time." She cut the feed, and the man disappeared.

Kane moved, rounding the desk to face her. "You want him dealt with."

It wasn't a question; Kane knew she did not tolerate incompetence. "I need you to find out who hired another team."

He inclined his head, and Miriam knew it would be done. "I'm calling our contact within the smuggling group. I don't want them to see you."

Kane silently slid into the shadows on the other side of the room as Miriam used her implant to call up her contact. A few seconds passed before the shadowy figure of the Broker appeared on the screen.

"I need to know where Striker's jet is headed."

There was a pause. "That isn't information I have or can get my hands on."

"I need you to find out." She bit out the words, making them snap like a whip. "Friday Jones is on that jet."

"Your team's failures have nothing to do with me. I gave you the information I had on their whereabouts."

"And now I need more."

"I don't have more. My job was to supply them with

transport and arrange the jet. Unless they need more transportation, they won't be in touch. However"—the figure leaned back in his chair, comfortable in his position of power —"I do have one piece of information that may be of use to you."

Miriam asked the only question that was relevant. "How much will it cost?"

The laugh was mocking. "Double."

"Done."

The figure leaned closer to the camera, as though sharing a secret. "Word is that your renegade scientist might not be a problem for very much longer. My sources tell me that she injected herself with Interferan-X before she left the Northern Territory. Apparently, the poison was on hand in her lab." He leaned back. "That's all I know. I'll be checking for a credit deposit shortly."

The image disappeared, and Kane manifested from the shadows.

"I want the person behind that voice found and dealt with once this is over," Miriam told him.

"It will be my pleasure."

Miriam sat back in her chair as she looked up at her most trusted confidant. "Interferan-X? What's the time between injection and death?"

"Five days, in total."

"And she met up with the smuggler roughly a day after taking the dose. That means she has about a day and a half to get to an antidote. What clinics in South America store the antidote?"

"There's only one. La Paz. You want me to arrange for another team to meet them there?"

"No. I want you to take care of this personally. I can't afford any mistakes this time."

Kane gave her a little bow. "How do you want it handled? Do you want me to have people waiting at the checkpoints to intercept them before they get into the city? Or do you want me to deal with them once they're inside?"

Her smile was slow and wide. "I'll leave all of the details up to you. I trust you will do what is needed."

And have fun while he did it.

CHAPTER 26

Friday woke up disorientated, but aware that she was moving. No, that her surroundings were moving and taking her along with them. A jet. She was in a jet, lying on a soft bed with a warm body beside her. Her heart rate shot through the roof. Who was beside her? Where were they taking her? What were they going to do with her? And the diamondback? What happened to it?

"Bébé, you got to remember to breathe when you're thinking."

She did the exact opposite and held her breath entirely.

Striker.

"Please be real," she whispered, her eyes still closed.

She felt the bed shift and warm, gentle lips press against hers in a soft, slow kiss. "That real enough for you?" His words were a breath against her mouth.

Her eyes drifted open, and she found herself staring into the comforting view of his mismatched gaze. "I thought my kidnappers had me and were taking me to the Northern Territory." At her words, disjointed memories of being hauled out of the crashed car came flooding back. He'd come for her, just as he'd promised.

Perfect white teeth flashed against warm mocha skin. "You think those assholes would have made you this comfortable for the trip?"

He had a point. "How long have I been asleep?"

"Couple of hours. We're eight hours from La Paz, 'cause we're taking the circuitous route." He stroked her hair off her cheek, taking his time to run the strands through his fingers.

She glanced at the clock beside the bed. "I only have thirty-two hours until my time runs out."

"If you take away the eight hours flight time, and the three hours it will take to get to the clinic, that leaves you twenty-one long hours to hang out in Bolivia after you take the antidote. We got plenty of time. Don't worry yourself none about the timing. But, if you want to put that big brain of yours to good use, you could come up with some ideas about what we should do with the eight hours we're stuck on this jet? Any thoughts?"

His fingertip traced the shell of her ear. She felt his touch ricochet throughout her body. There was only one thing she wanted to do with her time, and she was staring at him.

With a smile on her lips that only he could produce under such dire circumstances, she teased him. "How about we start researching your DNA?"

"That's one option, for sure." His lazy drawl was like warm honey on her skin.

He lay on his side, propped up on his elbow, and she could feel the heat of his body along the length of hers. Her eyes ate him up. His closely-shaven head, his stubble-roughened jaw, those mesmerizing eyes, and all that luscious bronze skin. His full lips quirked into a smile as her gaze scanned over them, down to his bare shoulders. She shivered at the sight of his muscles. Who knew shoulders could be that sexy?

"You like what you see." He'd asked her that before, back in the bar when they'd first met. This time it wasn't a question. It was the smug arrogance of a man who knew the effect he had on her. His fingertips traced her jaw to stroke down her throat. Everywhere he touched bubbled with sensitivity. Friday wondered if there were actual sparks flickering over her skin in the wake of his touch.

"Why are you naked?" She glanced down. "Why am I naked? And why does this keep happening to me? I lose consciousness around you and wake up naked." She glanced around the room. "At least this time we don't have an audience."

His eyes were on hers as his fingers lightly traced her collarbone. "You stop getting injured, and you'll stop waking up naked." He frowned. "Scratch that. When you're around me, you'll always wake up naked. But I don't like you getting injured, chère. This time you got banged up pretty bad when the car veered off the road."

His words brought back the memory of being thrown about in the back of the car while the diamondback dealt with her captors.

"Your diamondback saved me."

"When the talking handbag eventually wakes up, I'm gonna have a word with him 'bout that. I told him not to bite the damn driver. I told him the car would crash." He let out a sigh, heavy with exasperation. "He told me to go to hell."

She fought the urge to laugh. His words were at odds with his gentle touch. She felt decadent, lying there flat on her back with her arms at her sides, letting him touch her however he pleased. Letting him absently play with her as they talked. Her breathing became shallow, and her heart rate sped up. She wished his hands would roam some more. There were parts of her, intimate parts, that ached for his touch. She licked her lips. "To be fair. He didn't bite the driver. The driver was shot in the head when your rattlesnake bit the guy with the gun."

He let out a stream of creative curses, and she thought it

best not to tell him she'd been directly between the gun and the driver's head just before the shot went off. If she hadn't thrown herself to the floor, she'd have taken that bullet. It appeared logistics and forward-thinking weren't traits his diamondback possessed.

With bravery borne of desperation, she reached up and pushed the sheet from her body, watching as his eyes darkened at the move.

"Bébé? You're injured. Maybe you should stay covered until you're feelin' better. A man can only resist so much temptation before he snaps."

Trembling with need and nerves, she took his hand in hers and brazenly placed it over her breast. She gasped when their skin connected.

"I'm not *that* injured." His hand flexed on her breast, and she fought back a moan. "I like how you touch me. It takes me away from everything in my head."

"Bébé..." He sounded torn between his own need and worry for her.

"Please." She bit her lip and waited for rejection, almost expecting it, because her life hadn't taught her to expect anything else.

"You drive me crazy," he said on a sigh. "I'll touch, but we won't go further. You're bruised. You need to heal."

"I need you more," she whispered her confession.

His eyes blazed with emotion so intense, she needed time to figure out what it meant. He didn't give her that time. His lips covered hers in a slow, sensual kiss that stole all thought from her mind.

Lazy fingers traced circles around her breast, making it feel swollen. Making it ache for a stronger touch. With each circle, he inched closer to her taut nipple. If nipples had emotions, hers would have felt desperate. It pointed upward as though trying to catch his attention.

With clear reluctance, he pried his lips from hers. "You

feeling pain? The car rolled some ways across that field. I found you wedged under the back seat. With that damned rattler wrapped around you like you were his favorite toy."

She couldn't remember getting under the seat. All she remembered was the snake biting her kidnappers and the car speeding out of control.

"I'm a little stiff." She couldn't resist arching up to push her breast into his hand.

He shook his head with lazy amusement. "I see that, chère." His voice dropped an octave as his thumb rasped over her nipple. "But that's not what I meant. No headache anymore?" That deep drawl of his should have been registered as a potent aphrodisiac.

It took her a minute to focus on his words rather than his touch. He was circling the areola around her poor neglected nipple. "No headache."

"That's good. I gave you pain meds while you slept. Just in case. Then I used magic cream on your bruises. They're mostly gone now."

She couldn't stop the smile this time. "You were pretty busy while I was asleep. Magic cream, huh?" Her voice was unintentionally breathless as he abandoned one breast and moved on to the other. Her legs pressed together, and she began to squirm. It was hard to think. Hard to concentrate on anything but his touch.

"It makes bruises disappear. That shit is magic."

He trailed his hand down her stomach, slipping the sheet lower as he went. His movements were slow and controlled, a look of intense concentration on his face.

"You're going too slowly," she complained.

He smiled as he playfully dipped a fingertip into her navel. The heat in his eyes made her want to give him anything he asked of her. Give him everything.

"I'm learning you, bébé."

She licked dry lips. "Does that mean I get to test you on your knowledge when you're done?"

"Mm-hmm. I'm gonna ace that test for sure."

"Cocky."

He chuckled as his hand slid beneath the sheet to play with the curls covering her mound. Her hips automatically lifted into his touch, searching for more.

"Nuh-uh, bébé, slow. Remember you're bruised."

"I don't feel bruised." She cast around for the words. "I feel needy."

"Is that right?" His fingertips slid through her wetness.

She gasped. One hand flew up to clutch his shoulder, the other curled into the sheet beneath her. "We can't have that. People be sayin' I don't look after my woman if she's feeling so needy."

His touch was slow, languorous, torturous. Delicious.

"When do I get to learn you?" *When do I get to torture you?*

His finger circled her clit, making her moan, then the devil threw himself onto his back beside her.

"Have at it." His grin was wide as he clasped his hands under his head.

Friday glared at him. "That was mean."

His look of faux innocence made her want to laugh. He was playing with her, and she loved it. There hadn't been a whole lot of time to play in her life, and this man made up for it.

"I got no idea what you're talking about. I'm doin' everything I can to please you. I thought you wanted to learn me. All I'm doin' is accommodating you, chère. You think you'd be a little more appreciative."

"You're a devil." But excitement surged at the thought of getting her hands on his body. Muscles like those were made to be studied.

She knelt up beside him, uncaring that she was naked in

her eagerness to get her hands on him. He was an all-you-can-eat-buffet and she was a starving woman. Her eyes roamed over every inch of him. Over the strong line of his throat, across those overly muscled shoulders, down his rippling abs, and then they got stuck on his very impressive erection.

"I don't know where to start."

He chuckled, low and deep. "I find that hard to believe. You're looking at me like you're gonna eat me up."

She felt her cheeks heat, aware that she couldn't drag her eyes from his penis. Her mouth actually watered at the sight. It was long, thick, and curved up toward his stomach. A glance at his face told her he was watching her with a mixture of amusement and anticipation.

"Can I touch it?" Her fingers tingled at the thought. "I've only done this once before, and I didn't get to touch."

"You didn't get to touch?"

She shrugged. "No, he just told me to lie down on the lab floor and get ready. Then he lay on top of me and we were done a couple of minutes later."

He let out a stream of French curse words. "Please tell me he didn't force you."

"No. I wanted to see what sex was like." She looked up at him and gave him the truth. She didn't want him to be disappointed in her. "I don't think it's very good. Or, at least, I'm not very good at it. You should know that."

"What I know is that the guy you slept with was a grade A asshole, and if it wasn't good for you, then that's on him."

She sucked in a breath as his words flowed straight to her heart. It was clear he meant them. He was also angry—on her behalf. From the throbbing vein at the side of his jaw, she suspected her one and only previous lover might get a visit from Striker. One where he explained exactly what the guy should have done differently. She made a note never to tell Striker his name.

"Can I touch it, then?"

His eyes softened. "You can touch anything you like."

"Do I have to be gentle?"

"You planning on bending it in half, chère? Because it sure don't work that way."

"I'm worried that, you know, I'll hurt you."

"Gimme your hand."

She complied instantly. He took it to his hard shaft and wrapped her fingers around it—barely. He was wider than her wrist. He covered her hand with his, holding her to him. And then he squeezed. His hips came up off the bed, and he groaned.

She wondered how he could feel so firm and yet so soft at the same time.

"That's how hard you can touch me," he said hoarsely. He released her and put his hand back behind his head. "That help?"

"Yes. That was very helpful. Thank you."

Vaguely, Friday wondered if anyone had ever written a scientific paper on pressure tolerance in male reproductive organs. Would there be a standard level of pressure one could exert on all penises? Or would each have a different limit?

"Hey," Striker sounded amused. "You still with me?"

She blinked. "Yes." She still held him firmly, but not as tightly, in her hand.

"Good." He closed his eyes. "Then worship me. I'm waiting, chère."

What was it about that arrogant amused tone of his that let him get away with murder? She bet he'd charmed his way out of trouble for most of his life. "Does anyone resist that wicked charm of yours?"

He opened one eye, the one that didn't show his other half. "Don't see you complying right now. My cock is in your hand, bébé. You gonna do something about that? And I don't mean use it as a play mic for singing show tunes."

Once again, he'd lost her. "I only understand about half of what you say."

"Touch me, or I'm gonna end your turn and go back to playing with your sexy little body."

"You think my body's sexy?"

"You're holding my hard-on in your fist. It didn't get like that by accident. You caused it. Now, are you gonna do something, or what?"

She let go of him as she grumbled about his attitude. She pushed his thighs apart and climbed over his leg to kneel between his knees. Oh, this was a much better view. Her fingers squeezed thigh muscles that made her want to weep, then made her want to investigate why she'd had that reaction. She shook her head. This physical stuff was too confusing.

"I'm still waiting," he said.

"Stop pressuring me. I'm deciding."

His body was perfection, and she hardly knew where to start with him. But her inexperience was making her worry. Striker was her first official naked man. Well, outside of her genetics classes in college, where they had dead bodies to study. Did dead bodies count? She shuddered, hoping they didn't.

"I'm almost afraid to ask what you're thinking." He brought her attention back to him. Before she could answer, he held up a hand. "No. Don't. I know whatever it is, it's gonna lead us down some weird path and away from the good stuff. Just get your head in the game and touch me. You got one more minute before I give up and go back to playing with you."

"You are so impatient," she complained.

He arched an eyebrow at her and waited.

She looked down his beautiful body and felt completely out of her depth. There wasn't an inch of the man she didn't want to experience. Well, maybe a couple. She eyed the diamondback tattoo.

"Maybe you should get rid of your snake before we have sex. I don't want him watching us."

He heaved a sigh. "First, we ain't having sex. Right now, we're having nothing because you're too busy stalling. At this rate, we ain't never gonna have sex. Second, the talking handbag is out cold. Nothing's gonna wake him up." He leveled her with a stare. "Now. Do. Something."

"Fine!" With an irritated scowl, she leaned forward and took the head of his cock into her mouth.

"Fuck!"

His hips came off the bed, and his arm shot out from under his head. She felt his fingers tighten in her hair as she cataloged the sensations she was experiencing. He felt spongy and satin smooth. She tested the taste with her tongue, twirling around the mushroom-shaped head—salty, a little bitter, but not unpleasant. Striker groaned. His hips flexed, making him slip from her mouth.

"Stay still," she ordered before sucking him back into her mouth. This time she kept a firm hand wrapped around his shaft to stop him from sabotaging her play time.

With another lap at the crown of his penis, she decided she liked his taste. Although, it probably would have been more addictive if it were sweet rather than salty. Or flavored. Oh, chocolate would be great. She wondered if she could manipulate male genetics to make him taste chocolatey.

"Stop doin' fucking science experiments in your head and suck!"

She frowned as she twirled her tongue around the satin skin. How did he know what she was thinking? Was it a gift the mutated DNA gave him? Could he hear her right now? *Striker?* She thought hard. *Can you hear me?*

"That's it!" He arched up, grabbed her under her arms, and tossed her onto her back beside him.

He pinned her with a leg over her thigh. She tried to

decide his emotion, hoping it wasn't anger or disappointment. To her confusion, he mainly seemed frustrated and amused.

"I did it wrong, didn't I?"

His eyes crinkled. "What were you trying to do exactly?"

She felt her cheeks burn. "I thought that was obvious. I was trying to give you pleasure, um, orally."

He let his head fall, his eyes shut, and his shoulders began to shake. Was he laughing at her? This was mortifying.

"I told you I'd never done this before." What did he expect? Did he think all women were born knowing how to have sex? It wasn't like she'd taken a class on it. Were there classes in it? A distance learning course would be perfect. She could do it while she was stuck in Striker's lair for the next year. If she didn't die first, that was.

"And I've lost you again. You are murder on a man's ego. I can honestly say I've never had this much trouble keeping a woman interested when she's in bed with me."

"Really? Now we're going to talk about your many other women?"

He ignored her. "You're thinking too much. Sex is about feeling."

"I was feeling you," she protested. "With my mouth."

"I don't mean touching, I mean experiencing. You sat there with my cock in your mouth for about five minutes doing nothing. You didn't move. You just sat there. Your brain working so hard I could almost hear it. What the hell were you thinking about?"

Her cheeks were really burning now. "I was wondering if we could communicate telepathically. And..." She looked away from him, but her view was filled with overdeveloped shoulders instead. It didn't help. "I was wondering if it would be possible to tweak your genetics to make you taste like chocolate."

There was a pause before his whole body started shaking.

His forehead fell to her shoulder, and his laughter was deep and hard. Friday lay there, enduring his amusement and wishing she hadn't bothered to touch him in the first place. This sex thing was far too complicated. She should leave it to the professionals.

At last, Striker moved back to look at her. His eyes were sparkling, and his smile was wide. "I can see that big brain of yours is apt to derail us if we let it. I don't think you're ready for touching without supervision, so this is how we're gonna do things—"

"I don't want to have sex anymore," she interrupted. And yes, she was pouting. "I don't think it works for me. I'm fairly certain I won't enjoy it and you won't, either. I think we should forget about the sex thing and concentrate on the research part of the deal." She thought about it. That seemed a tad harsh. "We can kiss," she amended. She liked his kisses, and he hadn't complained about hers. Yes, kissing would be okay. "But nothing else. I don't like sex. I've tried it, and it was awful. It's not your fault. It's mine. So, do we have a deal?"

"Oh, we have something, that's for sure. I just don't know what to call it yet."

With that cryptic statement, he closed the gap between them and covered her mouth with his. His lips were soft and firm and delicious. Yes. She could do kissing. But nothing else. And then his hand slid down her throat to cup her breast, and Friday thought maybe she could do that, too. But nothing else. And then, his tongue delved into her mouth, and she lost track of all her thoughts. When he pulled away, she mewled her annoyance—sounding more like a disgruntled kitten who'd lost its favorite toy than a full-grown woman.

"From now on..." His voice was rough against her lips. "I'm in charge in bed." He cocked his head as though thinking about it. "And out of bed, too. But definitely in bed.

You can touch me all you like, but you don't get to take over."

That didn't sound fair at all. "Why not?"

"Because the only way we'll get your brain to shut down long enough for us both to enjoy this is if I make sure you're too lust-dazed to think."

"I'm not sure I like your attitude." Although, she couldn't exactly disagree with him.

"Bébé." He nuzzled at her throat, pressing into her and making her breasts flatten against his firm chest. Her hips rose up to meet him. Why did it still feel like there was too much distance between them?

"I want to touch you, too. You said I could play."

"Oh, you can play. You can touch me all you like. But you're a beginner, bébé. Your brain short circuits your body when you try anything beyond your level. Until you've reached the advanced level, you can only play when I'm touching you, too."

He bit the muscle where her shoulder met her neck and she gasped. Her fingernails dug into his shoulder.

"That doesn't sound fair." Her protest was breathless and distracted.

He kissed his way up her throat to her ear. "Don' worry, you're a fast learner. You'll reach the advanced level in no time at all."

Her body was undulating beneath his. His touch making her lose track of reality. She wanted to float away on the sensations he provoked. She actually had to fight to think straight. "Is there a textbook on this?"

He pulled her earlobe between his lips and nibbled. Oh! Why did that feel so good?

"I'll find one for you," he whispered against her ear, making her gasp.

His voice should be outlawed. It made her blood turn to molten honey.

"One what?" She arched her neck, exposing her throat for him.

"Exactly." He nibbled along her jaw and down her throat.

She hooked her leg over his thigh. She needed. Oh, how she needed.

"Striker?" It was a plea for something she didn't fully understand and instinctively knew he could supply.

"Don' worry, bébé, I got you."

She ran her hand over his smooth head, searching for hair to cling to and finding none. Somehow the frustration of not being able to hold his hair made her need heighten. She moaned as his mouth moved down her body to her breasts, tasting and biting and kissing. Her skin was on fire. She felt like she was burning up from the inside out.

"Please, Striker, please."

She didn't know what she was begging for, but he did. He captured her nipple with his mouth and sucked hard, pressing it against the roof of his mouth.

"Yes!" Her back arched, offering her body up to him.

Her mind was filled with fog. But this fog wasn't cold and isolating. It was a warm, delicious mist that carried her away from everything except his expert touch. She floated on sensation, desperate for more. Nothing had ever felt this good. The press of his body against hers. The feel of his wide, strong hands holding her firmly, anchoring her lest she float away entirely. And his mouth. His mouth was wickedly wonderful. He was a master at giving pleasure, demanding she take what he gave her, demanding she enjoy everything he did to her. And she was more than willing to comply to those demands.

His mouth moved lower as his hands shaped and caressed every inch of her. Little bursts of color flashed inside her eyelids. Fireworks, he was making fireworks. She felt hot. Needy. Desperate for more.

"Please!"

His reply was a grunt before he pushed her legs wide and angled his broad shoulders between them. One long lick and she lost her mind completely. She was pure sensation, moving in the rhythm he dictated.

"So good, so, so good…"

She couldn't stop the words or gasps or moans. His wicked tongue teased her higher and higher, making muscles tense and burn, making her feel empty inside, clenching for something that wasn't there yet and needed to be there soon or she would scream from desperation.

"I need you." A sobbing, begging plea.

"Shh, bébé, trust me. I'm gonna make you fly first. Just let go for me."

His words made no sense, yet meant everything to her. She clung to them. Clung to him. She wasn't sure what part of his body she was holding, all she knew was that there was firm, hot muscle under her fingers. She was going to burst. No, explode. It was too much. Too, too much. She felt his lips cover her most sensitive bundle of nerves. He sucked. Time stopped. And then everything exploded in a shower of lights and wails and desperately spasming muscles. She came back down to earth slowly, unaware of anything other than her limp muscles and panting breaths. She shook. She ached. She clenched. And she wanted more.

Striker's mouth descended on hers, and he claimed her in a punishing kiss that took everything she had left to give. She felt his body press against hers, covering her with his strength and heat. She fought to open her eyes, managing to get her eyelids up far enough to peer at him. And he was magnificent.

He held himself on locked arms, making his muscles bulge. His bronze skin held a glittering sheen that made him seem godlike. And his eyes. His eyes held a wealth of promise and depth of need that thrilled her.

"How do you feel? Tired? Sore? We can stop if it's too

much." His eyes scanned down her body, hardening at the sight of her bruises. "Maybe we should stop."

"No!" She clung to him. "Please, I want this. I want you."

It was reassuring to see he was torn, just as desperate as she was in her need for him. His throat flexed. "I'll be gentle, but if you feel pain, if you want to stop this, we stop. Am I clear?"

"Yes," she breathed.

The corded muscles in his neck flexed as he lined himself up with her. With energy she didn't even know she had left, her hands flew to his hips, and she held on tight. She felt every wide, hard inch of him as he entered her. Slow. Sure. Being careful with her. Thinking of her before himself. Melting her heart as he did so. His jaw tightening with restraint was the sexiest sight she'd ever seen. She couldn't look away. She was mesmerized. Captivated. Caught.

And then, without warning, his hips flexed, and he surged the rest of the way inside her. Friday clung to him, her fingers biting into flesh. Her head fell back. Her eyes squeezed closed. And a long, glorious moan of desperation and ecstasy left her lips.

"Let go, bébé," his deep voice rumbled as his hips began to move. "I'll make it good for you."

She let go. Flying with him. Losing herself in his touch. Because she trusted him to do exactly what he promised.

And he did.

CHAPTER 27

Without proper documentation, it was almost impossible to fly into La Paz's airport. That was why they landed on a small private airfield in the town of Oruro, three hours south of the capital. The permits to drive past the checkpoints and into the city were easier to get than the ones needed to land at the airport.

"You sure we won't have a problem getting into the city?"

With twenty-four hours until her time ran out, Friday was beginning to feel pressure in every single second.

"Relax, the paperwork is solid. We'll sail through the highway checkpoints no problem." Striker gave her a reassuring smile as they headed for their rental car. "Plus, nobody knows we're here. We flew under the radar, in a jet equipped with cyber repellant shields—"

"Is that another technical term? Like magic cream?"

He cocked the eyebrow over his unpatched eye, making her miss the strange iris that was now securely hidden. "You mocking me, bébé? After I spent the flight taking you to paradise? I feel used."

"About that." She climbed into the passenger seat. "I can't remember touching you. You mess with my mind, and then it's hard to remember what I planned to do. I didn't get my time exploring, and I want it—without you distracting me. When am I going to get to advanced level? When will it be okay for me to take the lead?"

"Uh, never." He pulled the car out of the underground parking garage beside the tiny airport.

"That's not what you said on the jet. You said all I needed was practice. That's why you kept waking me for more sex."

His laugh was so mischievous it almost made her smile. Almost.

"I woulda said anything to get your mind off the highway to crazy and on to what we were doing. Chocolate-flavored cocks?" He grinned over at her. "Let's face it, bébé. You ain't ever gonna be cut out for advanced level. Best you let me do all the heavy lifting when it comes to sex."

She stared at him, wishing she could see into his mind. He was far too composed for her liking. And then it hit her. "You lied to me! There aren't any levels, are there?"

With a huff, she folded her arms and tried to block out his laughter. She'd been conned. Admittedly, she'd loved every second of it, but that wasn't the point. She'd wanted to investigate him. To learn him. To get to know every inch of him. And that would never happen if he kept distracting her.

"I can't believe you told me there were levels."

"I can't believe you fell for it."

"You're evil."

"Bébé, I was desperate. You were planning genetic experiments to turn my cock into a candy bar. I had to do something to get us back on track."

"I'm never going to believe a word you say ever again."

He shrugged. "I can live with that."

Impossible man. She ignored his smug smile and focused on the scenery. Oruro was a nowhere place. Once famous for its mining—silver and tin—now it was a city overtaken by dust from the high desert. Even though it was still populated, it felt abandoned.

"The Technology War started in Bolivia," Friday said absently as she watched the crumbling brick houses zoom past.

"I know. I was around when it happened."

She felt her cheeks color. "I'm sorry, I forget."

"It's all good. You've had a lot to take in, and a short amount of time to do it."

She angled in her seat, turning toward him. "Did you join the fight down here?"

"No. I was deployed in the Middle East when the fight over Bolivia's mining operations started."

"They were mining for lithium." She searched through her memories. "The mineral found in the salt flats south of here. The one used in batteries for old cell phones."

He chuckled. "We considered them cutting edge at the time. But yeah, it was used for batteries. As far as I can gather, it was also in short supply, that's why the big companies started putting pressure on Bolivia to hand over its mining operations."

"But the demand for lithium didn't last long, it was only a few years later that they discovered lanthanum worked better. Now everyone's searching for ladmium."

"You know what bothers me?" He flashed her a grin. "The person who named all these minerals had no damn imagination."

She rolled her eyes at him. "The minerals are related, that's why they sound the same. Although, to be technically correct, ladmium isn't used for batteries."

"You're just aching to tell me what it is used for, aren't you?"

She tried hard to keep her mouth shut. To keep the information to herself. But it wanted to get out. "It's a conductor used in implanted data chips. It functions as a bridge between the brain and the data chip's receptor. The chip then converts the electrical pulses of the brain into other signals, which communicate with tech outside the body. Ladmium's a really fascinating element to study. It uses the electricity within the body as a power generator for the chip, as well as enabling the information to move smoothly between biological and technological elements."

"You make me want to kiss you when you go all geeky on me."

His words made her feel warm inside and embarrassed at the same time. "Lithium, the cell phone battery element, was found in huge quantities in the salt flats. Bolivia, back before the war, was an extremely poor country, but one with integrity. They didn't want to rape the landscape to get to the mineral, and even though demand was high, they slowed down output to preserve their landscape."

"Yeah," he scoffed. "They were all about integrity. Limiting the amount of lithium produced had nothing to do with driving up the price."

He had a point. "Whatever the government's motives, it was the fight over lithium that started the war."

"Because the companies tried to bribe Bolivia with free cutting-edge implants in order to get their hands on the lithium. I remember. They told Bolivians they would be ahead of the world, that they'd always have access to the latest gadgets. That they'd get their implants first— at a greatly reduced price, of course." He snorted. "The companies kept talking about how great it would be to be able to talk to your TV or make a call with just a thought. I remember thinking that only a complete nutjob would have a chip implanted into their head so they could talk to their TV. At the time, the news was full of stories about how radiation from your cell phone could fry your brain. Having that same technology inside your body seemed like a mighty irrational reaction to the radiation warnings."

"I have a data chip inside my head. More than one, in fact. Does that make me a nutjob?" She frowned. "I don't exactly know what a nutjob is, but it sounds insulting."

"Bébé," he said on a sigh as he reached over and threaded his fingers with hers. "We live in a different time, with different dangers. You said it yourself, when you were arguing with Mace, most of the problems we worried about then have solutions now. You aren't a nutjob." He grinned. "Mostly."

He pulled her hand to his mouth and nibbled on her knuckles, at once derailing her thoughts and stealing her irritation. She narrowed her eyes at him. Did he know the effect he had on her? Was he doing it on purpose? He looked innocent enough, but she could never really tell with him.

"I didn't think data chip implants were that common before the war."

"They'd taken off in the States." He frowned, remembering. "Even the military was looking into whether they'd be an asset for their men. Seemed like everybody was vying for the latest advance, something to give them the edge. Implants were everywhere for a few years, different companies bringing out new, improved versions every few months. For a while, it was like the smartphone competition years earlier. They all wanted to corner the market. Which made the big companies rush out their products. A lot of the first implants were substandard, and people got hurt."

"And that's what started the war."

"Yep. Not everyone trusted the implant technology. A lot of us thought they were rushing things. We figured there had to be repercussions from having a mini-computer in your head. Bad repercussions, of the fatal kind."

"It isn't a mini-computer. Data chips are more like storage devices with communication capability."

He arched his eyebrows at her, a look that said she was being too literal again. "The world split once the Bolivians refused the offer of cheap implants. Soon the two sides were protesting, then fighting. It got bad fast. The people who thought implanted tech was the next great advance for mankind wanted to force it on the rest of us. And the people who didn't want it were terrified the other half would manage to force it into them. Tension was building globally. The whole damn planet was a powder keg. The fight over mining rights in Bolivia was just the match that made it blow."

"I don't understand." She shifted some in her seat, still holding on to his hand. "You were in the army, working for the Northern Territory government, but you agreed with the Coalition Countries when it came to implanted tech. You were obviously against it. How could you fight for something you disagreed with?"

Striker's shoulders tensed. "First, I wasn't fighting for a cause. I was fighting for my country, which back then was the United States of America. The country was under threat, and I was sent to protect it. That's all there was to it. I did my duty. Second, back then, I lived in a country that had a democratic government. One that answered to its people. I never, not once, believed that any American citizen would be forced to accept implanted technology if they didn't want it."

"It's hard to imagine a government that fought for freedom of choice instead of profit. We haven't had that sort of governance for decades." And they might never have it again, not if the companies had their way. Not if the Freedom rebellion was squashed.

"It had its good and bad points, just like everything else."

"So, the war started, and it became clear that the side against implanted tech was winning." She knew this from her history books.

"Yeah. Their forces were pushing into the States. They'd taken over a chunk of Texas and were moving north. We were deployed to take the region back."

"And then the bomb fell."

"That sounds like it happened on its own, kind of by accident. The reality is that the big tech companies put pressure on America to drop an untested bomb, sacrificing their own military in the process. It did end the war, though."

"But you were the cost."

"Yeah, we were the cost."

"And"—she took a deep breath—"while you were asleep for a hundred years—"

"Just like Sleeping Beauty."

"—the big companies redrew the map into Territories and Coalition Countries."

"They also ousted the democratic government and installed themselves in its place." He glanced over at her. "Makes perfect sense. What else is gonna happen when companies have more power than government? There was no reason for them not to take over."

"It wasn't a coup," Friday pointed out. "It happened over time. People just started listening to the companies more and more, and their power and influence overtook that of the governments."

"I know, I read up on all those puppet governments you guys had until the companies got fed up hiding behind a fake democracy and got rid of them." He squeezed her hand. "And here we are. The companies rule the Territories, and the Coalition are doing their own thing. Basically, we have a dictator in charge of the former United States, and their only concern is profit."

"That's why Freedom is fighting."

"I don't think they're pure as the driven snow, either, bébé."

"Probably, but who else is there? They're the only ones fighting for change."

"I understand, but that doesn't mean I like how they fight. Terrorism is terrorism, no matter how you package it. People get hurt while the terrorists strong-arm everyone into doing what they want."

"That isn't how Freedom operates."

"We'll see." He pointed to the peaks in the distance. "La Paz sits in the middle of those—if this navigation system is correct. We're about halfway there."

She yawned loudly and saw his eyes soften.

"Tired again?"

"Yes." She glanced away. She wanted to sleep every couple of hours now.

"Catch yourself a nap, then. I'll wake you when we get to La Paz." He patted his thigh. "Use me for a pillow. I'll take care of you while you sleep."

She curled her feet up onto the bench seat and rested her head on Striker's warm and solid thigh. She fell asleep to the sensation of his fingers stroking through her hair, secure in the knowledge he meant what he said. He would take care of her for as long as she had left.

CHAPTER 28

Striker knew there was a problem the moment they hit the first checkpoint. The queue into the city was longer than it should have been for a Saturday evening, and it was crawling along.

"Maybe there's an event happening tonight?" Friday sounded as worried as he felt.

"Maybe." But his instincts were twitching, telling him something was wrong.

"Should we give up and try to find another way in?"

He glanced at his watch. Something he'd been doing increasingly over the past few hours, all too aware that time was slipping away fast. It was seven p.m., Friday had twenty hours until the poison activated in her system. More than enough time to drive into the city and get to the clinic. But it wasn't enough time to find a way to sneak over the monitored border fences. No, their only option was to stay on the road. He reached for her hand. Her fingers were icy cold. She'd been sleeping deeply for most of the trip, and there were dark purple circles under her eyes.

"No, we'll stick to the plan. This queue will move fast

enough. We'll get through the checkpoint, no worries." He hoped. "I'll make a call to the team, see if they know what's going on."

He pulled an old satellite phone from his daypack and hit the team's HQ number.

"What is that?" As usual, she was fascinated by his tech.

"Satellite phone. I'll let you play with it after we get out of La Paz."

"Another relic that should have been obsolete. I need to look into the tech your team use. I've never seen anything like it." She beamed at him. "I feel like an archeologist who's been thrown back in time when I'm with you."

"Thanks." He shook his head at her as someone answered the phone.

"Yo there, dude." There was only one person on the team who dared call him dude—Hunter, their tech expert.

"My radar is going off here. The queue into La Paz is backed up for miles."

"I'm on it."

There was silence as he heard Hunter type on his old-fashioned keyboard, something else that would no doubt fascinate Friday. They'd moved up two car spaces before he came back with an answer.

"There's been an attack of some kind in the city. They're tight with their information. Not sure if it's a domestic situation or terrorist."

"That explains the extra security. Is our permit gonna get us through this checkpoint?"

Friday stiffened beside him as he listened to Hunter type. He rubbed his thumb across the back of her hand to soothe her.

"You're solid," Hunter said at last.

A wave of relief rolled through him. "Has Friday's name come up anywhere outside of the Territories?" What he was really asking was whether Enforcement had made a deal with Bolivian security to pick her up for them.

"No. You're good to go, boss. Anything else?"

"One more thing. Any word on that issue Mace is looking into?" As the point of contact for all of their teams in the field, Hunter would know exactly what issue Striker was talking about. Mace had gone off hunting the mole on their team.

"He's following a lead." Hunter's voice was tight. "We think the leak is a guy calling himself the Broker."

"Seriously?" That was a relief. "At least we know it isn't one of our team."

"Yeah, nobody on this team would use that lame ass-name."

"Any idea of the identity of this 'Broker'?"

"Mace is checking out a hunch, and I'm hunting online. He thinks it's someone we use to arrange transportation and weapons. He's got Sandi for backup."

"Keep me informed." He ended the call after Hunter grunted his agreement.

Friday's eyes were wide when he turned to her. "Does your team have its own satellite, or do you piggyback on other people's?"

As usual, it wasn't the question he'd expected. Seemed nothing could derail her curious mind. Well, nothing but him. And didn't that make him feel ten feet tall?

They drove through a built-up, industrial area of the city, that seemed to go on forever. Friday watched it all pass as she held Striker's hand, fighting the ever-present weariness that made her bones ache. Tension was heavy in the car, as they were both painfully aware that each delay ate up time. She glanced at the clock on the dashboard. Nineteen hours until the Interferan-X activated. And they weren't even inside the old city yet. The roadblocks had stolen time from them.

"We're about half an hour from the clinic," Striker said. "We've got plenty of time to get you that antidote."

His gaze stayed firmly on the road in front of him, his eyepatch in place to hide his snake from the world. It felt wrong. He was magnificent in his entirety, both halves making up a fascinating whole. None of it should have been hidden from the world.

"How do you do that?"

"Do what?" He skillfully negotiated the traffic to make sure they were never stuck waiting behind another driver.

"Know what I'm thinking."

Oh, how she loved his smile. It was easy and charming, just like the man. "We're attuned to each other. You're thinking what I'm thinking. Plus"—his smile turned mischievous—"it's usually written all over your face."

"I thought I was good at projecting an expressionless demeanor." For goodness sake, her life had depended on the ability.

"You are good at it. I guess you just relax more around me." And didn't he sound smug about it.

The flat road they were on suddenly dipped and curved to the right. She couldn't help but gasp at the sight before them. They'd driven into a massive twinkling bowl, a valley filled with a billion multicolored stars.

"Pretty, eh?" he said.

The city had been built into a steep and narrow valley, spreading out and up the mountainsides. The result was mesmerizing in the dark. It felt like they were riding into a distant galaxy with swirling bright stars all around them.

"In the daytime, the mountain peaks are so close you can almost touch them." His voice was low, gentle, intimate.

"I didn't expect this, not after the flat area we just drove through."

"The high plains. In my day, that was a different city called Altiplano. It grew to join with La Paz proper."

"You were here a hundred years ago?"

His laugh was deep. A rich molasses. A decadent chocolate torte. A full-bodied wine.

"Now, that makes me feel old." He steered the car down into the valley, where the buildings that had seemed like glittering fairy lights from a distance became tall skyscrapers up close. And yet, even above the tops of the highest buildings, there were still more lights to be seen on the sides of the mountains.

"It's a serious question. Were you here before your sleep?"

"Yeah. Couple of friends and me, we came down here to South America to see the place. We visited all the Inca sites and did crazy shit like bungee jumping and caving."

"Bungee jumping?"

"You stand on a bridge, they tie a thick elastic band around your ankles, then you jump off and bounce upside down until you stop, then someone lets you down."

Friday's jaw dropped. "Are you nuts?!"

"Yeah, maybe. Don't think they do bungee jumping anymore."

"I should think not." What kind of idiot threw themselves off a bridge headfirst hoping a piece of elastic would save them? "You don't do crazy things like that now, right?"

He gave her a hot look. "Bébé, my life is crazy enough without seeking that shit out."

He had a point.

"Right, the clinic is round the next corner, at the end of the street."

She could hardly breathe. They'd made it. Eighteen and a half hours before the deadline and they'd made it. Her whole body tingled in anticipation as their car turned into the clinic's street.

And came to an immediate halt.

A police barricade blocked the road.

"Come on." Striker parked illegally in a loading zone. "We'll walk from here."

"Is this normal?" She tried to keep her hands from trembling as she climbed out of the car.

"I dunno." He took her hand and held it tight. "Let's find out."

Together, they walked toward the barricade.

The street was narrow, a testament to a city built in a different time, when cars were fewer. The road surface was new and looked out of place among the older buildings. Tall, narrow buildings that made her feel hemmed in, the lack of space compressing the anxiety growing inside her.

"What's going on?" Striker called to the officer standing by the barricade.

He spoke Spanish, one of the world's three official languages, the other two being English and Mandarin. Friday had learned all three as a child.

"Gas explosion. Several buildings have been damaged. There are many casualties. This area has been cordoned off for inspection. You need to leave at once." He turned his back on them, uninterested in whether they followed his instructions or not.

"What buildings?" Friday called after him as a sinking feeling started in her stomach.

The officer gave her a stern look. "I said, move along."

"Come on." Striker tugged at her hand. "We won't get any answers here."

"Where are we going?" She trotted along beside him, struggling to keep up with his long stride.

"Up. We need an overview. See what's happening and whether we can find a way in there."

He pushed through the doors of an old hotel and

approached the desk. Money changed hands, and the woman manning reception pointed them to the lifts. Once inside, Striker pressed the button for the top floor, and they sped upward. Friday wrapped her arms around her stomach. She couldn't voice her fears, worried that if she did, they'd become reality.

"Hey." Striker pulled her in against him. "It's gonna be okay."

She rubbed her cheek against the cool cotton of his shirt, feeling the firm muscle beneath it. "What if your spy found out where we were going and told CommTECH? What if this is just a way to smoke me out?"

"Then we deal with it." His voice was calm. Even. Full of confidence. "And you weren't supposed to know about the guy leaking information. I thought my conversation with Hunter was cryptic. Guess I need to be more careful in future, because you're a hard woman to sneak something past."

Future.

She wasn't sure she had one.

The lift stopped, and the doors opened, letting them out into a nondescript corridor that was badly in need of a makeover. It was hard to tell the pattern on the faded wallpaper, and the carpet had worn bare in places. She followed Striker through the emergency door at the end of the corridor and up the concrete stairs to the roof. There was a one-way lock on the roof exit, and he made sure to prop the door open, lest it slam shut behind them and trap them on the roof. Together, silently, they crossed the flat expanse to look down into the street.

Striker stood behind her, his hands on her shoulders as they looked out over La Paz. It took a minute for her to understand what she was seeing. The explosion must have been huge, as several buildings were damaged. But the one in the center of the devastation, the one where the explosion occurred, was entirely gone. There was nothing but a pile of smoldering rubble where it once stood.

It wasn't until she felt hands tighten on her shoulders that she forced herself to compare the scene before her to the map of the area she'd memorized in the car. Her knees went weak when she realized which building had been destroyed.

The clinic was gone.

CHAPTER 29

The Penthouse, New Amsterdam Hotel,
New York City, Northern Territory

"I'm telling you," Serge Abramovich said as he helped himself to some top-shelf Scotch. "Miriam knows we interfered. She knows we sent a team after the scientist."

"She knows nothing." Sandrine crossed her legs as she sat back in the corner of the sofa. Serge was wearisome. His lack of courage grated on her.

"You should have let me pick the team who went after the scientist. Yours obviously didn't know what they were doing." He sprawled in the armchair facing her, every inch of him screaming 'entitled rich boy'.

"There was nothing wrong with my team." She wasn't entirely sure what had gone wrong—seeing as none of her men had made it back to tell her. "Miriam's team didn't succeed, either. Last I heard, the scientist is still alive and on the run."

Serge chuckled. "You haven't heard the latest then." He pointed at her with the glass, making the whiskey slosh about. "Friday Jones took Interferan-X. She's hours from death and trying to get to the only clinic in South America that stocks the antidote. The thing is, Miriam beat her to it. She sent her pet ghoul to blow the building. The girl is dead. One way or another. The plan failed."

Sandrine raised one perfectly groomed eyebrow. Now that information changed things. She wished she'd had it before she'd gone to the expense of sending a retrieval team after the scientist. The chances of anyone picking up the woman before she succumbed to the poison were minute. A wasted effort.

"That would have been useful information to have at the start of this plan." She narrowed her eyes at the man. Had he held out on her?

He shrugged. "I only just found out myself. The same time as I found out Miriam suspects our interference. She isn't pleased."

Sandrine waved a dismissive hand. "Nothing pleases the great Miriam Shepherd."

"Yes, but she's particularly displeased that we intended to release the video and use it against her."

"She can't know that for certain."

"She doesn't need to, does she? Even if she suspects, it will cause problems for us."

Sandrine was unfazed. "She can't touch me." There was nothing in her life that Miriam could use against her. She had no family. No friends. No pets. Nothing. There were no weak spots for her enemies to exploit.

There was a knock at the door. "Oui?" Sandrine called.

Her personal assistant poked her head in, blushing at the sight of Serge and making Sandrine wonder if this was yet another woman the man had bedded. She frowned at Angela. "What is it?"

She snapped her eyes from the Russian. "We have a problem, Madame President."

"What problem?"

"May I?" Her assistant pointed to the screens covering one wall of the suite.

Sandrine nodded, and all Angela did was blink and send a mental command to the screens. A second later, several news channels filled the wall. They were all showing the same footage.

Sandrine shot to her feet, her hands on the hips of her exclusive designer dress. There was nothing she could do but stare in horror at the images of herself sitting behind her wide wooden desk. She knew exactly what she was looking at. A meeting she'd taken three years earlier when she'd first become president of her company. A meeting between her, the head of research at one of her companies, Jang Pharmaceutical, and Ju-Long Lee, CEO of Lee-Chan Medical. Ju-Long wasn't in the frame. In fact, the camera angle betrayed him as the one who had filmed their meeting. And it was a damning meeting.

"I must insist that you listen, Madam President," Leon Masters, the lead research scientist at Jang Pharmaceutical said.

"I am listening." Sandrine stared at the man coldly. "And I disagree. The antiviral will go into production as planned."

"But the side effects." The man pointed to the data pad in his hand. "They can cause long-term damage. You have to see that the good the medication can do does not outweigh the possible repercussions of taking it. We need more time in the lab. With more research, I'm sure we can come up with a way to minimize the risks associated with taking the pills."

"No." She folded her hands on the desk. "We stick to the scheduled release date. You are free to continue your research, but the medication will still be launched as planned. The risks are negligible compared to the financial benefits. We've already advertised this medication. If we don't release it on time, we will lose the confidence of our customers."

"If you release it early you risk more than customer confidence. You risk lives!" The little man waved his arm so fervently that he knocked over a potted plant sitting on the corner of her desk.

His face turned purple as he looked at the mess.

Sandrine arched her eyebrow coolly. "We release as planned." She stood and leaned over the desk toward him. "And do not forget you signed a confidentiality agreement."

"No, Madam President, of course." He backed away from her, eyes down, running for the door while Sandrine smiled smugly at his back.

"Our stock is plummeting," Angela said, pulling her attention from the covertly recorded meeting.

Of course it was. Sandrine eyed Serge. At least he wasn't crowing over her problems. "You have to excuse me. I need to head back to Australia. There's some damage control that must be done."

"Of course." He nodded, placed the empty glass on the table beside him, and headed for the door, winking at Angela as he did so and making her blush like a teenage girl. Before he closed the door behind him, Serge looked back at Sandrine. "Still think Miriam doesn't know about your plan?"

With that, he closed the door softly. Sandrine glared at her assistant. "Who released the file?"

There was no point in asking who'd filmed it. It had clearly been Ju-Long.

"We don't know, Madam President." Angela spoke to her feet. "But the location of the file was traced to New York." She glanced up and swallowed hard. "To the CommTECH building."

Sandrine clenched her teeth. It wasn't conclusive evidence, but it was just enough of a hint to let her know who was behind the leaked video. It was a message. Pure and simple. Miriam Shepherd somehow knew about Sandrine's interference, and by releasing this footage, she'd issued an order to cease and desist. Which Sandrine had no choice but to follow.

For now.

CHAPTER 30

No!

Striker staggered back a step at the sight before him.

NO!

Fires still smoldered among the rubble. Emergency services pulled bodies out of the mess. Nothing of the clinic remained. The antidote was gone.

Gone.

No. He gave a furious shake of his head. This couldn't be their only option. He looked at his watch. They still had eighteen hours left. More than enough time to get to another clinic.

He spun to Friday. She was stunned reactionless again. Just as she had been when he'd first revealed his other nature. She stared blankly at the bomb-site, her face expressionless. She didn't move. She barely blinked, her big brain working overtime to process the disaster in front of her.

He stepped into her view, placing his hands on her shoulders. "Friday."

No reaction. They didn't have time for this. He growled low in his throat and pressed his lips savagely to hers, ending the kiss with a reprimanding bite on her bottom lip.

"That hurt." Shaky fingers covered her lips as her dazed eyes morphed into glaring ones.

Better. That was better. "We need a backup option. Where's the nearest clinic that stocks the Interferan-X antidote?"

She blinked up at him, and he saw the bleakness in her eyes. She was defeated, giving up. He wouldn't allow it. Not now. Not ever. Not her.

"Where?" He squeezed her shoulders.

"Back in the Northern Territory."

His stomach turned bitter at the words. "You're telling me that there isn't another clinic with the antidote in the whole of South America?"

"No. The poison was developed in the Northern Territory. They control it and the antidote—especially outside of the Territories. They're worried it might be used as a weapon against them."

"Fuck." He wanted to roar. Rage. Pummel something. Anything.

His snake stirred from slumber.

What?

Friday's in trouble.

Mine.

It was a definitive answer. Friday couldn't be in trouble because she belonged to the diamondback, and he wouldn't allow it. Striker understood his reasoning and, for once, they were in complete agreement.

"Where are the clinics in the U.S.? I mean, the Northern Territory?"

"Houston, where I took the poison. New York and Seattle."

"Good. Good. Okay." He ran a hand over his smooth head. He could do this. There was still time. "If we get on a super jet, we can be in New York in seven hours."

He flicked open his satellite phone as he pulled his

trembling woman against his body. It was okay. Everything was going to be okay. He wouldn't allow anything else.

"What's up?" It was Hunter.

"Somebody blew up the clinic. We need super jet passage to New York. That's where the nearest antidote is."

He heard Hunter suck in a breath. "Enforcement behind the explosion?"

"I would say so. Have you started booking that passage?"

"You turn up in the Northern Territory, and Enforcement is going to be on you before you can get her to the clinic."

"Do you see another choice?"

There was a pause. He could practically hear their tech guy think. "Maybe we can break into the New York clinic, steal the antidote, and bring it to you."

"We looked into that when she first approached us. It isn't an option. It would take weeks to plan and days to execute. The security around the antidote in the Northern Territory is tight." He pressed a kiss to Friday's hair. Her eyes were still pinned to the clinic. "This is our only option."

He heard Hunter's fingers move over his keyboard. "There's a super jet flight leaving for New York in an hour."

The tension in his shoulders loosened slightly. They could do this. It was possible. He'd worry about Enforcement later. The main thing was to keep Friday alive.

"I've got the two of you passage to New York under assumed identities. I'll get Dominic to hack the system and change your bioscans. The new identity will come up when you're scanned at the plane. It's gonna cost a shit ton, dude."

"I don't care." All that mattered was getting it done. Dominic, their hacker connection, was a genius who lived on the fringes of Territory society. He was weird as hell, talented and loyal. He'd get the job done. "Tell him I'll bring him back some Inca Cola." The guy was also addicted to sugar and caffeine, two things that were seriously restricted and monitored in the Territories, but not in Bolivia.

"Good luck, boss." Hunter didn't wait for a reply. The line went dead.

He wrapped his arms around the woman who'd come to mean everything to him. "We've got to get out of here, bébé. The super jet leaves from La Paz International in an hour." Time was tight if they wanted to make that flight. And he very much wanted to make it.

"When I get to New York, Enforcement will kill me. I die here, or I die there, what's the difference?"

"No." He clasped her chin and angled her face up to him. "No. We'll assemble an army. We'll protect you. They don't know we're coming back. They don't know you'll be at the clinic. But we'll be ready if they find out. I'll keep you safe. I swear this to you. I swear it."

Her eyes went liquid as she buried her face in his chest and clung to him.

"Come on," his voice was soft. "We need to leave now."

She nodded against him before stepping back. Together they turned toward the door that led back into the building—and froze.

A man stood in their way, blocking their only exit off the roof. He smiled at them. The cold, dead smile of a killer. Friday began to shake and took a step closer to Striker, looking for protection, which he readily gave. There was no need for introductions. They knew exactly who had come for them. He was the bogeyman of the Northern Territory. Miriam Shepherd's pet psychopath—Kane Duggan.

Friday's hand curled into the waistband of his jeans as Striker scanned the roof, looking for an out. He felt her shake, knew she was terrified, but she didn't make a sound. More men came out of the stairwell behind Kane. They were all dressed in black. All wore military boots. All carried weapons. They spread out, forming a barrier in front of the door.

Every man present held a gun in his hand—including

Striker, who'd removed his from the holster on his thigh as soon as he'd turned toward the door. And although there was firepower aplenty, no one took a shot. There was only one reason for the lack of gunfire—Kane wanted Friday alive.

"Bébé," he barely whispered. "Hold on tight and run when I say."

He felt her nod against his back.

"Surrender." Kane's voice rang out. "Give me the woman, and you can walk out of here alive." He inclined his head, the gesture of a benevolent dictator. "In pain, but alive."

Friday's trembling increased. He reached back and wrapped a hand around her wrist, holding her tight as he waited for their moment. He could only see one way out of this, and they would have only one chance to make it work.

"You want money?" Kane spread out his hands. "I can give you money. Whatever the bitch paid, I'll triple. You're a smuggler, Striker. Not a fighter. Take the fee and walk away. She's dead, anyway."

A strangled sound of distress came from behind him, and Striker flexed his hold on Friday's wrist, trying to reassure her that she was his priority. Kane could offer all the riches in the world, and he would never walk away from her.

Never.

Kane made a tiny gesture with his right hand, and the eight-man team spread out. Slowly hemming them in. Their time was up.

He squeezed her wrist. "We're running left in three," he whispered. "One, two, three!"

He shot at the generator above Kane's head. It exploded in a shower of sparks. It was barely more than a distraction, but it bought them the time to run. And run they did. Straight to the edge of the roof, over the ledge, and into the night.

CHAPTER 31

THEY WERE FLYING. FRIDAY SCREAMED, BUT IT CAME OUT AS A squeak. They'd ran straight off the hotel roof. Ten floors up. Into nothing. A few seconds later they landed with a thud on the roof of the building beside them. Her knees jolted on impact, sending pain spearing through her. There was no time to process—they had to keep moving. They had to get away from CommTECH's enforcer.

"Run!" Striker hadn't let go of her wrist, even during their jump. He tugged her to her feet, dragging her along with him as he ran.

They didn't look back, heading straight at the door to the interior stairs. Striker shot out the lock before he hit the door hard. It gave way with a crash, swinging inward to slam against the wall. They took the stairs two at a time, moving fast enough for her to worry she'd trip and get them killed. Because they were being chased. Kane and his men had followed them.

They barreled through the first door they came to and discovered they were in an office block. Small rooms. Cubicles. An elevator. They raced toward it. Striker hit the button as he shoved her behind him, aiming his gun back down the corridor, protecting her. There was nothing she could do to help, other than stare at the lift doors, willing them to open.

The bell on the elevator sounded its arrival as their pursuers rushed into the corridor.

Striker pushed her into the lift. "Close the doors," he ordered.

She frantically pressed the button, glad the elevator was too old to use biolocks, which meant anyone could work it. The doors began to close. So, so slowly.

"Striker!" She reached for him, afraid he wouldn't make it in before the doors slammed shut.

He fired off several rounds before throwing himself through the closing gap. Her hands curled into the cotton of his T-shirt as she shook violently. He was a calm, confident port in a terrifying storm.

"Don't worry, bébé." He hit the button for the first floor and then the emergency override button, which meant they wouldn't stop until they got there. "I'll get us out of this." There was absolute conviction in his voice.

"Someone will be waiting for us at the bottom." It would be all too easy for some of Kane's men to backtrack through the hotel building to cut them off.

"I know." He flashed her a reassuring smile before he jumped up and pushed the panel in the ceiling, flipping it open. "Up you go."

Before her brain caught up with his actions, she was through the space and clinging to the top of the lift as they plummeted downward. He followed, slamming the panel closed behind him.

He wrapped an arm around her as he stood, taking her with him. "You aren't gonna like this next bit. Don't scream."

There was no time to figure out his intention. One second, he was staring at the walls as they flashed past. The next, he jumped, taking her with him. Friday opened her mouth to scream, but nothing came out. Fear had stolen her voice.

They landed feet first on the narrow ledge outside another set of lift doors. There was nothing to hold onto. Nothing to keep her on the ledge. She wavered. Her foot slipped. And she fell. Her stomach hit the edge of the ledge, and she grabbed Striker's ankle. Pure, unadulterated adrenaline swept through her, making her feel like everything happened in slow motion.

She dangled over the shaft, her free hand clawing at the ledge, her other hand biting into Striker's leg, clinging to him, desperate. Terror kept her silent, her focus on staying alive.

A hand wrapped around her upper arm. Muscles flexed, and Striker pulled her up beside him. There would be bruises where he'd grasped her, and she'd be grateful for every one of them.

"I could kiss you right now," she whispered as her body shook.

"Hold that thought." He transferred her hand to a recessed handle beside the doors. "Grip this while I open the doors. Don't move an inch."

That would be hard considering she was shaking so much. With a white-knuckle grip on the narrow handle, she watched him produce a multipurpose tool from his daypack. He unscrewed a panel to manipulate the wiring inside. A second later, the doors slid open, and they tumbled through. They were on the fifth floor. As the elevator doors closed behind them, Friday fought the urge to throw herself into Striker's arms. She wanted him to hold her until she stopped shaking, if that was even possible. But there wasn't time. Kane and his men were still looking for them.

"Come on. I need to see where we are."

They ran for the window at the end of the corridor. Buildings from this era had been built close together, with architectural details that no longer served a purpose, like the narrow Spanish style balcony outside the window.

"We're goin' out." He used his multi-tool to short-circuit the lock on the window before throwing it open.

They climbed out onto the old wooden balcony, and Striker sealed the window after them. In the street below, emergency services worked on the buildings damaged during the clinic blast. Lights flashed. People shouted. Smoke filled each breath. Friday swallowed it down, fearful she'd cough and attract attention. The buildings were so close together that there was only an inch between theirs and the one next door. A balcony jutted out above them on the neighboring building.

"If I stand on the rail, I can jump up to that balcony. Then I can pull you up."

She glanced down. The ground was awfully far away. What if they slipped? Fell? She kept her lips sealed. If there had been another option, he would have given it to her.

As he took a step toward their balcony rail, her hand shot out, fingers holding him hard. "Be safe. Please. Don't sacrifice yourself for me. I'm not worth it."

"Bébé." There was a wealth of emotion in that one word, all of it meant for her.

She found herself blinking back tears as he clasped her nape and pulled her in for a quick, hard kiss.

"You're worth it," he whispered against her lips. "Never think otherwise. You. Are. Worth. It."

With one last squeeze, he released her and climbed up to stand on the rail of their balcony. She held her breath as he bent his knees and sprang upward, gripping the base of the balcony above them with both hands. Biceps flexing, he pulled himself up. He made it look effortless, jumping between balconies five floors up with nothing beneath them to break his fall.

He fumbled with his pack before lying flat on his stomach. One end of a rope fell down to her.

"Wrap it around your waist. Tie it real good, chère. Then climb up to stand on the rail, and I'll pull you up."

She was about to follow his orders, but suddenly hesitated, her hand still on the rope. What was she doing? Risking his life to save hers? No matter what he said, she wasn't worth it. Especially not now, when it was too late to get to the antidote anyway. Her time was up. Kane was seconds away from finding them, and even if they did manage to escape and make it to New York, Enforcement would be waiting for them.

She had to face facts. She was dead already. The question was, did she want to take Striker with her when she went? She didn't even have to think about the answer. She didn't want him to die, sacrificed for her. She wanted to save him. He was more important than she would ever be. He was everything to her. He was…

She looked up into his gorgeous face, filled with worry. Over her. And it hit her.

He was the man she loved.

Desperately. Completely. Loved.

And she couldn't let Kane get his hands on him.

"Don't do it." It was the order of a commander, an urgent hiss, filled with pain and anger. "Don't you even think about doin' it. We're getting out of here. Together. You an' me. We've got a flight to catch. Don' you dare walk away. You hear me? Don' you dare."

Her heart ripped in two. The pain made her stumble. But she couldn't take him down with her. Her eyesight blurred, and she blinked hard to clear it. With a tiny moan, she released the rope and stepped back.

"No!" The fury in his word made her shake. Not from fear. From pain.

She fought to get the words out through her tightening

throat. "This is for the best. You're in danger with me. We both know we'll never make it to New York in time, not now. Not with Kane at our heels. And even if we did make it, Enforcement would kill us both. This way, you live."

"No." He sprang to his feet. His hands on the rail, ready to jump.

"Don't," she snapped the word at him. "This is just a job. I hired you to get me to La Paz, and we're here. Your job is done. Go home." Her stomach roiled with the lies.

His eye turned black. "Fuck that."

His arms tensed, ready to swing his legs up and over the rail, and then he froze. His body shook. His eye rolled back, and he collapsed into a heap on the balcony floor. Friday screamed. She scrambled onto the rail, desperate to get to the man she loved, desperate to help him, somehow. An arm wrapped around her waist and pulled her back against a hard, immovable body. She kicked and punched and fought, shouting for freedom, begging for Striker's safety.

A man's face appeared on the balcony above her, the one where Striker lay motionless. "What do you want to do with him, Boss?"

"Bring him along." Kane Duggan's arm tightened around her.

All she could do was watch helplessly as the other man hefted Striker's limp body over his shoulder. He wasn't unconscious. The neural stun gun had rendered him temporarily immobile. His unpatched eye was open. It stared at her with equal measures of fear and fury. She turned her head in shame, blinking away useless tears. This was all her fault. All of it. She should have given up on life in Houston and let the poison take her. She shouldn't have tried to find the antidote. No one would have missed her. No one would have mourned. And now, because she'd been selfish, Striker's life was on the line. More than his life—his secrets, and the secrets of his team, were on the line.

Because of her, his unique DNA was in the hands of CommTECH.

She erupted with the injustice of it all. "Leave him alone. Put him down. He's got nothing to do with this. Nothing. I only hired him to bring me here. You don't need to take him. Leave him!" She kicked back at Kane's shins as she dug her nails into his arms. Panic was a ferocious beast, eating her alive from the inside out. Kane had to understand that Striker had nothing to do with her. He had to let the man she loved go free.

"You're more fun than I thought you would be, little girl," Kane said against her ear. "Now, for every kick you give me, I'll make sure my associate kicks your smuggler."

She went still in his hold.

"I knew we'd reach an understanding." With a cold, hard laugh, he climbed through the window, back into the building, taking her with him.

CHAPTER 32

Last Stop Bar, Monroe, Texas

NO MATTER WHAT TIME MACE WALKED INTO THE LAST STOP BAR, day or night, it was always filled with desperate losers trying to drink away their existence. Some days, he felt like he fit right in.

"I hate this place," Sandi said as she strode beside him. "Reminds me of all the times I pulled my mom out of shitholes just like it." Her face didn't show any of the disgust Mace knew she felt. "I say we just shoot the traitor and be done with it."

"Can't." The crowd parted for Mace. Mainly because he was huge and built of solid muscle, but partly because there was murder in his eyes. "We need to know what information he sold."

"Then I can kill him?" Her tone held death.

"Then you can kill him." One betrayal in a lifetime was more than enough and they hadn't been able to exact retribution that time. This time, they could.

"This kills me. He was supposed to be our friend." She faked a pout. "I need one of those Cosmo articles—Ten Steps to Help You Deal with Trust Issues. Otherwise how am I ever gonna meet a man and fall in love?"

"Cosmo doesn't exist anymore, baby sis. You're on your own."

There wasn't a romantic bone in his foster sister's body. *He* was more romantic than Sandi, and that in itself said everything. She pouted again, but the humor fell flat. There was no getting past their reason for being in the Last Stop.

"He's at the end of the bar." Mace spotted their prey.

"Oh, to be unnaturally tall and able to see over crowds."

They stalked through the room, aiming straight for the end of the bar. The owner spotted them and gave them a chin lift in acknowledgment. Glen handed a beer to a local miner.

"Got a minute?" Mace said.

"Back room." Glen nodded toward it.

They followed the owner into the corridor that led to the back of the building, cold, stark rage driving Mace. He reined it in. He needed a clear head. There were questions that had to be answered. He flexed his hand, his knuckles bruised from his last round of questioning. The guy who'd known about "the Broker." The guy who'd known who'd sold them out. The guy who'd named Glen.

The office was spacious, but sparsely decorated and furnished with items that had seen better days. Whatever Glen was doing with the money he made selling information, it wasn't going into the bar.

The big, ex-military man walked into the room—confident in his safety, certain his double life remained well hidden. He waved them in, closing the door behind them. As soon as he turned, Mace was on him. He grabbed Glen's nape, holding tight while he pummeled his stomach. His blows were powerful. One would have been enough to disable their betrayer. Anger drove him to deliver more.

Glen doubled, groaning, unable to fight back. Mace

dragged him to the desk and threw him into his chair. Sandi had his wrists and ankles strapped down within seconds. Side by side, the adopted siblings stared down at their betrayer.

"We know all about your extra-curricular activities, Glen." Mace didn't try to hide his disgust.

"I don't know what you're talking about." The words were strained.

Mace glanced at Sandi. "Door."

She nodded and wedged a chair under the handle. She'd already blocked all transmissions from the room, visual or otherwise, using the jammer she'd brought with her. Nobody would come to Glen's rescue.

"We know you're the Broker. You've been sloppy. Too many people know your identity."

"And BTW," Sandi added, "your cover name is lame. It sounds like something straight out of a third-rate comic book."

Mace frowned at his sister. "Not helping."

She shrugged, clearly already done with Glen. She wanted it over. She wanted him gone.

"I don't know what you're talking about," the bar owner wheezed between words. "We're friends."

Just for that, Mace struck out, breaking his nose. Hating that he was reduced to this, hurting a man he'd thought was a friend.

"We know you're the Broker," he repeated. "There's no denying it. We're past that. We know you sold us out. What we don't know is who you sold us out to and what you told them. Start talking. You know I can make this last, and you know how painful it will be while I do it."

Glen's eyes flickered over the room, looking for an out, realizing there wasn't one. That's when his tactics changed from denial to cooperation. There was cunning in the man's eyes. Something he'd never before let the team see.

"I'll tell you everything I know, but you have to let me live."

Yeah, he was going to try to negotiate. The fool. He didn't have anything to negotiate with, but they'd play along to get answers. For now. "You sold us out. You deserve to die."

"I have information." Glen licked his lips. "I never told them anything about you specifically. Just the girl."

"What did you tell them?"

Glen shook his head, wincing with pain. "I want your word. I know you never break it. I want your word that you won't kill me."

The siblings shared a speaking look. Sandi gave a short, sharp nod of agreement.

"You have my word." Mace tried not to vomit at the triumph in the bar owner's face. "I won't kill you. But that's depends on you talking. You hold back, and all bets are off."

"I understand." The words were overflowing with fake submission.

"You told Enforcement Friday Jones was holed up in South Munroe." It wasn't a question. "You told them about the tunnels."

Glen nodded then grimaced in pain. "Yeah. I deal with Miriam Shepherd, among others." He tried to hide his pride over his lofty connections. He failed. "She wanted to know about your team, about the scientist."

"And you told her?" The urge to pummel the man into the ground was intense.

Out of the corner of his eye, he could see Sandi vibrate with rage over Glen's confession.

"I gave Miriam the tunnels and South Munroe, and that you were meeting the jet in Monterrey. But that's it. That's all I told her."

He said it as though it were nothing. As though he'd shared minor, throwaway information about the team. A muscle in Mace's jaw began to twitch wildly. Three times he'd almost been killed, because of this man. His friend.

"What else did you tell her about us, about my team?"

Glen's eyes flickered between them, calculating how much he should give up. Mace's fist shot out, hitting his jaw. There was a satisfying crack.

"Fuck!" Glen spat out a tooth. "We have a deal!"

"I said I wouldn't kill you. Not that I wouldn't hurt you. You were thinking of holding back information. I want it all."

"Fine. Fine." He licked his bloody lip. "I told her your team appeared three years ago, from nowhere. You have no background. None of you. I told her nobody's heard of you in the Coalition Countries. It's like you appeared out of thin air. I told her you can somehow get through the Red Zone. And that you have a base somewhere between here and Mexico, but I didn't know where. I told her you were the best in the smuggling business." His look said they should have been pleased he talked them up. "That's it. That's all I knew. That's all I told her."

Mace turned to his sister, knowing she had let her senses loose—the ones she'd gained from her animal. She nodded once. The bar owner was telling the truth. Sandi would have known otherwise. But from the look on their former friend's face, he definitely held back something more.

"What else?"

Glen's eyes narrowed as though he was still trying to figure out what he could get away with. Mace withdrew the knife he kept strapped at his waist and tossed it in the air. Like he'd said, he wouldn't kill him, but that left a whole lot of space for inflicting pain.

"I had another contact." The bar owner rushed to get the words out. "Sandrine Cherbourg, she wanted to know about the scientist, too. I told her about Monterrey and the jet."

That explained the second team. The leader of the Southern Territory had been after Friday and the information in her head. Sandrine had been making a power play. A poorly staged one at that. He flipped the knife, letting his eyes roam over Glen as though looking for a good place to stick the blade.

Glen's skin turned gray. "I told them about the poison the scientist took. I told them she was on a deadline to get the antidote."

"Who did you tell?"

"Miriam Shepherd, Serge Abramovich."

Fuck, the whole world was looking for Friday. This mess was much bigger than any of them had imagined. Whatever was in the scientist's head was obviously a threat to all of the Territory leaders.

"You told them she needed the antidote for Interferan-X?"

"Yeah." Blood ran from his mouth and down his jaw. "I overheard when she was talking to Striker."

"You overheard?" He arched an eyebrow. Glen had been at the other end of the room during that conversation.

The bar owner looked away. "I have all the tables bugged. Now let me go. That's everything I know, all the information I sold. I swear."

Sandi shook her head. "We know it isn't everything. We want every detail you have concerning Friday Jones."

Mace was done with this shit. Enough prevaricating. He swung his arm and embedded the knife in Glen's thigh. His scream was a high-pitched wail, even though the knife hadn't hit anything vital.

"No more," Glen shouted. "I'll tell you everything. The only other thing I know is that Miriam Shepherd sent her lapdog to La Paz to deal with the woman. He took a team with him."

The siblings froze. Kane Duggan was in La Paz. And Striker was alone with Friday, with no team to back him up.

"That's it, that's everything. I swear." Glen didn't look too manipulative now. "You have to untie me. We have a deal."

Mace crouched in front of his former friend. "See, here's the thing. Our deal wasn't for your freedom. Our deal was that I wouldn't kill you. And I won't." He stood, strolled over to the door, and pulled the chair out from under the knob. "But Sandi didn't make that promise."

"I hate scum like you." Sandi's voice was ice cold. She lifted her gun and aimed for Glen's forehead.

"No!" he roared.

She pulled the trigger. The bar owner's head shot back before it slumped forward, blood oozing from the hole in his forehead. The siblings didn't linger to look at the man. He was old news to them now. Instead, they headed out of the office and into the bar. Nobody stopped them. The gunshot was swallowed by the loud music.

Sandi glanced around, obviously taking one last look at the place. "Now we need to find somewhere else to drink. I hate looking for a new bar. It's like trying to find the perfect pair of shoes."

They pushed through the doors and out into the night. Once in their hover car, Mace hit the comm button for their base.

"Yo," Hunter said.

"Glen has been eliminated." He swallowed the feeling of revulsion. Of betrayal. Would there ever be a time when the people they trusted didn't turn against them? "Kane Duggan is in La Paz."

"That explains it." Hunter's words made the hair on the back of Mace's neck stand on end. "We've lost contact with Striker."

"Get us on a plane to La Paz." He started the car and headed for the airport.

"Already done. There's a jet waiting. Jeremiah, Doc, and Ignacio are on their way, too. They'll pick up their ride in Monterrey." That was still hours out. Hours where Striker was alone to fend off the butcher of the Northern Territory.

"It's worse, man," Hunter said. "Kane blew up the clinic. I booked Striker and Friday on a flight to New York. They never boarded."

Hunter was right. It was worse. No antidote. No backup.

And Kane Duggan.

If they didn't get to Striker fast, he was fucked. They all were.

"Do we have anyone in the area we can trust?" Someone who could act as backup until they got there.

"No."

"Is his tracking device enabled?"

"No."

"Damn it."

"Yeah," Hunter said. "Get to the jet. Save our boy."

Mace noticed Hunter didn't mention Friday. There would be no saving the scientist now.

They all knew she was already dead.

CHAPTER 33

Striker was seriously going to go Hulk on somebody's ass. He couldn't remember the last time he was this furious. Even when he woke to discover somebody had stolen his world and given him a reptile in exchange.

Kill! Save mine!

His talking handbag hadn't shut up since somebody had immobilized them. Apparently, the diamondback really didn't like having its body frozen.

As for Friday, as soon as he was able to move again, Striker planned to shake her until her bones rattled. Leave him? She'd been planning on leaving him?

Hell no!

Not gonna happen.

Not over something as dumb as trying to save him from her.

Kill! Save mine!

Shut up! I can't think with you screaming.

Save mine!

There was no shutting the damn rattler up. And to add insult to injury, he'd been tied hands and feet and shoved in the boot of a hatchback. It wasn't even a proper boot. It was the equivalent of putting the dog in the back of the car. At least he could see out the windows and knew they were heading south through the city.

Friday was in the car, too. He could see the back of her head. She sat, surrounded by muscle, in the middle row of seats. There were two guys in the back row nearest him, two on either side of his woman, and two in the front.

It occurred to him that they were driving in a people mover. He was stuck in a mom van on the way to soccer practice with his team. Oh yeah, and it was possible he was losing his mind.

Let me free. I get her.

He wished he could knock some sense into the diamondback. If he set the damn thing free in a car with Kane Duggan, he'd end up on a dissection table at a CommTECH research facility. And who would save Friday then?

No, he needed a better plan. A sensible plan. He hadn't been immobilized for long, but he knew they'd missed their flight to the Northern Territory. They still had time to get to New York and get the antidote before the deadline. He was sure of it. All they needed was nine hours. An hour to get to La Paz airport, seven for the superfast jet to New York and another hour to get to the clinic. Sure, he'd have to break every speed limit on the planet, but it was doable. He just needed to get out of his current predicament with nine hours to spare.

"Where are you taking us?" Friday's voice cut through his thoughts.

Of course, she was going to ask questions. And more than likely, those questions were going to piss their captors off. If only he had a telepathic link to her instead of his other half. It would have been a whole lot more use.

Go to hell, the diamondback said helpfully, having read his mind.

"Somewhere secure." Kane's voice was easy to recognize. It was a flat, emotionless void.

"To download the data from my chip?"

"Nobody wants the information on your data chip. We're more interested in stopping it from getting out."

There was silence as Striker watched the buildings zoom past. He struggled against his bonds, but he couldn't break them. His fingers felt along the strap securing his hands. It was the equivalent of an old zip tie. It could be cut, but the goons had relieved him of all tools and weapons.

"You're going to kill me." Friday sounded calm. Far too calm.

She sounded like she'd accepted her fate. Her death. The anger he'd been fighting to contain surged.

Kill. Save Friday. Save mine.

Not helping, he told the rattler.

"I don't need to kill you," Kane said. "You've done that for me. All I need to do is watch it happen."

Over my dead body, he told his diamondback.

For once, the rattler agreed.

If I call you out, you need to follow orders. We need to work as a team.

Kill!

He almost screamed in frustration. It was like dealing with a stubborn two-year-old. *Not kill. I need you to bite through the bonds around my wrists and ankles. Then I need you to come straight back onto my skin. If you don't, they'll know you're here, and they'll kill Friday. Do you hear me? They won't give us a chance to save her. They'll kill her.*

There was silence for a beat. *I follow.*

He fought the sigh of relief that wanted to escape. *Okay. Here goes. Do exactly what I tell you. We need to work together to save her.*

Okay.

Against his better judgment, he called the diamondback

from his body, hoping the slight snapping sound wouldn't attract anyone's attention.

Don't rattle! He ordered before sending the snake images of the bonds and telling him what to do.

He felt the diamondback slide over him to where his hands were tied at the base of his back. He kept watch as the rattler gnawed at the bindings. They passed an armed checkpoint, where Kane was addressed as "sir" before they were waved on through. Where the hell were they taking them? And why was someone showing Kane Duggan deference in a Coalition country?

"Why aren't there any company logos on these buildings?" Friday asked. "What is this place?"

Their captor barked a cold approximation of a laugh. "Welcome to CommTECH's top secret ladmium mine."

There was a pause. "CommTECH isn't allowed to mine in Bolivia. The Bolivian government only allows state-owned mining operations."

"Is that right?" Kane drawled, making his men chuckle.

"What's that in the sky? It's a grid. No, wait… There are too many drones, it's a—" She gasped. "It's a holomatrix. This whole area is shielded from satellite screening. You're hiding this operation from the world."

"That's what top secret means." The CommTECH enforcer was as close to amused as the man probably ever got.

"No! You can't do this. There are international agreements in place. You can't mine here." Her head turned frantically as she tried to get a better view of the site.

She needs help! The rattler shifted as if to go to her.

No! Finish what you're doing, then we can both help her. He put as much authority as possible into his words. The diamondback grumbled but went back to gnawing at the zip tie.

"You've destroyed most of the lower city. The historical buildings, the people." Friday's voice was shaking with her distress. "Oh my goodness, you've done this by force haven't you? You're forcing the people to work for you? You've enacted war on the Coalition Countries by doing this against Bolivia's will."

The laughter that filled the car was superior and cruel. As soon as he heard it, he knew exactly what had happened. The Bolivian president had gone behind the backs of the Coalition governments and made a deal with CommTECH. He'd sold out his country.

"Nobody even knows we're here," Kane said. "Except the very welcoming Bolivian president."

She gasped. "The holomatrix. It projects an image for the world that shows the city the way it used to be, doesn't it? They'll find out about this. You can't keep something this big secret for long. The Coalition Countries will find out."

"Are you going to tell them, Ms. Jones?" There was that cold amusement again. "Before or after the poison gets you?"

Done, the diamondback said.

Striker felt the band give and his hands were loose.

Ankles now. Fast.

With slow, tiny movements, he rubbed his wrists before inching his hand to his belt. He pressed his thumb against the center of the buckle, activating the tracking device built into it and hoping the damn thing worked. He then moved his hands back behind him, in case someone checked on him. It was best if they all thought he was still bound.

"You bastard!" Friday snapped, making him blink. He didn't think she knew any curses. "You think you can get away with anything, but you can't."

"That's where you're wrong. I can do whatever I like. Who's going to stop me?"

Striker felt the tension around his ankles give way, and he shifted his feet. *Get back on me, he ordered his rattler.*

I help.

You help by getting back in position.

I kill. Save mine.

Get back! If they find out about you, you risk all of us. And you'll get Friday killed.

With a grumble, the snake crawled up his body and snapped into place. *You better save her. She mine.*

Yeah, yeah. You keep telling me. You're a different species, you realize that, right?

The reply was silence, which was way better than listening to more rubbish from a talking reptile. This was his life. He now talked to snakes.

———

Friday couldn't think. Her brain had been fried from data overload. She knew any sane person in her position would focus on having mere hours to live, but all she could think about was the man she loved. He was hurt, bound and immobile in the back of the car, and there was nothing she could do to help him. She'd begged her captor to release him, but all he'd done was laugh.

She should never have dragged Striker into her mess. She should have found a hole to sit in after she took the poison and waited for death to come find her. After a lifetime of struggling against her circumstances, she should have learned that there was no happy ending for women like her. Women who were born without options.

From the moment she'd been dumped in front of the CommTECH headquarters as a baby, her life had been overshadowed by the company. Her education had been furnished by CommTECH at the expense of her freedom. Her work revolved around CommTECH. Her only friends, well, acquaintances, were all CommTECH employees. Hell, she'd even lost her virginity to a fellow CommTECH scientist on the floor of the company's lab.

Her death would be courtesy of CommTECH, too.

Sure, she'd taken the poison, but they had done everything they could to make sure she didn't get to the antidote. And now, it was too late. They'd won. CommTECH had won. And all her pathetic little rebellions were for nothing. Kane Duggan was right. There was no one to stop him, or CommTECH, from doing exactly what they wanted to do.

"Pull over there." Her captor pointed at a generic cube of a building in an area that once had been filled with Spanish era houses. Now it was the staging post for a vast mining effort. They were raping the country under the noses of the watching world and getting away with it.

Kane's eyes were flat and dull, his mouth a cruel line. "I've got a nice cell waiting for you and lover boy. It's going to be entertaining to watch what you do with the few hours you have left. And then, when you're gone, I'll get rid of the infamous Striker. The Territory's most famous smuggler. The man who can do anything, go anywhere—for a price." He inclined his head. "But he couldn't save you, could he? He couldn't do that. I wonder what you paid him." He gave her a slow considering look. "Did you promise him information or access to your body?"

She couldn't stop the flush that hit her cheeks as she snatched her gaze from the monster.

Kane's laugh was chilling as the car drew to a halt. "Tell me this, Ms. Jones—do you think he'll mourn when you die?" He cocked an eyebrow. "Do you think anyone will mourn?"

She couldn't hold his eyes and looked away. No. She didn't think anyone would mourn her. Mainly, she thought they would feel relief that she was gone. Striker's team as much as anyone else, because of all the trouble she'd brought down on their heads.

That would be her epitaph—Friday Jones, thankfully gone.

"Get them out," Kane snapped. "Take them to the holding

room. There are plenty of cameras in there. I think I'll record your last hours together for my boss to watch later."

She tried to stop the shudder his words provoked but didn't succeed, which seemed to delight him further. The two men sitting behind her climbed out and walked around to the rear of the car. The man beside her grabbed her arm, pulling her from the vehicle.

She looked over to find the other two men had retrieved Striker from the boot. His body was limp, still paralyzed from being stunned. His hands were tied behind his back, his head hung down, and his ankles were crossed and secured. He was helpless.

Or was he?

His shoulders flexed. His hands clenched. Friday sucked in a breath. He was faking his weakened state. Why didn't anyone notice? She glanced around as she was led from the car. Nobody was watching him, that was why. Nobody but her. And even then, she didn't believe her eyes when she saw him move.

One second, he hung limply in his captors' hold, the next he had one of their guns in his hand. Three shots rang out in quick succession. The two men beside him collapsed. It wasn't until he grabbed her hand, pulling her with him as he ran, that she realized the man who'd held her was dead, too.

"Stop them!" Kane roared as they ducked between two buildings.

Blasts hit the wall above her head. A man ran at them. Striker fired, and the guy hit the ground. More blasts shook the building beside them. There were running footsteps. Shouted orders.

They headed to the rear of another small building, hitting the door at a run. It crashed open, and he wedged it shut behind them. They were in a vast storage unit. There was drilling   equipment,   generators,   diggers,   scanners—

everything the well-equipped pillager would need to plunder a country of its resources.

Striker tugged her down behind a large piece of machinery. "We need to get out of here. We need a car, something that can get us to the airport."

It physically hurt to look into his eye. She felt the pain right to the very center of her being. To her soul. This amazing man was still trying to save her when he should have left her behind and saved himself.

She placed her hand on his cheek. "You need to leave me here. It's too late to get to the airport. It's too late for me. You need to save yourself."

He shook his head, furiously. "No. Don' even say that to me. I'm takin' you to New York. We're gonna get that antidote."

"Striker, honey." Tears stung her eyes. "It's only twelve hours until the poison kicks in. We won't get to New York in time."

"We will." He grasped her shoulder with one hand. The other held the gun he'd stolen from his captor. "I worked it out. We only need nine hours. There's still time."

"We're in the middle of CommTECH's illegal mining operation. The sky is filled with a holomatrix. That means they can project whatever image they want up to the satellites, at the same time as watching every square inch of the land beneath it. They already know where we are. We can't hide. We can't run. Our only hope is that I surrender and distract them enough for you to slip out of here."

"Listen to yourself! You're tellin' me to leave you. Do you hear that? How can you tell me to do that?"

"This was just a job. You did your job. I'm here in La Paz. It's time for you to go."

"This wasn't a job, and you know it." His unpatched eye flashed with fury, as the muscles in his jaw visibly throbbed. "Deny it. I dare you. This wasn't just a job."

"It was." The words made her nauseous, but he had to believe her. He had to save himself.

Anger leeched from his face. "If it was just a job, bébé, why are you crying?" He cupped her cheek and swiped away the tears with his thumb. Tears she hadn't even realized she'd shed.

She bit her bottom lip to stop from blurting out exactly what he was to her. Words wouldn't change anything. Their situation was hopeless. Completely and utterly hopeless.

"Please don't die with me," she whispered.

"Nobody's gonna die."

Saying the words wouldn't make them true. But she knew there were some things you couldn't fight. Like destiny. Like love. And she very much feared that the amazing man in front of her loved her just as much as she loved him. Which meant, he wouldn't leave her, even to save himself. Stubborn, hard-headed, amazing man.

Their heads snapped to the door as they heard someone try the handle.

"Locked," a voice shouted.

"They definitely came this way. Try it again."

He leaned in to whisper. "Follow me."

Quickly, and as silently as possible, they made their way across the room to a door in the corner. She'd hoped it would take them outside, but it held a staircase down into the basement.

"We can't go down." He closed the door. "We don't know what's down there and we can't risk getting trapped underground. There—" He started jogging. "A window."

"Look." She tugged at his hand and pointed to the wall. There was a map of the complex with evacuation points highlighted.

"Perfect." He studied the diagram. "If we head this way, we should see the main gate. We can hotwire a car to take us to the airport."

If they got through the gate. "You're forgetting the guards, and the surveillance, and the barricades…"

"I ain't forgetting anything. I just haven't figured that part of the plan yet." He inched the window open and peeked out. "We're clear."

Before she could protest, he lifted her up and over the ledge, climbing out after her. She stood, still and silent, pressed against the wall, listening for trouble, hoping it would pass them by.

He put his lips to her ear. "That way."

Together, keeping low, they ran in the direction of the main gate. The very well-guarded main gate. At this rate, Striker was going to get himself killed. She didn't care about herself. She was already dead. They ducked into an alcove that housed an emergency exit, one that could only be opened from inside the building.

"You need to listen to me," she hissed at him. "You need to leave me here. You have more chance of getting out by yourself."

One second, he was scanning their surroundings; the next, he had her body pressed back against the cool metal door. "Stop. Sayin'. That." His words were barely whispered and still managed to convey his anger. And he was furious. With her. Every tense muscle in his body screamed it.

But she wasn't afraid of him. She was more afraid *for* him. Before she could argue, before she could explain why he was being completely illogical, he covered her mouth with his. The kiss was equal parts fury and passion.

"No more talking about me leaving you." A whispered order. "Let's go."

It was impossible to talk sense into him. He was determined to stay with her until the bitter end, holding out foolish hope that he could somehow change destiny. She wished she could spare him the pain of finding out he couldn't. Wished she could save him from Kane and from himself. Wished…

She shook her head. With hours left to live, there was no point wasting precious time wishing.

———

Striker was closer to panic than he'd ever been in his life. Everything Friday said was true. The odds were hopelessly stacked against them. They were outgunned. Outnumbered. Outplayed. And stuck in the middle of enemy territory.

Basically, they were screwed.

But he couldn't let her go. He wouldn't stop fighting. Not ever. Not while there was even the slimmest chance he could save his woman.

Mine, the snake reminded him.

Ours, he answered, because there was no getting around it. From the first moment he'd set eyes on her and felt that strange pull toward her, he'd known in his soul that she was his. And he couldn't, wouldn't, let her go. Not while there was still a chance to fight.

But there was no denying the odds were against them. Guards were scrambling around, looking for them. Traffic into the mine had picked up as workers arrived to start their day. There were too many people around, and the sun was climbing higher every minute. They couldn't hide for long. Someone would eventually spot them.

He tried to ignore the loud ticking clock inside his head. Reminding him that every second took him one step closer to losing Friday. He had to find a way out of the compound. And he had to do it fast. They didn't have the fire power to blast their way past the gate, and his only weapon was the gun he'd taken from his captor. Their only option was to sneak out.

As he looked for a way out, one of the Bolivian workers

drove into the compound, parked her car within feet of them, and headed into the nearest building, leaving the vehicle there for them to take.

"We're going to that car. Crouch down. Run fast. When you get there, keep low beside it while I crawl underneath and hotwire it. Got it?"

She nodded and gave his hand a squeeze. Her face was far too pale. The dark circles under her eyes were grotesque purple bruises, marring her perfect skin. She looked fragile, and he felt panicked at the sight. If he lived forever, he'd never forget how panic tasted. It was bitter, and the taste lingered. He needed to get her out of Bolivia. He needed to get her to New York, even if it meant hijacking a jet to take them there. He couldn't watch her fade away in front of him. He just couldn't.

He forced his eyes from hers to scan the area. There were a few windows overlooking the parking area, some people standing by the nearest building—talking with their backs to the carpark. There was no sign of Kane or his henchmen. It was as good as it was going to get.

"Now!"

Together, they ran for the car. Crouching beside it, out of the sight of the people standing around talking, Striker pressed his gun into her hand.

"Cover us while I hotwire this thing."

With her back to the car, she aimed, watching for trouble. With one last look around, Striker slid on his back under the vehicle and rewired the damn thing. It took barely seconds, but he felt each one of them as though it was a year.

As soon as it was done, he shimmied out from under the car and came to his feet.

Friday wasn't where he'd left her.

His head shot up. And his heart stopped.

Kane Duggan stood behind Striker's woman, his hand wrapped around her throat and a gun at her temple.

CHAPTER 34

"You there?" Hunter's voice cut through the darkness Mace felt smothering him.

"I'm here. What's the news?" He leaned into the comm unit as Sandi did the same in her seat opposite him.

"We have a signal from his tracking device."

"Where are they?" He'd been hoping for this. Praying for a place to start in their hunt for Striker.

"La Paz." Hunter paused. "This is weird though. The tracker is giving me the coordinates. But according to the map, the boss is literally sitting inside a two-foot-thick wall."

"How is that possible?" Sandi leaned farther forward.

"I don't know. But I'm looking at satellite imagery, and the spot where the tracker is located is smack-bang in the middle of a solid stone wall built about six hundred years ago."

"Maybe there's a secret passage within the wall?" Sandi looked as confused as Mace felt.

"The wall's only two feet thick," he reminded her. "Any passage that fit in a space that size wouldn't accommodate Striker." He didn't mention Friday, because he already considered her gone. He was surprised at how much that thought bothered him. Seemed the little scientist had won him over after all—mostly.

"Is the signal stationary?" Sandi asked.

He looked over at her. "You thinking maybe a rat or something small has the tracker?"

"It's possible."

"No," Hunter said. "It isn't. The signal's moving back and forth over the same ten feet. It looks like he's pacing. And, according to the satellite imagery, he's doing it through a water tank and an Incan wall. Unless our boy's genetics mean he can dematerialize and walk through solid objects, the satellite feed is off."

"Explain," Mace barked.

Hunter let out a sigh. "This satellite imagery is nothing like the stuff we were trained on. You could literally count hairs on heads using this system, it's that detailed. And accurate. That's why this doesn't make any sense. According to this, the boss is walking through walls."

"Maybe it's the tracker that's off," Sandi said. "Could it be giving out a faulty signal?"

"It's state of the art and was checked before he left on this trip. That tracker is in perfect working condition." Hunter sounded worried.

"What about a laser blast, would that affect the tracker?" Mace asked.

"Doofus." His sister leaned forward and smacked him on the head. "If the belt was hit by a laser, the thing would be completely fried."

He rubbed his head as she glared at her. As usual, she wasn't intimidated. "What about another electrical current, would that affect the tracker? Or maybe cause signal interference?"

"I don't see how," Hunter said. "Those things are pretty indestructible."

It didn't make sense. Unless… "This is a long shot, but what if the satellite is wrong?"

There was silence, then Hunter spoke. "You think someone is faking out the satellite to hide something there?"

"Is that possible?"

"I guess so. I'm the second-string tech guy. If Zane were here, he'd know for sure."

"Can we contact Zane and ask him?" Their teammate was on a sensitive job and had gone radio-silent.

"No. He's still dark."

Mace ran a hand through his hair. "Then I think we have to assume the satellite is off and there's something fishy going on in La Paz. We go in with extreme caution because we sure as hell don't know what we're heading into. What's the rest of the team's ETA?"

"They're three hours out," Hunter said.

"We'll meet up at Oruro airport. They bringing weapons?"

"Yeah."

"Lots of weapons?" Sandi amended.

"Yeah," Hunter said with long suffering.

"You arranged a helicopter to take us straight to La Paz?" Mace added.

"Do I look like an amateur?" Now Hunter was just getting pissy.

A chopper would cut down their time travel significantly. The only reason Striker hadn't taken one was because it attracted attention. Mace didn't care about that. All he cared about was bringing his friend home. "Dig around, see what you can find on La Paz. Anything that can give us a better idea of what we're walking into."

"Got it." With that Hunter cut the connection, obviously done with them.

Mace leaned back in his chair. "I've got a bad feeling about this."

"The kind of feeling you didn't have before you woke up changed?"

"Yeah."

"Then we definitely go in cautious." She paused. "And armed to the teeth."

He might hate their new world and the genetic crap that came with it, but it had its perks. One of them was the strange sixth sense his animal had given him. It hadn't steered him wrong yet. And that sixth sense told him Striker was in trouble up to his neck.

The sooner they got to La Paz, the better.

CHAPTER 35

They'd been thrown into a holding cell, which was nothing more than a bare concrete room with one high, narrow, heavily barred window and a thick steel door. There was a toilet and sink in the corner, a mattress and blankets on the floor. Nothing else.

Well, except for the four cameras taking up space in each corner of the room. They were placed high up against the ceiling, protected behind shatterproof glass, ensuring they couldn't be tampered with. There wasn't one inch of the cell that wasn't covered by surveillance. Striker had checked. He'd been pacing the cell, looking for weaknesses since the minute they'd been thrown into it. He glanced at his watch, for the millionth time. Nine and a half hours until Friday's deadline. They could still make it to New York. If he could just get them out of this cell.

Friday sat on the mattress, her knees pulled up tight to her chest, her arms wrapped around them. It didn't take a genius to see she was hugging herself. She didn't move or speak. She just sat there, watching him pace. The fight had gone right out of her. Seeing her like that was a knife to his heart.

He tore his eyes from her and examined every inch of the

room, one more time, paying particular attention to the door. There was no way out. At least none that he could see. All the while his diamondback kept sending him images of them running free. It didn't help.

I'm trying! he snapped at his other half.

There had to be a way out of the room. He just had to try harder to find it.

"It's pointless," Friday said softly. "Even if you find a way out, it will be too late."

"No." He refused to believe it. Refused to give in.

There was no handle on the inside of the door. No lock, either. Which meant nothing to pick. Another dead end.

"Come talk to me. Take my mind off things." It was a gentle plea that made him want to punch and scream with frustration. He had to get her out of there!

"I'm a bit busy here." He examined the ceiling. It was flat, solid concrete, with one strip light wired into it. They were trapped in a concrete box. Floor. Walls. Ceiling. All solid concrete. The only gap was the solitary window high on the wall. The one that was barred, and too narrow for them to get through even if it wasn't.

"Honey, come sit with me."

"No!" The roar echoed off the walls. "No! We need to get out of here." He looked at his watch. Nine hours. It was still possible. It had to be.

She rose from the mattress and came to stand behind him. He felt her palms on his back and jerked forward, everything within him exploding. There was nothing to hit out at except the door, and he gladly whaled on it with his bare knuckles. He struck it hard. Again, and again, and again, until blood soaked his fists. He didn't feel any pain. The rage inside was so loud it drowned out everything else.

Soft fingers gripped his forearm, gentle in their touch. He reeled back, opening his mouth to roar, but nothing came out.

Friday stood beside him, her blue eyes wide with distress, tears streaming down her cheeks.

"Fuck!" he huffed. His hand hooked the back of her neck, and he pulled her against his body. "Fuck," he whispered.

She trembled against him as she cried, not once making a sound. It humbled him like nothing else could have done, and the rage seeped away, only to be replaced with agonizing fear.

"I'm sorry, bébé. I'm sorry." He kissed her hair and cooed nonsense to her, trying to soothe something that couldn't be soothed.

They stood like that for what seemed like forever, swaying in place as Striker held her tight, hoping his hold alone would be strong enough to keep her with him. Against all odds. Forever.

As Friday's silent sobs eased, he cupped her cheek and angled her face up to him. "I'm sorry, bébé." He smoothed away the tears.

She pulled her bottom lip between her teeth, and the look she gave him would have brought him to his knees if she hadn't been holding him up. Her tears weren't for herself. They were for him. She was crying for him. Fuck, but she tore him up inside.

He opened his mouth, intent on promising that he'd get her out of there. That he'd do something to make things right. That he would fight with his last breath to save her.

Trembling fingers pressed against his lips as one lone tear slid down her already stained cheeks. "It's over," she whispered. "I know you don't want it to be. I don't, either. But even if a miracle happens and we get out of here, we won't make it to the antidote in time."

"No." He shook his head. His stomach tightened. "No. It's still possible."

"I want..." She took a shuddering breath that went straight to his soul. "I want to spend these last few hours with you. Concentrating on you. I want to feel every single minute I have left. With. You."

"No, bébé, it isn't the end." He couldn't accept it. He wouldn't. His throat was tight, the ache making it hard to get the words out. His eyes stung and he blinked furiously. "No, bébé."

"Please." There was no guile in her expression, only the bare honesty of raw emotion. "Please give me this."

It hurt to swallow. Striker looked up at the ceiling, staring at the blank gray concrete until he felt he could speak again. When he looked back down at her, he saw the most beautiful woman alive. She was so fucking brave. There was no hatred in her. No resentment. No anger.

He didn't deserve a woman like Friday.

But if this was all he had, he'd take it.

Take it and beg for more.

"I let you down." He could barely get the words out. It was a first. He didn't fail. Never. And in this, the most important job of his life, he'd failed spectacularly. He'd failed her. He'd failed them.

"No." Her hands clasped his face. Her expression earnest. "Is that what you think? You silly man. You did exactly what I hired you to do. You brought me to La Paz before the deadline."

"I promised I'd save you." It was a confession. All he had left was his honor, and now that was gone, too.

"This isn't your fault. None of it. If anyone's to blame, it's me. I knew what I was doing when I took the poison and ran. I knew the risk, and that the chances of survival were slim. There had to have been another way to stop Enforcement from tracking me through my implants, but I didn't look for one. I did it anyway." She stroked his face, from the eyepatch to his lips. "Do you know what? I wouldn't change a thing. I would do it all again just to have these last four days with you."

He shook his head as his eye closed. "You can't say that. Not after everything that's happened. Everything you've been through. Not after it led to this."

When he opened his eye again, she was smiling. Her eyes were red and glistening, her cheeks blotchy with tears, and yet she was smiling. "I spent four days with a man who makes me feel completely alive." She took a shaky breath. "I've never lived. I've only existed. Hoping that, somehow, tomorrow would be different. I never experienced real joy, or fear, or exhilaration, or passion, or ecstasy, or genuine laughter. Not until I met you. You gave all of that to me. You gave me four days of a full life. You let me taste freedom. That's all I ever wanted. And you gave that to me."

She swallowed hard, steeling herself, gathering her courage when there was no need. Didn't she know by now that he was her safe place? She didn't need courage to do or say anything to him. He wouldn't hurt her. Never her.

She looked up at him through those long, black lashes that were a stark contrast to her pale, pale skin. "I never knew love until I met you."

She slayed him. Completely and utterly devastated him with her courage and honesty. With her fearless emotion. All directed at him. All for him.

With an animalistic growl that shocked him, he clasped the back of her head and slammed his mouth down onto hers. There was no resistance. She willingly gave everything he demanded. He kissed her with every word he couldn't say. He kissed her with every emotion he didn't know how to express. He kissed her with a desperate, furious longing for a future that was fast slipping away. He gave it all to her in his kiss.

Fight. His rattlesnake demanded. *Fight. Save mine. Save Friday.*

He couldn't answer. Couldn't even think about what was coming. Couldn't get the words out that told his other half it was too late. The words cut like knives, ripping his soul to shreds.

The diamondback showed him a string of images where he slunk out of the window and came back into the building to open the door from the other side, and Striker stiffened. His head snapped up, ripping his lips from Friday. He examined the barred window. The glass was open to let air circulate. His diamondback could get outside without any problems, but would he be able to open the door? His reply was an image of the rattler biting Striker for doubting him.

Okay. We'll try it. It wasn't like he had any other options. *But I need to set up some cover first, otherwise your escape is gonna be on camera.*

He leaned in to whisper against Friday's ear. "The diamondback wants to try sneaking out and opening the door for us."

She started to shake her head, and he stopped her. He knew what she was going to say—that it was pointless to try to escape. And maybe, in a secret part of him that he couldn't acknowledge, he knew it, too. But his diamondback was desperate to do something, and that Striker could understand because he felt the same way.

"Let him try to get you out of here. Let us both try to give you somewhere else..." He couldn't say the words. He couldn't. He could barely even think about the fact he was trying to give her somewhere better, nicer, to die. Damn it to hell. He blinked to clear his stinging eyes. The muscles in his throat were tight and raw.

"Okay," she whispered. "Okay, Striker."

His fingers tightened in her hair. He couldn't let her call him that. Not now. He leaned close to whisper against her ear. "Luke. My name is Luke Boudreaux."

She sucked in a breath. "It's beautiful."

He stared into her sky-blue eyes. The color of freedom. "It's yours. Only the team know it. I'm giving it to you."

He may as well have given her diamonds from the look of wonder on her face.

He cleared his throat and turned toward the mattress. "I need the bedding. Can you help me?"

"Of course." She gathered the blankets as he dragged the mattress over to the area under the window, beside the sink. Taking a blanket, he tied one corner to a bar on the window farthest away from the sink. He then secured the opposite corner to the sink. He stood the mattress on its side and wedged it against the sink so that it stood out at an angle from the wall. He then draped the remainder of the blanket over the edge of the mattress and stepped back to consider his work.

With the mattress making a wall and the blanket forming a lopsided roof, they had a space where they could sit out of sight of the cameras. More importantly, he had a section of window that was hidden by the blanket—a secure escape route for his rattler. Taking the last two blankets and the pillow, he made a pallet on the floor inside the little hut.

"Come on." He held out a hand. "We can have some privacy in here."

Her fingers were small and fragile in his. "Kane will probably knock it down."

Since there was no lock or handle on the door that could be jammed to stop someone coming in, and nothing in the room to use as a barricade, there wasn't much he could do to stop Kane. But at least their privacy would give them the time needed to set the diamondback free.

"We'll worry about that later." He helped her into the shelter.

Once he'd settled her on the pillow, with her back to the wall, he pulled down the rest of the blanket. Now they were completely hidden from the cameras.

"They can't see us right now, but they can still record sound. Don't say anything important."

She nodded. Without hesitating, he sat back on his heels, widened his arms, and called to his rattler. He felt that familiar pulling sensation inside his body before there was a burst of pain and the snake emerged.

Get going, he ordered.

Although the damn reptile knew the situation was urgent, he still took time to rub up against Friday before he headed up to the window. They watched it disappear, a silent and deadly phantom, completely hidden by his makeshift tent.

Friday reached out and lifted his hand, examining his torn and bruised knuckles. "We need to see to these. At the very least, we should wash the scrapes."

He studied his beaten hands. "They don't hurt."

She gave him a cute little frown. "I'll dampen a tissue and wipe them for you."

"No, I'll wash them." He didn't want her moving around, not when she looked this close to exhaustion.

He crawled out of their tent and washed his hands in icy water, drying them off on his jeans. Her eyes were closed when he crawled back into the tent. He sat beside her and pulled her to him, wrapping his arm tight around her. When her cheek rested over his heart, he swore he heard it miss a beat. This was where she belonged. In his arms.

"Tell me about your life, from before, when you were a child." Her tone was sweet, soft, intimate.

He rested his head back against the cool wall with the warmth of Friday's soft curves pressing against his side. He could feel her heartbeat against his thumb as he caressed her neck. It was strong. Vital. Alive. He couldn't think about the time when that would change.

He cleared his throat and gave her what she wanted. The only thing he was able to give her. He gave himself. "I grew up in a house on the bayou. There was a big old gator that slept in a hole at the bottom of our yard, by the water. Mon

Père wanted to shoot the thing, but Maman told him the gator had as much right to be there as we did…"

As he whispered, she relaxed into him. He told her all about his younger sister, who tormented him night and day, but needed a keeper, seeing as she had the worst taste in boyfriends. Not that she ever got far enough with any of them to get hurt. Striker chased them away long before it could happen. He told her about his Maman's famous cakes and how she had a special one for every occasion. It had been his job to deliver them—a spice cake for good news, an angel cake for births, a strawberry torte for weddings, a fruitcake for funerals.

He told her about apple pie Sundays during the season, after he and his sister had collected the fruit from the neighbors' trees. And how, when they were feeling particularly wicked, they would throw the bad apples at that old gator, stirring him up enough to make him mad. Those were the days his Père would take a switch to his behind for being dumb. Then he'd feel bad about it and take him fishing out in his boat, with his Maman shaking her head because her husband was soft.

He didn't know how long he talked, remembering a life long gone, but he stopped when he heard Friday's breathing deepen and knew she was asleep. He ran a hand over her hair. The golden silk comforted him, as did the beat of her heart against his chest.

"You can't die on me, mon amour," he whispered.

Four days he'd known her, but it felt like she'd been wrapped around his heart for an eternity. There was no way to imagine the rest of his life without her. It just wasn't possible.

She was everything he didn't know he'd been looking for. Her insatiable curiosity and her astounding bravery. Her kindness in giving everything she had to the people whose house they'd broken into. Her self-sacrifice when she'd thrown herself into the mist to save him. Her unexpected reactions and big brain that derailed everything else.

He chuckled at the memory of her wanting to turn his cock chocolate flavored, and his arms tightened around her. The world would lose something wonderful if it lost Friday Jones. He would lose something wonderful. Something he knew he would never be able to replace.

Still holding her tight, he twisted his wrist to look at his watch. Six and a half hours. In desperation, he reached out to his snake.

You have to do something. We need to get out of here. If nothing else, he could at least give her daylight and sunshine. He clenched his jaw tight enough to ache. *Hurry. For Friday.*

And then he rocked his woman as she slept.

CHAPTER 36

THE WESTERN DIAMONDBACK FELT COLD AS IT MOVED STEALTHILY through the corridors of the building. He was used to being warm. His other half provided that for him—a nice consistent temperature where the rattler could doze all he liked.

The diamondback wasn't sure how he'd come to be part of the man. He remembered a time when he was separate. But he had to admit, he liked this new existence better. He knew things now that he'd never known before. And he had someone to talk to. He'd never felt alone, not before his human half came along, but it was better being part of a pair. And now they had Friday. They were a family. He'd known she was the right person for them as soon as she appeared. Mate. That's what she was. The one person who could complete both man and snake. She was special.

She was theirs.

And he wasn't going to let anything happen to her.

The rattlesnake wasn't stupid. What the man knew, he knew, too—in as much as he could understand it. But even if the man hadn't told him Friday was sick, the rattlesnake would have known. He could smell it on her. Taste it on the air around her. The snake knew toxins. It knew she had one inside of her. One that didn't belong there. One that was sleeping, waiting to take her from the rattler and the man.

He wasn't going to let that happen.

That was why he was sneaking through the corridors looking for the man who'd hurt Friday. He had to save her. And to do that. He had to eliminate the threat. He had to kill the man.

He'd told his human that he was going to open the door. That he would get them out of the room. But he'd heard the human's thoughts, the ones he didn't even acknowledge to himself, let alone say out loud. The human knew that the door needed a special key. A biological key. And there was no way the rattler could get it. The human had been lying to himself. Clinging to hope that wasn't there.

The diamondback knew better.

The rattler couldn't free them, but he could eliminate the threat. And then he would go back to the room and help his human take care of their mate.

Because Friday belonged to both of them.

CHAPTER 37

Kane Duggan was amused by the nest the smuggler had built for himself and his woman. Amused enough to allow his captives the illusion of privacy, for the time being. It was hours until the poison activated and Friday Jones expired. According to the records at the Houston facility, she'd accessed the controlled substance cabinet at six p.m. five days earlier. That meant she'd taken the poison close to the same time. Which gave her less than six hours to live.

Kane smiled at the monitors showing the couple's cell. In an hour or so, he'd send a team to rip apart their little sanctuary. And then he'd record every last emotional minute for Miriam. He knew exactly how much she'd appreciate his efforts.

Satisfied with his plan, he turned his back on the monitors, but he could still hear his prisoners whisper. Kane couldn't quite make out the words, but from what he did manage to hear, they were talking about Striker's family.

Not a topic that interested Kane. Family was nothing more than sentimental weakness. It was why he'd rid himself of his as soon as been able. He'd learned early that a man with his skills made enemies easily, and it was best not to have anything those enemies could use as leverage. Not that his useless parents would have been much in the way of leverage, but it had been wise to eliminate the possibility—in the most permanent way possible.

Of course, he'd made sure that the right people heard about what he'd done to his family. In the end, his useless parents had served a purpose—they'd furthered his reputation as a man to be feared. Mm, maybe he was sentimental after all, because listening to Striker talk about his childhood had brought back the happiest memory he had from his youth—watching the life drain from his parents.

He tapped the console in front of him and connected with CommTECH's head office. He hated the Coalition Countries. Hated that his implants were useless outside the Territories. He wanted to go back to New York, where his will was carried out with the merest thought. After a moment's delay, Miriam's face appeared on the screen covering the wall.

"Is she dead?"

Kane smiled. Miriam Shepherd always got straight to the point. It was one of the things he loved about her, in as much as he could love anyone.

"Nearly. They're locked in a monitored cell."

Her gaze sharpened, his meaning at once clear. "Are you recording it?"

"Of course."

"No chance of escape?"

"None."

"I knew you wouldn't let me down." She practically purred the words, and not for the first time, he wished he found her even remotely attractive. He considered Miriam to be his soulmate, but she didn't arouse him sexually. His needs lay in other directions.

"When can I expect your return?"

"Tomorrow. I need to clean up this mess. After that, I'll

meet with the mine management, to ensure ladmium production is on track. Then, I'll be back."

"I look forward to it." The communication ended.

The CommTECH CEO was a piece of work. He'd never met anyone as intelligent or as ruthless. Aligning himself with her, instead of against her, was one of the smartest moves he'd ever made.

He checked the monitors again. There was no movement from inside the little tent. No sound coming from the room. If the bioreadings for the cell hadn't been telling him there were two bodies in the space, he might have assumed they'd escaped. But there was no escape. Not for them.

Settling in at his desk, Kane went through the reports on the mine. It had only been running a year, and already it had supplied half the amount of ladmium they needed for their new data chips—at a fraction of the cost of buying the mineral legitimately. CommTECH would make a fortune from this deal. And not only in the Territories. If Miriam was right and her plans were successful, CommTECH would rule the world.

And Kane would be the new world leader's second-in-command. He liked that title very much. Leading had never appealed to him. He didn't want the attention. No, he liked the ability to slip into the shadows when the need arose.

Two hours later, Kane looked up from the reports to check the monitors, and found no change. Still, it was time to rip away their shelter and lay them bare for the cameras. Since his commlink didn't work in Bolivia, he reached for the comm button on the console to call his security staff.

Only, he never made it.

The attack happened with blinding speed. The first he knew about it was a series of stabbing bites to his leg. He reacted fast, striking out at his attacker. But it was too late. He knew that when he felt the poison moving up his leg. An excruciating burning pain that made his vision blur. He reached for his gun as sweat broke out on his brow. Another bite. This time to his arm. Something moved behind him, crawling across his chair. No, not crawling. Slithering. Nausea assaulted him, and he vomited over his desk.

His fingers turned numb first, and his gun fell to the floor. The pain was blinding. His arms and legs began to swell as he felt another stabbing bite to the back of his neck. Too many bites. Too much venom. Blood rushed through his veins, propelling the poison through his system at the speed of light. His head fell to the desk in front of him with a thud, and he couldn't lift it again.

Antivenin.

He needed antivenin. He let out a sound that was a mixture of laughter and screaming.

He'd blown up the antivenin with the clinic.

He'd killed himself.

His heart surged, and it felt like it might burst. Agony wracked his body. His throat closed tight, trapping his screams. He couldn't breathe. His limbs were swollen to the point where he felt like they would explode. His tongue filled his mouth as he gulped for air and got nothing. He gasped. Desperate. Unable to breathe. Unable to move. With one last shudder, his heart stuttered and stopped.

CHAPTER 38

Striker knew exactly what his diamondback had done. He'd lived through the experience along with the rattler. And he'd taken great satisfaction in seeing justice served. They'd both known, man and snake, that there was no way the reptile could free them from their cell. Striker had sent it out hoping for a miracle—desperate for one. But he would settle for revenge. Knowing that Kane Duggan died in agony was small comfort, but he would take it.

"You should have woken me," Friday complained as she pushed up from where she'd been plastered to his body. "I don't want to sleep my time away."

He suspected she was past having a choice in the matter. When he'd tried to rouse her, she'd grumbled and carried on sleeping. Her system had run out of fight. All it wanted to do was rest. He gently rubbed the blue smudges under her eyes. Her movements had slowed now, as though the slightest thing took the greatest effort.

"What time is it?" she asked.

"You sure you really want to know?" He didn't. He wanted to live in denial. Happy in a world where Friday had all the time she deserved.

She considered his question before nodding.

He glanced at his watch, hating the timepiece for what it had to tell him. "It's almost three."

She tried to hide a wince, but he saw it. "I took the poison just after six."

They sat there, in their little makeshift tent, looking at each other, neither of them wanting to acknowledge out loud that there were only three hours left. There was no lying to themselves now. No avoiding the fact that there wasn't a place on earth they could get to fast enough to save her. And that was if they even managed to get free of CommTECH.

She cleared her throat. "I need to use the toilet. Can you put your fingers in your ears and promise not to listen?"

He burst out laughing, something he could have sworn would be impossible given the circumstances. He laced his fingers through hers. "The room is full of cameras and sound equipment." There would be no privacy for her, no matter what he did.

Her cheeks turned the cutest shade of red. "I know. But I can pretend they aren't there. I know you're here. Will you do it for me?"

"Don't you know I'd do anything for you?"

She blinked hard, her eyes filling before she looked away. "Okay, then. Operation Toilet commencing." The humor in her voice was forced.

His brave, beautiful woman.

He brought her hand to his mouth and kissed it before she scrambled over him and out of their tent. Feeling foolish, he put his fingers in his ears because he'd told her he would. As he sat there, he felt his diamondback return. The snake was satisfied and strangely determined. It slid to the floor beside him.

The threat is gone, it declared.

I know.

There was nothing more to say. The threat of Kane might

be gone, but they were still locked in a cell, watching Friday waste to nothing. The blanket shifted, and she crawled back into their tiny cocoon. With a smile, Striker made a production of taking his fingers out of his ears. Her laugh delighted him. And then her eyes fell on the rattler and lit right up.

"Oh, you're back!" She scooped up the deadly snake and cuddled it to her, as though it were a kitten.

He shook his head. He couldn't imagine any other woman on the planet accepting him and his other half the way she did. Not once had she made him feel like a freak. It was a gift he hadn't expected to receive, and one he could never give up willingly.

"Who's a pretty boy?" she crooned to the rattler, and the damn reptile preened.

"You're spoiling that poor excuse for a handbag."

She shot him a querulous look. "Don't call him that." Her brows puckered, and a tiny line appeared above her nose. "Does he have a name?"

"Why the hell would I name him?" Sometimes women were a mystery.

"Because you can't keep calling him 'the handbag.' He needs a name. Don't you, boy?"

Yes, the suck-up hissed in his mind. *I like her better than you.*

He snorted a laugh. Of course it did. He didn't baby the damn thing.

"How about Sid?" she said.

"As in Sid Vicious?"

"I don't know who that is. I just like Sid."

"No."

"Okay, what about Sheldon?"

"What? No!"

"Slinky?"

He couldn't help his laugh. "Are you gonna work your way through all the names you know that start with S?"

"Maybe." She blushed again and stole his breath. She was so beautiful. He could look at her forever. A sharp pain made his heart clench. They didn't have forever. He forced the thought from his head.

"Sparkles?" Her eyes were alight with amusement.

She was playing with him. The woman who'd grown up without play was teasing him. His chest tightened at the thought.

I like Sparkles, the reptile said as it rubbed its head against her cheek.

"I'm not calling my other half Sparkles. Damn it, woman. I might as well change my name to Fairy, so we match. He's a deadly predator. He needs a strong, manly name."

She petted the diamondback while she thought about it and Striker felt her touch down the length of his back, where the reptile normally sat.

"Satan?" she said. "He took the form of a snake in the Garden of Eden."

No relation, his diamondback said.

"I'm not calling the snake Satan."

"It's strong. Manly. Strikes fear into people."

"No."

"You know," she considered him. "I didn't know you were this contrary. It's a character flaw."

"I'm okay with that."

"Okay, Mr. Difficult, what about Sam? He looks like a Sam."

He looked like a damn snake, that's what he looked like. "I can live with Sam."

I like it, the reptile practically purred.

"He says he likes the name."

With clear delight, she stroked the rattler's head. "Do you, honey? I'm so pleased. You are such a beautiful boy. Aren't you, Sam?"

Striker wanted to vomit as the rattler crowed about how much she adored him.

"You never pet me like that." Yeah, he'd turned into a jealous four-year-old.

She fought a smile. "Are you feeling neglected?"

"Yeah." Damn it. He really was. He wanted her close, not fawning over a bad-tempered diamondback.

"Well, we can't have that, can we?" She kissed the reptile's head. "Go on back to Striker now."

And damned if the reptile didn't do exactly as he was told.

You are such a suck-up, he told it.

You're jealous because she likes me better.

He felt that familiar sharp burst of pain as his body merged with the reptile. *Damn straight I'm jealous.*

Friday crawled the short distance between them to kneel beside his hip, her fingers tracing down his cheek. "You are such a beautiful man."

"Only you would call me that."

"Will you take off your eyepatch for me? I want to see all of you. I love your unusual eyes."

He didn't hesitate, removing the patch and placing it in the pocket of his jeans for safekeeping.

"Thank you, Luke," she whispered.

He sucked in a breath at the sound of his name on her lips. It seemed different coming from her. More special, somehow.

"Thank you for everything." She cupped his cheeks and leaned into him, pressing a sweet, gentle kiss to his lips.

Her words unleashed the helpless rage inside of him. His hands went to her hips, and he held on tight. She couldn't leave him. She was his, damn it!

"Don't," she whispered against his lips. "There's time for

anger and grief after. This time, the time I have left, it's for us."

He rested his forehead against hers. "You're killin' me, bébé."

Each word was a blow. A nail to his heart. A brutal wound from which he would never recover. Never. He'd keep walking and talking after she was gone, but he wouldn't live. He knew that. His life was wrapped up in hers, and a large part of him would cease to exist when she did.

"Do you think," she hesitated, her voice a whisper. "Do you think there's anything there after you die?"

It took a minute to answer. To make his voice work. "My Maman believed in Jesus. She said if you believe in him, you get to hang out in heaven forever. She wasn't afraid to die. She said she'd get to live in Paradise." His heart squeezed at the thought of his mother. He hoped she was right. He hoped she'd been living it up somewhere wonderful these past eighty years.

"I like that. I never did believe in anything. But I like that. I don't really know anything about Jesus, but maybe he wouldn't mind letting me in, too. I'm sure if I knew him, I'd believe. And if I get to carry on after this life, in heaven, then maybe I'd meet your Maman there."

"You'd love her." His voice was tight, and it hurt so damn much to use it.

"I already love her son." His heart stopped entirely at her softly-spoken words. She leaned back to look into his eyes. "It's true, Luke Boudreaux. I really do love you. You slammed right into my heart the moment I met you, and you've been making yourself at home there ever since. I've never loved anyone before. Not one person. I always thought that, maybe, it wasn't because I didn't have anybody to love, but because I wasn't capable of loving. I was wrong. I've been storing up my love all these years, keeping it safe, because it was meant for you. Only you."

"Friday," he croaked the word. His eyes stung. His fingers flexed on her hips. His throat ached. "Bébé."

"These past four days. They've been a gift for me. More precious than you can ever know. I've tasted freedom and learned how to love. All because of you. I wouldn't take a minute back. Not one minute."

He couldn't speak. It was impossible because he knew if he did manage to get a word out, it would be to beg her to stay with him, something neither of them could make happen.

"Make love to me, Luke. One last time. Please."

She didn't have to ask. He was hers as much as she was his. And he would have told her so if any of the words in his head would make it out of his mouth. But they wouldn't leave his lips. It would make it all too real. So, instead of words, he pressed his mouth to hers and enfolded her in his arms.

His kiss was reverent. He needed her to know how precious she was to him. That he needed her. Wanted her. Loved her. So. Fucking. Much. Too much for words. Too much to let her go. How was he going to go on without her? How was it even possible?

His arms tightened as though trying to hold her to this life. "I wish…" he managed to croak out.

"No." Her fingers touched his lips as she stared deep into his eyes, seeing his soul, knowing all of him. "No wishes. No regrets."

He kissed her again, tasting every corner of her mouth. Memorizing her, the feel of her satin-soft lips, the small sounds of need she made when his tongue danced with hers. He kissed her with everything he had. Giving her all of him. Because he was hers. Only hers.

With a glance to make sure they were still hidden from the cameras and she was protected, he reached for her shirt. This was their time, no one else's. He hated that he'd failed her.

That she was spending the last precious minutes of her life locked up when she'd desperately wanted to be free. She should have been in a palace, in a bed of satin, with the sun shining through the windows onto her golden hair. He felt his body tense at the injustice of it all, and the rage he fought to suppress began to bubble up again.

"Shh," she whispered as she cupped his cheek. "It's just us. That's all that matters."

He forced himself to relax and concentrate on the woman in front of him. He had to make every minute of the present count, instead of being angry at a future he was helpless to change.

"Yeah, bébé, just us."

He helped her wriggle out of her clothes, and she knelt before him, a feast for a starving man. And that's exactly what he'd been before she came along. His eyes trailed down her body, lingering on her soft curves and porcelain skin. She was perfection. And he needed to feel her skin to skin. He reached down, grabbed his shirt, and tugged it off. His pants and boots followed fast. She studied him, watching every tiny movement.

"I love the color of your skin." Her voice was husky with desire.

He knelt facing her, placing his palm on the curve of her stomach. Enjoying the contrast of her moonlit skin against his earthy tones.

"And your muscles." She sounded awestruck as she ran her hands down his chest, tracing each muscle. "They make me want to bite." The confession made her eyes widen, as though she'd surprised herself.

"You can bite all you like. I might even enjoy it."

Her eyes darkened to midnight blue. "Yeah?"

"Oh yeah."

———

Friday didn't want to think about a future she couldn't change. She'd known the chance she took when she'd poisoned herself. What she hadn't known was that a man as wonderful as Luke Boudreaux would come into her life. She'd thought she would die alone, with no one in her life to regret leaving. She'd been wrong. If she could have one wish granted, one miracle, it would be to stay with this man. To live a long and full life in his arms. But wishing was foolish. And miracles were myth.

It was best to deal with reality, rather than unrealistic hope. And reality told her she had just over two hours to spend with Luke Boudreaux. Two hours to touch him. Two hours to love him. She ran her hands up his chest to his shoulders, feeling the firm muscle beneath the smooth, warm skin. He was a living sculpture. A study in perfection that would have been at home in any ancient art collection.

Slowly, keeping her eyes on his, she leaned in and bit his pec, just above the nipple. She felt the tension of the muscle under her teeth and heard him gasp. Strong hands threaded into her hair, holding her to him. Empowered by his reaction, she soothed the bite with her tongue before licking her way to his tiny nipple. Male nipples were such odd things, completely purposeless, yet strangely compelling.

"You're driftin' again." She felt the sound rumble through his chest and into her lips. "You'd better not be planning on making my nipples strawberry flavored."

She couldn't help but smile against his skin. "I like your taste just fine."

His hold tightened in her hair. "You sure? Maybe you should sample some more before you decide."

Delighting in him, she did exactly that. Kissing and licking and biting her way down his stomach to the firm length jutting toward her.

He tugged at her hair again, angling her head to make her

look up at him. "You taste my cock, bébé, and this is gonna be over before it starts."

She arched an eyebrow at him. "And here I thought you had more stamina than that."

"Smart-ass," he grumbled, then groaned as she sucked the head of his shaft into her mouth. She liked the taste, but it could definitely be improved with chocolate. If she'd had more time, she would have played with his genetics. Or, at the very least, bought a bottle of chocolate sauce.

"That's it." His hands were under her arms and hauling her up to kneel facing him. "There's too much thinking goin' on in that head. Time for the expert to take over."

"Expert, huh? That must be one of those levels you were talking about on the jet. Tell me, how am I going to make advanced level if you keep taking over? I need the practice."

The words landed between them like a lead balloon. There would be no practice. Not for her.

"Fuck!" Striker clasped the back of her head and slammed his lips down on hers.

The kiss stole her breath along with her sanity. And then there wasn't any space to think. Only feel.

His arms were around her, holding her tight. The heat from his skin penetrated hers, making her warm where she'd always felt cold. Firm hands brushed over sensitive skin. The scent of musk and earth filled her senses. The taste of passion made her mouth water. He kissed her until her lips felt bruised, and then he lowered her to her back on their makeshift bed. The concrete floor was hard beneath the pallet of blankets, but she didn't care. All she cared about was the man above her.

He moved over her, touching, kissing, tasting, biting, fingers teasing her nipples while he nibbled at her throat. Her body pressed up into his. Her leg hooked over his hip. She felt herself open for him. Felt his hard length against her. Needed him inside her.

She moaned—a begging sound, filled with longing. His teeth grazed her nipple in reply. His other hand massaging her free breast.

"I need you, Striker." She didn't know if she whispered. She was past caring who heard them. All she cared about was wanting him. Needing him.

"Luke. Call me by my name." And then he sucked her nipple hard.

"Luke!" It was a groan. A demand. A plea.

"That's it, bébé. So fucking gorgeous. I could spend hours teasing these beautiful breasts of yours. Hours."

She heard it in his voice. The pain he couldn't hide it. The agony of knowing they didn't have hours. She clasped his head and held him tight against her. Could he feel her heart beat? Did he know it was only for him?

She was panting now, climbing higher with every teasing, torturous touch. "I need…"

"I know what you need, bébé. I bet I could make you come just from playing with your breasts. You're sensitive for me, aren't you, chère?" That low drawl of his would be enough to make her climax. She didn't even need his touch.

"Luke." It was agreement and complaint. He drove her past desperation. She couldn't think. Couldn't concentrate. Couldn't breathe.

His lips moved lower. Her legs opened for him, and her hips arched.

She felt his chuckle as he kissed her inner thigh. "Demanding little kitten. You needing petting, bébé? You gonna purr for me?"

She couldn't answer. Couldn't think. She just wanted. Needed. Desperately. And he didn't make her wait. His intimate kiss was slow and languorous, taking his time as he tasted and teased her.

"Please, please, please, please…" Her fingernails pressed into his shoulders, and she knew she'd left marks. There was no stopping the primal thrill she felt at leaving her mark on the man. She wanted to brand her name on his soul. Mark him for eternity as hers. Only hers.

"Please!"

He rumbled against the little bundle of nerves, making her wail. Fingers slipped inside of her, seeking that secret spot she'd only ever heard about. And then he stroked her as he licked around her clit. She didn't think it was possible to climb higher, but she did. She soared high on the tension of ecstasy, desperate for the snap of release only he could give her, the one that would tip her over and make her free fall.

"You gonna come for me, bébé?"

Answering was an impossibility.

"Yeah, you're gonna explode for me." He sucked her clit hard and everything stopped, snapped, and detonated.

She fell back to earth in amongst a meteor shower. Lights flashed around her as she fell, weightless, through space. It was a timeless falling, and she never wanted it to end. The closer to earth she came, the more she became aware of Striker's weight covering her. His hand on her cheek was a brand. His lips against hers were slow and sensual and delicious. She clasped his waist as she fought to open her eyes. Her eyelids were so heavy, but she didn't want to miss a second of anything at all to do with Luke Boudreaux.

His thick shaft pressed into her as she lifted her hips in welcome.

"You feel good." His voice was a rasp. "Never felt anything this good."

Slowly, deliberately, he entered her fully. She wrapped her legs around his hips, holding him to her the only way she could. They were trapped in one another's gaze. The need to keep him forever was a physical thing. She could almost feel it reaching out to him, tendrils intended to bind him to her for eternity.

"Mine," he whispered.

"Mine," she answered.

She saw it then, in the depths of his eyes, the possibility of everything she'd ever wanted. And it was all just out of reach.

His movements were slow, deliberate, as though he didn't want their joining to end. Their mouths tangled in a kiss that was heavy with meaning. Each taste was a feeling too deep to express in words. Each touch of lips to lips was a promise that couldn't be kept. Each teasing bite was a reprimand for a future filled with loss.

Friday felt tears on her cheeks as she clung to him and realized they weren't only hers. One lone tear had rolled down his face to fall and mingle with hers. He reached up, wiped his face, groaned, and then surged into her. Her throat began to ache with repressed sobs. His kisses left her mouth and made their way across her cheek to her ear.

"I love you," his voice was hoarse.

Her tears fell faster, as her body soared higher under his touch.

"It will always be you," he whispered. "Only you."

A sob escaped her, and his mouth was there to capture it. She wanted to scream at the injustice of it all. She wanted to beat something, anything, to release the anger at leaving this man. Her man. Instead, she fought the anguish back and pushed her love for him outward. She pushed it through her fingers as they clung to him. Through her lips as she kissed him, taking his taste deep inside of her where it would always live.

"I love you, Luke Boudreaux," she said against his lips and watched as he swallowed, taking her declaration into him, making her a part of him in a way. Maybe, just maybe, she would live on in this man, a part of his heart, his soul. Forever.

Their kiss became desperate; their movements, frantic with need. Together, they shattered. And when they reformed, they did it as one. For always.

CHAPTER 39

"WHAT THE HELL AM I LOOKING AT?" MACE SAID INTO THE comm unit strapped around his throat.

The team was in the hills, south of the location marked by Striker's tracker. They should have been looking out over the built-up suburbs of La Paz. Instead, they were staring at a gash in the landscape and a shit ton of digging equipment.

"Mining," was Sandi's droll reply.

"The images you're sending me don't match up to the ones I'm getting through the satellite feed," Hunter said over the comm.

"Secret mining," Sandi amended.

Hunter typed in the background. "I'm checking all records, but there are no official mining operations running in the south of the city."

"I don't think they would have hidden it if it'd been legitimate. Just sayin'," Sandi said.

"Not helping." Mace frowned at his sister.

"What?" She shrugged at him. "Somebody needs to educate the rookie."

"The rookie is over a hundred years old," Hunter said.

"And still ignorant." Sandi smiled mischievously at her brother. "That must chafe."

Mace wasn't amused. "Could you two focus for a minute? Has the signal from the tracker moved?"

"Nope. It's still at the coordinates I sent you."

He hit a button on his binoculars, and a coordinate grid came up, superimposed over the area in front of him. "He's in the third building from the left, beside the gate."

"The one that's surrounded by guards?" Ignacio Morales, the leader of the other half of their team, asked. His people were positioned two streets up from the main gate.

"Yeah."

"I can deal with the guards at the gate," Gray said over the comm.

There were at least ten heavily-armed guards at the entrance, with about a dozen more stationed close to it. Going in alone was a suicide mission.

"No." They weren't going to lose anyone on this mission. Especially someone who was practically begging to die. "We go in from the side, over the fence. We make this a snatch and grab, not a full-out war."

"Still too many armed guys wandering about," Sandi said. "One way or the other, we're gonna take fire. Unless, maybe, we wait 'til dark and move then."

The weight of her words landed heavily on all of them. Nobody argued that they rush in there to save Friday. It was almost six. They all knew she was already gone.

"Eh, boss?" Ignacio said. "I found out who's running the mine. They aren't exactly hiding it; there's a company logo plastered to one of the crates they're unloading. I'm sending the coordinates."

When they came through, the team shifted their binoculars to the building.

Gray let out a low whistle. "CommTECH." The word dripped with disgust.

"This shit is illegal," Ignacio said.

"I don't think they care," Sandi said.

Things had just gotten a whole lot more urgent. If Striker's DNA fell into CommTECH's hands, there was no telling what they'd do with it—or with him.

"No waiting until dark," Mace said. "We need to get him out of there fast."

"I have grenades," Jeremiah said cheerfully into the silence. "I say we blow the gate sky high and ride out of there with our boy."

"We can sneak along the fence and plant timed explosions," Ignacio added. "Attack on several fronts at the same time. Take out as many of them as we can."

It was as good a plan as any. "Ignacio, Gray, set charges. Jeremiah, get the cars ready and arm everybody. We go in with two vehicles. First car lays down cover, the second finds Striker." There was agreement. Mace checked the time. "Thirty minutes to set up charges, then we move."

He hoped Striker was still in one piece when they got to him—otherwise, they would have to burn down the mine and everything in it to prevent their secrets getting out.

CHAPTER 40

Friday fell asleep as soon as they'd finished making love. Striker knew she wouldn't wake up again. Her time had run out. Part of him was relieved, for her sake, that she wouldn't wake. He didn't know what the poison would do to her, now that it was active, and he didn't want her to experience any more pain. This was better, he assured himself. She could sleep through it. That was good, right?

No.

Nothing about this situation was good.

Nothing.

He sat with his back to the wall, the blanket tent covering them and the woman he loved in his lap. One arm was wrapped tight around her, the other pressed flat over her heart, counting the steady beats. They were strong, her breaths even. There was no visible change—yet. Her lips were still the palest pink. Her skin was still warm. Only the darkening circles under her eyes indicated something was very wrong.

He'd dressed her in his T-shirt because he didn't want anyone to see her naked. Someone was bound to check on them at some point, especially when they found Kane

Duggan dead. As soon as she was covered, he'd pulled his jeans and boots back on, ready to run with her if the occasion allowed. And he hoped it did. He wanted to take her back to the Red Zone. He wanted her in his bed. He didn't know how long the poison took to work, and he wanted her somewhere safe. Somewhere he could watch over her. Somewhere with people who cared whether she lived or died.

He wanted to take her home, to mourn her.

"Damn it." His eyes stung, and he blinked them hard. He needed to focus. He needed to watch over his woman.

She's just sleeping, the diamondback said.

Yeah, buddy, she's just sleeping. He swallowed the knot in his throat.

We take care of her. His reptile snapped free of his body without being called, something Striker didn't like one bit. It meant he didn't have as much control over the diamondback as he'd thought.

The rattler slid under Friday's shirt and curled around her.

Warm here. The diamondback almost purred the words. *Don't worry. I take care of her.*

It was impossible to reply. Instead, he brushed Friday's silken blond hair from her forehead. She was so beautiful, inside and out. Four days. He'd only had four days with her.

"This is bullshit!" He roared the words, hearing them echo off the walls.

Everyone he loved had been taken from him. Three years earlier he'd woken up to find out his family had been dead for decades. Now this. Friday. The only woman he'd ever loved. More than that—she felt like the only woman he ever would love. She felt like she belonged with him.

She does. She belongs to us.

What will we do when…? He couldn't finish the sentence. Not even as a silent whisper to his other half.

She just sleeping.

Pulling her closer, he willed it to be true. Willed her to wake and laugh with him again. He poured the full force of his personality into his desire, thinking that maybe his will alone could keep her with him. How could someone completely change his life in just four days? And she had. She'd turned it upside down. He was a different man with Friday. One he liked. She gave him something to live for in this new and strange world. Something other than the fear of being discovered, or the drive to protect his team.

She gave him hope.

Hope of a future filled with love. How was he going to live when she took that hope with her? He would be half a man, because she had the rest of his soul tucked deep inside of her.

"I love you so fucking much," he whispered. "Don' leave me, bébé. Please don' leave me. I'll do anything. Just don' leave me." He pressed his forehead to hers. "Please, God, please."

He'd never felt as helpless in his life. He couldn't save her. He couldn't do anything for her except hold her and love her. And beg. "God, please…"

He'd do anything to keep her there. "Maman told me you did miracles, God, please…"

A shuddering blast made the earth rock beneath him. His head snapped up. He held Friday tighter. There was shouting, running. Another blast from farther away. Two more. This was no mine accident. His senses were sharp. Alert. He strained to listen, to make sense of the chaos. He heard tires squeal, and adrenaline surged through him. Gunfire. Another blast, this one much closer. The walls shook. He called to his diamondback, and the reptile returned to his skin.

Striker pushed himself up the wall and out of the tent, until he stood with his woman in his arms. He waited. More gunfire. This time from inside the building. Another blast. It sounded like a grenade. Hope soared. His hold on Friday tightened. He heard running feet. Shots fired. Something slammed against his cell door.

And then it swung open.

And Mace walked in.

Striker's knees almost gave way.

"About fucking time," he snapped at his second-in.command as he strode toward the door.

"Good to see you, too." His eyes went to Friday.

"She ain't dead yet. We need to get back to base. Maybe there's something Doc can do."

His best friend didn't say anything, but he also couldn't look Striker in the eye. No matter. Striker didn't care if anyone thought his efforts were wasted. She wasn't dead yet, and he was taking her home.

"We got a car out front," Mace said as they jogged along the corridor to the sound of a war raging outside.

"I hope it's armor plated."

"What would be the point if it wasn't?"

Together they pushed through the doors into the twilight. At the sight of his team guarding their car, he swallowed hard. This was his family, and they'd come for him. They provided cover while he ran for the car and secured his woman inside.

Mace climbed into the driver's seat. "The rest of the team will meet up with us at the airport. Sandi and I will cover you two." He hit the accelerator.

They wove through chaos, past burning buildings and guards firing weapons. The main gate had been blown to hell. Jeremiah crouched behind what remained of the wall, picking off the enemy with his rifle. He flicked a salute at the car as they raced past.

"Duggan?" his second-in-command asked as he slammed past a makeshift barrier, making the guards dive for cover.

"Dead. My diamondback took him out."

"Any evidence?"

They couldn't afford for even a hint of their genetics, or abilities, to get out.

Striker shook his head. "Nothing. We're good."

Sandi glanced back at him, her eyes filled with sympathy. He looked away. This wasn't over yet. He couldn't, he wouldn't, give up hope entirely until...

Looking down at the woman in his arms, he whispered, "We're going home, bébé."

Then held her close as Mace sped through the streets of La Paz.

CHAPTER 41

CommTECh Headquarters, New York City,
Northern Territory

Miriam Shepherd stared at the images of Kane Duggan's dead body. He lay sprawled, face down, across the desk in the head office of the La Paz mining operation. His body was swollen and bloated, almost beyond recognition. There were patches of black skin on his bare arms and neck. And he was lying in his own vomit.

"What killed him?" She kept her voice perfectly flat.

The holo-image of the man standing on the other side of her desk shuffled nervously. And he was smart to be nervous. The La Paz mine had been attacked. Buildings were destroyed, the mine had collapsed in places, the security team had been decimated, and Kane was dead. On top of that, the smuggler and the scientist had vanished. It didn't take a genius to figure out his team had ridden in to rescue him. That put them right at the top of Miriam Shepherd's wanted list. The only good news was that the little scientist was either already dead or hours from it.

"It seems to have been a snake bite. Um, several snake bites."

Miriam dragged her eyes away from Kane's brutalized body. "Snake?"

"You can clearly see it in the other footage I sent you. A rattlesnake made its way along the corridor before attacking Mr. Duggan."

She brought up the security footage and watched the snake stalk Kane. It was almost as though the reptile had entered the room with the purpose of killing the man. It didn't wander, it didn't investigate its surroundings, it simply headed straight for Kane.

"There have been reports of South American rattlesnakes in the area, Director," the security guard said. "One must have made it into the compound. They're known for being vicious and deadly. We've tried hunting the snake, but it's either long gone, or was killed during the bombings."

Miriam tuned him out as she watched the battle between Kane and the rattler. Kane almost seemed to be laughing toward the end of it. Miriam felt a stabbing sensation where her heart should have been. She was going to miss the man. No one could best him for loyalty and a willingness to get the job done.

"What are your orders regarding the mining operation, Director?" The security guard dared to interrupt her thoughts.

She turned a glacial look on the man. "I want production back on track by the end of the week."

"But Director..." He swallowed hard, and she noticed sweat beading on his forehead. "Half of the compound was destroyed. We've lost a lot of workers."

"Find more. You have twenty-four hours to bring me good news." She cut the feed, uninterested in his excuses.

Kane wouldn't have argued. Kane would have nodded and then done whatever it took to get the job finished. She sent a command to her console to rerun the footage and watched the snake attack all over again. It was too convenient. Kane dying hours before the mine was attacked? She didn't think it was a coincidence. Someone had set that snake loose. Someone had led it to Kane's office. Which meant there was a traitor on her La Paz team. Or, someone had infiltrated the site.

She brought up the security feed from outside Kane's office. The snake had been alone, no handler in sight. The reptile made its way along the bottom of the wall before climbing through Kane's window. Miriam rubbed the back of her neck. Something wasn't right. It was almost as though the snake knew where it was heading.

She sent a message to what was left of the La Paz security team, telling them she wanted all of the security footage from the site for the time leading up to Kane's death.

It took hours, but Miriam managed to follow the path the snake had taken before entering the office. She froze the image of the its earliest appearance and sat back in her chair. She'd kicked off her shoes hours earlier, and the meal an assistant had delivered was sitting, uneaten, on her desk.

She stared at the screen. It didn't matter how hard she looked, she couldn't find an earlier image of the rattler. But what she was seeing didn't make any sense at all.

The rattlesnake had first appeared slithering through the bars of the cell where Kane's captives were being held. From there, it had made a beeline through the compound, straight for Kane—as though it knew exactly where to go, and what to do once it got there.

She leaned forward and drummed her fingers on the desktop. It couldn't be a coincidence. She flicked to the images from inside the cell itself. There was no sign of the reptile, but it was clear that the man and woman were still very much inside, although hidden by their makeshift shelter.

So where did the rattler come from? Had it been hiding in

the room? Then how did it know to seek out Kane? Because that's exactly what it'd done. The reptile had passed several easier targets without so much as a glance, let alone an attack. Yet, when it got into Kane's office, it had bitten the man repeatedly.

Miriam poured herself a glass of sparkling water and worked her way through the security footage of the time after the snake killed Kane. It took hours and when she finally had the answer she was looking for, she stood to stretch her stiff muscles.

Two images filled the screen on the wall opposite her desk, the first showing the rattler slipping out of Striker's cell. The second showing it slip back in.

The rattler definitely belonged to the smuggler. Whether the reptile was a real snake that had somehow been modified to do its owner's bidding, or whether it was a synthetic creature that the smuggler could program with commands, she didn't know. What she did know was that it was a weapon she'd never seen before, one that was capable of getting past the tightest security. One she very much wanted to get her hands on.

She strode back to her desk as she mentally called for Kane's second-in-command. A few minutes later, the door to her office opened, and the twins strode in. Miriam sipped her water as she considered the two men. They were identical in every way, including their sociopathic need to kill. And, although she hadn't known them as long as she'd known Kane, they had yet to disappoint her.

"Congratulations," she told them. "You are now head of security. Kane was assassinated in Bolivia."

There was no reaction from the brothers. She hadn't expected one.

"I want you two to have his body transported to our Houston lab. Have the poison team run a thorough investigation into the toxin that killed him. I want to know if there are any signs of a synthetic delivery system. I also want to know if the poison is natural or manmade." She waved a hand, and footage of the snake attacking Kane filled her office wall. "I want to know what kind of weapon that snake is. It was programmed to find Kane and kill him."

That got their attention. The duo's eyebrows arched slightly, in perfect unison. Miriam changed the image. A security shot of the smuggler filled the screen.

"This is Striker. I want to know everything there is to know about the man and his associates."

The twins didn't acknowledge the order. Instead, they waited to see if she had any more instructions. She only had one. "Move your things into Kane's old quarters. You're living with me now."

Again, there was no response, and the door closed silently behind them. In the darkness of her office, with only the image on the wall for light, Miriam studied the man responsible for killing Kane.

If she couldn't get the reptile weapon he owned, she'd take the smuggler.

CHAPTER 42

"Is he eating?" Mace watched his friend from the tunnel outside of his room.

Striker gently brushed Friday's hair back from her face. The scientist looked like she was sleeping. There were no outward signs that one of the most dangerous poisons on the planet was at work within her.

"Sandi's been forcing him to eat." Doc stood beside him. "Last I heard, she pulled a gun on him and told him there were easier ways to die than starving. He ate the soup."

"When we were growing up, my sister was known for her soft heart and her kind, subtle way with words."

Doc's answering grin was subdued.

"What's the latest?" Mace hated seeing the toll this took on their team leader. With Friday stuck in the no-man's-land between life and death, Striker held on to hope that she'd pull through. Everyone on the team, except their leader, thought it was a false hope. She might as well have been plugged into life support for all the signs of life they saw. Mace worried that one day soon, one of them would have to pull the plug.

"I'm damned if I know." Doc let out a weary sigh. He'd been burning the midnight oil in his search for answers. "She should have died weeks ago. Every research article I've read said the longest someone lived after Interferan-X activated was three days. We're on seven weeks. She's breathing on her own, and there are no physical changes. As far as I can see, the only sign that something isn't right is the fact her temperature is elevated and she's been unconscious since we brought her here."

"Coma?"

"It looks like it, but I'm not sure. There are anomalies. Equipment readings I wouldn't expect to see if she were in a real coma." He let out a huff. "I'm a medic. Not a specialist, not even a doctor. I'm in over my head here."

"What if we try giving her the antidote now? I can take some guys, we can hit the lab and lift some."

The medic shook his head, clearly at a loss. "I don't think it would make any difference. The blood tests I've been running are becoming increasingly strange. The Interferan-X is still there, but it's mutating. It looks like there's something else too, some other foreign body in her blood that I can't quite identify."

And just when Mace thought it couldn't get any weirder. "When you say the Interferan-X is mutating, what do you mean, exactly?"

"It's morphing into something else, that's what I mean. Don't ask me what, because I don't have a clue."

They stared at the pale-skinned woman. Each of them at a loss as to what to think.

"We need to do something," Mace said. "We can't leave him like this. He's scared to move from her side in case she dies while he's gone. He hardly eats, we have to force him to shower, and he isn't interested in anything but Friday. I bring him news about the team, about jobs we're running, and he turns away." He ran a hand through his hair and lowered his voice. "I'm worried that when she eventually goes, he's going to follow."

"I don't know what to tell you. I think that's a distinct possibility. I've never seen anything like this before. He's acting like they've been joined at the hip for years instead of knowing her for only four days before she slipped into unconsciousness." He cast Mace a sideward glance. "In the middle of the night, when he thinks no one is around, he spends his time whispering, begging God to let her live. *Begging.*"

The words sent Mace reeling. Their team leader didn't beg. None of them did, but Striker especially wouldn't bend to anyone.

"There's a lab in New Zealand," the medic said, of one of the Coalition Countries. "They could run more extensive tests than we can here. I could send out some blood. See what they come up with."

"We can't. I've had Hunter flag incidences of accidental poisoning using Interferan-X. There haven't been any cases since Friday took her dose. If we send out her blood, the fact there's Interferan-X in it will cause a ripple. We can't afford for anyone to think she's still alive." If that was even what they could call her current state.

"Is CommTECH still searching for them?"

"Striker, yeah. They think she's dead."

Since the imprisonment in La Paz, Miriam Shepherd's team had been turning over every stone in their path looking for information on Striker. She was desperate to get her hands on him, which set off all kinds of alarm bells. The kind that made the team think their leader had somehow given them away.

He stared at his friend, willing him to fully reenter the world. They needed him. "The Mercer twins are running the hunt."

Doc reeled back on his heels. "Then we can't let Striker out of the Red Zone. The world needs to think he's dead along with his woman."

"I don't think that's a problem right now. We can hardly get him to leave her bed, let alone the zone."

"But later, when…"

Yeah, none of them wanted to talk about what would happen when she eventually slipped away. But that didn't stop Mace from planning. Somebody had to be ready to contain Striker when he lost his mind and went after CommTECH.

"Doc!" Striker shot to his feet. "Doc! Get in here!"

They ran into the room. Striker was leaning over Friday, his hands shaking as he gently held up her limp arm.

"What is it?" The medic was at his side, Mace behind him.

"Look." Their team leader elevated the scientist's arm slightly, turning it so that the inside of her bicep was visible.

"What the hell?" Mace snapped. His eyes shot to Striker's. "That wasn't there yesterday."

"No." His voice trembled. He couldn't take his eyes off Friday's arm. "What does it mean?"

The three men stared at the tiny tattoo on the inside of the woman's arm.

It was a perfectly coiled rattlesnake.

A diamondback.

A baby diamondback.

"I need blood samples." Doc's voice shook. "I need to check something." He rushed off to get the equipment he needed.

Striker leaned over Friday and kissed her lips. His touch was so gentle that it made Mace ache for something he knew he'd never have and had never thought he wanted.

"You're coming back to me, aren't you, bébé?" he whispered.

Mace cleared his throat and took a step away from the bed. He felt as though he was intruding. This moment was private, just for them.

Doc came running back into the room. He unhooked the

IV line running to the bag of fluids above Friday's bed and attached a vial to the cannula. They watched it fill with blood. Once he had all he needed, he hooked the IV line back up to her arm.

"I need your blood, too, boss," he said to Striker.

"Why?" Striker asked, looking bewildered.

"Seriously?" Mace said. "You are beyond sleep deprived if you don't know the answer to that question. There's a baby snake on your woman's arm. That shit had to come from somewhere. Guess who's the prime suspect? Lack of sleep has made you stupid. Give Doc your blood."

With a growl of irritation, Striker stuck out an arm, the other hand still stroking the image of the baby snake. "You think I infected her? How? Kissing her? Having sex? I've had sex with other women since I woke up. Far as I know, none of them have snakes."

Now that comment was like a kick in the gut. If having sex meant infecting women, then Mace hated to think what he'd left in his wake. When he'd first woken up, he'd anesthetized himself to the shock of being in a new century by sleeping his way through most of Texas.

"Don't be an idiot. We aren't infectious. This is something else. Something new." Doc put the vials on the table behind him. "Help me get her undressed. I need to check her skin."

Striker glared at Mace who let out a sigh and turned. Like he planned to ogle an unconscious woman. He couldn't wait until his best friend was well rested and back to his old self, just so he could knock some sense into the man.

Once Mace had turned his back, Striker relaxed some. He didn't want anyone to see Friday naked or vulnerable. It took all of his self-control not to punch out the medic, and he was only doing his job. Doc took the sheet from the bed as Striker careful removed the button-up shirt he'd put on his woman. His hands shook, and his fingers fumbled. His mind was all over the place, making it hard to think straight. He didn't dare hope that she was on her way back to him, but what else could the snake image mean?

"Turn her over," Doc said once he'd studied the front of her body.

Only the fact his attitude was professional and detached kept him from earning a black eye. Slowly, gently, Striker rolled her onto her side with her back toward their medic.

"There!" Doc pointed at something low on her back.

Mace turned to see what had excited their medic and Striker snarled at him. With a shake of his head, the big guy held up his hands in surrender and turned back around.

"What is it?" Striker was fast running out of patience. He wanted answers *now*. And not just any answers, he only wanted good ones. Ones that told him she was coming back to him.

"See for yourself. Come around. I'll hold her."

When he glared, the medic amended. "One hand on her hip. Another on her shoulder. Just to keep her in place for you to see what I'm talking about."

Reluctantly, he released his hold and circled the bed. There, in the small of her back, were the telltale puncture wounds of a snakebite.

He sucked in a breath.

"There's no swelling," Doc said. "No blackened skin, no redness. If the puncture wounds weren't still there, we wouldn't know she'd been bitten. Here, cover her back up. I need to look at the blood."

Striker eased Friday's slight form back into the bed. She'd lost too much weight since she'd fallen asleep. There was only so much nutrition they could feed her using a tube. He hated seeing the tubes coming out of her, taking care of bodily functions until she could do it herself. Even though they kept her alive, they also reminded him that he'd failed her.

"It's gonna be okay, bébé," he cooed as he covered her up.

"Can I turn now?" Mace sounded like he was losing patience.

Tough. "Yeah, but be warned. I plan on hitting you later for being a pain in my ass."

"Funny, I was thinking the exact same thing." His best friend covered the distance to stand beside him. "What's your rattler say about this?"

"He's been hibernating, or whatever the hell you call it when a reptile decides to go to sleep for weeks. He ain't been talking much."

"You telling me he's been asleep as long as Friday?"

Now that he thought about it, that did seem kind of strange. "You think there's a connection?"

"Damned if I know what to think about any of this. She should have died weeks ago. Instead she looks like Sleeping Beauty waiting for her prince. Meanwhile, Doc says her bloodwork is showing weird results, and there's a baby snake on her arm. We're in the Twilight Zone, man. I have no clue what's going on."

He had a point. Striker traced his fingers down her arm. It was soft and warm and very much alive. That alone had been the one thing to keep him from losing his mind completely these past few weeks. The fact she hadn't deteriorated in any way gave him hope. Blind, desperate, hope.

"I'm gonna have a word with the handbag." And he was gonna be pissed if the rattler was holding out on him.

"Have at it." His friend sat back in the chair beside the bed and stretched out his legs.

Striker focused inward and found the presence of the sleeping diamondback. *Wake up, asshole! Did you bite Friday?*

The reply was a testy grumble.

He didn't have patience for this. *Yo! Sam! You talking handbag, did you bite Friday?*

Stop yelling. He felt the reptile yawn and stir within him.

Did you bite Friday? Striker demanded.

You know I did. I saw it in your mind. There's a bite mark.

That made him clench his teeth. *Why did you bite her?*

He got the distinct impression that his reptile thought his human half was dumb as dirt. *To save her.*

He sucked in a breath, drawing Mace's attention. "What?" his friend demanded.

Striker tried to process what he'd just learned. "He said he bit her to save her."

"How the hell would he know to do that? His bite is poisonous. It kills people. How would that save her?"

I know poisons. The rattler sounded more than a little superior. *I knew my poison would eat hers.*

"He said he knew his poison would eat the one inside her. And I think he added a silent asshole on the end of that just for you."

Mace shot him the bird, but he wasn't offended. He figured it was meant for the diamondback, anyway.

And, the rattler said, *she's our mate. My bite doesn't work the same way on our mate as it does on other humans.* He said the last part as though it was common knowledge.

Everything within him stilled. *I don't understand.*

I'm tired. Wake me when my mate is here, the rattler said before curling back to sleep.

It wasn't the first time his other half had referred to Friday as his mate, but now Striker was beginning to suspect something else entirely. Something that made adrenaline flood his system. "Snakes don't mate for life, do they?" he asked Mace.

"No. They're horndogs. They jump any snake in their path."

"That's what I thought." He sat on the edge of the bed and

caressed the image on his woman's arm. "Then why is it telling me to wake him when his mate gets here? Why is he saying that his bite doesn't affect her the way it would other people—because she's our mate?"

Mace sat up straight. His eyes going to the image of the baby snake. "I thought that was his child. You think it's his mate? You think there was something special about Friday that meant biting her would create a mate for him instead of killing her?"

"I don't know what to think."

"I've got it." Doc ran into the room, waving a data pad. "The other foreign element in Friday's blood is definitely the diamondback's venom. I didn't recognize it because it interacted with the Interferan-X, essentially consuming it. But there are a whole lot of other things going on in her blood that I just don't have the skills to interpret."

Striker ran a hand over his head. "I don't care about the details. Is there anything in her blood that's going to kill her?"

"I don't think so."

It took a minute for that to sink in. "She's gonna live?"

"I think so, but I don't know for sure. Don't get your hopes up. I'm totally out of my depth here. Hell, I'm not sure there's anyone on the planet that could tell us what's going on. Your reptile's poison isn't exactly normal. The red mist changed it somehow. It's something the world hasn't seen before."

"But she's gonna live, right?" That was the only question he needed answering.

"Yeah." Doc's smile was slow in coming, but when it got there, it was wide. "I'm pretty sure your woman is going to live."

That was all he needed to hear. With an answering grin, he climbed onto the bed and stretched out beside her. "In that case, wake me up when things change. I haven't slept for weeks."

He tuned out his friends' laughter as he wrapped himself around his woman and closed his eyes. Seven weeks he'd waited, prayed, and begged, desperate for a miracle. And now it was here. He hadn't dared to hope, but he hadn't been able to let her go, either. He took a deep breath, filling himself with her soft springtime scent. His whole body shook at the news. She was going to live. He wasn't going to lose her. Thank you, God, he prayed.

She wasn't going anywhere. She was his.

Thanks, he added to his diamondback.

Dumbass, was the reply.

CHAPTER 43

It was three more weeks before Friday woke. Striker sat beside her bed going over reports that detailed the massive hunt underway to find him. Somehow, he'd managed to compromise his team during the op in La Paz. He wasn't sure how he'd done it, exactly, and until they knew for sure, he'd confined himself to the caves.

Not that he cared. He wouldn't leave his woman anyway.

The air around them stirred, and Friday let out a tiny moan. She'd been doing that a lot the past few days, and they all thought it was a sign she was getting ready to wake. Striker put his computer tablet aside as he reached for her hand. The diamondback, who'd been curled on top of her stomach, raised its lazy head and stared at her face.

Her eyelashes fluttered as Striker held his breath.

She's waking! the snake said.

Yeah. He smiled at the excitement in the rattler's voice. He felt a little light-headed himself.

Hours, he'd spent, staring at this woman, wishing he could climb inside her and fight the poison for her. He'd never felt more helpless in his life. And he sure as hell wasn't going to let anything harm her, ever again. From now on, he was gonna stay glued to her side. Hell, he'd get her to invent a special protection suit. One she could wear twenty-four-seven. Because she was never getting hurt ever again. Not if he could stop it.

She let out another little moan as her eyes slowly opened. Striker's heart stuttered within him, coming back to life when it'd been in stasis along with his woman.

"Hey, bébé," he said softy, "it's good to have you back. You scared me. Don' ever do that again."

Her head turned slowly toward him, and she blinked several times. His world tilted at the sight before him. Instead of two blue eyes, there was only one. The other eye was yellow, with the distinct elliptical pupil of a snake.

"What is it?" Her voice was hoarse from lack of use.

He forced himself to breathe. "You're beautiful."

Her gaze was soft and unfocused. "Are you real? Or am I dead?"

"I'm real, and you are nowhere near dead." He pressed a gentle kiss to her lips and felt her hand tighten in his.

"I'm not dead?" she whispered when he broke the kiss, searching his eyes for the truth. The eyes that were a match for hers. "Or dreaming?"

"This isn't a dream, and you're very much alive. I plan on keeping it that way, too." He kissed the tip of her nose. "No more playing with poisons. You hear me? There's gonna be hell to pay if you pull a stunt like that again."

"Are you sure this is real?"

"You want me to pinch you?"

"What would that prove?" Her brow puckered in confusion.

"Trust me, you're alive. The poison didn't kill you, but everybody thinks you're dead. We're in the Red Zone, and nobody can get to you here. You're safer than you've ever been." He caressed her silken hair. "You're free, bébé. No more CommTECH."

Her eyes filled with unshed tears as she searched his face, the beginnings of belief and hope in her gaze. "Really?"

"I wouldn't lie to you about something this important." He rested his forehead on hers. "Don't you ever try to leave me again, you hear?"

He felt her tremble, and her hand came up to cup his head. She was weak, but she was alive, and he'd make sure she got stronger. She was his first priority. The reason he'd found for living in this strange new time.

"Did you get the antidote to me in time? Is that what saved me?"

"No." He leaned back to look at her, hesitating because he wasn't quite sure how to tell her she'd changed. Not only changed, but become like him.

No, like us. She's our mate.

Not helping!

"Whatever it is, just tell me." Her voice shook, and he was instantly angry with himself for scaring her. "I need to know what happened. I need to know this isn't a hallucination brought on by the poison."

He let out a sigh. There was no easy way to say this. "The handbag bit you when you slipped into unconsciousness in the cell."

"Sam?" She looked down at the rattler, who practically preened.

Tell her how brilliant I am, the diamondback demanded. *Tell her I saved her. Not you. Me.*

Smug pain in his ass. Striker scowled at the reptile before turning back to Friday. "Far as we can figure, when the rattler bit you, his mutated venom ate the Interferan-X."

She blinked at him a couple of times, thinking. The sight made him want to shout from the rafters because it meant she was back. "I need a blood sample and access to the lab."

He couldn't help his grin. "DNA study has to wait. You need to get your strength back first."

"I have questions."

"I bet you do, and I'm sure you'll be able to find the answers to them. Later. Once you're better." He paused before deciding just to spit it out. "I have to tell you something else. The venom changed you a little bit." Her eyes went wide, and he rushed to reassure her. "They're good changes. You look real cute."

"Striker?" Her tone was losing some if its weakness. Which was good. Mostly. Unless she started shouting.

"Hey, look who's awake."

He almost sighed with relief when Doc walked into the room. The medic headed straight for the bed and came up short when Friday looked up at him.

"Holy crap," he said.

"What's wrong? What is it?" Her gaze moved rapidly between them.

"Thanks a lot," Striker grumbled. "I had her all calm, and you blew it."

He had the decency to look sheepish. "Sorry."

"What's going on?" Friday struggled to sit up, and he reached over to help her. "What aren't you telling me?"

"Let's get you out of bed, and I'll explain everything." Or better yet, put her in front of a mirror and let her see for herself.

"Yes. Good idea," Doc stopped gaping long enough to say. "I need to unhook you from the equipment."

Friday pinned Striker with a glare. "You will tell me everything and answer all of my questions."

"Promise." He lifted their entwined fingers and kissed her knuckles. "You just woke up. Let's get you sorted first."

She wasn't convinced, but she nodded.

Tell her about the snake, the rattler demanded. *Tell her she carries my mate.*

Reptiles don't mate. How many times do I have to tell you this? You sleep around. It's what you do.

I mate. The rattler hissed at him and started shaking his tail.

He rolled his eyes. *You're an embarrassment to your species.*

And you are a dickhead.

I liked you better when you couldn't talk.

The rattler narrowed his eyes and struck out, biting him on the shoulder. "Hey, that hurts. You're damn lucky the poison has no effect on me." He rubbed the bite. "I swear, if I thought I could survive without you, I'd turn you into a pair of boots."

"Striker!" Friday was outraged as Doc chuckled.

He shrugged. "That talking handbag is a pain in my ass. He never shuts up, and he's got an ego like you wouldn't believe. You try listening to him all the damn time. His only saving grace is that he likes to sleep."

The rattler rubbed its face along Friday's jaw, cuddling into her. She softened, smiling down at him and petting him. *Asshole.*

"You need to stop being so mean to him. You're much bigger, and I'm sure he's just as confused as you are about the way you're merged together now."

See? I told you she likes me better, the snake crowed, earning another glare.

Doc cleared his throat and, wisely, hid his smile. "Right, that's all the machines unhooked. You're free to go. Striker can take you to the shower. I'm sure you'd like to get cleaned up." He took a step back and folded his arms. "Far as I can see, you don't have any health issues other than what you'd expect from being bedbound for weeks. You'll feel weak, you've lost weight and some muscle mass, but that's about it. Take it easy for a while, eat, rest, and you'll soon be back to normal." He shared a look with Striker. "Or better than normal." His laugh was forced, and Striker made a mental note never to send the medic into an operation that required undercover work. He wasn't fooling anyone.

Especially Friday. "What aren't you telling me?"

While the medic turned red and looked like he might bolt from the room, Striker threw back her covers and shifted her legs around, getting her ready to stand. "Nothing I can't explain once you're all cleaned up. Let's go."

With one last glance that promised the topic wasn't closed, she let him help her to her feet. She swayed in place, and he held her waist tight to steady her. She was there. Alive. In front of him. Overwhelmed by emotions he couldn't fully comprehend, he wrapped his arms around her and squeezed her tight.

"Never again," he forced the words through his closing throat. "You hear me, bébé, never again."

"Never again," she promised, the words muffled against his chest.

———

Friday was glad Striker carried her to the shower room. Not because she felt weak, although she definitely did, but because she didn't want even an inch to separate them. She wrapped her arms around his neck and rested her cheek against his chest.

Hers.

Her other half. And she'd almost lost him. She blinked hard, willing the tears back, focusing on the present. She'd prayed for a miracle, and that's what she'd received. It was a second chance, and she wasn't going to waste a moment of it.

"I want to get married," she blurted. "To you," she added, just in case there was any confusion.

"Bébé, I'd tie you to me with rope if I could get away with it. Marriage is definitely happening. So is tagging you with a tracking device and possibly handcuffing you to the bed at night. There's no way I'm letting you slip away from me ever again."

Laughter bubbled up inside of her. This must be what happiness felt like. "I'm not sure about the handcuffing thing. That sounds uncomfortable."

"We'll see." He looked down at her, his eyes sparkling. "I already ordered wedding bands."

"Oh, that's good." Although she'd had something else in mind.

"But?" He read her face far too easily.

"I thought we might get matching tattoos, instead. They're about as permanent as you can get. You can take off a ring. You can't take off a tattoo. Well, not easily anyway."

He threw back his head and laughed hard. Although she wasn't sure what she'd said that was so entertaining. His laughter vibrated through her body, like bubbles inside of her. It was the most glorious feeling, one she never wanted to end.

As they made their way down the corridor, his team began to converge on them. She turned her face into his neck, worried what reception they'd give her and a little embarrassed at being carried.

"Hey, girl," Sandi said. "Glad to see you awake. I went shopping for you. Now you have clothes that will fit."

The kindness melted away her worries, and she pulled her face out of Striker's neck. "Thanks, Sandi."

As soon as their eyes met, Sandi jerked with shock. The reaction was gone in a flash, replaced by a wide, welcoming smile. "You're more than welcome." She shared a look with her team leader that Friday couldn't quite read.

When she looked up at Striker, his face was an innocent mask. Oh yes, there was definitely something strange going on. And as soon as she got her man alone, she'd make sure she got to the bottom of it.

"I'm cooking," Mace said by way of hello.

Friday looked up at him, waiting for his reaction. Sure enough, shock registered in his face, too, before he quickly covered it. Her stomach tightened. There was something very wrong with her. Mace's eyes shot to Striker, who grinned, evidently pleased with himself. Whatever shocked his team, didn't bother him. Her eyes narrowed at him. Sneaky man. What had he done?

"I'm glad you aren't dead," Mace said, pulling her attention back to him.

"Smooth, brother," Sandi said. "Real smooth."

"Thanks?" What else was she supposed to say to that?

"I'm cooking," he said again. "Tell me what you want to eat, and I'll make it."

"I thought you could only make chili?"

"I'll adapt."

She blinked at him, and then something mischievous yawned and stretched within her, waking from a lifelong slumber. She gave him a sweet, overly innocent smile. "You'll make anything I want?"

"Yeah," he ran a hand through his hair, "it's the least I can do for being an asshole to you."

Her smile widened. "In that case, I'd really love some lobster."

"Lobster?" His jaw fell. "We're in the middle of the Red Zone. The coast is miles away. How the hell am I supposed to get my hands on lobster, and how the hell do I cook it if I do?"

She forced her lower lip to tremble, and felt Striker's chest shudder as he fought back laughter.

"Damn it!" Mace threw up his hands. "Never mind. I'll figure it out." He stormed back down the tunnel toward the kitchen.

"That was evil," Sandi said. "I'm impressed." Then she followed her brother.

She grinned after them. "I've never had lobster. I hope it's nice."

Striker's wide answering smile was so sexy it made her feel faint—which made her grateful again that he carried her. One smile from the man was enough to make her crumple.

The shower room was empty, and Striker left her to brush her teeth while he ran the water to warm it. Then he stripped.

"What are you doing?" She licked her lips at the sight of him, giggling when he puffed out his chest a little at her reaction.

"I'm gonna get you showered."

"I can shower by myself."

He pointed at her death grip on the sink. "Yeah, I'd be more inclined to believe that if you could stand without help. You're weak right now, bébé, your system has been through a lot, and you've been unconscious for weeks. Let me help you."

How could she resist him when he talked to her like that? She reached for him, and he came to her instantly. Slowly, reverently, he unbuttoned the shirt he'd dressed her in. The pale blue cotton came to her knees like a dress and smelled of him. It fell from her shoulders to puddle on the floor, his warm hands trailing after it, making her cool skin burn under his touch.

"I can't believe you're here," he whispered. "I keep thinking it's all a dream."

"I'm not sure it's real, either." She pressed a kiss to his chest, right above his heart. "But even if it isn't, I like this dream."

"I thought I'd lost you." His hands tightened on her. "I don't know what I'd have done if that happened. I think I might have gone insane."

She felt more tears pool in her eyes and put it down to being weak from unconsciousness. She turned her face up for a kiss, and he didn't disappoint her. It was sweet, soft, and lingering, because now they had all the time in the world. With reluctance, he broke the kiss and led her into the steaming shower, where he took his time washing her, caring for her. Loving her. He lingered to kiss and tease until she complained he was leading her on when she was too weak to do anything about it. With a chuckle, he wrapped her in a towel and took her back to his room. She was grateful to find it empty. She wanted to be alone with her man. He pulled the curtain over the doorway to let people know they wanted privacy, and then he carried her over to the mirror in the corner.

She looked at the large bed, which someone had thoughtfully remade with fresh sheets, and wondered why he hadn't taken her there, instead. Then she remembered the shocked looks on the faces of his team and her stomach clenched. This was it. He was going to tell her about the damage the poison had done to her. She touched her face. There wasn't any scarring. It had to be something else.

Placing her in front of the mirror, he stood between her and her reflection. He looked nervous, which made her stomach knot. Striker was never nervous. The diamondback, which had followed them, crawled over to sit at her feet. Unlike the man, the rattler didn't seem worried in the least.

"What is it?" She trembled, wishing he would just get it over with and tell her the bad news. The anticipation was killing her. She wanted to move on.

He took a deep breath. "We think that the red mist, the diamondback venom, and the poison you took interacted to cause a different effect than you had expected."

"Well, yes. I expected to be dead."

He cocked an eyebrow. "Really? This is the time for sarcasm? Can't you see I'm worried here?"

"Sorry. Carry on."

"Right, so, the thing is…" He ran a hand over the top of his head, a sure sign of anxiety. "Ah, to hell with it, see for yourself."

He stepped away from the mirror. She felt him come up behind her and hold onto her waist to steady her. Or perhaps catch her when she passed out. Which wasn't unlikely. Because Friday was stunned by what she saw.

Trembling, she trailed a fingertip under her left eye. The eye that was now a mirror of Striker's reptilian one. As she moved her hand, she spotted the image of a tiny diamondback coiled inside her upper arm. It was smaller than Striker's tattoo, but there was no missing the fact it matched his. Her heart stuttered. This had to be a dream. Right?

"Oh my goodness…" She ran her finger over the image on her arm, barely touching it. Her eyes met Striker's in the mirror. "Is it a real snake? Like yours?"

"We think so. It's a baby right now, but the handbag said it will become a full-grown female a year from now."

The diamondback rubbed against her legs in an affectionate move.

"The handbag says you're welcome," Striker said in disgust.

Friday took a step closer to the mirror, studying her eyes. It was strange to see herself with one blue and one yellow. "How did this happen? It took a hundred years for you to change."

"We don' know, bébé. That's what you need to find out."

A surge of excitement rushed through her, and her ever-curious mind started to overrule the shock. "Will I be able to see heat signatures like you do?"

"We think so, but you're in the early stages. The snake is still developing within you."

"You know, I kind of knew this," she muttered as she studied the image of the snake on her arm, "I felt something happening inside me. I thought it was the Interferan. I didn't realize it was this. Now it makes sense. Will my snake talk to me, too? Will I be able to call it out the way you do with Sam? Will I have to eat rodents? Are we permanently joined because of this? You and me, I mean.

Not me and the snake, because that's obviously permanent."

With a grin, he covered her mouth with his palm and cocked an eyebrow at her. "Welcome back, chère. I'm sure you're gonna have lots of fun playing around with your DNA. It should keep you occupied enough so that I don't have to worry about waking up with chocolate-flavored balls."

She barked out a laugh against his hand. This was real. She was alive. Changed, but alive. And, to be strictly honest, she was more than thrilled with the changes in her genetics. She matched Striker now. They were a pair. Just like their rattlers. No wonder he'd laughed at the matching tattoo idea. They had something far better than that; they had matching animals.

She turned in his hold and threw her arms around his neck. "I'm alive!"

"Yeah, you are."

"And I have my very own snake. How cool is that?"

"Super cool." He laughed.

"I have a snake!" she shouted excitedly, and laughter echoed back up through the caves to tell her the team had heard.

"Oh." She wriggled from his hold and reached down to pet the diamondback. "We need to think of a name for my diamondback."

"I'll get right on that," Striker said drolly, as he picked up his other half and headed for the closet in the corner.

"Where are you going? What are you doing with Sam?"

"Getting rid of the audience." He threw the hissing snake into the closet and slammed the door. He stalked back toward her, his eyes filled with molten heat that melted her insides. "You can name your snake later. Right now, you have other things to do."

"Like what?" she teased.

He flashed a sexy smile. "Like anything I want, anytime I want it. We have a deal, remember?"

"Oh yes." She nodded solemnly. "I would never shirk on a deal. What exactly do you want, Luke Boudreaux?"

He clasped the nape of her neck and pulled her to him. "You, Friday Jones. I want you."

EPILOGUE

IT TOOK TWO MONTHS TO ORGANIZE THE COVERT TRIP TO NEW
Zealand's research facility, where Friday's data chips were
removed, something that made her incredibly relieved.

"You ready for this, bébé?" Striker wrapped an arm
around her shoulder as she stood staring at the monitors
Hunter had set up in the main cavern. Now that they were
back in the Red Zone, it was time to see exactly what was
stored on her chip.

"Absolutely." She kissed his throat because, even though
he didn't show it, she knew he worried about her. "I want to
know what we're dealing with."

"That's my girl." He tipped her face up to kiss her lips.

She would never get used to his kisses. They were like
chocolate, diamonds, sunsets, and silk all wrapped up into
one. They were priceless.

"Will you two give it a rest," Mace complained. "You
make me want to vomit."

"Have at it." Striker grinned at his friend. "Make sure to
clean up when you're done."

"Asshole."

"I hear that a lot," he said drolly, making her laugh.

His diamondback was always telling him he was an ass. She traced over the image of her own snake. It was growing nicely as it slept, and she couldn't wait to meet it. The image of the diamondback made her feel like she belonged. Like she was really part of the team. Of the family. The feeling made her giddy. Instead of dying, she'd been blessed with everything she'd always wanted. Some days she couldn't quite believe just how much love was in her life now. She wrapped her arms around her husband's waist and hugged him tight. He kissed her hair. Striker knew exactly what she felt about her 'second life'.

"Right, here we go." Hunter grinned over his shoulder at the rest of the team. "Should we look at this in private first, Friday? Are we gonna see some stuff you'd rather we didn't share with the team?" He waggled his eyebrows at her.

There were chuckles, but she was lost. "Like what? Sex? I only do that with Striker."

The laughter increased.

"Let's keep it that way," her husband grumbled.

"Right, here we go." Hunter tapped at his old-fashioned keyboard. "We're going to speed through the twenty-four-hour period before Friday stupidly dosed herself with poison."

Striker's hand flew out, and he cuffed Hunter across the back of his head.

"That hurt," their tech guru grumbled, but his focus stayed on the screen.

There was silence as the team watched her former life inside CommTECH. She didn't speak to anyone, she simply focused on her work. The sight made her shift uneasily, ashamed that everyone could see exactly how pathetic her old life had been.

"You're not that woman anymore," her husband whispered, making her wonder, yet again, if he could read her mind.

She smiled her thanks and held him closer.

"That's the fourth nutrition bar you've eaten," Mace pointed out. "Your diet has improved dramatically since you've been here."

"I'm still waiting for my lobster, though," she reminded him, to the team's amusement.

The man mountain shook his head, but there was a smile on his face.

Her focus went back to the screen, which showed an empty corridor behind the data pad in her hand. She'd been hurrying, rushing to get back to her work, and going over her research notes while she walked. Her whole life revolved around her job, to the point where she used to sneak back into work when she wasn't even supposed to be there. It made her even more grateful that things had changed.

Striker's body stiffened against hers. "Go back," he ordered. "Then take us forward, slowly."

Friday held her breath as they watched the slow-motion footage. They saw everything through her eyes, as though they were inside her head with her on that day. She was focused on her data pad, and then suddenly the view became blurred. She'd stumbled over her own feet. When the image came into focus again, she no longer looked down at her data pad. Instead, she'd glanced to the right—straight at a group of people meeting in the lower level conference room.

"Freeze that," Striker snapped.

She sucked in a breath at the image in front of her. A murmur of shock rippled through the team. On the screen were the four most powerful leaders in the world—Ju-Long Lee, Serge Abramovich, Sandrine Cherbourg, and Miriam Shepherd. They were smiling and shaking hands with two other people. Miriam held out a credit chip toward one of the other men, and Friday shook when she recognized him. Arnold James, one of the three leaders of the Freedom organization. The image changed slightly as Hunter walked it to the next frame. The last unknown man in the image grinned as he slapped Ju-Long on the shoulder. It was Matías Delagado, president of Bolivia and the unofficial leader of the Coalition Countries.

Friday staggered back a step, felt the chair behind her hit the back of her knees, and sat down with a thump. Striker placed his hand on her shoulder.

"We got sound with this?" His voice was harsh. She liked to think of it as his commander mode.

"Yeah, but that's a different file. The data chips were damaged a little, and the files aren't running simultaneously like they should do. Give me a minute."

She reached up, took hold of her husband's hand, and held it tight. He caressed her hair, letting her know she wasn't alone. She'd never be alone again.

"Right, here it is." Hunter played the audio, but it was too low to hear, telling her that she'd picked it up in the background but hadn't consciously listened to the conversation. "Wait, let me enhance it."

The images on the screen were mesmerizing. This was the reason half the world was after her. The reason she'd almost died. All because of this. One split second where she'd seen something she shouldn't have and heard something she hadn't even realized she'd heard.

"Okay, here goes," Hunter said.

Miriam Shepherd's voice filled the room. "I don't want any mistakes, Arnold," she told the leader of the rebellion group.

"Don't worry. There won't be any. Not for this much credit." He laughed.

"Make sure you get the prototype," a male said.

"Of course." Arnold sounded smug. "Your new chip won't be worth much if the competition still has their prototype. Don't worry. We'll make sure it all goes up in smoke."

"We need to talk about ladmium output," another female voice said—Sandrine. "We need to increase production to meet the market demands in time."

"Especially seeing as we're guaranteed a monopoly in the market once our friend here gets done blowing crap up." A male voice sounded amused.

"Serge!" Miriam reprimanded.

"The ladmium needs to be refined before use," a new voice said.

"There's no time. We'll use it as is."

"Then the chips will be compromised."

"But the profit won't." There was more laughter.

The voices faded as Friday had obviously moved out of range of the meeting.

There was silence in the Red Zone cavern.

"They're going to implant faulty data chips," Ignacio said. "They're willingly endangering people."

"And Freedom is helping." She felt ill at the thought. "Without their competitor's product, everyone will jump at updating to the new implants from CommTECH." She felt herself pale as she looked up at Striker. "People will die. You have no idea how dangerous unrefined ladmium can be. We have to do something. We can't let this happen."

"No," he said. "We can't."

And then he kissed her and took all the worry from her head.

For now.

ABOUT THE AUTHOR

Janet is a Scot, living in New Zealand and is married to a Dutch man. She writes contemporary romance and romantic suspense with a humorous bent – this is mainly due to the fact that she has an odd sense of humour and can't keep it out of anything she does! If she wasn't a writer, she'd like to be Buffy the Vampire Slayer, or Indiana Jones. Unfortunately, both of these roles have already been filled. Which may be a good thing as Janet has no fighting skills, wouldn't know a precious relic if it hit her in the face, and has an aversion to blood. When she's not living in her head, she's a mother to two kids and several pets.

Janet loves to hang out with her readers. You can chat with her in her Facebook group, which is full of awesome readers. And don't forget to sign up for her newsletter too!